THE DAY DEATH STOPPED

REBECCA THORNE

THE DAY DEATH STOPPED

Copyright @ 2023 Rebecca Thorne

Cover Illustration and Front Lettering by Esther Bellefontaine
https://www.instagram.com/sublme_/

Back Cover Lettering by Amphi
https://amphi.studio/

ISBN 978-1-962597-09-8 (*print edition*)
ISBN 979-8-9866924-9-4 (*ebook*)

1 2 3 4 5 6 7 8 9 10

www.rebeccathorne.net

To anyone who was told that you can't do the thing.

Prove them all wrong.

Chapter One

The Day Death Stopped

Time is a funny thing.

It exists in twists and turns and tangents instead of a simple, straight line—a weaving road of misery and confusion that could have been rectified if one would just *stop for directions.* In that way, time is quite similar to the stories we tell: the most curious ones happen out of order, for sometimes we only understand a crucial, world-stopping decision in hindsight.

And this decision *was* world-stopping.

Or rather, death-stopping.

Outside of Eugene, Oregon, a red Honda Civic turned too soon, colliding head-on with a speeding motorcycle. Under the force of the bike, the car's windshield shattered, crushed into thousands of tiny, interconnected shards that buckled like warping plastic. After the hissing, screeching metal settled on the hot asphalt, breathless seconds ticked by in eerie silence. Then, the Honda's driver, a young woman, kicked open the door and crawled out.

Blood gushed from a deep, glass-embedded gash on her forehead, past her caved-in cheek, beyond her grotesquely angled neck. Torment coursed through her, and she sobbed in pain, but her windpipe was crushed and there was no physical way to push air beyond it.

She should be dead.

Across the street, the motorcyclist staggered to his feet, his organs slipping through bloody fingers.

He should also be dead.

Around the world, a 103-year-old man in Athens had his ventilator pulled amidst resigned family members, but when the nurse checked his pulse, his heart beat strong—even though his body had already failed.

A hiker in the Himalayas stepped on a bad patch of ice and crashed into a ravine, down, down, a hundred meters down, wedged between two massive sheets of ice. His skull was crushed, but terribly, his soul remained, forcing consciousness in the dripping throes of agony.

A tsunami slammed into an island in the Philippines, and dozens were pulled with the tide. They drifted, perpetually drowning in a tumultuous sea with no hope of rescue, choking on seawater while their souls ached to rise, to leave, but were forcibly tethered to these corpses instead.

Reports like this surfaced all over the world, in simultaneous panic. That's because, on October 1st, at precisely 5:12pm Western European Summer Time, death on the planet Earth ground to a halt. If that sounds idyllic, near utopian, we've had a terrible miscommunication, because of the two constants in life—death and taxes—death is arguably the most necessary.

"In hindsight, there really was no other way," Ozarik, our villain at this moment, muttered, his eyes bright with power, his face flushed with fever.

The huckleberry smoke of the teleportation spell wafted and disappeared as he oriented himself in the cavernous study of his castle retreat, striding across the stone floor to his overcrowded desk. Looking on, one might think he'd gone certifiably insane, swimming in sacred texts and spellbooks witches hadn't touched in decades.[1]

---

1. Not since the invention of e-readers, and, more recently, the creation of the Windle app, a comprehensive compilation of all resources witchy, easily accessed through any phone, computer, or scrying mirror.

This would be the correct assumption.

The Almost-Zaro—leader supreme to all witches—Ozarik continued to whisper, flicking through pages of notes while his magic pulsed around him. The castle walls reverberated with it, deathly silent in a point of irony. To be quite frank, the castle, proudly nestled in the High Tatras of Slovakia, wanted absolutely none of this nonsense. When Ozarik first stumbled upon it, the crumbling walls did the exact opposite of falling over themselves, desperate to reconstruct some semblance of centuries past. *A Zaro*, it bragged to the nearby Oravsky Castle[2] in the way old buildings sometimes do. *The leader of the world's witches studies here.*

Now, harboring their greatest villain, the castle wasn't bragging anymore. It swallowed Ozarik's words, stuffing them in the darkest corners and hoping the cobwebs kept them there.

(Far in the distance, the Oravsky Castle trembled in laughter.)

Ozarik, being a touch distracted, noticed none of this. After all, the magic required to stop death is immense. Imagine all the flowers in the world unfurling at once, coupled with a symphony of singing birds and the stalwart glory of a snowy mountain range. Now imagine all that beauty was funneled into Ozarik... and then expelled in dark waves of increasingly unnatural instruction.

Stay in your bodies, that instruction said. *There's nowhere else to go.*

This was a lie. But newly dead souls didn't know better, and Ozarik was supposed to be the next Zaro, the symbol of light and good in the world, the bridge between magic and humanity. If he said it, why wouldn't it be true?

Ozarik was, unfortunately, rather persuasive.

---

2. Which, in the nameless castle's opinion, had gotten a bit too knotty for its wood after the whole Nosferatu nonsense.

And unfortunately for him, Claire Bishop was equally persistent.[3]

At 5:26pm, fourteen minutes after death stopped, Ozarik's cell phone rang. This came as a surprise, since before that moment he hadn't possessed a cell phone, not even to contact human leaders regarding their affairs. Zaros—future and present—simply nudged a conversation into the air, and it landed right in the mind of those with whom they wished to speak.

But Oz's mind was preoccupied, so Claire had to get creative.

He gritted his teeth as it howled, a ringtone closely mimicking an air-raid siren coupled with a cat in heat. It was not a pleasant sound, which was absolutely Claire's point.

"Busy right now," Ozarik shouted, hands trembling over the yellowing pages of a leatherbound journal, one stamped with the simple initials *ZV*.

In Hong Kong, a sick child slated to donate his little heart drew another shuddering breath, much to the anxiety of the surgeon standing by. The parents, watching beyond the glass, allowed themselves to hope that maybe their prayers were answered. (They weren't.)

The phone's ringtone increased in volume, adding the roar of a chainsaw to the screeching. For a brief second, Ozarik faltered, and thirty-two lucky souls snuck through his persuasion, soaring upwards in crippling relief.

Claire's voice filtered over the phone's speakers, even though Ozarik hadn't touched the device. *"You've gone too far, Oz. Stop whatever you're doing, or I'm coming over there."*

Her voice was music to his ears. Ozarik's heart pounded, his irritation at the interruption melting away. He whispered, gratitude in every syllable: "But it worked. You're still alive."

This simple fact solidified his actions in Ozarik's mind. Not only had he *not* gone overboard, oh no. He was on the path to protect every single

---

3. This is the time where Claire Bishop should possibly, probably, be introduced—but she appears often enough later on... or rather, earlier on... and thus her entire introduction will be a full name and nothing more.

person in the world, witch or not, from the grief of losing a loved one. A pleased smile spread across Ozarik's lips.

He was helping. *Finally*, after one month of perilous uncertainty, Ozarik knew without a doubt he'd fulfilled his duty to Reiki, to his magic, to the Universe.

This was entirely false. As such, Claire's sympathy had fled long ago, her tone anything but kind now. "*Yeah, well, if you keep this up, you won't be. Either the magic will kill you—or I will.*"

Ozarik stared in blank incomprehension. In his power-sought, feverish state, all he could think was, *Kill me? Well... that won't work.*

What he said was, "I was trying to fix what I've messed up. People keep dying. My parents, Reiki, and—and y-you." He choked on the words. Like bellows stoking a fire, his anguish fanned the flames of magic. Efforts redoubled across the world, and any souls that squeaked through were a thing of the past.

"*I haven't died!*"

Except she had.

He tried to speak rationally, tried to reason with her, even though his voice trembled under the weight of his actions. "The spell went further than expected, but—this is a good thing. Death doesn't need to happen, Claire. Wouldn't it be great if sickness or crime or unfortunate accidents didn't remove a loved one entirely?"

"*No,*" she said, flatly.

Claire was so smart, the most intelligent person he'd ever known. It was shocking to him that she didn't understand. Ozarik tried again. "Without death, a new Zaro won't be born."

"*Or they'll be born right on schedule—again and again and again. You stopped death, you moron, not life. If that happens, the 'one Zaro for all witchkind' problem won't just be ours anymore.*"

Ozarik shook his head. "No, that won't happen." He had no basis for that statement, just an increasingly infallible belief that this—stopping death—would solve all of his problems. "I'm ceasing the cycle. With two halves of our magic, we can *finally* rule... side-by-side."

Imagine, if you will, an old-timey balance scale. Go ahead. Think of something ornate, something you might see in a museum, something bronze with perfectly sculpted pans suspended by the finest chains. In this metaphor, the Zaro—who's essentially a pope, if said pope possessed immense natural power and the ability to shape time and space—is the beam holding the chains. This person represents a stationary point of balance amidst ever-changing forces. It is because of this person that witches live harmoniously in every culture on Earth, instead of all that nastiness about stakes and burning.[4]

Now imagine that scale was snapped out of existence, and what replaced it is a pendulum, a weight of gold that swung between two potential Zaros: Claire and Ozarik. The push-pull of their power could annihilate the world—case in point.

You could understand Claire's concern.

But in Ozarik's mind, now that Reiki was dead, ceasing the cycle meant he and Claire could command the world's magic, protect the world's witches, side by side. There would be no more dramatics.

They would rule.

Forever.

But that was cliché, so he finished with, "Isn't that our job?"

"Stopping death was never supposed to be my job, and it sure as hell isn't yours," Claire hissed, suddenly present in the cavernous, bookshelf-lined study.

He'd kindly left a drop of magic within Claire's control, and immediately Ozarik regretted it. Partly for the interruption, but mostly because of how she *looked*.

Her eyes were sunken, face pale and drawn with pain. Her hand pressed against a wound on her side, one deep enough to stain the royal blue robes

---

4. The nearly 300 years of witch burnings were a PR disaster for the Zaros of that time. Of course, most witches are too clever to be captured for silly reasons like that, so the people targeted were, unfortunately, just normal humans.

dark crimson. It was a far cry from the stage-worthy Magnificent Claire Bishop, and it twinged his heart. She staggered a bit, although whether that was because of her injury or the magic Ozarik stole was anyone's guess.

That very magic rippled the air, mingling with the smell of musty books, and she inhaled sharply as she confirmed the extent of his spell.

The extent of what he'd done.

Ozarik turned to face her fully—and she slapped him with a bloodstained hand, so hard he dropped to his knees.

"I'm taking *this* back, thank you." Ruthlessly, while he was incapacitated, she jerked on the power that push-pulled between them. The pendulum swung, silently, in the opposite direction. Her steps were steadier now, although the bloodstain was growing bigger, drenching her heart in copper and betrayal.

"*No.*" Ozarik hadn't meant to give Claire an opening to seize his magic back. Cheek stinging, he desperately grabbed at the waning power—as futile as snatching sand in a sieve. "Give it back!"

She wouldn't. Strands of Claire's ponytail had fallen from its meticulous hold, framing her ice-blue eyes as she glared at Ozarik with the practiced ease of a woman scorned. Blocks of golden light cut through square windows, highlighting her devastation. "This isn't you, Oz. You need to stop."

"I won't." The words were snarled.

Her eyes narrowed. "Then I guess it's my job to make you."

Claire acted strong because, in his daze, Ozarik wouldn't respond to anything less. But in reality, beyond the encompassing fear for her own life, her heart was breaking for him. They'd been best friends, yin and yang, sun and moon, since they were born. All her life, she knew he existed somewhere in the world. Like monarch butterflies perfectly navigating to

Mexico every winter, their meeting—at thirteen years old, when Claire fled the devil and slammed into Ozarik's life—was only a matter of time.[5]

And once they met, it was a relationship for the ages. All those afternoons spent together, all those stolen moments on the Strip, the shared secrets and whispered laughter that accompanied two halves of a whole... Claire was asexual and had little patience for intimacy, but she loved fiercely, and loved how Ozarik showed her the difference between independence and vulnerability.

Facing Ozarik's death-defying choice, her memories wilted, edges blackening and curling like paper in a fire. What he'd done was *unforgivable*, something so drastic it made him the villain after all—and Claire couldn't bear it.

But while Claire's future crumbled, Ozarik's was solidifying. To him, that history was background noise: always there, the one constant in a sea of change. Claire Bishop was something that just *was*, like the audacious size of the Grand Canyon or the derision of a disapproving mother. Of course, Ozarik thought Reiki *was* too, and look how that turned out. Murdered by his own machination.

And then today, Claire. Attacked, *killed*, revived only by his hand.

Ozarik would never again be placed in a position of failing to protect those he loved. Today's events were the final straw. He was done living in fear, mourning his inaction as death happened around him.

He would never lose her again.

Whether she agreed was irrelevant.

So, when Claire said, "This isn't you, Oz," his heart warmed at the nickname, even as his motivations solidified into something dark and dangerous.

---

5. Scientists have since discovered that monarch butterflies use the sun to navigate, processing its position through their internal "time-compensated sun compass." To be clear, this is not the method Claire used.

When Claire said, "You need to stop," Ozarik realized that in this moment, she wasn't just his friend, his love, his half. She was also a distraction. An interruption.

And when Claire said, "Then I guess it's my job to make you," Ozarik immediately thought, *Good luck.*

And the pendulum swung again.

Chapter Two

24 Days before Death Stopped

T o truly understand those events, we need to back up. The beginning of the end of the world happened the way most horrifying experiences occur: on stage, in front of an audience.

Of course, although the stage was perfectly normal, it should be remembered that there were many kinds of audiences. The non-engaged audience of a Hollywood audition, for example, wherein the actress was fresh out of the drama program at Wichita Community College and the role was actually for a very talented, highly obedient iguana. The glassy-eyed stares of passengers on a dual-engine jet when the flight attendant spoke faster than the plane could fly, and therefore no one really understood how to fasten a seatbelt when he finished. Or the typical over-eager parents, cooing beyond their recording device while their little one stumbled his way through *Annie,* in a production that would surely haunt him in ten years' time.

With that in mind, it was important to emphasize that *this* audience was of the breath-holding kind, the waiting-to-be-amazed kind, the I-spent-$200-on-this-ticket-and-$20-more-on-a-vodka-cranberry-so-this-magic-show-better-be-worth-it kind.

So, when the death of a goddess caused a ripple that became a world-destroying tsunami of time and space and the magic inside souls—and on stage the Magnificent Claire Bishop collapsed to her knees while her previously "just an illusion" galaxy of glimmering stars burned bright and crashed around her like a day of biblical reckoning—this particular audience cheered.

And Claire couldn't even tell them it wasn't part of the show, because her hair had caught fire. Also her deep red, utterly flamboyant, "seems a bit much" stage outfit.

Also the stage.

But that was hardly Claire's concern, considering her soul currently felt like an ant writhing under a magnifying glass and a child's malicious smile. It took several seconds to catch her breath. Several more to stagger to her feet.

If the death of their Zaro hit her this hard, she could only imagine what Ozarik was going through.

"Whew, look at that," she exhaled into the microphone. (Said microphone, having realized three years ago that Claire Bishop was no ordinary[1] magician, and therefore didn't need its voice-projecting capabilities, had taken an extended vacation, and Claire didn't have the heart to tattle on it. Luckily, the microphone was correct and her voice echoed through the auditorium speakers anyway.) "There's a light show you won't get at the Bellagio, folks!"

The audience chortled. A few leaned forward, sipping their vodka cranberries.

Meanwhile, the very real fire was creating a newfound relationship with the polished stage—a sibling relationship, where the young fire kept poking the older, annoyed strips of wood, until they buckled and blackened in a hiss of "stop iiiit," which only incited the fire more.

Peeking from backstage, her manager, a wibbly man with a short mustache and terrible control of his bladder, understood this wasn't part of Claire's act and was very close to wetting himself.

Claire's chest and left pinky were aching with the sudden loss of... well, everything, but she smiled brilliantly for the audience, surrounded by

---

1. Fake

crackling flames and waves of heat. Inside, a dark fear bloomed, one where she questioned whether or not her magic still *existed* now that Reiki was gone—or if Ozarik had somehow stolen it all, as Reiki had hoped.

"Guess we got a little too close to the sun, eh? A tad dramatic, if you ask me." An ironic pause. "And I should know. I'm in the business."

While the audience chortled, Claire waved a hand to gather the flames, much to the groaning relief of the assaulted stage. It worked, and she breathed an internal sigh of relief. Then she shooed flames from her clothes and hair, winced at the charred sequins and the cameras capturing her very public failure.

Four years in Vegas, and she'd never ruined a show.

Leave it to Reiki to die in the middle of the first act.

Heart pounding, head spinning, Claire compressed the fire into a tiny ball in her palm, then extinguished it like one might snuff a birthday candle. Murmurs of approval rippled through the audience, people with no idea how close they'd come to melting flesh and tortured screams. Only Mr. Hiddles, Claire's manager, seemed appropriately traumatized. She flashed him a reassuring grin—which didn't reassure him at all—and cleared her throat.

"Stars are overrated, I think." Claire stomped the stage, and a massive tank of boiling water rose from the depths. "Let's try swimming instead. Wagers on how long I can hold my breath?"

After all, the show must go on.

By that disillusioned September evening, Claire Bishop had lived in Las Vegas for four years and forty-seven days. She'd been the Strip's best-selling star for four years, eight days. She hadn't expected that kind of success, but in hindsight, there was no alternative. As someone tied for the title of "second-most powerful witch in the world," where else but the Las Vegas Strip could Claire win the hearts and wallets of drunk, magic-loving customers?

Of course, her deal with Ozarik still stood. Even though she *could* use magic—possessed so much of it that a flick of her finger could burn cities or heal forests—in her partner's words, "That would be cheating."

"I dunno, Oz. Cheaters prosper," Claire said, spinning a pink poker chip on the lacquered surface of the 24-hour diner's bar top. That was three years, 308 days ago, back when Claire and Oz were inching towards adulthood and Claire's show was nothing more than a footnote in the Vegas brochures[2].

Ozarik sighed. She was joking. He had to believe she was joking. But the truth was, Claire often said things like this: risky statements wrapped in sarcasm accompanied by a dazzling smile. Things that went against everything the Zaro stood for—everything *they* stood for—and she seemed to care less and less about the blasphemy.

In Ozarik's deepest, darkest soul, there was a whisper that maybe Reiki was right in banishing her.

He'd gotten very, very good at ignoring that whisper.

"That's hardly the point, Claire. Look, you're insanely clever." Oz smiled warmly, his fingers fluttering across her palm. She twisted her hand to intertwine their fingers, and the spark between them was so powerful the diner's florescent lights flickered.[3] "If you tried, I'm certain you could fabricate illusions that *look* real. Mirrors and tricks of light and whatnot."

Between them, Claire's poker chip spun and spun and spun, far longer than physics should allow.

Claire pressed her lips together, offended. "Mirrors and lights?"

---

2. For exactly eleven more days. After a visit from a very well-known celebrity we won't mention here, who raved about the "outrageous and incredible" feats of magic on Claire's stage, her show became the destination on the Strip. A certain magical pair of comedic performers—whose names we also won't mention—were not pleased.

3. To be fair, their magic made a lot of lightbulbs uneasy.

"If you wanted. Better than your audiences knowing the next Zaro is five meters[4] from them."

Claire leaned across the table, propping up her chin with her free hand. "Didn't know you'd be up on stage with me, Oz."

Ozarik glanced over his shoulder, as if Reiki could hear them from halfway across the world. Which was ridiculous; a Zaro's power was immense, but eavesdropping had a 453 foot[5] limit. Claire and Oz knew. They'd tested it.

"What if Reiki's wrong, Claire? Where does it say two people can't be Zaros together?"

"Um, everywhere. Every sacred text she makes you study. 'One Zaro to lead Earth's witches.' That's how it's always been."

"Until now."

An uncomfortable beat passed between them, and all the while that existential pendulum loomed.

Claire cleared her throat, her fingers warm against Ozarik's. Her blue eyes, however, never left the poker chip spinning between them. "Did you know Nevada passed a law in 1973 barring witches from performing magic shows?"

"Because it's cheating," Oz said again.

"Because the humans were afraid of someone stealing the limelight." Claire sniffed, removing her hand from his. She took a delicate sip of her coffee, and the steam formed condensation on her nose. "When you think about it, I'm doing your job. Ensuring equal opportunity for our people and all that."

---

4. Ozarik was born in the newly independent Slovakia. Therefore, Oz, like most civilized people, used the metric system. Claire had been raised with the American education system, which was baffling on the best of days, and thus used the imperial system. She insisted it was normal. Ozarik assured her it was very much not.

5. Rather, 138 metres, to the rest of the world.

Ozarik's lips pinched together, but his words were steady as always. "And the paycheck that comes with it is, what? A bonus?"

"Exactly." Claire flashed a charming smile.

Ozarik, who'd denounced all earthly possessions when Reiki began his training, sighed again. He sighed a lot around Claire, truth be told. "If anyone finds out you're not really a stage magician, they're going to contact the Order. And Reiki has your name earmarked, so it'll go straight to the top. And then she'll send me to discipline you, and you know how I hate that."

Now Claire's smile turned vaguely wicked. "Really? I kind of like it."

Even though they were seventeen days from becoming official, from truly trying this *dating* thing, Claire's statement was empty and they both knew it. Claire Bishop was not a touchy-feely person. She was, however, a flirtatious person, and thus Oz's cheeks flushed at the words. He plowed ahead. "Promise me you won't be too over-the-top, Claire."

A waitress strolled towards them with a notepad, fishing a pen out of her apron. While she was distracted, Oz hastily tugged the poker chip from its dizzying spin. It settled to a perfectly normal stop.

Claire smirked. "Buzzkill."

"Claire."

"Oh, all right. I promise. But only because you said I was clever."

So, until the night Reiki died and the stage caught fire, Claire's show didn't utilize real magic. As far as Las Vegas was concerned, the Magnificent Claire Bishop was something of an engineer. When confronted about her tricks being too "fantastic," she'd walk the accuser through an elaborate display of pulleys and weights and, yes, mirrors and lights, and they'd leave her stage more impressed than when they arrived.

That was the beauty of illusion.

Vegas and Claire got along swimmingly, and she had no intention of leaving. After tonight's show, after the falling stars and fire and the screaming space between souls that reverberated with the loss of their Zaro, when Claire *could* have snapped her fingers and magicked to Ozarik's location—which would surely be Reiki's deathbed—, instead she went home and waited.

Waited for Ozarik to visit yet again, bearing bad news.
But Ozarik never came.

Chapter Three

19 Years and 102 Days before Death Stopped

While we explore the circumstances around these events, it's important to note that Zaro Reiki was generally considered a kind soul.

Most Zaros were, to be fair. Their entire existence focused on resolving witch/human conflict, or witch/witch conflict, and—on the rare occasion—human/human conflict. People who dedicated their lives to helping others rarely became anything but kind, selfless, and empathetic. Indeed, the Zaro might be the one example where power does *not* corrupt.[1]

Some postulate this is the sole reason the Universe, in all Its glory, bestows one person with such magic.

But for every Zaro that exists, another is born towards the end of their reign, a new shining star to carry the magic. Over time, the original Zaro's power ebbs into the younger child, until they become old enough, strong enough, to Assume the title.

And because the Universe recognized this magic is a Terrible Thing to give a temperamental toddler, It installed a failsafe, crudely speaking. There is a gravitational pull between Zaros, stronger than the planets with their

---

1. And absolute power does not corrupt absolutely.

sun. The Zaro *knows* the moment a successor is born, and is propelled on a journey to find them.

Two decades ago, Reiki found hers.

"Call him Ozzy," his mother cooed, hovering as the Zaro examined the baby.

The power radiating from him wasn't as fierce as Reiki expected, a ripple instead of a wave. But she wasn't about to tell Zuzana Krajovičová that. The woman was puffing like a sparrow in the bath at the fact that *Zaro Reiki* made a house call. (And all the better that her neighbors had seen the most powerful woman alive strolling through her front door.)

Her husband, Marek, was not as impressed. He hovered at the doorway, watching Reiki warily, discontent and irritation curdling at the witch's proximity. Gruffly, he asked, "What does this mean? For *us*, you understand."

They had a luxurious two-story house on the outskirts of Poprad, a nondescript mountainous town within the Spiš Region. Poprad was nothing special outside of its breathtaking views: immense snow-capped mountains that framed its skyline.[2] But their lives seemed nice. It was perplexing that they desired more.

Of course, Reiki shouldn't have been surprised. The exterior of the house had expensive upgrades: a tile roof in a community of wooden thatches, colorful, painted accents around the front door, and meticulously maintained rose bushes leading up the concrete-stamped walkway. Their grassy backyard backed to a picturesque meadow, and had been specifically landscaped to draw attention to their view. Had the couple offered half that reflection inside, Reiki wouldn't be sneezing past decades-old carpet dust.

Not that she'd voice it. Instead of responding to Marek, she merely ignored him, which ruffled *his* feathers in a far different manner.

---

2. Zuzana, who refused to accept she'd be "nothing special," or, horror of horrors, "nondescript," continually praised her hometown—much to the amusement of anyone who heard.

"Is his full name Ozzy?"

The wife brushed a dark curl from their baby's face. "Well, it's Ozarik. Ozarik Krajovič."

Thank the Universe, that was better than some silly nickname. Reiki hummed. "Just Ozarik, then. The Zaro belongs to no family."

Perhaps too late, Zuzana began to wonder the real reason the Zaro came to visit. Suspicion, cultivated through many years of maintaining appearances in her social circles, flared to life.

She tried to be tactful. "Well, I don't believe that's—"

Her husband did not: "You come into *our* home, tell us *our* son is a—a *witch*, and now you try to say he isn't even ours anymore? Who the hell do you think you are?"

There were moments in Reiki's life where she wished the Universe, in all Its magic, wasn't so excellent at translation. A Zaro needed to be fluent in every language on Earth[3], but was it necessary to interpret that tone?

Reiki inhaled, stepping away from the crib. The baby, Ozarik, blew spit bubbles under a tightly wrapped sports blanket that boasted the words *Naši chlapci* in decorative red, white, and blue. Reiki, who didn't follow sports and couldn't care less about competitive championships, thought it seemed awfully strange to declare a days-old baby a fan of any form of athletics.

Her words were level. "I understand your concern. My parents felt the same."

Zaros *were* allowed to lie for the greater good. In truth, Reiki's parents hailed from Kyoto, a city centered around tradition in a country that valued the whole over the one. When her predecessor, Zaro Arjun, arrived at their home, they were deeply honored and remained so until the day they died.

---

3. In fact, most conversations between Ozarik and Claire happened in two languages simultaneously. Usually their native Slovakian and English, but sometimes they'd switch it up just to confuse people.

Now, Reiki smiled, nudging a bit of calming magic into the air. It settled over Ozarik's parents like a blanket, soothing their dark thoughts. "But the decision has already been made. Your son Ozarik will become the most outstanding person alive. He alone will carry my title, and with it, the hopes and dreams of every culture on the planet."

"Every *witch* on the planet, you mean," Marek said, grumpily.

It should go without saying that neither of Ozarik's parents were of the witchy variety.

"Well, yes. Witches are born in every nation. In fact, I have several right here in town who are anxious to meet their future ruler. They've offered to monitor Ozarik from afar until his power grows out of your control."

With this, Reiki cast another, slightly doubtful glance at the baby. He was obviously the one she sought... but his magic felt too weak. She couldn't dispute the curdling hesitation in her soul, the one that whispered, *there's another.*

But that was impossible, so Reiki pointedly ignored it.

"Out of control?" Ozarik's mother repeated cautiously, pressing a hand to her chest. "What do you mean?"

"He will be able to persuade the wind and rain, communicate with time, influence souls. Eventually your home will not contain him, and Ozarik will join me on our sacred island of Javarini for full-time training."

His parents were growing distressed about the way Zaro Reiki spoke—in absolutes, like there was no other future for their four-day-old baby. Imagine growing something for nine months, living through the uncertainties and hardships of pregnancy, the exhaustion of labor, only to discover their child was the Chosen One.

This was quite the scandal.

Maybe in witch circles, a future Zaro under their roof was a status symbol, but Marek could imagine their very human neighbors whispering. Suddenly, he couldn't stomach it. "So, we deal with the baby-ing, the crying and diapers and spit-up, and you get him before he can carry on our name? You have to know we can't stand for that."

"Indeed." His wife sniffed.

Reiki inhaled slowly, meticulously. Zaro Arjun never had to deal with this drama.

"I realize you aren't familiar with our customs," she began, choosing her words carefully this time, "but I am merely a tool of the Universe's desires. My role doesn't change the fact that your son *will* grow into something far greater than yourselves. You may be proud or live in denial, but that choice is irrelevant to his future."

There. Even they should comprehend that.

As someone who'd never had children herself, Reiki didn't quite understand the fuss. After all, she wasn't trying to take the baby *today*. She had absolutely no need for a thing so young. They would have many good years together.

But Ozarik's parents gaped at her words. Zuzana quivered, although Reiki couldn't tell if it was rage or devastation.[4] Marek's face purpled, and he shoved a shaking finger at the bedroom's door, floorboards creaking beneath the blue carpet as he shifted his weight.

"Get out."

Nothing here felt resolved, so Reiki hesitated. "I'm afraid—"

"Don't question me. Surely with all your 'magic,' you can find your way out! *Go!*"

Reiki sighed, but there was no use arguing with them. She'd return in a year, and hopefully in that time they'd come to their senses. She smoothed her kimono and strode past them.

The front door slammed behind her, and Marek drew the curtains in a defiant manner. Reiki shook her head, passing their perfectly pruned roses to rejoined her aciradaan—who acted as the chief acira, commanded the Zaro's staff, *and* ensured the world's safety in the event a Zaro went insane. Reiki's aciradaan was named Clementine, and she waited vigilantly with the rental car.

It was a rainy day, but none of the drops dared touch Reiki. The Zaro waved a hand, and the car started, warming the interior.

---

4. It was rage.

Clementine furrowed her brow. "Is the future master everything we hoped for?" Her anticipation had been aflutter ever since Reiki had suddenly declared the new Zaro had been born, and now Clementine held her breath. Foreboding rose as Reiki's expression turned pensive.

"He's something." The Zaro paused mere steps from the vehicle. She glanced again at the house, testing the gravitational pull that strengthened the moment she left Ozarik's proximity.

But his wasn't the only pull.

There's another.

Water streamed down the aciradaan's face, and Clementine wiped the bangs from her eyes. But the aciras—especially the *lead* acira—didn't move until the Zaro moved. Feeling distinctly out of the loop, Clementine dared to ask, "Is something wrong, Kio?"

Another.

"My dear, I'm so sorry."

Clementine's breath caught, and she reminded herself again that Reiki didn't *mean* anything by such terms.

Reiki had already moved on: "I have to go."

With a frown, Clementine repeated, "Go? Where?"

Reiki concentrated, magical fingers plucking at the secondary pull. From their previous position on business in Kyzyl, it blended with Ozarik's, a sudden and insatiable desire to go *west*. Now, standing in front of the baby's house, she could identify this was something of a pitstop. A lovely and important sideshow, but not the destination.

The thread stretched out of Slovakia, over Europe, the ocean, and into—

"America," Reiki said, softly.

Clementine was definitely out of the loop now. They'd found the Zaro. Was there more pressing business?

But Reiki looked so concerned that Clementine didn't want to worry her further. If it was important, Reiki would tell her. Clementine was, after all, the Zaro's closest confidante. She wiped rain from her eyes. "Should I prepare the jet?"

Reiki nodded. "Back to Javarini. I'll return shortly."

And with a snap of her fingers and a puff of huckleberry smoke, Reiki vanished from Central Europe, leaving Clementine alone in the rain. Feeling distinctly abandoned, the aciradaan drew a breath and slipped inside the rental car.

Chapter Four

20 Days before Death Stopped

As we're starting to grasp, the end of the world didn't happen on a dime.[1] Something kicked it off, and that something was the unfortunate, untimely death of the Zaro Reiki. To a person like Ozarik, this held a gravitas weight. Even Claire, who swore to loathe Reiki until the day the woman died, suddenly had no reason to bear a grudge. But not everyone was affected as such.

In truth, only 7% of witches had the pleasure of meeting their Zaro. Of that number, most could only boast a polite handshake. (A select few boasted more, such as sending family-held spells or a trained familiar the Zaro might make use of... which was why the Zaro's sacred island of Javarini had both a library of spells and a separate castle for the cats, of which there were currently one hundred and thirteen.)

---

1. Funny phrase, "on a dime." Most people assume it applies to racecars or boats—things that need to accelerate quickly and efficiently to make headway—and their turning radiuses. In reality, it's mispronounced; the true idiom is "on adime," which refers to Adime Webler, the witch who invented a potion that accelerates time in one location... say, a racecar or boat. It's a common mistake, and one she was rather bitter about.

So, it made perfect sense that three days after the Zaro was killed, Henry Ballard, a witch in Good Order Standing, held a wedding.

It was barely planned, but to be fair, that was the case with most Las Vegas weddings. This one took place in a chapel off the Strip at exactly 10:14pm, which was their pre-ordained slot as decided by the receptionist. The groom brought his best friend, Milo, and the bride's parents drove here in their pajamas when they realized their lovely daughter, Jenifer, was absolutely serious.

Drunk, but serious.

"But a witch?" her mother whispered. "Did you know she was dating a witch?"

Her father grumbled, "A shotgun wedding. And not an Elvis impersonator in sight. Can't even do *this* respectably." He smoothed his superhero pajamas and glared at the priest.

Behind the podium, said priest, a practicing Catholic, was too busy fidgeting to glare back. Suddenly, his "Fool's Guide to Witchy Matrimony" certificate didn't seem quite as relevant as the website promised. He'd been led to believe witches liked to marry under the stars, close to nature, not—not here, in a crumbling chapel one street north of the Strip.

When in Vegas, he supposed, wringing his hands as Henry—the witch—flashed him a smile. The priest's eyes drifted to Henry's friend, Milo, squinting as he tried to discern if *he*, too, was a witch.[2]

Must be. The website said they flocked together in... covens, and whatnot.

The truth wasn't any of that. Witches didn't much care where they got married, any more than a lark preferred a certain tree branch to sing. And covens were grossly appropriated in modern media—humans simply preferred to label groups of people different from themselves.

Which was just fine, since witches also had a name for humans in small gatherings. They called them *popaloos*, mostly because the word was rather fun to pronounce.

---

2. He was.

25

"Look at 'em," Milo whispered in Henry's ear. "Two more and we'll have a right popaloo here."

"Be nice." The bride, Jenifer, giggled.

Jenifer Shields, soon to be Jenifer Ballard, wasn't a witch, but rather an accountant who was fascinated with the statistics of witchery. For example, only one in eleven people were born with a magical ability. The chances of hereditary magic were slightly better, one in eight people, but still not a guarantee. Jenifer had eleven siblings, making her the twelfth, and she found it fascinating none of them possessed an inkling of magic.

"If we're ready to begin?" the priest said, trailing off hopefully. His 10:28pm slot had just filled, according to the red light above the chapel doors. Still, his eyes settled on Henry, just in case he'd forgotten some witchy procedure that needed to happen before the ceremony.

But Henry just handed Milo a comically large, half-drained margarita and took Jenifer's hands. Milo took a deep swig himself as the priest drew a breath.

"Dearly beloved—"

"It's just, how do we know he's not bewitching her?" Jenifer's mother persisted, frantic. She slapped her husband's arm, even though she had everyone's undivided attention now.

The priest closed his eyes. This was why he didn't recommend *parents* at the ceremony.

Jenifer snickered. "Mom, that's not how it works. Witches can't control peoples' minds."

"But the spells—!"

"I mean, anyone can do those spells with the right ingredients," Milo said helpfully. "They're frighteningly easy."

Jenifer's mother paled, and the bride hastened to say, "All witches have one thing they can do, Mom. It's not a free for all."

"Except for the Zaro. Not much the Zaro can't do," Milo added, nudging Henry, who in this moment happened to be the 7% who'd politely shook hands with said Zaro.

Henry tried damage control. "It's okay, Mrs. Shields. Look, my magic has nothing to do with love. All *I* can do is find the prettiest rock." At this he puffed his chest, rather proud.

Jenifer gestured towards him, like this made everything better.

Her parents stared. Where her mother stammered for a reply, her father sweltered in fury. "Finding the best *rock*? What is this? Corpus Christie, out by the beach? Hunting for seashells and the like? How will that provide for our daughter?"

"Seashells aren't rocks," Milo said, yet again helpfully.

The clock ticked ever closer to 10:28pm. The priest cleared his throat. "If we might continue…"

"Dad, use your imagination," Jenifer said. "You know the odds of me finding a diamond in the bedrock outside Vegas? So far less than zero you can't quantify the number. But Henry here can snag one the first time he smacks a shovel in the dirt."

"Well, I could if diamonds were pretty." Henry sniffed.

Jenifer leveled a stern gaze at him.

He stiffened. "For you, love, I'd find the prettiest diamond." When she smiled, he leaned to Milo and murmured, "There's an oxymoron if I've ever heard one."

"If you *please*," the priest said, since his receptionist got rather snippy if he didn't wrap up the ceremonies in a timely manner. He thumped his Bible on the podium and tried to look strict.

"Of course, of course." Henry waved a hand.

The priest glowered at the bride's parents, who settled back into their seats. When everyone was silent, he drew another breath. "Dearly beloved, we are gathered here—"

"Wait, I'm so sorry. How could I forget? Jen, by witch tradition, before we say our Christian vows, we have to drink goat's blood from the bleached skull of an anteater."

The priest paled. How did the website fail to mention *that*?

"Milo, you brought the anteater skull, right?"

"Ah." Milo patted his pockets.

Jenifer's mother moaned, sliding into a faint.

"I do," Jenifer said, and tugged Henry into a passionate kiss.

The priest flipped through the pages of his Bible, heaved a sigh, and watched the clock tick to 10:27pm. "Yes, fine. I now pronounce you man and wife."

"And for my beautiful wife, a bonafide alexandrite I found outside the Bellagio." Henry dropped it into her open hand.

Her eyes widened. "It's on a ring and everything."

"You sure he's not a thief?" her father barked, fanning her mother rather dramatically as she slowly surfaced from the throes of unconsciousness.

"I find the pretty rocks. Just so happened this one already had a ring. Lucky, right?"

At this point, one might be wondering why this wedding is an event of importance to Claire and Ozarik's story. Well, it all ties together, because at that moment, the double doors of the chapel slammed open and a blonde woman with piercing blue eyes strode down the aisle.

"Luck?" Claire said. "I'd call it magic."

She waved a hand at Jenifer's parents. They vanished in a puff of huckleberry smoke, leaving a vague fragrance of petrichor. When Jenifer squeaked in surprise, Claire flashed a smile. "Don't worry. They're back at home, all tucked into bed. Mazel tov, by the way."

"Oh. Thanks." Jenifer gripped Henry's arm.

The priest cleared his throat. "A-Ah, so sorry, m-ma'am. But I have another appointment—"

"Giggling couple in the lobby? Yeah, they were *not* ready to tie the knot." Claire glanced over her shoulder, where the receptionist was fluttering in obvious distress, raising a phone to her ear—only to have it vanish with a snap of Claire's fingers. The snippy receptionist squeaked and fled.

Claire turned back to the priest. "And if you don't want to wind up at the Trump Hotel, you'll show yourself out."

Apparently that online certificate didn't tell him everything about witches. The priest inhaled sharply, tapped the sign of the cross against his chest, and scurried out the open doors—which took it upon themselves to lock resoundingly behind him.

Milo's jaw dropped. "W-Wait. Are you the—but you can't be the next Zaro. Ozarik is supposed to Assume—"

"Yes, that's right. Just call me the unwanted step-child." Claire's tone was light, but her eyes flashed to Henry Ballard. "Speaking of, Oz hasn't contacted you, has he?"

Henry frowned. "It's concerning you think he'd call me first."

Milo had begun to sink into a bow, and Henry now elbowed him in a desperate attempt to stop the motion—which would have been awkward in the best situation, but now might be a disaster considering the giant margarita he still held.

Claire sighed, massaging between her eyebrows. "He hasn't come to see me. It's been three days."

"Well, that's because he's at Javarini, preparing for the Assumation Ceremony to become the next Zaro," Milo said, ever helpful. In truth, that was his magical ability—knowing just the *wrong* thing to say in a conversation, but always thinking it was right.[3]

Henry inhaled through his nose. "Can you two wait for me outside? I'll catch up."

"Some honeymoon." Jenifer pouted.

"I'll have my manager send you something nice," Claire said, even though she currently lacked the brunette hair, brown eyes, and general bone structure of the Magnificent Claire Bishop, and therefore the comment only prompted curiosity and furrowed eyebrows.

Still, Jenifer flipped her tiny gauze veil over her ponytail and strolled outside. Milo, at the doors, caught Claire's eye and rubbed his arm. "Hey. I'm not sure if you or... or the Future—ah, Almost-Zaro Ozarik want a new familiar, but—"

"I'm allergic to cats," Claire deadpanned.

---

3. There's a great debate about what constitutes a magical ability, and thus a witch. Milo is a prime example: is it magic that propels him to say these things, or is he just terrible at conversation? The world may never know.

"Well, that's convenient, 'cause I'm training a ferret and I'd be happy to ship him—"

"Milo." Henry said.

"Never mind."

The doors slammed closed again, slightly miffed at all this locking and unlocking they suddenly had to do.

Alone in the chapel, Claire's bravado vanished, and she sunk into the front pew. Her voice was vaguely miserable. "He hasn't come to see me, Henry. Reiki *died*, and he's not here."

"She didn't just... die. You know that, right?"

"Whatever you call the process, the result was the same."

Henry perched on the raised platform opposite her, his back against the priest's podium. Their relationship was an unspoken oddity, one where Henry saved Claire from some particularly nasty casino bouncers, and in the months afterwards Henry was astute enough to realize that Claire, for all her power, was quite lonely when her other half wasn't around.

Much to his befuddlement, Henry had somehow become the closest thing Claire had to a friend.

Still, he tread lightly. "Claire, I... well, I don't think I'm qualified to help here. The aciras have Ozarik's Assumption well under control. Maybe Milo's right. Maybe he's just busy."

In reality, Henry did think it was strange that a Zaro passed, and there was barely any news on the subject. Someone killed her—but no one knew more than that. Henry comforted himself by acknowledging that the matters of goddesses and gods were far above him, and proceeded with cautious grief into their new future.

Claire, clearly, was not following that tactic.

"He's not busy. He's avoiding me," she snapped, and outside thunder boomed on an otherwise clear night.

Henry wasn't impressed. "People drift, Claire. It's a fact of life. Hard to be close emotionally when you live so far away."

"Not with Oz and I. We're different."

And they were.

Claire buried her head in her hands. "I always used to hope that when Reiki died, my magic would siphon into Ozarik automatically. Magic is weird. Just once, I wish it'd work for *me* and cut me loose."

Henry frowned. "Do you really wish that you weren't a witch at all?"

A huff. "No. I guess not."

Silence passed in several, weighted minutes. Henry ran a hand through his carefully gelled hair and tried a different tactic. "Okay. Look. If Ozarik won't come to you, why don't you go to him?"

"You know I don't *go to him*. Reiki made sure of that."

"Well, Reiki also told you to keep your magic under wraps, and you ignored that tonight." He gestured at Jenifer's missing parents, towards the lobby and the receptionist's empty desk.

Claire followed his gaze, obviously one second from rolling her eyes. "That's different."

"Is it? She's not here to stop you anymore." Henry winced as if he'd spoken blasphemous words, but cleared his throat and moved on. "Maybe the world has changed all around. Maybe now... things can be different for you."

For all that he'd prefer to be out finding pretty rocks, Henry Ballard was a very astute and equally empathetic person. They were possibly his best qualities.

Claire considered this, then pushed to her feet. "Oh, fine. *Fine*. But when Clementine gleefully peels my corpse off the floor of the Cat Castle's foyer, I'll make sure she ships my ashes to your doorstep."

"Please don't," Henry said, good-naturedly.

"I left you a zero-gravity room at home. Make sure Jenifer takes off her shoes first. Happy wedding." And with that, Claire strolled towards the lobby. With a heaving groan, the double doors heaved themselves open one last time to bid her adieu.

"Wait, what? Zero—Claire. Hang on!"

But she snapped her fingers, and in another poof of huckleberry smoke and petrichor, the chapel was suddenly empty. Above the gaping double doors, the red light flicked off.

Chapter Five

19 Years and 102 Days before Death Stopped

Across time, decades earlier, all Zaro Reiki could think was: the house seemed mild.

The key word here was "seemed." Many things *seem* mild at first: the smattering of rain that preceded a category five hurricane, for example, or the warm glow of a campfire before the embers drifted into a bone-dry forest. They were quiet, subdued things, almost pleasant... right until they weren't.

Reiki hadn't realized it yet, but "seemed" was the perfect word to describe the tiny American bungalow.

Exactly 6 minutes earlier, she'd left Clementine on that quaint suburban street in Slovakia and poofed her way around the globe, landing in this oddly normal neighborhood. Based on the pines scenting the air, the heavy fog, the thick, gangly foliage, she guessed somewhere in the American Northwest. Washington, perhaps, or Idaho. Her nose wrinkled. Hopefully not Oregon—the witches in Oregon were *odd*, to say the least.

Drawing a slow, maybe even nervous breath, Reiki stepped through the neighborhood, an older area with decaying houses and overgrown yards. Nothing about this place impressed her, but Zaros came from all walks of life. That was the very point of their existence.

And there was no denying the magic here. It emanated from one particularly mild home, pulsing like a tiny baby's heartbeat.

Bum-bump, bum-bump.

It was overwhelming, far more powerful than anything Reiki expected to feel from an infant. Which meant it was *exactly* what she should have felt at Ozarik's crib. The facts solidified: two magical babies. Two future Zaros.

Her stomach churned at the prospect.

The house was silent, which was odd when Reiki considered the toys littering the front yard. Silence and children did not mix, in her vast experience. Harnessing her own magic the way she might prepare for war, Zaro Reiki climbed the crumbling concrete steps. The porch creaked under her slippered feet. Slowly, carefully, she knocked.

This was her duty, after all.

But even the tensest situations don't always deliver, and this was one of those moments. The front door remained closed. She might have thought no one was home, except for the pulsing thrum of magic.

Reiki set her jaw. Although her personality and culture of origin urged her to *turn around, walk away, don't inconvenience anyone*, this was an exceptional case regarding an exceptional baby. Someone was inside this bungalow, and by the Universe, she'd have an audience with them—even if she had to break down the front door.

At that, the deadbolt squeaked and unlocked in a tizzy, swinging open before the Zaro could do anything rash.

"Oh. Thank you," Reiki told it, and stepped over the threshold.

Based on the state of the front yard, she wasn't surprised to see the owners cared little for their property. While outside was obviously for the children, the interior was an adult's playground. Playing cards carpeted the floor in front of an ancient television. Microwave dinners had been left to mold. Her sharp brown eyes slid over crayon markings on the walls, a wooden end table pieced together with duct tape, a hole in the drywall beside the grimy bathroom.

In the eyes of witches everywhere, the Zaro is a benevolent being who lives above judgement.

But nobody's perfect.

Reiki wrinkled her nose, pausing just past the threshold. The shag carpet curled around her satin slippers, and she lifted her kimono skirts around an oozing stain beside the door. "Ah, hello?"

Silence.

Reiki raised her voice, pushed a tiny ounce of magic into the words so absolutely everyone in the residence would hear. "This is Zaro Reiki, Ruler of Witches, Harnesser of Magic, Imbuer of Hope. It is imperative we speak."

In the back of the bungalow, a baby started to cry.

The unease in Reiki's chest twisted into something that stole her breath. With a ripple of magic, she confirmed her horrific suspicion: that aside from the days-old baby radiating power with every heartbeat, the house was empty.

They were alone.

It's important, in the following moments, to know that Zaro Reiki, hailing from Kyoto and Buddhist parents, prided herself on a calm demeanor, an infallible ability to maintain her composure in the most trying situations. Every Zaro acted as an arbitrator, but none in three centuries had been so highly preferred to resolve conflict, even in human affairs.

Which was why, when Zaro Reiki lost her temper for the first time in decades, the ground literally trembled underneath the house's cracked foundation. Ninety-seven miles east, chaos erupted at a research facility as seismologists tripped over themselves to report the earthquake.[1] The

---

1. Upon later examination, they discovered the epicenter was a measly house in Spokane, and despite the earthquake registering higher than anything in the last 23 years, there was no damage. What they couldn't know was that, with Zaro Reiki in her state, everything from the roads to the homes were too terrified to rattle to pieces. The seismologists eventually chalked the quake up to malfunctioning equipment and moved on.

bungalow, contrarily, stayed perfectly still, even as Reiki stormed to the back bedroom, leaving smoldering footsteps in her wake.

The baby was lying on a bed.

Not in a crib. Not even properly swaddled. It was tiny and red-faced and screaming discomfort, one precarious moment from rolling the short distance to the floor. Reiki's temper flared, and the lightbulbs in the living room shattered.

The baby cried harder.

As furious as she was with the parents, she knew this child had done nothing wrong. "Come here, little one," she whispered, scooping the baby, a girl, with gentle hands. The near-violent thrum of their combined powers settled into something serene as Reiki drudged a nursery song from her childhood. When she sang, magic offered weight to the words—and slowly the baby's eyelids eased shut.

Safe and sound. Reiki continued singing as she wrapped the child in the folds of her kimono, stepped back into the living room.

A bubble of magic is a wonderous thing, a protective cocoon that muffled sounds and emotion and instilled contentedness instead. Zaro Reiki saved it for the most hysterical cases, but she swaddled the American baby in one now, protecting her from the storm to come.

The ground trembled again, renewed in its terror as Reiki's eyes settled on the open front door. She snapped her fingers, and the space between souls snapped in response.

A set of people slammed into existence, crashing to their shag carpet with little decorum. The wife held a shopping bag while the husband clutched a toddler's chubby arm, and neither of them seemed prepared for the sudden change of scenery. The wife screamed, which Reiki silenced with a whisper of, "Quiet. You'll wake the baby."

The baby wouldn't wake, not unless the Zaro released the bubble, but she felt it fair to offer an explanation as to why the woman's mouth had suddenly zipped shut.

Panic overrode the wife's features, and she clawed at her lips as the man shoved the toddler behind him.

As if *Reiki* were the threat.[2]

"Who are you? How did we get here?" the husband demanded.

His aura made her pause. Reiki surveyed him with rising fury. "You're a witch."

The man stiffened. "Don't say that word in my household. How *dare* you—"

"I am Zaro Reiki."

He clamped his mouth shut.

If Reiki were a snide woman, she'd sneer, *so you have an inkling of intelligence.* If she were less benevolent, she'd say, *magic is only for those who deserve it, and you clearly don't.* If she were vindictive, she'd merely strip his Universe-given ability[3], leaving him a hollow shell of a human—only fair, since he seemed so vehemently opposed to the word "witch."

But Reiki was none of those things, so she simply said, "What is your name?"

The toddler sniffled pathetically behind him, and his wife had tears leaking from her eyes. The man straightened. "Kyle Flanderson. What the hell do you want?"

"Is this your baby?" Reiki uncovered the child from the folds of her kimono.

Both parents flinched. The wife slapped his arm, and when Reiki looked at her, she magically regained the ability to speak. "I told you. I told you we shouldn't have left—"

"And I told you, I needed *him* to make it work," Kyle snarled, yanking the toddler back into view. Reiki surveyed him as well, but this child wasn't a witch, and therefore wasn't her jurisdiction. While her heart wrenched

---

2. To be fair, she was. Yet as previously stated, Reiki was a benevolent witch; even furious, she'd cause no lasting damage. But she saw no harm in letting these people think she was capable of more.

3. Which happened to be breathing underwater, but only above sea level.

for the little boy, she couldn't just go around removing *human* children from their parents.

Still, an anonymous tip was immediately filed at the local CPS office, marked *URGENT*. It would have to be enough.

"What were you trying to make work?" Reiki asked, narrowing her eyes. "What was so important you left your newborn alone?"

"None of your business," Kyle snapped, in that defensive way people do when questioned about less-than-legal activities. Of course, that might have been a supposition.

Reiki didn't care how Kyle Flanderson and his family filled their inconsequential existence. What she cared about was the future Zaro in her arms. She gestured to the baby. "What is her name?"

The mother seemed taken aback. "Ah, C-Claire."

"All right. Claire contains all the magic of a Zaro, which would be dangerous enough without her lack of supervision. Therefore, I'm taking her, but you can comfort yourselves that she will accomplish greater things in life than you have."

For a long moment, there was silence. Then the mother screamed again, sounding on the verge of a hysterical breakdown. It was understandable, considering the Zaro's level words, but Reiki was beyond compassion for this family.

Kyle clenched his fists. "Now hang on a minute—"

"I assure you, Mr. Flanderson, that I am done 'hanging on.'"

"Y-You can't take my baby." The wife sobbed, staggering forward, shopping bag and toddler forgotten. "It was just for a moment. We weren't gone more than a minute, and she was *fine*. We were on our way b-b-back when you—you can't *take my baby*!"

The reaction was extreme, in Reiki's opinion.[4] Especially when the woman collapsed at her feet, grappling her kimono with desperate hands. "It was just for a minute. She's our baby. We h-have t-toys for her. Food.

---

4. Keep in mind that Zaro Reiki renounced familial ties, and thus had no children of her own.

Diapers! Look at him!" Now she pointed at the toddler, wailing, "We're good p-parents."

The little boy didn't seem physically harmed. He was plump and terrified, but didn't bear bruises or other signs of abuse. Reiki shifted, suddenly uncomfortable. Her anger cooled, and her calm demeanor returned in time to see herself in this situation: an ultra-powerful witch breaking into a family's home, plucking their baby out of bed, then threatening to kidnap her with little explanation.

This went against everything the Zaro stood for. The worlds' presses would—what was that American phrase? Have a field day?

In her arms, fast asleep, Claire drooled. Her magic thrummed softer now, content around the current Zaro.

"We'll call the cops." Kyle looked seconds away from starting a fight, face screwed in anger, shoulders trembling. "We'll tell everyone what you did. You won't be able to hide this."

Reiki could, in fact, hide it. But she was supposed to be benevolent.

The Imbuer of Hope.

She clenched her jaw, drew a breath through her nose, and met Kyle's gaze. Magic sparked as her eyes pinned him, boring into his very soul. He paled, and when she spoke, the walls shook with her words. "You will never leave her alone again. You will never put her in an unsafe situation, and you will treat her with love and respect until her powers manifest. At that moment, I will collect her for training, and she will no longer belong in your household or to your family. Is that clear?"

The wife began to wail again, like a banshee with a horrific toothache.

Kyle, on the other hand, pressed his lips into a thin line. "You really think our kid is the next Zaro?"

There was an undercurrent of greed to his words, and Reiki narrowed her eyes. "It is inevitable." At least, it would be, if Reiki didn't have Ozarik to contend with as well. But that was a problem for another day, one where she wasn't threatening a witch and his wife to properly care for their child. In fact, she already felt irate at the gleam in Kyle's eyes now.

He watched the baby in Reiki's arms like she were a bar of gold. "Holy shit. Okay. We're—um, we're very sorry for the inconvenience. I swear, it won't happen again."

"It absolutely won't," Reiki said, and the words floated into the popcorn ceiling, flooding the bungalow with magic. And for added measure: "Let me be clear. You will not speak a word of her fate to anyone outside this room. If you or your wife try, it will fall on deaf ears. Your daughter deserves to be raised without the weight of the world on her shoulders."

This wasn't what she'd told Ozarik's parents, although in hindsight, she probably should have. Based on how Kyle's lips tilted upwards, how his eyes had illuminated, Reiki could only imagine what Claire would endure if Kyle were allowed to spread this around.

It was purely to protect the girl. Everything she did in this moment was to protect Claire. She told herself that over and over in the coming weeks, and stamped her fear so far down it became a distant memory.

"I will be checking in. Don't forget." And Reiki handed Claire to her mother.

The woman sniffled pathetically, but took the baby in a proper hold, cuddling her as if love really were present in this home.

Reiki chose to believe it.

That was what one might call "a devastating oversight."

Chapter Six

24 Days before Death Stopped

As we know, Reiki died, and the power of it shifted the very heartbeat of the Universe.

Although Ozarik was physically inside the musty hotel room... when the gunshot echoed, his mind immediately distanced. And no wonder: the death of a Zaro was a powerful thing. As it happened, time seemed to buckle and the screams of space reverberated through the spirits of every witch alive—but it was nothing compared to the tsunami of magic suddenly transitioning between old Zaro and new.

At precisely 9:12pm Mountain Standard Time, three hundred miles from Claire's fiery performance of falling stars, Reiki collapsed to the moldy carpet... and a mere breath later, Ozarik slammed to his knees.

His mind was ripping itself apart, and it had nothing to do with the magic.

It seemed to Ozarik like the room was flickering in and out of focus, a shaking camera in an amateur horror film. Moments that immediately became memories assaulted him: a spray of blood misting the air, sprinkling on Reiki's body as she settled.

That human—no, that witch—no, that *murderer*—crashing to the floor under Ozarik's unconscious command, bound in impossible, invisible chains. He was trapped, and would remain trapped for as long as Ozarik drew breath: first in magic, then within the local justice system.

The motel room's front door slamming open at the exact wrong moment—*too late, five seconds too late*—as Aciradaan Clementine burst in from the outdoor breezeway. The way her bloodcurdling scream saturated the air.

Ozarik was screaming too, but no one could hear underneath the wave of his own agony. Inside his mind, a devastating mantra began: *Reiki is dead. Reiki is dead. Reiki is dead.*

He reached for her, his Zaro, his leader, his goddess, grasping at her indomitable life force with his magic. Briefly, for one fleeting, world-altering moment, he touched her soul—a bright flare of light, incomparable warmth, a loving touch. And then... it slipped from his hold and vanished.

All that remained was the echoing expanse of silence in a cruel Universe.

Back in reality, Clementine's desperate hand grabbed Ozarik's shoulders, but he didn't recognize her. In fact, neither of them could tear their gazes from the blood staining Reiki's lips. Her dark eyes were unfocused, unseeing.

Reiki's magic, suddenly and undesirably Ozarik's now, *burned*.

"Ozarik—" Clementine started.

His instincts flared. *Reiki is dead.* Ozarik was yanked back to the moment he gazed upon his parents as they desperately tried to wash off his accidental, magical flames, both of them writhing in agony, skin bubbling and splitting. His childlike horror as he reached for them, desperately confused at why the magic somehow protecting him wasn't protecting them too. How, after a few awful seconds, their hysterical, animalistic screams fell silent, and all he could comprehend was the stench of their bodies smoldering.

He couldn't bear to see *their* corpses either. He fled, then.

And he fled now.

In a poof of huckleberry smoke, Ozarik slammed into existence on the other side of the world, in an unknown forest in the dead of winter. The cold assaulted him, ruthlessly biting his exposed skin, his blurring eyes, freezing tears onto his cheeks. Overhead, the sun shone limply through the snow-drenched pines. Behind, the shadows caressed his shoulders.

He took a second to orient himself, one bleary second to stare through the purple smoke, recognize the churning of his gut as a residual effect of the teleportation spell—and then he *screamed*.

And this time, anything within a fifty-meter radius heard.

The shockwave of his grief blasted through the forest like an explosion, rippling the trees and sending birds flying as loose snow erupted, clearing the area at his knees all the way to the ice-encrusted dirt. The magic swirled overhead, creating angry storm clouds that blotted the watery sky, like thick bruises on pale skin.

Ozarik gasped for breath, and his magic gasped with him.

Reiki is dead. Reiki is dead—

A second, more horrific thought solidified: *—and it's your fault.*

At that, Ozarik collapsed, hunching over himself as he slammed his fists into the ground. To truly understand what he was feeling in this moment, step back and imagine an astronaut facing the glimmering stars above, the pure blue planet far below. Imagine her wonder as she faces all that's ever been and all that could be, and knows she's a true, honest part of it.

Now imagine her oxygen tank ruptures.

Cruel, isn't it?

Ozarik gasped and coughed and spluttered and fumbled for something that never would be again, and his magic formed a barrier around him as the clouds he forced into existence became a blizzard of his own fury and devastation. Across the world, simultaneously, stars were raining around the Magnificent Claire Bishop. It was quite dramatic, and not at all in keeping with how Reiki had been. But no matter how diligent one is in life, death has a way of changing everything.

And sometimes, even the dying gasps of a forest chipmunk can determine the fate of the Universe.

The creature in question had merely been in the wrong place at the wrong time. A chance happening had it emerging from its cozy den, squinting at the predator far below. Perhaps it was curiosity, perhaps fear, but the chipmunk ventured further along the tree branch, turning black eyes on the storm overhead instead.

When the shockwave hit, absolutely nothing stopped its little body from slamming into the branch above it—fracturing its spine, sending it crashing to the dirt clearing.

For several moments, Ozarik was too blind to notice reality... but slowly, that faded. His world inched back into view—and a tiny, pained chittering caught his attention. He scrubbed frost off his eyelashes, daring a glance over his shoulder.

There, in the shadows, was the chipmunk. Its velvety fur was sticky with blood, its eyes darting back and forth as it struggled to correct its sudden paralysis, struggled to inhale between failing lungs.

Ozarik had seen too much death today. Blankly, he stared at it, not a flicker of sympathy to be found in his deadened expression. The Future Zaro simply couldn't spare it.

The chipmunk wheezed.

An inkling of humanity finally found its way into his soul, and he shifted his weight to face the creature. With gentle hands, he scooped it up, rubbing his thumb along its soft ears. A little coaxing of magic eased its pain—but it was still dying.

Its eyelids fluttered shut.

Ozarik's heart surged as he felt its soul slip away.

"No," he breathed. "No!"

And with a vicious yank, he clamped magic around its soul and dragged it back into its body.

For a brief moment, nothing happened. The chipmunk was still.

Then, desperately, it jerked back to life. Inside, its spirit was tied in chains, wrapped so tightly it could barely feel, barely exist. A perpetual ache of *wrongness* centered in its mind, but of course, a chipmunk didn't have the brain capacity to analyze this. It simply stared up at Ozarik, the greatest predator it had ever known, and tried to scamper away. But of course, that didn't work. Its spine was still unfused.

Ozarik failed to notice any of this. All he saw was that the rodent had been dying—and then, suddenly—

It wasn't.

This was a dangerous turning point in Ozarik's journey, in case that wasn't clear.

"You're still alive," Ozarik murmured, more fascinated than pleased. His heart had shattered and was still lying on the ground in pieces, and the memories of Reiki collapsing to that grimy motel floor invaded his mind without warning.

The moment he grasped for her soul, a child lunging for a baseball soaring overhead, and *missed*.

Ozarik's jaw set. He probed the creature with magic, feeling what he'd done.

Now, one might assume this would reveal the horrors of his actions, the true state of the chipmunk and its never-ending woe. Regrettably, instead, this was the moment where Ozarik's mental narrative veered off course.[1]

Where the creature had been truly happy to die, considering the alternative, Ozarik saw a new, permanent lease on life.

Where the chipmunk's physical functions had been demolished in the fall, Ozarik assumed it was stunned into gratitude.

And where the Universe and everyone within would hope that his magic would wear off, that this poor animal would fade into a proper death in hours, possibly days, Ozarik could tell that he'd tethered its soul firmly, unerringly. The planet Earth itself would crumble and crash into an everblazing sun before this chipmunk's spirit would dare try to escape its own decaying flesh.

Because of this, Ozarik decided that he'd *helped*.

This was irrevocably and unforgivingly false.

Drunk off this newfound power, he placed the paralyzed chipmunk on the ground again and pushed to his feet. As he turned his back to the creature, Ozarik allowed a desperate smile to curl his lips. The blizzard magically calmed as he faced the sky. The snow began to gently and

---

1. The result is what literary experts refer to as "unreliable narration," and it would become the bane of Claire's life... and death.

peacefully fall, dusting his empty patch of icy dirt with a fresh coating of white.

"It's within my power." His fervent whisper sliced through the hush. Fresh tears spilled over his cheeks, and he scrubbed them off before they could freeze again. "But that means... I could have *saved* her."

The admission was lost to the wind.

On the ground, the immortal chipmunk ached to curl into a tight ball, breathing far too fast, eyes wide, desperate and cornered. Ozarik didn't notice.

To be fair, no one was present to comfort Ozarik, either. In Las Vegas, Claire had just summoned a tank of boiling water from the depths of her stage, further impressing an audience who had recently cheered at their own imminent deaths. In Denver, Clementine was still crouched over her Zaro, sobbing as her entire purpose in life remained limp in her arms.

The rest of the world progressed as normal, inching towards a headline that would make international news.

Ozarik shuddered, maybe from cold, maybe from anguish. He couldn't return to Reiki—not now. He wouldn't return to Javarini, not alone, not now. And Claire...

Well. Claire was at risk, too. If today had taught him anything, it was that no one and nothing Ozarik loved was safe.

Yet.

Drawing a shallow breath, Ozarik compartmentalized his grief for a moment, and prepared for experimentation. A chipmunk was one thing, but if he was going to utilize this ability in truth, he'd need to research. Scrolls, textbooks, compilations of ancient records. Some Zaro, sometime, must have recognized this as a possibility.[2]

Ozarik just had to find the spell.

---

2. She had indeed. Her name was Zaro Victoria, and some of you might know her.

Leaving the immobile chipmunk behind, he began his journey down the path of failed recovery. And one month later, the entire world would weep.

Chapter Seven

20 Days before Death Stopped

Traveling through magic wasn't pleasant. It was convenient, certainly, and far faster than any airplane or automobile. But it did leave the user feeling vaguely discombobulated, like their colon and spleen had swapped locations, which resulted in a functioning uneasiness for most of the afternoon.

So, when Claire poofed into Ozarik's room with all the suddenness of a... well, a witch with a teleportation spell, she felt sick for two reasons. The first was obviously the spell. The second was a slick, dangerous fear that she'd wind up incapacitated, drained, or dead.

Claire waved away the huckleberry smoke, holding her breath—but there was no shocking lance of pain.

Which meant Reiki was truly gone.

Good riddance.

Addressing the first cause of discomfort, Claire coaxed a can of grape soda to abandon the kitchen. No one knew why grape soda in particular soothed a Zaro's post-teleportation chaos—mostly because Claire was the only Possible-Zaro who'd tested it, which meant it was a shockingly small sample size.

It was entirely probable that Claire just liked grape soda, and looked for excuses to drink it.

Tapping the aluminum of the soda can, Claire surveyed the bedroom she hadn't seen in four years. It hadn't changed, still sporting mild beige curtains, a dark blue bedspread, and scuffed hardwood floors. Very few personal effects implied anyone lived here.

The only real hint of Ozarik's life was a single picture frame beside the bathroom, a photo Ozarik snapped the first day thirteen-year-old Claire came to live on Javarini. Dressed in ripped jeans and a graphic tee, Claire was pointing at the main castle, jaw unhinged. To be fair, the castle itself was something of an international icon: after generations of Zaros brought architectural influences from around the world, it represented the absolute mish-mash of cultures and preferences. A second, far less impressive castle—for the cats—perched in the background.

It was a lovely time for them, back before Reiki inserted herself into the dialogue. Claire admired it fondly.

Meanwhile, Ozarik dropped his mug in utter shock. "*Claire?*"

"Oh, hello." She popped the soda can open, ignoring the *hssssk* to squint at the brand. Some Norweigan label, which meant it would lack the distinctly colorful[1] flavors of the US. Claire took a swig and wrinkled her nose.

Ozarik, meanwhile, had leapt to his feet. "Y-You can't—Hang on, here, let me help—" With little decorum, he shoved his magic into her soul, which was something akin to smashing a person on the head with a gravy boat.

To understand this, we must examine why the benevolent Zaro Reiki was driven to the point of dangerous warding in the first place. While Javarini had been threatened in centuries past, the world generally regarded it as a sovereign state, belonging in totality to the Zaro, their aciras and staff, and the witches of the world. A revolving number of witches resided there at any given time, with a few keeping permanent residence. The island itself was merely the two castles, a few guest houses, some generous swells of forests, and a private airport.

---

1. Read: artificial.

It had been a peaceful place... right until Claire, dirtied and abandoned, locked eyes with Ozarik on that brisk New York City afternoon, and magic sparked between them. Even though she was rambunctious and arrogant and infuriating, Reiki had no choice but to bring Claire home.

For three years, she raised this chaotic child alongside Ozarik... as if they both had a chance at the title of Zaro.

Claire never had a chance.

It was Reiki's one true failing in life.

Which is why, after an argument whose echoes sparked immense fury—and a little bit of guilt—whenever Reiki recalled it, after Claire abandoned Javarini and Ozarik and the possibility of becoming Zaro, Reiki decided to make triply certain the young teenager would never rescind her bold decision. And considering the magical ability of a Zaro, her security measures were less "wiring the doors" and more "conjuring a black hole to drain the magic of a particular genetic sequence... and the witch attached to it."

When Claire said she "didn't" visit Ozarik, what she meant was she *couldn't*.

Although Ozarik's current defense was well-intentioned, Claire gasped anyway, staggering under the combined weight of their power. She grabbed the corner of his bed as magic flooded all the way to her toes. Her soda crashed to the floor, about to create a matching stain to Ozarik's tea, but her magic stilled the can before it could spill.

"*Christ*, Oz, warn me next time."

Her voice tapered out as she faced that breathless moment where an uncomfortable pain shifted into something almost pleasurable, like basking instead of burning. Claire wasn't a fan. With a huff, she coaxed the magic back to Ozarik, far smoother than he'd shoved it onto her.

He sank into his chair, but even as his aura brightened, an incredible sadness settled over him. They both knew what this meant: if Claire was able to speak, much less conduct magic as usual, then Reiki's wards were gone... forever.

Claire scooped up the soda can, taking a tentative sip. The vibrations after teleportation slowed, like an anxious dog finally drifting to sleep. The soda still wasn't sweet enough, but it helped.

Instead of apologizing, Ozarik simply said, "That was a risk."

(He meant, *teleporting to see me, even though it could have killed you.*)

"You weren't answering my calls."

(She meant, *you're worth it.*)

After all, no matter how badly Reiki wanted to keep her protégés apart, keep Ozarik on the path of goodness and magic and eliminate any mention of Claire from the history books, the fact was that nothing on earth could fight the gravitational pull between them.

Two halves. Same whole.

In Reiki's mind, the Universe really screwed up.

"I was busy. Lots of—um, lots of things to wrap up. No time to drop by Vegas, not with—burial rites and..." Ozarik gulped, choking on the words as tears leaked from his eyes. "And—"

"Okay. Oz, it's okay."

Ozarik buried his head in his hands. His elbows rested on a thick spread of newspapers from all over the world, each detailing whatever limited information Clementine and her aciras had released about Zaro Reiki's death. Claire, who hadn't bothered to read anything about the event because she simply didn't care, now regarded the newspapers with malice. The corners of the pages curled in fear.

She faced him again. "Oz, this isn't healthy. Reiki's dead. Lamenting won't change that."

Ozarik flinched.

Claire was never great at commiseration. Or conversation.

But she *was* right. Dark bags hung under his brown eyes, and his very skin seemed to sag with the effort of staying awake, staying alert. He gloomily nudged the papers aside, into a neat pile with a Moroccan headline on full display: ZARO REIKI MURDERED?

"I couldn't face you," Ozarik muttered.

Claire quirked an eyebrow. "Because I'm so scary?"

"No, because of—of Reiki." His breath hitched as he met her gaze. It was like looking into the eye of a hurricane. "Claire, it was *my fault*—"

That's when footsteps thundered down the hallway of the squat castle, and Oz's wooden bedroom door was thrown open. Because in this kind of story, timing is everything, and several of the Zaro's aciras were infamously terrible at both appropriate introductions and reading a room.

"Future-Zaro Ozarik, we felt a disturbance of magic."

"Are you alright?"

Aciras Bao and Jorge clamored to push into Ozarik's room before the other... at least until their eyes settled on Claire Bishop, standing by his bed. Bao recoiled, an action that left Jorge crashing to his knees just past the threshold.

Claire waggled a few fingers.

"Hello, Jorge. Bao. Long time, no see."

When Reiki brought a young teenager home from Times Square, her staff noticed. Hard not to, the way young master Ozarik and this new girl gallivanted through the mismatched hallways. They were perplexed, but Clementine reminded them that the Zaro *was* known for benevolence—and the girl was clearly too thin, unaccustomed to supervision, nearly... orphan-like.

They drew their own conclusions.

And then drew new conclusions when, three years later, Reiki announced Claire Bishop "returned" to America. At that time, fully fed and clothed and decidedly *not* orphan-like anymore, Claire had outgrown their sympathy. Mostly because she was something of a terror.

Which explained their disdain as they comprehended just who, exactly, was sitting on the future Zaro's bed.

"You!"

"How did you get in here?"

She flashed a charming smile, the kind that won all manner of favors on the Las Vegas Strip. "Well, obviously Oz let me in."

Only the Zaro could teleport through the magic between space and souls, so Bao and Jorge nodded like that made sense. Of course, they would have been told if there were visiting guests, and Javarini's airspace was carefully monitored, so it didn't *really* make sense... but it was easier than facing the alternative.

Bao frowned. "Certainly. And Future-Zaro Ozarik, you've, ah... well, I suppose you've accepted her company." Obviously, their charge was fine—and in Bao's mind, security detail for a Zaro was absurd anyway. They could move mountains or incite volcanoes if they chose. Bao's personal magic was limited to sparking rather dangerously from his fingertips whenever he needed a fire in his pizza oven.

But guarding the Zaro was a large, roughly ceremonial, responsibility of the aciradaan, and Clementine was both fiercely protective of the boy she'd raised, and excellent at delegating when she couldn't be physically present.

Bao knew better than to dispute her orders.

Meanwhile, Jorge fiddled with his collar, wondering when he could return to his card game. If he hadn't submitted his application on a dare and actually been *chosen* for the honor of becoming an acira, he would have moved to Las Vegas long before Claire set her stage there.

"Ah, Future-Zaro?" Jorge prodded out of obligation.

It took Ozarik far too long to reply. Claire cleared her throat dramatically, which made him blink and tear his gaze from the newspapers. "Of course, I've accepted her company. Claire is my greatest friend."

Bao gaped. It was a little-known fact[2] that Bao considered himself the Future-Zaro's greatest friend.

Jorge, who realized last year none of them were Ozarik's favorite, stifled a chuckle, then straightened to assume control of the conversation. "Understood, my lord. Then we'll just leave, shall we?"

"Uh, sure. Thank you."

But before they could step away, a third set of footsteps thundered down the hallway. Clementine shoved her subordinates aside, panting for air. "Ozarik, we've just received an urgent message from the Japanese emperor. The witches in Kyoto are rioting!"

Ozarik stared at her.

---

2. To Ozarik.

Silence.

A *long* silence.

It got very, very awkward.

"Oh, for God's sake." Claire said.

"The *Universe's* sake," Jorge replied, then stiffened at the unimpressed look on Claire's face. What he thought was, *Americans*, but what he said was, "Apologies, Ms... ah..."

"Bishop. I go by Claire Bishop now," Claire remarked, leaning casually against the bedframe now. "You might have heard of me? The New York Times called me the 'best act on the Strip'?"

Clementine, who was steadfastly pretending Claire didn't exist[3], repeated, "Japan, Ozarik. How would you like to handle it?"

Ozarik didn't seem inclined to reply, so Claire pushed off the bedframe and flicked his head. The aciras gasped, and Clementine in particular moved forward in fury[4], but he just turned his dazed look on Claire instead.

"This is where you say something, *Future-Zaro Ozarik*." The title was only partly sarcastic. She waved a hand, prompting him along.

"I—But I—" Ozarik choked, eyes widening in a perfect imitation of a horse who'd seen a snake slithering through the grass. "I can't. I *can't*." And just like that horse, Ozarik reared out of his seat and bolted.

Past the aciras, down the hallway.

Out of sight.

Without pause, Jorge and Bao followed, scrambling to help their leader, shouting condolences and solutions. Clementine shot a brutal look at

---

3. And had been, on and off, since a particular prank six years ago that involved two chickens, a tub of Jell-O, and a paintbrush.

4. Injuries to Ozarik were one of the few times Clementine decided it was better to acknowledge that Claire did exist... so she could protect him properly.

the trespasser and stomped after them, completely missing the stubborn tongue Claire stuck in her direction.

After they left, silence resonated in the room. Claire sighed. "Well, then. This is more serious than I thought."

Her blue eyes caught the newspapers on Oz's desk—and something beneath it. A note, scribbled in Ozarik's penmanship: *locate missing spellbook!* Claire squinted at it, glanced around the room for said spellbook, but clearly it was, indeed, missing.

What did he need a specific spellbook for?

Her eyes drifted to the newspapers. They trembled under her scowl, but this time she wasn't satisfied with curling the edges. This time, the words literally bled from the articles, staining the wood with ink, dark as night.

Only when all mention of *murder* was erased from Reiki's obituaries did Claire trash the emptied grape soda can, mutter some calculations, and poof to Las Vegas.

Chapter Eight

19 Years and 95 Days before Death Stopped

Seventeen centuries ago, in the vestiges of the Western Jin Dynasty, the Tibetan Tribes, the Persian Empire, and the Arabian Nomads, etc, etc, the Zaro was less public relations and more hero of myth. Whispered-about figures of magic and power... and the plural form of that is intentional. Back then, the general consensus was that the Zaro wasn't a person, but a *group*, a collection of witches who appeared from the shadows, swathed in auras so strong even non-magical folk recognized them.

In reality, popaloos were generally confused about the ever-changing ethnicity of the Zaro[1], and this was further exasperated by the fact that the Zaros of old were required by oath to teleport with one other: the aciradaan.

This might seem strange, as the aciradaan—and thus, the aciras of Javarini—were almost never witches of diplomatic sway; that was the *point*

---

1. This misconception could be corrected, but witches decided it was a clever way to present themselves as power-adjacent, and many spent their lives pretending to be a Zaro themselves. Ironically, this subsect wound up collecting humans who craved power, too—and eventually evolved into the secret "society" we know as the Illuminati.

of these witches. They were unknowns, nameless, people of every culture brought together on one island to prove that peace could be created, that the countries of the world could, in fact, cooperate.

But the aciradaan served another purpose.

And it began with the ancient Ti. Zaro, or Tiberius the Zaro of the Roman Empire, who was both patriotic to a fault, and a general asshole. After all, "—of the Roman Empire" should *not* have been a part of his title. Even back then, Zaros renounced their family of origin and, while most nodded to their home countries, they lived their lives representing the whole, not the one.

Ti. Zaro, of course, did nothing of the sort. This was because Tiberius wasn't intent on being a hero, a myth. No, Tiberius the Zaro of the Roman Empire wanted to be a *god*.[2]

So began a long, drawn-out process of mistaken identity, where the humans of the Roman Empire began to fear the Zaro as a physical coming of Jupiter, the witches were inclined to agree, and the aciras watched in horror as conflict arose and tribes crumbled under their warlord's magic.

It ended with one acira named Kù Yuan. Yuan was from a small village in China, and joined Tiberius the Zaro to escape the chaos and infighting of the Western Jin Dynasty. Although Yuan's family were shopkeepers, he spent much of his early childhood pining over an imperial metallurgist's daughter, and eventually graduated into apprenticing at the forge. As a result, Yuan moved to Javarini with an uncanny knowledge and skillset for smithing.

The story that followed was a classic of danger, intrigue, and overthrowing power, one so fantastic that it morphed into legend. Considering we're pressed for time, the abbreviated version is that Yuan forged a Chinese dao, a steel sword with a slightly curved, single-edged blade, stamped a circle into the hilt to signify the world's will, and tracked

---

2. This was wholly redundant, to be clear. By definition of their power, Zaros are gods. But none before were so arrogant as to proclaim such.

down a Persian witch with a rare ability—a *Universe*-given ability—to transfer the magic of others.

This ability was infused into the dao, a final fuck-you to Ti. Zaro.

And when Tiberius the Zaro of the Roman Empire returned to Javarini one spring afternoon, Acira Yuan followed him to the cliffside overlooking the sea—and plunged his sword into Tiberius's heart.

The dao fulfilled its role as this transfer agent, sucking every ounce of magic Tiberius desperately called to heal himself. This magic expelled into the Universe with the force of a lightning strike, and in the sands of the Sahara, a Pastoral nomad went into labor. At Yuan's feet, Tiberius crumbled, blood staining the grass.

The god was dead, and the cycle began anew.

The Dao of Magical Allocation, set inside a plain leather sheath and cleaned of Tiberius's blood by now, lay discarded on the grass at Clementine's feet. If the current aciradaan had her way, it would be stashed in a locked chest, deep in the musty cellar of the castle, or possibly thrown into the sea in its entirety. The weight of it pushed against her ankle, familiar and unwanted, and she kicked it further away as she sipped the tea in her ceramic cup.

Zaro Reiki, seated beside her as they admired the sunny skies, the blue, blue ocean, mimed the motion, drawing another sip of the matcha she'd so carefully prepared. Then again, she always appeared content—it was Clementine's job to see past that, to push the real problems to light.

And this was a real problem.

"I always assumed finding the child would be a happy time," Clementine finally said, breaking a half hour of silence. She'd expected Reiki to address the Slovakian baby in the week since they'd located him—but her Zaro had given only stoic silence.

Now Reiki glanced at her, raising one delicate eyebrow. "Do you feel differently?"

It was a weighted question, one very cleverly posed. Clementine redirected, although a wry smile tweaked her lips. "All due respect, Kio, but this isn't about me."

"Mmm." Reiki set her teacup back on the table, tilting her face towards the sun. Clementine could practically *see* her recalling the dreary day, the stamped concrete path to the child's house, the magic pulsing inside. It had felt weak compared to Reiki's aura—but then again, Clementine expected nothing less. Ozarik was, after all, a baby.

A baby destined to replace Reiki—to carry the world into a new era.

It made Clementine's heart clench.

And of course, Reiki noticed. "I would argue, my dear, that this is about both of us. All of us."

She inclined her head towards the nearby dais, a stone circle surrounded by nine perches. During the Assumation Ceremony, they would choose nine cats to lend magic, fill the grassy knoll with chairs for visiting dignitaries, and Clementine herself would coach Ozarik through the ancient script of Assuming a Zaro's power.

Or rather, whoever replaced Clementine as the aciradaan would perform that task—because Clementine herself refused to exist in a world without Reiki.

As if reading her thoughts, Reiki set a hand over hers. The woman's fingers were warm, her smile soft and knowing. "Clementine, this is the natural order of things. My title is forever, but... all life ends."

Clementine swallowed past the sudden lump in her throat. She tried to be present in this moment, tried to appreciate the sun's warmth contrasting the cool ocean breeze, tried to symphonize the melody of the birds with the undertone of ever-present waves. She was *here, now*, with Reiki—the future didn't matter.

But Clementine had never been great with meditation, and the raw knowledge that *it did, it absolutely does, shit, nothing else matters more than this baby and what he signifies* gnawed at her chest.

"I know," she replied, and the words were choked.

Reiki squeezed her hand. "I would not trade my time with you for the world, my dear. And the new Zaro will do wonderfully. Of that, I am certain."

And funnily enough, for the first time, she did *not* sound certain.

Clementine glanced sharply at her. "He wasn't what you expected?"

Reiki withdrew her hand, and Clementine missed the touch instantly. The Zaro took another cautious sip of her tea, staring at the ocean. "Your magical ability is something to behold, my dear."

Clementine told people her magical ability was a flawless talent for spellwork. In reality, she possessed an uncanny ability to discern emotion in others—and everything inside her was screaming that Reiki, the Zaro, her love, wasn't telling the full truth about this boy.

"Kio. You can tell me anything. You know that, right?"

Let me be your confidante.

Zaro Reiki looked at her properly. This moment held weight, a point of divergence where one path led to honesty and a plan—and the other led to Reiki's greatest failure in life. Had Reiki opened up about the truth, told Clementine there were *two* Zaros born, not one, told her why she'd really teleported to America, why she'd spent the last week strangely withdrawn, why she would spend the next nineteen years wrestling to convince herself that this was the *right decision* when it so clearly wasn't—well, the world would be very, very different.

And that was what scared Reiki, if she were being honest.

So that's exactly what she said.

"I am afraid of the unknown. Change is a constant in life, and yet it remains the one thing we all try to stop." Reiki drew a breath through her nose, acknowledging the fact that she was trying to avoid change by lying about Claire Flanderson... and discarding it for the Greater Good. "Because of this, I am afraid of Ozarik. What he represents, what he will do with our world, and what will happen to you when I'm gone."

This, at least, was the truth.

Clementine's concern faded, her magic accepting this explanation and tucking it away. It wasn't difficult, considering the aciradaan herself had that same fear.

"I agree," was all she said.

Reiki glanced towards the ground, her dark eyes landing on the sword abandoned at Clementine's feet. A prickle of foreboding slipped up Reiki's neck—this was not magical, or witchy in nature, but rather acknowledgement of a flaw in her otherwise flawless aciradaan.

"My dear," she said. "I humbly request you keep that dao on your person at all times. It should not be discarded as such."

Clementine's cheeks warmed, and she snatched the antique off the ground. As always, in her hands, it felt warm and powerful. Dangerous. Even unsheathed, it was just a sword—but if she were to slice its blade along a witch's skin, draw blood, it would also draw magic—and keep drawing magic until that witch perished.

"Reiki, I would never use this," Clementine said, for the hundredth time.

She was, by all intents and purposes, a terrible aciradaan.

Reiki knew this, and that was why she kept Clementine in that position. Every decision Reiki made as Zaro, she made with the knowledge that *Clementine* would have to reel her in, control her, *kill* her if it came to that. And killing Reiki would almost certainly kill Clementine too.

Truly, it was a flawless failsafe for this pair.

"You swore to uphold the duties of aciradaan when you accepted the title," Reiki replied, for the hundredth time. But this time, her voice softened. "From now on, there are two in your charge. You must be prepared to keep *any* Zaro from going mad with power."

Reiki meant Ozarik and Claire.

Clementine utterly missed this.

Her fingers tightened around the worn hilt of the dao, tracing the circle stamped there. "I will do my best to intervene before it ever reaches the point of needing this sword."

"And if we *do* need it...?"

"Then—" Clementine pressed her lips together, glancing at the dais again. "Then I will do what is necessary, my Zaro. As I promised."

If this sounded foreboding, it absolutely should.

Chapter Nine

19 Days before Death Stopped

"So, what you're saying, sir, is that she's gone."

Mr. Robert Evan Hiddles, manager and agent to one fantastic stage magician, tugged at his suit's collar. His partner favored bowties, which was why, facing down Ms. Finch, Paris Las Vegas's feared Director of Entertainment, he was losing air due to a too-tight argyle monstrosity.

He couldn't even summon the wherewithal to be angry, partly because Mr. Hiddles rather loved his partner, but mostly because Mr. Hiddles was, in all honesty, a mild man with mild intentions.

He did not fit here, in the cutthroat corner office of a top-performing hotel.

(Of course, when he signed Claire Bishop as a client, he never expected she'd become the most desired act on the Strip. His ambitions for her, much like his ambitions for himself, had stretched as far as Laughlin, or maybe Carson City if they felt lucky. But it was too late to complain about that.[1])

Mr. Hiddles cleared his throat, tugged at that infernal bowtie, and said, "My client's contract clearly states—"

---

1. Much as he might like to.

"Hold on, Mr. Hiddles. I must have misheard, because there is no way *you* are claiming to have a better comprehension of the most lucrative contract in Nevada than I do." The very idea offended the woman to her core. Ms. Finch, after all, had graduated top of her class at Yale.

Mr. Hiddles tried again. "Until last night, Claire has never missed a show—"

This would be the moment where a self-discerning citizen might ask, *wow, is she all right? Should we call the police?* But Ms. Finch wasn't a self-discerning citizen. Ms. Finch was upper management at one of the biggest hotels in the world, and if someone presented Ms. Finch with Claire Bishop's charred corpse, her first thought would be, *great, now I have to find a replacement act.*

Which was why she held up a hand, silencing Claire's manager with a scowl.

"Do you have any idea what occurred at our theater last night? We nearly had a riot, Mr. Hiddles. Thousands of people flying from all over the world to see the best magician alive, and she doesn't show. Imagine that."

Mr. Hiddles had been out to dinner with his partner, and they had a strict "no cell phones" policy on date nights, so he didn't realize Claire vanished until the following morning. And by then it was too late to do anything about it, so he spent his time calling her, leaving messages, and upon hearing Ms. Finch's furious voicemail, picking a bowtie for this meeting that didn't make him want to melt into the floor.[2]

Ms. Finch glowered at him. "Let me explain something. I'm paid to ensure our guests are entertained, at exceedingly high cost. When something like this makes the news, I have to do damage control. Refunding tickets. Rebooking rooms. Shuffling VIPs. Statements to the press. Mr. Hiddles, it's what you'd call a *shitshow.*"

"I—I can imagine."

"You really can't. Every day that Claire Bishop isn't on stage, we're losing upwards of half a million dollars."

---

2. He still did, but the bowtie had nothing to do with that.

Sweat dripped down his neck. "That's a lot."

"It is." Ms. Finch steepled her fingers, leaning over her expansive desk. Although the rest of her hotel emphasized European luxury, her office was strictly corporate America, decorated with steel accents and faux black marble that made her seem cold and powerful. In truth, Ms. Finch hated it, preferred more rustic chic herself, but she couldn't argue the results.

In the low-sitting metal chair opposite her, poor Mr. Hiddles hunched against her gaze.

Her voice remained level, icy. "Allow me to be brutally honest, sir. If you don't produce a top magician before we hit two million in losses, Claire's disappearance will be the least of your worries."

Mr. Hiddles felt faint, and was thinking his partner's bowtie wasn't as lucky as promised when the office door flung open in a grandiose display.

And Claire Bishop strolled inside.

"Did someone call for a magician?" she asked, although there was no Earthly way she could have heard Ms. Finch through the thick walls.[3]

"Ms. Bishop!" Ms. Finch blinked. She forced a bright tone, a happy smile. "Ah, welcome back."

Claire crossed her arms, her sharp gaze pinning the Director of Entertainment in her chair. She then proceeded to do the worst possible thing to Ms. Finch: she ignored her.

"Mr. Hiddles, I'm terribly sorry for last night. A dear friend needed me, and I had to be certain the visit wouldn't kill me before I popped in to say hello."

Her manager nodded, quite understanding even though he understood exactly none of it.

Across her desk, which suddenly seemed laughably large, Ms. Finch stiffened. People didn't *ignore* her, especially some street performer who happened to get lucky. She tried to reinsert herself into the dialogue.

---

3. There was, however, a magical way, wherein Claire was less than 453 feet from Ms. Finch and therefore fully able to eavesdrop as she strolled through the hallway.

"It is unfortunate, Ms. Bishop, that you missed last night's show. Per the contract, and since advance notice was not provided, we will not be distributing pay—"

"Interesting. I could have sworn the contract says I'm allowed a vacation day. No notice required, full pay," Claire said, casually.

"That's impossible."

"Is it?"

The two women stared at each other, until Ms. Finch sniffed and plucked a massive folder from the locked drawer at her desk. She maintained eye contact as she flipped through the top pages, then tugged a thick section of the contract up for examination.

She didn't see the contract's language shift the moment Claire ordered it so, but as certainly as the sky is blue, the ink reassembled itself under her will. Ms. Finch did, however, see what it *now* said, under Subject Compensation, Section C, Subsection 2, Paragraph 15.

"Read that aloud for me, will you?" Claire dug a finger in her ear, then flicked her nail. "Just to make sure I'm not crazy."

Ms. Finch felt faint. "'The subject will be entitled to vacation days. No notice required, full pay.'"

"Huh."

If it seemed like Claire was enjoying this immensely, it's because she was.

Mr. Hiddles tugged his bowtie again, but the sweat had dried. He always felt more confident when Claire was in the room, arguing to executives *for* him.[4] He even had enough reckless conviction to straighten in his chair.

Meanwhile, Ms. Finch was trying to save face. She primly closed the contract, lips pressed in a thin line. "Be that as it may, Claire, you have to understand we can't have you gallivanting off whenever the whim strikes."

"Gallivanting. There's a word." Claire leaned against the armrest of Mr. Hiddles's chair, flashed another smile. "Look, if 'whim' has you in a tizzy, call it a family emergency."

---

4. Were he representing anyone else, Mr. Hiddles would be an absolutely terrible manager.

"Family is more important than your work?"

There was a reason Ms. Finch wasn't *Mrs.* Finch, after all. The last man to try was some trust fund baby with one grand idea: the Snot Blot, a winter glove equipped with absorbent fingers for, well, blotting snot. It lacked all the decorum he did, and Ms. Finch didn't have any problem showing him the door.

Claire quirked an eyebrow.

Mr. Hiddles coughed, suddenly struck with the urge to call his partner and profess his love.

Ms. Finch cleared her throat, abashed. "All right, Claire. I suppose we can't change the past, so griping about it now fixes nothing. Let's look ahead and promise it won't happen again." It didn't take much to add a plea to her voice, considering that, contractually, Claire owed her nothing—which meant someone really messed up in negotiations. And since Ms. Finch drew the contract, it was her head on the chopping block.

She didn't remember screwing up so royally when her company sat Claire down at a long, mahogany table and handed her a ballpoint pen, but apparently she had.

Magicians. Just the worst.

Claire rubbed the back of her neck. "This is awkward. I actually came here to tell you I'm taking a brief sabbatical."

Mr. Hiddles began to sweat again.

Ms. Finch stared. "I'm sorry, what?"

"A sabbatical. A holiday. Whatever you'd like to call it, I'm leaving again."

Mr. Hiddles, imagining all the calls he'd be fielding with his star client gone, dared to ask, "H-How long, exactly?"

This was the multi-million dollar question[5], and one that made Claire pause. Everyone grieved at their own pace, and Claire couldn't say how long Ozarik would be incapacitated. All she knew was that Japan's witches

---

5. Literally.

65

weren't happy—and she didn't care to be reading about Oz's failures in every worldly newspaper before he even had the chance to Assume his title.

He'd always been that person for her, an impending strength when she felt weak, a calm word when she panicked, a friendly smile when she was alone. The least she could do was return the favor.

She shrugged. "No more than two weeks, I'd say." Paused, considered the date of the Assumation Ceremony, then amended, "Well, maybe three."

Ms. Finch looked like she'd swallowed a lemon. "Absolutely not. We can't sustain that type of loss—"

"Our contract says you don't have a choice."

Ms. Finch stiffened. She really, really didn't like Claire—uppity little actress thinking her talents were worth more than a law degree from Yale—which was probably why she said, "Reputation is everything on the Strip, Ms. Bishop. If you walk away from this for three weeks, you're telling everyone you're unreliable and self-centered. Without Paris Las Vegas vouching for you, you'll never work in this city again."

"Threatening isn't a good look for you," Claire said.

But unfortunately, Ms. Finch was right. Maybe not in such a dramatic manner, but Claire had a sparkling reputation and everyone on the Strip knew it. It was a point of pride; Reiki kicked her out, but Claire still made something of herself. She *was* somebody. Not even a Zaro's power could alter someone's appreciation of character.

Claire was raised in the shadow of a poor reputation. She would never repeat the experience.

So, she sighed and held out a hand. "Give me three weeks. Then I'll be back, and I'll remove that clause about vacations."

Ms. Finch, still stubbornly annoyed about the contract, sniffed. "Two weeks. The clause is removed. *And* I want a return show with all new tricks, something I can promote to recoup the extensive losses you're causing us."

"New illusions, the clause removed, three weeks," Claire said.

"Fine."

They shook hands.

Mr. Hiddles untied the bowtie, pushing to his feet. "Then, ah, I'm also taking a vacation. I deserve it."

"Right you are, sir," Claire said, patting his shoulder. And that was that.

Chapter Ten

16 Years and 93 Days before Death Stopped

"Shut up. Don't you know how *rich* we're going to be?" Kyle Flanderson told his wife, taking a long swig of the canned beer. It tasted like piss—some lite beer that was more water than alcohol. If he closed his eyes, he could imagine it was an amber ale, or maybe an IPA.

Soon, he'd be able to buy those kinds of growlers whenever he wanted. His eyes gleamed as he regarded the toddler in Noelle's arms. Claire, now a feisty three-year-old, squirmed, face wrinkling in fury as her mother tried to coax her into bed.

Claire's bed was shoved in the corner of their room. After all, the Zaro refused to remove the caveat of "you will never leave her alone again." While Maxwell, his son, slept down the hall, Claire was perpetually at their side.

Well, Noelle's side. Kyle wasn't really a *kid* person.

This was a prime example. Claire burst into furious tears, shoving at her mother's shoulders and screaming louder as Noelle tried to tuck her under the sheets. "No! No, I don't wanna. I wanna see Max!"

"Don't talk to me like that, Claire," Noelle hissed, shoving her harder than necessary against the mattress.

At that moment, the magic flared to life. After all, Reiki had given this house an assignment. The walls had ears, and it paid attention to how baby

Claire was treated. And in that moment, it recognized an all-too-common response: violence.

In an equally violent burst of magic, the house lashed back. The lights flickered as magic flowed from the popcorn ceiling to hit Noelle like a truck. She gasped, staggering under the weight of the pain she'd just caused Claire, multiplied tenfold. Tears sprung to her eyes, furious ones, as she slammed to her knees.

"I'm sorry—I'm sorry," she screamed, as if the house cared. Then, more desperate: "Kyle, *do* something."

"Look, just don't push her around." Kyle knew a Zaro's magic was nothing to mess with, and absolutely impossible to overcome.

Noelle, much to his exasperation, was struggling to come to terms with that.

"We're losing control! She's not listening and we can't discipline her. What do you want me to do?"

"She stops when I say 'enough.'" Kyle took another swig of his beer. "We just gotta make sure she knows that's non-negotiable. We'll be able to keep her in line."

"*Bullshit*," Noelle seethed.

"I wanna see Max," Claire cried again.

"Max is sleeping!" Her mother raked her hands in her hair. "Fine, Kyle. If you're so good at this, make her shut up, will you?"

This was a woman on the brink of insanity—and she hadn't been that far from insanity *before* she birthed the next possible leader of the world's witches. Noelle also wasn't a witch herself, and thus resided firmly in the category of humans who regarded the entire Assumation process with derision. She didn't give a shit about the Zaro and her daughter's future.

All she wanted was to *not* have this wailing, complaining child around, for once.

So when Kyle said, "Calm down, Noelle. Think of the money," Noelle saw red. She abandoned the child on the mattress—damn kid had a better bed than she did—and shoved her husband's arm. Her voice was loud and unforgiving.

"What the hell is that supposed to mean? She's three. She hasn't shown us any magic, so how are we supposed to profit off it?"

"She's the next Zaro," Kyle replied. "Even if we can't tell anyone, it's true. We just need to keep her alive long enough that she takes that bitch Zaro's place, and then we're riding high!"

On the bed, Claire stopped crying, the way she always did when her parents fought. Trembling, she inched off the mattress, eyes darting to the door. In her little mind, this room wasn't safe, and never really had been. The house didn't let them shout *at* her, but shouting *around* her was just as bad.

She couldn't tell the difference, most days.

Noelle didn't notice her movement; she was too busy smacking the beer can out of Kyle's hand. It bounced off the shag carpet, adding yet another putrid stain to their floor. "I can't take it anymore. I don't give a shit that she might be famous later. Thanks to that woman, we can't leave her alone. How the hell am I supposed to parent like this?" Now Noelle's eyes narrowed dangerously. "This is your fault, you—you goddamn witch."

"Hey, she's not *my* ruler." Kyle stepped closer, pulling his shoulders back menacingly.

Claire reached the door, peeking into the hallway. And just as she expected, Maxwell was there. In three years, he'd lost a lot of his chubbiness, but he still had friendly, round cheeks and kind eyes. He cast a glance over her shoulder at his father, arguing with his step-mother, and wordlessly took the toddler's hand.

In a rare blessing, the magic Reiki placed on the house allowed Claire to leave her parents' vicinity under the watchful eye of her older brother.

They stumbled into Max's bedroom, but Max led them past the bed and straight to his itty bitty closet. Claire's eyes widened at what he'd done: blankets strung from the hanger bar overhead, secured to the walls with thumb tacks. Inside, he'd found a little battery-powered light, and when he turned it on, the place became something truly magical.

"I made this for you," he said, letting her sneak into the fort first.

"So, um... so pretty," Claire gasped.

A pleased smile crossed his face. He crawled inside after her, gently shut the door, and padded the space underneath with pillows. Then he plucked a juice box from behind him and handed it to her. "They gave me this at school."

"Ooooh." Delighted, Claire fumbled with the straw. Max moved to help her, puncturing the box with practiced ease. He handed it back.

"Two hands," he said, as their parents' argument escalated. Both kids tried not to listen when a loud *crash* echoed through the room next door, or when her father shouted, "Just *leave*, then."

Tears brimmed in Claire's blue eyes as she sucked on the juice box.

Max scootched next to her, pulling her against his side. "I don't like it either. I wish—I wanna be the witch."

"Why?" Claire sniffled. "Why?"

"Cause then they'd be fighting over me, not you."

Claire hunched at the reminder. Her parents fought about a lot of things, but most often, her magic was at the center. She didn't even know what magic felt like, or what it was. Daddy said it was like having a third lung, as essential as breathing, but she didn't know what that meant.

"Can you—give me magic?" Maxwell asked, cheeks coloring in embarrassment. "Do you think you can? Dad said you're powerful. I bet if you tried—"

"I don't know how," Claire sniffled, shoulders shaking as she started to cry in earnest. "I don't—umm—I don't—" she cut off, eyes dropping to her juice once more. Fat tears rolled down her cheeks.

"Okay, it's okay. Shh, it's fine," Maxwell pressed a kiss to her temple, flinching when another round of shouting echoed through the house. Now they were screaming about selling the property.

For a brief moment, Max imagined moving down to Arizona, where his mother lived. She hadn't wanted him before, but maybe now—maybe something changed. Where was she from? Skitsdale? From what she'd told him when she called two years ago, it sounded sunny. It must be better than here.

But he wouldn't go if she didn't take Claire, too.

"I wanna," Claire mumbled against his chest. "But I dunno. I don't know how."

Max wasn't a witch, so he didn't know either. But he patted her head and tried anyway. "Can you feel something, deep in your chest? Like—like how your heart beats, but bigger?" His guess was eerily accurate, but at six years old, he had no way of knowing that. To emphasize, he put her hand on his chest, over his heart.

She felt the beats for a few seconds, sniffling. Closed her eyes. Sipped her juice. Then—then the air shifted.

A push-pull of magic between Claire and Ozarik.

Working in her office in Kyoto, Reiki paused in her shūji, the brush inadvertently pressing harder against the rice paper. A Zaro-level utilization of magic, particularly the persuasion brand. Unfortunately for this moment, Reiki assumed it was Ozarik. After all, the house in Spokane promised to alert her of true magic at the Flanderson residence.

What Reiki didn't anticipate was a three-year-old possessing the ability to *hide* her magic.

And so, Reiki made a note to visit Ozarik at her earliest convenience... while Claire Flanderson unknowingly persuaded the minds of her family.

To be fair, Claire wasn't intending to manipulate people. She *wanted* to give Maxwell a magical ability—Max always helped her, and she wanted him happy. But focusing on a spell at such a young age was nearly impossible, so although she did have the power to give Max a magical ability... that wasn't what happened.

Instead, Claire yanked magic from Ozarik, halfway around the globe, right as her mother began to scream again. And her little mind got distracted, and as she twisted the power under her will, her only thought was, "Make Mommy go away."

In the next room, instantly, Noelle said, "I'm leaving."

It was so abrupt that Kyle thought he misheard. But when she began shoving her clothes into a ratted backpack, almost on instinct, Kyle panicked. "W-What? Babe, you can't leave. What about the kids?"

"Only one of them is mine, Kyle." Noelle's tone was blank, lacking all her usual passive aggression. Instead, it was merely facts. "Call Maxwell's mother if you're so scared to be left alone."

"What about Claire?" Kyle grabbed her arm, forced her to look at him.

Noelle smiled serenely, mind dazed with magic. *Leave. Leave now.* The words pushed against her soul, and she was perfectly content with the decision. "Claire's your problem now, witch. Enjoy your long-term investment scheme."

Without another word, Noelle shouldered her backpack and walked out of the house forever.

In the closet, Claire finished her juice box. "Do you—um, do you have magic?"

Maxwell didn't feel any different. "How will I know?"

"I dunno," Claire replied.

The two children sat in silence for a moment, and then Max said, "Well, it sounds like they're done. Come on. You can sleep with me tonight."

It would be the first night Claire didn't sleep in her parents' bedroom. She perked up at the thought. "Okay." He took her juice box, and she crawled on sticky hands and knees out of the closet, blinking in the abrasive light of his bedroom. Maxwell had just closed his closet door, hiding their secret space, when Kyle staggered into the room.

"Claire, you—" he stopped short, staring at her. "You're... here. Away from me."

She stared up at him. "Hi, Daddy."

"Hi," he replied, eyes flicking to Max.

"She wasn't alone," Max offered helpfully.

A long, slow smile spread across his face. "I see that." Now he approached, ignoring how both children flinched as he picked up Claire. He handled her with the gentle love of a banker hugging a bar of gold. "Mommy left, Claire, but she'll be back once she cools off.[1] Until then, maybe you and I can work on some magic."

---

1. She wouldn't.

Kyle wasn't attuned enough to feel the shift, not the way Reiki had. But he also realized that if he wanted to make money off his magical child, he needed to make sure she *actually* had magic.

After all, she seemed old enough to understand him now.

Claire stared passively, understanding far more than he gave her credit for. "Mommy's not coming back."

"Of course she is."

Maxwell rubbed his arm, thinking again of Skitsdale.

Claire just shook her head, and Kyle planted a sloppy kiss against her wispy blonde hair. "Don't you worry about that. Tomorrow, we're going to find your magical ability, okay?" Then his eyes cut to Max. "And you're in charge of her until then."

He put her on Maxwell's bed, patted his son's head, and strolled from the room to crack open another beer.

The house didn't intervene.

And by Claire's standard, it was a good night.

Chapter Eleven

25 Days before Death Stopped

Reiki's end began with a letter.

In a digital age, a physical letter seemed almost comical. But international calls were a bitch, especially regarding ultra-powerful witches who possessed both the ability teleport anywhere in the world with a thought—and the utter lack of knowledge to own and operate a cell phone.

Which was why the Zaro required multiple aciras to be hired for the sole purpose of sorting through the incredible volume of fan mail that arrived on Javarini each day, identifying the important letters, and delivering them to said Zaro... wherever they may be. If it sounded pleasant, consider that while a Zaro could teleport anywhere in an instant, the rest of the world's witches—including these aciras—couldn't.

It basically resulted in the world's largest, most chaotic game of cat-and-mouse.

Which would explain Acira Min-Ji's exasperated, exhausted expression when she staggered up to them in a Canadian hospital as Zaro Reiki assessed patient zero of a hyper-infectious disease.

Inside the sickroom, Ozarik had settled a blanket of magic over the woman, containing her in an invisible bubble of calm while Zaro Reiki worked. Eradicating illness was a spell attempted by Zaros over the centuries, especially after the Black Plague fiasco. Of course, Zaro Arjun's predecessor had forgotten the majority of it—much to the dismay of everyone locked in battle during World War I. Arjun himself perfected it after the fact.

It involved highly concentrated magic, a pinch of reassurance, and lots of lemon juice.

Okay, the reassurance was voluntary.

That was part of the reason why Ozarik, in charge of maintaining that bubble of calm, had no problem breaking concentration when Min-Ji hesitantly tapped on the window. Two doctors scowled over her shoulder, irate at the interruption, but she just waved a letter at Ozarik and mouthed, "*Gingeubhan,*" which—for those of us without translational powers—meant "urgent" in Korean.

Across from the patient—who was shaking with a viral fever and had the tendency to stop breathing if left unsupervised—Reiki frowned at her protégé.

"We're busy, Ozarik," she said, pointedly.

Ozarik pressed his lips together and reinstated the calming bubble, tweaking his magic around the patient—whose name was Cynthia—as the acrid scent of lemons cut through the air. He felt Reiki nudging around Cynthia's soul, locating the tiny black nugget of illness in a sea of blinding white optimism. With magical fingers, she plucked it out, carefully bundling it up in the space between souls so it couldn't bother anyone again.

Almost immediately, Cynthia's fever broke. Seconds later, she inhaled without gasping, and a moment after that, she felt nearly back to normal. It was truly a miracle, and the less altruistic doctor beyond the glass sent a silent prayer that the Zaro would never change career paths.

Meanwhile, Reiki clasped Cynthia's shoulder, offering a warm, encouraging smile. She nudged her own magic into the woman's chaotic brain, a spell designed to soothe an erring soul.

"You're going to be fine, my dear. We'll make sure no one else was infected along the way. Is there anything else we can do for you?"

Cynthia normally would have been aghast with anxiety over the future suddenly staring her down, but Reiki's magic was strong and effective—and that particular spell was one of the reasons people regarded Zaros with high esteem. Curing a plague was flashy, but it was these little moments of comfort that told the world, *your Zaro cares.*

And she did.

Cynthia shook her head. "Ah, n-no ma'am. Thank you."

Zaro Reiki cast a glance at her protégé, her successor, the young man who was *supposed* to be learning from these experiences, channeling this empathetic, encouraging energy. She'd taught him that spell years ago, but she rarely saw him use it.

Now, Reiki raised one delicate eyebrow—but Ozarik didn't even notice. His spell had already collapsed, and he was gone before anyone could blink, wrenching the door open to retrieve the letter from Min-Ji.

This was an incredibly rude thing to do, but no one would say so with the Zaro standing right there.

Reiki had every intention of addressing this, but not publicly. The world adored their Future-Zaro, and she would not deprive them of that—even if he seemed to be slipping as the months wore on.

A dark part of her heart whispered, *it's probably Claire's doing.* But that was awfully impressive, considering Reiki knew for a fact they'd ceased their relationship, and at this moment, Claire was preparing for yet another of her "not real magic" magic shows.

Acira Min-Ji lifted her chin and said in Korean, "It's from Flanderson. I brought it straight here, as ordered."

Ozarik grinned wide, tearing into the envelope. The paper was thin, striped in blue lines and clearly ripped out of a cheap notebook. In scrawled handwriting, it read, "I'd be honored to meet the Future-Zaro." And an address for a cheap hotel in Denver.

The world shifted into certainty.

Foreboding tickled Reiki's neck as she eased the door shut, staring at Ozarik with growing dismay. But they had a job to do here, so instead of speaking to him, she smiled at her acira and turned to the doctors.

"It is done. The sickness has been eradicated, but I will follow up and ensure no one else suffers the same fate."

"I thought you only helped witches," one of the doctors blurted.

He was, unironically, not a witch.

Reiki smiled, folding her arms in the sleeves of her kimono. It had been an honored gift from a reputable craftsman in Kyoto, and she was thoroughly pleased to display it. "The world's witches are my priority, but I will not turn a blind eye towards those in need. And a sickness like this—" she paused, glancing over her shoulder at Cynthia, who still looked befuddled. "Well, this was worth our time."

Now she glanced again at Ozarik.

He faltered, eyes darting from the letter. "Ah, yes. We're happy to help."

Outside, Min-Ji joined Clementine for an impromptu Meeting of the Aciras—which sounded impressive, but was essentially coordination on how they'd be getting back to Javarini, depending on whether the Zaro and her pupil would poof home beforehand or fly with them.

Said Zaro and her pupil followed them out of the hospital's double doors. Reiki paused in a lovely patch of shade under a broad pine tree, taking a moment to inhale the crisp Canadian air. Then, to business.

"Ozarik," she said, quietly.

He stopped short, bowing his head at her tone. "Ah, apologies, Reiki. I was distracted."

"A Zaro cannot afford to get distracted while handling something of this importance," Reiki replied, and her voice was curter than usual. She realized it, drew a breath, and centered her mind. "What were the contents of the letter?"

Now he sheepishly tugged it out and handed it over.

She scanned the message, a frown on her features. "Fan mail?"

"An agreement to meet. Reiki, this is from Claire's *father*."

Zaro Reiki stiffened. The years had not been kind to her mind, nor her soul, in regards to Claire Bishop—nèe Flanderson. What had once seemed like a very wise and appropriate decision had become, in hindsight, a coward fleeing responsibility. And as much as Reiki tried to make it right, Kyle Flanderson was a direct link to the mistakes of her past.

In the most benevolent, stately way possible, she hoped he'd die alone.

"You're meeting him?" she asked.

Everything in her mind screamed that it was a bad idea.

He grinned, bright and confident, offering a glimpse of the little boy she'd trained a decade ago. He'd shown such promise then. Now he waved the letter like a white flag. "He's willing to make amends. He wants to reconnect with her."

That wasn't what the letter said, but Reiki didn't know what Ozarik had previously discussed with Kyle Flanderson. Clearly, she should have been keeping a better eye on things.

"He is dangerous, Ozarik."

It was a bold declaration, and stopped Ozarik cold. "He can't hurt me, Reiki. And if you're worried, maybe you should come with me." His expression slipped into true determination. "Actually, you *should*. Claire always said you hated him, but—but I know it'd mean a lot if you two reconciled."

This was incredibly, fantastically false.

Reiki, however, had no way of knowing that. She pressed her lips together, watching the zealous approach her protégé was taking with a known criminal. "Kyle Flanderson is not the type of person to reconcile with, Ozarik. I suggest you forgo this discussion and leave it alone."

"He's a *witch*, and he's requesting an audience," Ozarik snapped, angry now.

So fast to change his temper.

"Many witches request audiences. We do not have time to oblige them all. Or are you willing to tell the people of Argentina why we missed their celebration?" Now she uncrossed her arms, brow furrowing as he seemed to consider which was more important.

She recognized the moment he arrived at the wrong conclusion.

"Claire's father takes priority. It's the least we can do for her," Ozarik said. "If you really don't want to come, then *you* can handle Argentina."

Between a thriving country requesting her presence for a holiday, and Ozarik meeting a criminal, Reiki knew where she'd be. She also knew, deep down, that this meeting would go horribly wrong—felt the magical certainty of it like poison through her veins. But Zaros never feared their own deaths—they were too busy, too important, to mourn themselves beforehand. The Universe would propel itself the way it always did, and their lives would pass as they should.

It was a lesson she worried Ozarik hadn't yet learned.

Meanwhile, Ozarik shoved the paper in his pocket and stomped off to Min-Ji and Clementine, interrupting their session. They listened with rapt attention as he said something curt, and then he vanished in a cloud of huckleberry smoke.

Clementine stepped to Reiki shortly after, frowning. "He's getting touchy lately, isn't he?" Now her expression darkened. "Probably Claire's fault."

Reiki suddenly felt sick, off-balance.

She rubbed her forehead. "I must take a brief sabbatical. I will return to Javarini tomorrow."

And before Clementine could interrupt, could insist on coming with her, Reiki poofed to Japan—and began the long trek to a very holy shrine.

Chapter Twelve

18 Days before Death Stopped

Claire escorted Mr. Hiddles out of Ms. Finch's corner office and bid him adieu, then stopped briefly by her condo in Mandalay Bay.[1] This was more of a formality than anything, as she could poof home at literally any point—but the condo was already feeling slighted at the idea she'd be traveling for weeks.

Her condo embodied a lavish life in Las Vegas. Sweeping penthouse views through gold-tinted glass, a wrap-around balcony overlooking the absolutely blinding Luxor pyramid, heavy granite countertops that cost more than a yacht, leather and brick accents hidden by a few towering plants that had no business thriving indoors.

It was everything a Zaro *shouldn't* be.

Which was absolutely the point.

---

1. Technically, Mandalay Bay didn't have condos. Technically, it was a hotel... at least, that's what the manager thought, until Claire Bishop strolled through the doors with an absurd amount of cash and told him which unit she desired—at which point four celebrity suites merged into one condo that the building hoped would suit her fancy. To this day, the manager isn't certain how this happened.

She packed a few things in her bedroom, spreading outfits across her Nevada King[2]. Perhaps with a hint of malice towards Reiki and her ideals, Claire chose whatever would raise eyebrows: high midriffs, plunging necklines, ostentatious jewelry. She'd look like a drunk bride at a bachelorette party, but hey. When from Vegas.

Shouldering her bag, Claire heaved a longsuffering sigh and told the ceiling: "Don't wait up. Something tells me I might be a while." A pause, a thought, then, "And don't let my plants die."

The condo, feeling vaguely miserable at the whole thing, stubbornly decided maybe it *would*. In response to that traitorous thought, the palm trees growing in huge pots beside the front door shivered.

Claire noticed none of this, and with a snap of her fingers, poofed to Javarini. Completely by chance—or subconscious luck—she landed in her old bedroom. Her whole body tensed as the familiar wood floor and stone walls took shape around her, but of course, Reiki's protective spells never hit.

Force of habit.

Ignoring her stomach twisting over the teleportation, Claire surveyed the room, wrinkling her nose at the barren walls, the plain bed, the space where her desk used to be. It was a near identical copy to Ozarik's bedroom across the castle. The mattress had lumps she couldn't magic out, a perpetual draft seeped through the stone, and despite the castle having electricity and outlets everywhere else, Reiki had removed any form of technology from her exiled prodigy's space.

"Well. This won't do," Claire told the bedroom. "When I get back, I want a widescreen TV."

She didn't watch or particularly care about television shows, but the act of defiance almost settled her nerves.

Almost. Because the truth was, the Magnificent Claire Bishop was a stage name, and one she only took after Reiki's exile. She didn't belong in

---

2. Which was a mattress similar to a California King, but twice as wide and three times as expensive.

the Zaro's headquarters any more than an atheist belonged in a convent. Even standing in this room, vivid memories crashed into her: memories of Claire's magic yanking posters off the wall, of splintering the wooden desk, of books soaring around the room.

And Reiki, looming in the center of it all, that perpetual look of disappointment settling over her features.

The physical remnants of their fight had long been cleaned—by Aciradaan Clementine, in fact—but Claire's anger still echoed through the air.

Suddenly suffocating, Claire spun abruptly from the room, stomping into the hallway. After all, she was here for *Ozarik*, and damn it if she'd spend her paltry three weeks wallowing in this forbidden space.

Of course, she managed two steps down the hallway before Ozarik poofed onto her.

Literally.

She crashed to the ground under his weight, and her elbow slammed into the unforgiving floor. Claire hissed, but Ozarik was so engulfed in his panicked daze that he didn't notice. Instead, he gasped, "Claire! Thank the Universe. You have to help me."

In a puff of huckleberry smoke, he magicked them to the study.

Reiki's study.

If Claire thought her bedroom was bad, this place sent a literal shiver up her spine.

The room was in total disarray. Papers—more articles about Reiki's murder, Claire noticed with distaste—were strewn about the worn wooden floor. Differing timekeeping devices, everything from candles with hour markers to a genuine Roman sundial had been spread across the far wall, hidden in shadows. The windows were foggy, odd considering it was a rather lovely day outside, and the ominous nature of it seemed to lend an air of desperation to Ozarik's already frantic mood.

"Changing things up from your castle in Slovakia?" Claire drawled, feeling through space to locate a single can of grape soda deep within the kitchen. With a snap of her fingers, she yanked it into her hand instead. "I thought you needed a retreat that 'wasn't on the island.'"

Six years ago, Ozarik noticed that while Reiki did indeed work out of Javarini, she seemed to spend much of her time pouring over documents in the privacy of her embassy in Kyoto. Ever-determined to be a good Zaro like her, Oz declared he needed a retreat of his own, and upon locating the crumbling castle in the towering mountains of his home country, created a drafty "office" that Claire absolutely hated.

Having an office elsewhere in the world seemed silly, in Claire's mind. A temporary fix. Zaros were worldly beings, but they always returned to Javarini. It was inevitable, like the perturbed barking of a dog drowning out an ambulance's wail, or the fizziness of the beverage in her hand.

Of course, that could simply be because Claire herself had never felt connected to Spokane. Not like Ozarik with the Tatras Mountains, or Reiki with Kyoto. If she'd been allowed to stay on Javarini, Claire probably never would have left.

Regardless, Claire now sipped the grape soda and resolved to steal an American brand next time: her favorite had six times the sugar and was seventeen times as delicious.

Ozarik waved off her comment. "I needed some research from—well, never mind. Please, Claire, tell me you're here for good." His tone was pleading. A bit of his magic seeped into her, a barely imperceptible bribe.

Claire quirked an eyebrow, raising a solid barrier to keep his magic where it belonged. She rubbed her smarting elbow, somewhat petulantly. "I'm here for now. Why are you panicking?"

"Because I don't know what I'm *doing*." At his wordless intention, a few candles in the dark corner flared to life, illuminating a dusty computer Claire hadn't seen before.

To be fair, the entire corner was new to her—as was the room. Reiki's study in Javarini had been so sacred, so private, that the Japanese woman never bothered to have a door installed.

The only access was a window five stories off the ground, or teleportation.

And since only two other witches in the world had that ability, Reiki put the fear of... well, *herself* into them. Claire had convinced Oz to sneak inside exactly once, and the immediate result was Reiki poofing them into the middle of a herd of sheep.

In Scotland.

And then she siphoned the magic required to get home, so they had to use human methods to stagger back to Javarini. Which, as one might expect for a sacred island with one private airport, was *very hard*.

Regardless, Claire wasn't pleased to be yanked here now. But Ozarik seemed perfectly at home—which, of course he was. He'd been raised in this castle. No one within had ever viewed him as an intruder, an imposter. Ozarik was the world's beloved prince, and anything that belonged to Reiki belonged to him by extension.

Watching him bustle about, a long-buried spark of anger flared in her chest. She shouldn't even *be* here. All of this was Ozarik's duty; her job was delighting audiences once a day, twice on Saturdays.

Claire drew a deep breath, calming her emotions.

Not the time.

"Look," Ozarik said as the computer booted up with an ancient screeching sound[3] that made Claire wince. He jammed his thumb at the images that flickered to pixelated life: fires in Belfast, angry crowds in Buenos Aires, the grim-faced pope addressing people in the Vatican. "The world is in chaos."

"Sure. Because it was so orderly before."

He shot her an exasperated look. "Not like this. Rioters are swarming in big cities. Alliances are fracturing. The witches of the world think a human killed Reiki, and I—I can't convince them otherwise."

Claire, who had heard surprisingly few—*magically* few, in fact—details of Reiki's death, quirked an eyebrow. "Did a human kill her?"

It was the wrong question to ask. Ozarik hunched under her gaze, fresh tears spilling over his eyes. "Does it matter? S-She died. But it was my fault. *My* fault." He shuddered, and the ancient computer sparked under his

---

3. For the youngsters out there, that sound was dial-up.

grief, smoke slipping through the vents on its chassis. An acrid scent filled the air.

Claire yanked his magic out of the machine, and the screen went black. She stepped closer, daring to put a hand on his arm. If the gesture felt weighted, it should—this was the first time Claire had physically touched him in months.

Ozarik glanced at her hand, and she hastily removed it.

"It's not your fault," she said.

It actually was, but Claire didn't know that.

"I don't know what to do," he whispered. "I wish... I wish I could bring Reiki back." He moved to the foggy window, surveying the witchy staff swarming the castle grounds like ants, positioning the black mourning banners of a Zaro passed. His voice was quiet, somber. "She always had a plan."

Claire snorted. "Well, that's a lie."

One might assume a person like Claire should have respect for the dead—but one would be mistaken. While Claire grieved the loss of their Zaro for Oz's sake, she's spent the better part of four years alone and loathing Reiki's worldwide presence. The only good news was that Reiki had avoided Las Vegas like the plague, and now, her death opened the entire world.

It was *freeing*.

Ozarik didn't think so. He stared at Claire, a little hurt. "Reiki was doing her best. She always did her best."

Claire could argue that point too, but she chose not to. Instead, she strolled towards the old woman's desk. It had to be here somewhere: the object of their desire at 13 years old, the reason Claire convinced Ozarik to sneak into the study as teenagers, right before their odyssey in Scotland.

Where was it?

"What are you doing?" Ozarik asked.

Claire shrugged, tugging open the creaky wooden drawers of Reiki's desk. "The world's witches couldn't care less how Reiki died: what they *want* is to know that you're stepping up. There's a reason we have a Zaro,

Oz. It's not fancy displays of magic." Much as the words tasted like poison on her tongue, Claire forced out: "It's peace."

And for all her mistakes, Reiki was excellent at keeping the peace.

Frustrated at the lack of progress, Claire tried a different method, pressing a hand on the desktop, searching through its contents with her magic. The prize revealed itself immediately, and the hidden drawer hastily popped open under her prying gaze. She tugged out a thin black tube, then tossed it at Ozarik.

"Use this."

He fumbled to catch it, twisting the lid. "What is it?"

"The map."

It was all she had to say. His eyes widened, and reverently, he tugged it out. The parchment was ancient, dating back to the 16th Zaro.[4]

The world—as current witches recognized it—appeared in soft black ink. All along it, pinprick dots gleamed yellow. Claire, who had never actually seen the map, blinked. "Wow. Didn't expect so many witches in Wichita."

Ozarik laughed, a watery sound. "I mean, the alliteration can't be beat."

She flashed him a charming grin, then stepped back.

After all, this was the Zaro's responsibility.

Communicating with the world's witches was a tricky subject, with so many people moving or thinking or sleeping at any given point. The map acted as a focusing point, one Ozarik now used to concentrate his power.

Claire winced as he tugged at her magic, too, depleting it enough that she felt weak in the knees. Reiki, a fully-fledged Zaro, could use the map on her own. Ozarik didn't have that luxury—not as long as Claire was alive. She casually, subtly, took a seat in an old wooden chair as Ozarik closed his eyes, pressing his hands on either side of the map.

---

4. The 15th Zaro also used a map, but stupidly left the original—for safekeeping—inside the Library of Alexandria. It caused quite a conundrum for the 16th Zaro.

His presence touched her mind, and in that moment she was linked with Ozarik alongside every witch alive. It was unsettling, simultaneously connecting to the heartbeats, hopes, and fears of an entire species. She gripped the chair and hissed, "Talk fast. Everyone hates this."

"Oh," Ozarik winced, and a fresh wave of his panic swept through the connection. "Um. Right. H-Hello, everyone. This—this is F-Future-Zaro Ozarik, coming to you live from—ah, from the Holy Castle. In Javarini. My home. Yes."

This was, quite obviously, a disaster.

Although she tried her best to hide it, Claire's exasperation was palpable. Ozarik tugged at his collar and desperately tried to refocus his attention. "I am reaching out to confirm that—that Reiki is d-dead." He choked on the word, and Claire pushed swiftly to her feet, shoving more magic into him. He reeled from the force of it, but recentered it to strengthen his voice. "But we do not mourn her. I—I mean, we do. Mourn her, that is. But her legacy, um... her legacy is peace. So—don't fight."

Under Claire's horrified stare, Ozarik cut the broadcast with a panicked squeak. The map, mortified by second-hand embarrassment, curled into itself. In all honesty, that debacle was *nothing* compared to the 75th Zaro's Black Plague speech, but of course, the map couldn't tell anyone about that. Claire shoved it back into its thin black tube and resolutely twisted the cap.

"Christ, Oz, what was that?"

He wilted under her stare, burying his head in his hands. "I don't *know*. Claire, I can't—I don't think I can do this. Being Zaro. Every time I try, I think of Reiki. She s-shouldn't have died. I shouldn't be doing this!"

Claire slapped him upside the head. It wasn't an aggressive hit, but it certainly stopped him cold. While he blinked at her, she slammed her hands on the desktop, bending so they were eye level. Her blue eyes burned like the base of a flame, and her mouth set in a determined frown.

"This," she said, quiet and intense, "is what you've been working towards your entire life, Ozarik. Don't you *dare* imply you can't handle it. Reiki gave you every opportunity to succeed, and now it's on your shoulders. Got it?"

Ozarik nodded, glumly.

Claire sighed, pushing upright again. "Come on. Something tells me we need to get to Kyoto."

"Y-Yeah. Okay," Ozarik said.

But nothing was okay, and they both knew it.

Chapter Thirteen

86 Days before Death Stopped

Ozarik only experienced true love once in his life, and he realized it the moment Claire Bishop broke up with him.

Reiki was in a particular mood that morning, although she hid it well. In fact, the only reason Ozarik discerned something was wrong was because the popes—even Clementine—had made themselves scarce, and across the grassy knoll, the cats in their second castle were yowling like a pack of wolves on the hunt. Rather than trying to soothe the temperamental creatures, Ozarik carefully constructed a sound bubble around the castle for some peace and quiet.

Meanwhile, Reiki strolled crisply towards the kitchen with a newspaper tucked under one arm, ignoring him outright.

"Everything okay?" he dared to ask, trailing behind her.

Reiki's movements were controlled... almost *too* controlled. Her hand seemed to tremble as she set the newspaper on the kitchen island. The head chef—an Indian witch who'd quickly become an expert at Japanese cuisine—wasn't present, but he'd left a plate of melonpan on the counter. Reiki carefully removed the plastic wrap, choosing the crispiest-looking one.

The way she bit into it was almost vicious, if a woman as kind and mild as Reiki could be anything close to the word.

Ozarik chuckled, but there was no mirth in the sound. "Ah, should I go?"

"I knew she couldn't stay out of the limelight," Reiki said tightly.

The only "she" they ever discussed was Claire. Ozarik, who'd secretly been dating Claire for almost four years, stiffened. This was a careful line to walk. Reiki deserved his respect and trust, but Claire had earned his devotion, and Ozarik wasn't sure where his loyalties fell when they clashed.

"Her show is a hit, but they proved she isn't using magic." *Probably*, Ozarik thought, but he wasn't about to say that. "She's making a name for herself. Something that isn't tied to the Zaro title." He let that linger between them, a passive reminder that Reiki specifically ordered that the day Claire left Javarini forever.

What Claire did with her time after that moment was entirely her choice, in his mind.

Reiki was under a different opinion. With an uncharacteristic, hollow laugh, she pushed the newspaper in his direction. The *New York Times*. Huh. That was a lot further than Las Vegas. Brow furrowing, Ozarik unfurled the paper to see the headline.

FUTURE-ZARO OZARIK STOPS WILDFIRE, SAVES TOWN.

The blood drained from Oz's body.

Across the table, Reiki was watching him carefully, her expression unreadable as always.

The Zaro was no fool: she knew he wasn't behind this... and the only other person with that kind of magic was Claire. Which meant this was open defiance of every tenuous peace they'd managed in the last four years.

Claire's freedom was fading. Ozarik scrambled for an explanation, desperate to keep Reiki from confronting her in Nevada.

He settled on a lie: "I was hoping you wouldn't hear about that."

"Indeed." Reiki's gaze was uncomfortably intense, even as she took another bite of the doughy ball in her hand.

Oz cleared his throat, continuing the ruse. "I didn't have a choice. After all, the point of being a Zaro is *helping* people." He gestured to the image that accompanied the headline, running his fingers over an ashen-faced citizen standing beside his untouched house, staring dramatically into the burnt woods mere steps away.

Claire must have worked all night to stop that fire. No wonder Ozarik's magic had been low yesterday—he should have known.

He should have *been* there.

But something else soured in his gut too: irritation. Claire had intervened, but the world didn't know *Claire the Almost-Zaro* existed. Of course she'd use a disguise. Of course she'd manipulate the magic to make herself seem like Ozarik. He was the hero. He could easily save a village from total destruction.

And yet, knowing he hadn't had a choice in this matter, knowing Reiki was now infuriated at him, made him resent Claire for that choice, just a little.

He forced a laugh. "At least we'll get some good PR from this."

"Enough." Reiki's voice was final, and the word rang through the kitchen. Across the knoll, even the cats went silent inside Ozarik's bubble. Reiki set her melonpan back on the plate, rubbed her hands on a nearby napkin. "The Zaro does not intervene with natural events. We do not *stop* towns from burning. If we quell an earthquake, a larger one amasses in the depths of the Earth. If we extinguish a wildfire, the underbrush doesn't burn, and one of greater devastation will take its place the following year."

"I was protecting citizens—" Ozarik tried to say.

Reiki's eyes flashed. "*You* were studying the civil unrest in Comoros."

Oz clamped his mouth shut, something akin to fear curdling in his gut. For even though he was a verified adult, Reiki was the closest thing he had to a mother and a mentor, and failing her made him feel like a failure, too.

Which made her next sentence so hard to hear. "I am finished, Ozarik. Finished with how you protect her and her poor choices. Finished with her ambition, her desperation for recognition and glory. She has always been a negative influence on you."

That same protective instinct flared to life, and Ozarik crossed his arms. "All she ever wanted was a chance. You never even gave her that!"

"I gave her three years in my home, under my tutelage."

"You gave her a quarter of my education, then expected her to perform to the same caliber. None of this is Claire's fault, Reiki."

"A good witch must live with the choices they make, rather than hiding behind excuses." Reiki drew a breath, held it for five seconds, and released it. "You're in love with her, but she will cause you nothing but harm. The Zaro cannot form earthly attachments for this reason. I will give you one week to choose where your loyalties lie, and then I will be taking matters into my own hands."

And with that, Reiki swept from the kitchen.

Ozarik barely waited until she'd left the room before poofing to Las Vegas.

The late afternoon sun shone through Claire's gold-tinted windows, and perhaps it was Ozarik's imagination, but the entire apartment seemed gaudier today. He stood alone in her living room, eyes flicking to the red leather couch, the absurdly thick granite countertops, the house plants three times taller than he was. The ceiling soared, the floor glistened, and everything was bold and unnecessary.

Ozarik was fuming, but even he could recognize why maybe, *maybe*, Reiki thought Claire Bishop hadn't been right for the Zaro role.

He still didn't *agree* with her, but he could see it.

It only took a few minutes for Claire to emerge from her bedroom, dressed in an embroidered bathrobe as she ran a towel over damp hair. She stopped short, quirking her head. "Oh, Oz. Didn't expect you today. I don't have a lot of time to talk; curtain's in a couple hours."

She sounded reserved, tired. Although there were no physical scars on her, Ozarik could feel her depleted magic. She'd worn herself to the bone quelling that wildfire. He cleared his throat. "You're still going to work?"

That was the moment Claire noticed the newspaper in his hand. She paused, a frown deepening her features. "Heard about that, hmm?"

"Hard not to." Ozarik tossed it on the kitchen counter and strode to her, pulling her into a too-tight hug. She stiffened up, tense. Like she was waiting for him to start yelling.

All his anger bled away instead. "I wish you hadn't done it alone."

"Well, it's the same amount of magic either way." When he pulled back, she held his gaze, blue meeting brown. She looked beautiful, somewhat pink from the hot shower, damp hair crimping under the press of the towel. "Hopefully you weren't planning any big displays last night."

"No, I was studying." Reiki's ultimatum rested on his shoulders. Ozarik stepped back, suddenly wishing he'd formulated a battle plan before popping into her condo and disrupting her life.

Claire noticed. She tilted her head. "Something's wrong."

"No. It's fine."

It didn't take a magician to see through his lies. Claire draped the towel around her neck and gripped the ends, expression coolly ambivalent. "Reiki's pissed, isn't she?"

"She's, ah—yeah. A bit."

"Because I took your appearance?" Claire scoffed. "I have no idea what that woman wants. She tells me to lay low, and then gets irate when I cover my tracks."

"Claire, how is extinguishing an entire wildfire *laying low*?"

It came out wrong, and he instantly cringed. But it was too late; Claire had spent most of her life under disapproving stares, and she wasn't about to tolerate it now. Her walls slammed into place.

"Henry's aunt lives in that town, Ozarik. They were *choking* on smoke." Claire whipped the towel from around her shoulders, slapping it towards the ground. "What did you want me to do?"

What *did* he want from her? Ozarik thought about it. "You could have helped with evacuations. Or pulled the smoke from their lungs at the hospital. Humans fight fires every day, and you—" he drew a breath, bracing himself. "You went overboard. There's a reason Reiki isn't occupying every headline in the world."

"Because she doesn't *do* anything," Claire replied stiffly.

"She helps people every day. Just, in subtler ways. Ways that won't have sweeping ramifications."

"I can handle ramifications."

"*You're* not even the Future-Zaro," Ozarik exclaimed, too loudly, but he couldn't stop. "The consequences of this will be my problem, not yours."

The words hung between them. Claire held his gaze, blue eyes glistening with unshed tears. Then, abruptly, she spun on her heel and stomped into her room. Without a word or a twist of magic, the door—indignant on her behalf—slammed shut behind her.

The sound echoed in her wake.

Ozarik pressed against the other side of the wood, quietly cursing himself. "Claire. That—that wasn't what I meant."

"Oh, I don't think that's true," she called, voice muffled. The slamming of dresser drawers filled the room, then angry silence.

"Big displays of magic should only be performed after careful consideration. I'm just... asking for a little decorum." Ozarik scrubbed his eyes, feeling a hundred years old. How many times had they fought this fight?

Too many, he realized.

And beyond the door, Claire was buttoning her collared shirt and thinking the same thing.

Moments ticked by, and finally Claire emerged. Her hair was magically dry and styled, and her eyes smoldered. "It's my magic too, Oz. Just because you're Reiki's golden child doesn't mean I'm not entitled to use it how I see fit."

"But a Zaro doesn't interfere—"

"Damn good thing I'm not a Zaro, then."

This was careening out of control, but Ozarik couldn't stop it. He lacked Reiki's self-control, her ability to recenter herself in an argument. It was one of his greatest weaknesses—and what propelled him to snap, "Honestly, it probably is."

Claire's eyes widened.

Never, not in nearly twenty years, had Ozarik outright agreed with Reiki. He'd broken the unspoken rule—the one that said Ozarik basked, uninhibited, in the blessed glow of adoring witches everywhere... and in exchange, Claire could remain silently convinced that she'd do *just* as good a job, had she been given the chance.

"Well," she said, quietly.

"Come on, Claire," Ozarik exclaimed, gesturing to the heavy furnishings, the ridiculous plants, the windows and countertops and even her gold-imbued outfit. "Zaros aren't selfish. We don't fall prey to greed or material objects, and we certainly don't prioritize the needs of our friends over the safety of the world's witches." He tossed his hands into the air. "Can't you see why Reiki's upset?"

Claire crossed her arms, her chin jutting out stubbornly. In truth, she was wondering—for the first time—if she *was* wrong. Claire Bishop wasn't a person with an overwhelming sense of duty. If it hadn't been *Henry* begging for her help, she honestly wouldn't have lifted a finger for something so dangerous, so draining.

Claire prioritized number one—because if she didn't, no one else would. That was the real reason why, the day Reiki exiled her from Javarini, Claire didn't argue.

And that was something Ozarik could never quite reconcile about her.

"Claire, say something," Oz pleaded.

She arched an eyebrow, even as her heart fractured. "What would you like to hear?"

He rubbed his face. "I don't know. Something that tells me you won't do this again. Something concrete, so I can prove to Reiki you're not using magic with reckless abandon."

"Oz."

Very suddenly, Ozarik regretted visiting Claire at all.

But she took a step back, holding her arms tight against her chest, brows knitting together. "This—this isn't working. We're too different."

The words hung between them.

"What?" That didn't track. In Ozarik's mind, they were two sides of the same coin. Two halves of a whole. One swing of a pendulum's weight.

But even he was beginning to realize, gazing past her remorseful expression to her perfectly-styled hair, her gaudy pre-stage outfit, her absurdly lavish condo, that maybe she was right. Maybe they'd grown apart in more ways than one.

He just hadn't let himself consider it before this moment.

Claire buttoned the cuffs of her shirt, carefully avoiding his gaze. "You were raised on Javarini, groomed for royalty and power with no shortage of people who loved and challenged you." She shook her head. "*I* was raised in a bad suburb of Spokane. My dad's favorite pastime was running cons on anyone stupid enough to believe him. Including me."

She kept her childhood, her parents, carefully guarded, and Reiki was notoriously tight-lipped about it. It was the one looming question mark in the life of Claire Bishop, the one avenue Ozarik couldn't seem to discover.

Her final two words spoke volumes to him.

"That happened a long time ago. It doesn't define you now." His words were desperate.

"Sure. Because the past always stays where it belongs," Claire replied, neutrally. "Come on, Ozarik. We're not the same people anymore. We've grown up—and grown apart."

They were breaking up.

It slammed into Ozarik with the force of a tsunami, dragging him into the depths. He couldn't breathe. Couldn't think. Even as she waited for his response, he floundered. "That's not... Look, she wants me to choose, but—but Claire, it's always you. *Always.* I don't mean—" he cut himself off, inhaling a shaking breath. "You're my best friend. Please."

Please don't go.

But she was already gone, and they both knew it. Claire took his hands, squeezing them gently.

He wanted to kiss her: an intimacy she'd never really enjoyed, but would do occasionally because it made him feel happier than all the magic in the world. He wanted to hug her again, to feel her heart thumping against his chest. He wanted to beg. Plead.

But Ozarik just stood there, paralyzed.

Claire was shaking a little, but her level-headed—dissociative—voice never wavered. "Oz. You're right. The Zaro can't have ties like this. You can't *prioritize* me, especially over Reiki... and I won't apologize for the person I've become."

"I'd never ask you to—"

"You do. Every time Reiki disapproves of me, you ask me to change a little piece of myself."

She might as well have electrocuted him.

Claire gestured around her condo. "You know what I feel when I come home every night? *Pride.* I'm delighted by what I've accomplished in Las Vegas. This is me. And it's nothing that you actually want."

His breath caught.

Now she stepped close, hugging him, gone too soon. She offered a sad smile and whispered, "So, what are we doing?"

Neither of them had an answer. And that was the hardest part.

Chapter Fourteen

15 Years and 2 Days before Death Stopped

Kyle Flanderson knew many things about the world—and almost all of them were flawed. We'll refrain from calling them *wrong*, since he was intelligent enough to comprehend the basic functions of society. However, humans and witches alike were persuaded by pesky things like experience, memories that gradually applied a colored veil over the world, shifting plain knowledge into blue, green, orange, red.

If Kyle's life experiences put a color over the world, it would be gunmetal grey. The color of uncertainty, of fear, of violence as lines were drawn and people crashed to either side. Things were generally unfair, and color only splashed into existence when someone grabbed the problem and shook it until candy came out.

We won't get into Kyle's tragic backstory, as it likely wouldn't justify the events to come. But understanding Kyle's point of view *is* important—especially as Claire aged from a toddler with two negligent parents to a little girl who wished her remaining parent was merely negligent.

On this sunny winter day, the air warmed enough that Kyle could banish the children outside without the neighbors calling CPS again—and from his point of view, they had jackets, it wasn't snowing anymore, and kids liked to run and play—what better way to get the blood flowing while he had a drink or five?

The house's magic had its limitations, boundaries Kyle pressed every chance he got. Inside the house, Claire was protected. But Reiki's spell didn't comprehend cold weather, which meant the magic didn't see an issue with Claire and Maxwell sent outside without gloves, hats, scarves. Even though it was sunny, the wind was fierce, yet Kyle slammed the door in their faces and locked it tight.

"What—what do we do now?" Claire rubbed her reddening nose, hunching into her ripped, too-large overcoat.

Max tossed an arm around her shoulder, bending over her as the wind roared through the pine trees. "Well," he cast a surreptitious glance at the house, but their father was gone. Despite everything, relief flickered to life in his chest, and he smiled. "I have something to show you."

Maxwell coaxed a shivering Claire through the overgrowth of their backyard, to the dilapidated shed in the back corner. It was crammed full of yard equipment that hadn't seen use in years, and he lifted a plank up enough that Claire could crawl through on her hands and knees. The wind died, at least, and they huddled together in the spider-webbed shadow of an old lawnmower.

Although Maxwell was growing—and learning—far too fast, he was still young enough to view the world in shades of blue. Bright like the sky, full of potential, bursting with beams of yellow as he coaxed his sister closer.

"I got you something," he whispered, blowing dust off the grocery bag he'd stuffed between a broken leaf blower and a muddy trash can.

Claire, eyes wide, inched into his lap. He tugged open the bag, revealing a colored storybook, one with cartoon images and text she was only barely starting to understand.

"Ooooh." Claire ran her fingers over the book, flashed a baby-toothed smile. She loved story time, and Maxwell loved reading to her. They made a good pair. "What're you readin' this time?"

He stole another glance through a knotty hole in the decaying wood shed, towards the house. The curtains were still drawn, and he was moderately confident their father wouldn't find them here.

Mildly confident.

With a rush of fear and exhilaration, he opened the book and read the title: "*The World's Most Powerful Witch.*"

"That's me," Claire exclaimed, giddy.

"Someday," Maxwell agreed.

"Daddy said I'll be the most powerful—the most coolest witch ever." Claire twisted to meet Maxwell's eyes, swept up in the vision of grandeur. "He said that. I can—I could stop wildfires. Or bring storms! I can make someone sad or make them forget when—when Daddy takes groceries without—"

Maxwell's expression fell, and Claire tapered off, chest twisting.

He was disappointed in her.

Her own worldview, a cautious grey-blue with deep flecks of ruby, flickered into existence, and panic welled. Maxwell was her favorite person in the whole wide world. Maxwell meant *everything* to her.

"Is—Is that bad?" she whispered.

Maxwell forced a smile, but she saw right through it. "No. No, Claire, it's not bad. It's just—not what you're supposed to do. That's not who you should be."

The words, spoken with kind confidence, derailed her.

She shouldn't be magic.

She shouldn't be the most powerful witch.

She shouldn't do any of the things Daddy said, because between Daddy and Maxwell, Claire would always, *always* listen to her brother first.

Suddenly, shockingly, she shoved her magic away, pushing it back towards Ozarik across the globe. She hadn't rationalized that it was a person on the other end of this connection, not yet, but she knew that when the magic went there, it wasn't *here*. And that was what Maxwell wanted.

"Okay. I won't—" she stumbled, fumbling for words, before pointing at the book. "That's not me."

Max cocked his head. "No, no. I think it *is* you. This book is you. Not—not what Dad says." With a flourish, he turned the page. Claire returned her attention to the colors and drawings as he began to read.

He read about Javarini, about the aciras from around the world, about the aciradaan and their duty in stopping a rogue Zaro. Simple sentences and cartoon people gave way to complex ideas of peace and good and diplomacy, and slowly, his words sunk into Claire's mind.

She'd never thought hard about her role, her magic. Until now, she merely accepted her father's words, his lifestyle, his greed, and assumed it as her own. Whatever Daddy wanted, Daddy got, so if Daddy said the Zaro manipulated minds—well, she would.

Now, shame settled over her chest like a blanket. Even though her magic nudged at her core, quietly asking to return home, Claire again shoved it away.

Maxwell stopped on the book's final page, a portrayal of the Zaro standing at a stone podium on a seaside cliff while people of every ethnicity smiled. He pointed at the Zaro here. "My teacher said this is called the *Assumation Ceremony*, and it'll happen when we're older—Zaro Reiki will pass away, and Ozarik will become Zaro."

Ozarik.

It wasn't the first time she'd heard the name, but her father had never bothered to explain who, exactly, the boy was. Now, after reading this book, the answer was clear: he was her competition. A grey tint flared as she glared at the anonymous drawing of a young man, awaiting his moment to Assume the title.

"What about me?" she asked, because she suddenly didn't trust Kyle's viewpoint.

Maxwell smoothed her hair, rubbing her arms as she shivered in the cold. "I think it could be you. If you wanted. But no matter what—the Zaro is good. She's nice and helpful and loving. Is that what you want to be?"

Nice and helpful and loving.

Claire scrunched her nose, wondering if she truly were all those things.

"Okay. I'll try," she said, and Maxwell's bright smile was well worth the effort.

Exactly one week later, Claire put her new ideals to the test. She and Maxwell were sitting on a park bench, and her father casually glanced across the street at the mailbox cluster. The postman slammed his truck shut and started the engine, and the second he pulled out of view, Kyle stood.

"Claire. Showtime."

Claire had learned to coax open locks about four months ago, and her father had made full use of the talent. A sinking feeling slipped into her gut as she glanced at Maxwell, who was frowning. He thought she was a hero—but a hero didn't steal mail.

She hunched over her peanut butter and jelly sandwich, as if it might keep Kyle from noticing her.

Unsurprisingly, it didn't work. Kyle tapped her shoulder, ignoring her flinch. "Kid. Come on. Hurry up."

"She doesn't want to—" Max started to say.

Kyle silenced him with a vicious look. "Shut up."

Claire had gone still, the bread in her mouth getting soggy. She didn't dare to chew, didn't dare to move. Her eyes were plastered to the wooden table, to the crumb-filled plastic bag that held the other half of her lunch.

"*Claire.*"

Silence.

Kyle bristled, grabbing her arm roughly. The house's magic was far from protecting her here, and she yelped, manhandled out of her seat. Her own magic pulsed in defense, like a gasp of panic. Kyle released her like he'd been burned—not because he was in pain, but because if *he* felt her magic pulsing, Zaro Reiki almost certainly did.

Intent on keeping the Zaro out of this, he stepped back from Claire and turned his attention to Maxwell.

The boy hunched his shoulders. "D-Dad," he said, shakily. "She doesn't want to do it."

"I. Didn't. *Ask.*" His words were hissed, dripping with malice. "She never had an opinion about this before. What the *fuck* did you do?"

Claire swallowed, fear prickling her belly. "Daddy, I—I want to be good."

"Good?" Kyle barked a laugh. "Baby, no one is good. Everyone's out for their own gain. You gotta take what you want in life, because if you don't, someone else will trample you on their way to the top. Get it?"

She didn't, not really, but she definitely understood Maxwell's yelp of pain as Kyle's hand clamped around his shoulder. Kyle saw the way she stiffened, the way her eyes widened, and his final mode of control clicked into place. He smiled, sickly sweet.

"Claire, baby, use your magic to get the packages out of that mailbox."

She didn't move.

His smile remained as he released Maxwell's shoulder—only to wrap his hand around the back of Max's neck. His fingers were long enough, Max skinny enough, that the tips almost touched above Max's sternum.

Max choked a gasp, going very, very still. His breaths came short and fast, and tears pricked his eyes. "C-Claire," he whispered, but she wasn't sure if he wanted her to stand her ground or *save him*.

She went with the latter, out of pure desperation.

"Daddy, *stop*."

"You have somewhere to be, don't you?"

Tears poured down her cheeks too, and she turned too fast, nearly ran to the mailboxes. Her magic was clumsy with fear, and it took long, too long, to get the packages. Her heart raced, her hands shook, and she finally pulled two large boxes and several envelopes out.

Her father hadn't removed his hand from Maxwell's neck. From a distance, it almost looked like he was comforting his son—but Claire knew better.

She ran back like the devil was on her heels.

Kyle smiled, finally standing, leaving Max to ruffle her hair. She went utterly still, but his touch was fond, nearly loving. "Good girl. You listen to me, you hear? Not Max."

"Okay," she said, numbly.

Maxwell met her gaze, and all she saw was fear.

Together, they trudged home, and the world became a little more grey.

Chapter Fifteen

18 Days before Death Stopped

With a snap of their fingers, Claire and Ozarik poofed to Reiki's embassy in Kyoto[1].

Right in the middle of what seemed to be a riot.

To be clear, this was *not* a riot, but it was difficult to tell the difference when confronted with impassioned crowds voicing their grief past the embassy walls. Police made a show of blocking the entrance to the inner courtyard, but the witches beyond seemed less concerned with rushing inside and more interested in protest via noise. The chaos seemed to freeze Ozarik to the spot.

"Wow," Claire commented, which certainly didn't help.

Sweat glistened on Ozarik's forehead. "W-What do I do? How did this happen?"

Claire strolled to the windows and drew the shades. It didn't drown out the sound, but it offered a bit of privacy. She cast her eyes around the room, hunting for anything useful Reiki might have left behind. But, of course, the previous Zaro maintained a meticulous office, and anything useful had

---

1. The official witchy embassy was in Tokyo, but a secondary one had been created here thirty years ago in honor of Zaro Reiki specifically. She'd been humbled to receive it.

105

been retrieved by her aciras after her death. Boxes stamped with Javarini's shipping label lined the back corner, essentially forgotten in light of the people outside.

"Well, it began when someone shot the Zaro," Claire offered unhelpfully. Her patience with Ozarik's antics were dwindling. "And it'll end when you get your shit together and make a public appearance."

Ozarik grabbed his hair, clenching his eyes shut. "I can't—"

While he bemoaned his life, Claire eyed an oddly lavish piece in the corner of the room: a hand-carved wooden chair, made of a rich reddish wood. Three-dimensional dragon carvings lined the top of the chair and the two armrests. The carving on its back was intricate, depicting a long, Eastern dragon swallowing a circular disc undoubtedly meant to represent the sun. Although to her uncultured mind, it looked like it was vomiting a ball.

It was probably a metaphor. Claire wrinkled her nose.

But this was just the sort of piece that Reiki would have positioned in the hallways of Javarini's main castle, then forbid Claire to touch.

So, of course, Claire *had* to touch it.

"—go out there," Ozarik finished, desperately.

The chair was flat and uncomfortable as hell, but Claire heaved a satisfied sigh as she wiggled against the worn leather cushion. If Reiki were here, she'd undoubtedly have magicked the dragons on the armrests to wrap around Claire's wrists, maybe turned a blind eye as the dragon behind her head tugged out a few strands of hair. But she *wasn't* here now.

Claire might never move.

Finally comfortable—in spirit, if not in body—Claire returned her attention to Ozarik. "Why can't you go out there?"

His irritated sigh made her think he'd answered that question already.

(In fact, he had. Twice. All the while padding it with varying degrees of excuses that had no relation to his duty as Zaro.)

"I can't make an appearance without telling them what *happened*," Ozarik said.

"So... tell them what happened." Claire quirked an eyebrow.

Ozarik paled, scrubbing his face again. "N-No. No. If I tell them how she died, they'll want to know who *did* it. And that'll lead back to—" He cut himself off, eyes flicking to her before he fastidiously turned away.

Claire squinted at him, a prickle of intrigue setting root in her mind. "Back to who?"

"It's not important."

"Actually, it sounds like the most important thing in the world right now."

Face red, Ozarik spun towards her. "It's nothing, Claire." When she opened her mouth to push, his temper snapped, and he shouted: "*Forget it!*"

The words slammed into her with all the magic of his desperation. Greedy, shadowy tendrils formed in her brain, racing along her synapses until they discovered her growing curiosity about Reiki's murder. In the span of a millisecond, the tendrils opened hungry mouths and swallowed the idea whole.

Then they vanished, leaving Claire's mind blissfully blank.

Content.

Claire shuddered, though she wasn't sure why. Her spine prickled under Ozarik's gaze, but she just tilted her head. "Forget what? What were we talking about?"

Her own magic, meanwhile, had spread from her soul to her fingers and toes, desperately trying to uncover what had gone wrong. Like a defective immune system, it hadn't recognized Ozarik's magic as a virus—although in that moment, it probably should have.

"N-Nothing," Ozarik said, sounding dazed. "I'm—I'll figure it out."

If he sounded guilty, it's because he was.

He swept from the room, leaving Claire to puzzle through the sudden unease she felt. Her magic begged her to poof back to Las Vegas, back to safety, but Claire couldn't rationalize why—and thus, she didn't budge.

Instead, now alone, her fingers ran along the intricate dragon carvings on the armrests. "You'd hate me sitting here, wouldn't you?" Claire asked aloud, as if Reiki's spirit were still lingering.

(To be clear, it wasn't.)

Claire smirked, rubbing her fingers deep in the crevices of the dragon under her right hand. Her oils were probably going to discolor the finish, and the chair wasn't happy about it; she could feel its dissatisfaction from here. And yet it remained inanimate. Unmoving.

Except, of course, for a tiny switch Claire discovered under the dragon's chin. Her eyes cut to the door, but Ozarik hadn't returned. The witches beyond the gates were still shouting, so he clearly hadn't stepped outside yet either.

Claire bolstered her motivation, preparing yet again to dive into the fray. But—first thing's first. She pressed the switch, and a tiny *pop* echoed through the room.

This was, what one might call, a plot device.

"Very curious," Claire murmured, and slipped off the chair to investigate its legs. On the back left, facing the papered wall, a tiny trap door had unlocked. Inside was a thin scroll, bundled around a cylindrical rod. The knobs had been carefully carved as well: the Eastern dragon curled into a ball on one side, and the cylindrical disc—now with the pitted holes of the moon—adorned the other.

The start of a hunt. Claire grinned. "You sly witch." For all that she loved defying Reiki, she could respect the woman's ingenuity. After all, there was a reason people were crowding the streets outside.

But just as Claire was about to unravel the scroll, the door slammed open. She straightened, glancing at the man sprinting towards Reiki's desk with the fervor of an oncoming train.

Jorge, one of the aciras. He must have flown ahead to handle public relations until Ozarik arrived. Claire waited for him to notice her, but he was obviously panicked, rifling through papers stacked on Reiki's desk with a manic eye, and she didn't want to scare him shitless.

"—is it... Where is it?"

Claire cleared her throat.

He spun towards her, and everything stilled as he processed her presence. Then he exploded in a different kind of chaos.

"Du—" Jorge's native Norwegian slipped out, and he quickly corrected himself to the current default language of Javarini: English[2] . "How did you get in here? No one is allowed inside unless they're an acira or—or the Zaro himself!"

She almost responded in flawless Hungarian, just to mess with him. But Jorge looked flustered, and she'd already given him a shock the previous day on Javarini—rather than raising further suspicion, she replied in the language he expected. After all, she didn't have a problem with Jorge.

"I came with Ozarik."

She flashed a charming smile.

Jorge stiffened. "He didn't mention you."

Claire shrugged, subtly pocketing the scroll from Reiki's chair. Her jeans were too form-fitting to accommodate such a piece, but with a bit of magic, she made it work. "Well, I imagine he's focused on other things."

It wasn't a good enough excuse for Jorge. He narrowed his eyes. "He is, and this speech could have dire consequences. Clementine warned us that you distract him; you must—"

Now Claire had a problem with him.

Indignant, she waved a hand and Jorge froze in place, his mouth open, tongue peeking through his lips in the beginning of the word "leave." The magic it required to freeze someone in place rippled through the embassy. Ozarik would surely feel it, so with a sigh, Claire forewent Reiki's scroll for another day.

She left Jorge standing there, frozen, and went to find Oz.

---

2. This language had a propensity to change on the whim of the Zaro. For a brief period during Arjun's reign, it had been Swahili, which caused a fair amount of chaos—followed by an impressive uptick in people attempting to learn the language.

Tatami mats lined the welcome room, a relaxing space where Reiki used to entertain everyone from diplomats to florists.[3] A superb artist from Hakone had painted a mural along one of the sliding doors: yet another Eastern dragon, this one flying high over a small village. A single, exquisite kimono had been carefully hung inside a glass display: a plaque denoted it was a gift from Chiso Kimono. Claire admired it for a moment, then plowed ahead.

Ozarik was perched by the welcome area, standing next to Jorge's black shoes. The door out of the embassy was a simple wooden piece, but he stared like it was made of fire, or might swallow him whole.

Claire strode past the low table in the center of the room, passingly noting how the elegant bonsai's green leaves were shifting to dense, dry brown, literally wilting under Ozarik's panic. She cast a protective bubble around it—best not to anger the florists—and gripped Ozarik's shoulder.

He seemed paralyzed.

"They just want to know Reiki will be honored, and who better to honor her than you?" Claire nodded towards the door. "All you have to do is be sincere."

"I'm going to mess up again," Ozarik said, shaking a little.

Claire wrapped an arm around his shoulders, pulling him close. He drew a few deep breaths, calming himself through her touch. It reminded her of the nights when she'd first arrived on Javarini, scared and unsure of everything except this nice boy who'd poofed into her bedroom to make her feel better.

"This isn't you, Oz. Remember the kid who used to practice his speeches in the mirror? I laughed at you, but what'd you tell me?"

"That someday, they'd be counting on me," he replied, quietly.

"Today's it. So, are you going to stumble... or deliver the speech?"

---

3. Never underestimate the power of a floral witch. Reiki's predecessor, Zaro Arjun, offended one from Singapore in 1932, and every third Tuesday for decades he would awake to a massive carrion flower outside his bedroom window.

For a moment, it almost worked. He pulled his shoulders back like he was finally brave enough to try. And then it all collapsed; Ozarik backpedaled out of her grasp, shaking his head. "J-Jorge was going to get me his notes. He recorded their concerns earlier—I need it to prepare for the address—"

Claire realized in that moment that she wasn't helping. Not the way she'd hoped.

And considering she'd taken time off *her* life, reorganized *her* entire performance schedule in Vegas, left *her* apartment, *her* home, only to watch him fail at the one thing Reiki swore he'd do better?

"Ozarik. You don't need notes." Irritation prickled her skin. "Enough. Get out there and *say* something."

But the more she pushed, the more he backpedaled. Ozarik shook his head fiercely. "I can't." Then, the nail on the coffin: "You go talk to them. You're half-Zaro too. Why is it only *my* responsibility?"

Claire's sympathy vanished.

"Because *you're* the only Zaro they know. The Prince of Witches," she hissed, stepping into his space. "Don't you dare pull this bullshit on me now, Oz. Not after all the years I begged to be your partner, your equal."

"Reiki refused that, not me."

"I didn't see you fighting her."

Silence.

Ozarik clenched his jaw. "Well, Claire. Now's your chance to prove her wrong." With a snap of his fingers, he poofed away, leaving the distinct whiff of huckleberry and a swirl of purple smoke.

"Looks like you're already doing that," Claire muttered to the empty space.

Outside, the people shouted with continued fervor. If she concentrated, she could almost make out their individual demands. They weren't going away, and she'd seen enough fights on the Strip to know that without intervention, these kinds of things only escalated.

Her eyes swept the tatami room, stopping on the browned bonsai.

Something momentous slid into place, centered bold and determined inside her soul.

It wasn't because she *owed* Reiki, mind. Claire couldn't care less about any debts between herself and the old Zaro.

But the world's witches deserved more than this. They deserved a Zaro who wasn't fleeing at the first sign of conflict. A ruler who spoke with confidence, grace, and poise—kind of like a performer on a stage.

Claire Bishop knew all about that.

With little decorum, Claire cast an illusion on herself. She became someone else.

She *became* Ozarik.

And when Jorge thawed and staggered into the courtyard, he found the young lord calming the masses, charming Kyoto's witches in their native tongue, reassuring them that although Reiki was dead, her legacy lived on, and the devotion of the witches of Japan wouldn't be forgotten.

Claire-as-Ozarik put on a show.

And the world was captivated by her lies.

Chapter Sixteen

14 Years and 300 Days before Death Stopped

Managing two possible Zaros in their young age was a true balancing act, and one Reiki didn't get nearly enough credit for. This was because Reiki's "balance" meant spending 90% of her time with Ozarik, and 10% with Claire—and really, "with Claire" was a misnomer, since all she ever did was visit Kyle unexpectedly, and watch Claire from afar.

This could be because facing Claire in person meant facing her own indecision—which was quickly growing into something far harder to handle. Secrets fester over time, after all, and this was the biggest secret in the known Universe; the flesh rotted to bones, and Reiki shoved it so far away from her daily life that she had plausible deniability to the scent.

But sometimes, *sometimes*, the resulting whiff was too strong, and it arched eyebrows. Which was why, when Ozarik, crouched in the Krajovič family garden during a frigid Slovakian winter, asked, "Am I the only Zaro?" and Reiki had to fight every urge to stiffen.

Briefly, her eyes flicked to Clementine, who was knitting a scarf on the garden's stone bench—but although the English woman dabbled in several languages, Slovakian wasn't one of them. She smiled back at Reiki, encouragingly, oblivious to the wretched stench suddenly lingering in the air.

Reiki drew a calming breath and lied. "Aside from myself, that is correct."

Ozarik, only five years old, frowned, his forehead wrinkling in confusion. Before he could open his mouth to ask more questions, she nudged his attention back to the flower seed in his hands. It was freezing today, but she'd settled a bubble of warmth over the garden when they stepped out, and the temperature here remained in a pleasant range.

"There is magic in everything. Probe this seed. Can you feel the magic within? Like a hot coal inside a thick shell."

Ozarik focused very, very carefully—for even at this age, he was a dedicated student. He poked the seed with his magic, cautiously enveloped it, and his eyes lit up. "Yes, I feel it." Without prompting, and with little finesse, his magic sliced the shell open. The seed's magic spilled out, weak at first, then strengthening with sunlight, and a thin green tendril snaked around Ozarik's fingers.

Reiki frowned. Already, the tendril had doubled in size, thickened to be larger than his fingers—his arm—his leg—and before it could consume the boy entirely, Reiki's magic slipped around it, gently guiding it towards the ground instead. While Ozarik's magic offered the seed limitless potential, hers reminded the plant of its proper shape, it's proper size, and the tendrils buried in the soil until all that remained was a single, unmoving tree.

From the window, Ozarik's mother, Zuzana, frowned. She wouldn't say it aloud, not while the *Zaro* was perched in her front yard, in full view of all the neighbors—but that tree just didn't go with her garden décor. Quietly, she contemplated framing it as a display of powerful magic from Ozarik, and wondered if it'd be possible to order a plaque so passersby understood the significance.

Meanwhile, Ozarik swallowed. "Was—Did I make a mistake?"

"All things desire to grow, Ozarik," Reiki replied soothingly. "Of course, for some, that is a dangerous path. Your magic offers unlimited potential to the Universe at large—and you must be able to set confines around what can use your magic, and how."

Now she gestured to the tree, which pulsed with her own magical aura. "Analyze these confines, and we'll try again."

This might be asking too much to a five year old, but Ozarik gaped at the tree nonetheless.

Then, he stepped back. "But—it's not—this isn't just my magic."

Clementine was sitting too close. Reiki *knew* she couldn't understand their conversation, but the aciradaan's magical ability was strong. All it would take was one flair of emotion, and Clementine would begin asking questions again.

Reiki emptied her mind, acknowledged her fear, and held it close. Her voice was steady, almost perplexed. "That is correct. Our magic belongs inside everything, and thus, we find magic everywhere." She offered him another seed. "Let's try again."

"No!" Ozarik shoved her hand aside. "No, that's not what I meant!"

Clementine glanced at them, expression confused. Reiki offered her an encouraging, placating smile, and turned back to the disturbed boy. "What did you mean then, child?"

"My—my magic. It isn't mine." Ozarik's expression screwed into one of intense thought, and Reiki felt him prodding his magical connection. And to her horror, in response, Claire prodded back from halfway across the world. They were *communicating*, and it was likely that neither of them understood the significance of that.

Reiki's carefully crafted narrative unraveled. She should have known this day would come.

Seeing his distress, Zuzana opened the kitchen window and called out, "Is everything alright, Zaro Reiki?"

She was far more polite now than she'd been in years past.

Reiki offered a slight smile, even as her mind whirled. "Yes. I believe it's time for Ozarik to feel the sensation of our teleportation spell, if that is all right with you?" When Zuzana's eyes widened in fear, in desperation, she hastened to frame it in a way the mother would understand. "We won't be gone but a moment. This is about the age where I developed the skill, and it's a vital spell for his future."

Zuzana looked doubtful now, but she said, "Well, I suppose. If it's fast."

"Merely a few minutes. And then our session today will conclude."

Those were Zuzana's favorite words, so she nodded and closed the window again. Ozarik frowned at Reiki, who offered her hand as she pushed to her feet. Her bones were getting older, and her knees creaked as she straightened.

At the bench, Clementine did the same. "My Zaro? Is there something I can assist with?"

"No, my dear," Reiki replied in English. "I'm simply going to take Ozarik to the park and back. Exposure to our teleportation spell is vital at this age."

Another lie. Reiki could count them like beads in a necklace, now.

"Stay here, and we'll return shortly."

Clementine's fingers ghosted along the leather scabbard she'd set on the bench an hour ago, brushing the circle stamped into the dao's hilt. "Do you believe it's a wise idea to go alone, Kio?"

Reiki smiled serenely, even though panic was fluttering like a butterfly in her chest. "It will just be a moment," she reaffirmed.

"Bye, Teenie," Ozarik chimed, since when he was younger, "Clementine" was a bit too long for a toddler, and he liked how she smiled at the nickname.

Clementine broke into a smile now, waggling a few fingers at him. "Goodbye, Ozarik. See you soon."

Reiki took the little boy's hand and poofed them to a meadow fifty kilometers away.

The boy yelped in surprise, then groaned as his stomach caught up to him. He doubled over, and Reiki soothed his nausea with a push of healing magic. She waited while he gained his bearings, discomfort overtaken by the awe of their new scenery.

"Wow! We're—How did you do that? Can I do that?"

"Ozarik."

He snapped his gaze to her, for she rarely used that concerned tone. The weight of this settled on him, and even at such a young age, Ozarik realized this wasn't merely a magic joyride. "Yes, Zaro?"

"You are right. There is another end to your magic."

Now the boy stilled, eyes widening. "I knew it."

Reiki sighed, kneeling to his height. The meadow was crisp, white with snow, and thick pine trees towered in the distance. Behind her, the Tatras mountains arose around them. She looked into his curious green eyes, staring at the boy who had been lucky enough to be found *first*, and guilt wrenched her insides.

"I have a secret, Ozarik. But it's of vital importance that you—and only you—know it, or people might get hurt. You cannot tell anyone. Not your mother, not Clementine, not *anyone*. Okay?"

Ozarik bobbed his head. "Okay. I won't tell."

Reiki twisted their magic around that word, infusing it with meaning. "You *cannot* tell. Do you understand the difference?"

He didn't.

Reiki hated herself for doing this, but she simply could not trust a child to recognize the gravitas of this moment. So she said, "If you speak about this, it will fall on deaf ears. When you are older, I will lift this spell. All right?"

"O-Okay." Now Ozarik looked vaguely scared.

Reiki smoothed his hair, pressed a kiss to his forehead. "There is another. A girl. Her name is Claire. When you pull magic through that bond, you're borrowing it from her. And she occasionally does the same to you."

"Claire," he tested the name, poking his magical connection at the same time. This time, Claire didn't poke back, and he seemed disappointed. "Aww. Where'd she go?"

"I couldn't say," Reiki replied. The reality was that, in America, Kyle had just forced Maxwell to skip breakfast, and Claire was a bit preoccupied puzzling through that. Reiki, crouched in that Slovakian meadow, realized none of it, far too focused on the task at hand.

"Ozarik, there is only supposed to be one. *You*. You are the Future-Zaro. Claire was born with your magic, but like the seed, she will grow into something dangerous if you allow it to happen."

Ozarik frowned, and a pulse of fear made its way through the air. He rubbed his fingers, where that vine had wrapped too tight. "Really?"

"She's a good person, Ozarik. But you have to be better. Your magic is a wonderful thing—but in the wrong hands, it can breed chaos and fear. It is my hope that, as you age, you'll be able to siphon this magic into yourself, and Claire will go from what she is... to a normal human."

Ozarik's brow furrowed. This went against everything Reiki had taught him up to this point—that witches were to be protected, that he wasn't to decide anyone's fate. But apparently that only lasted as far as Claire, the opposite swing of his pendulum.

"Does this make sense to you?" Reiki asked quietly.

Even the Zaro could act out of fear.

Ozarik swallowed hard, and slowly nodded.

Reiki pushed upright again and took his hand. "You're going to be wonderful, dear. The greatest Zaro our Universe has ever seen."

It made him uneasy, but he slowly accepted the words. He would be great. And Claire, his other half, his partner, his future—well, she would be happy. Ozarik didn't question this again until the day he locked eyes with Claire in New York City and it became apparent, all at once, that Reiki hadn't been telling him the full truth.

Of course, by then, the die had been cast, and it was too late.

Chapter Seventeen

16 Days before Death Stopped

Rather than track Ozarik down after the Kyoto fiasco, Claire poofed back home. When that proved maddening, she poofed again to the one place where she loved to relax: Henry Ballard's living room.

There was something about Henry's apartment that calmed her nerves. Perhaps it was his modest energy, something even his decorating sense exuded. Unlike her own place, nothing here was pretentious or fake. His walls were mostly bare, but the pictures that hung were milestone moments in his life: here, a graduation photo, there, a date with Jenifer. His furniture was second-hand, worn to perfection and decorated in earthen tones. It was messy in a way Claire had never quite managed, yet clean enough to feel cozy.

But what was better, Henry proudly displayed his witchy culture. What the living room lacked in style, it found in earnest tributes to magic. Drying herbs hung off a shelf nailed to his wall. Vibrantly green plants she couldn't even name filled every windowsill. Claire's eyes traced the books on his coffee table—*The Magick of the Universe: A Study,* and *1000 Spells for the Curiously Adept*—then admired the chemistry set and apothecary supplies stacked on a desk by the window. A pendulum[1], quartz on a simple cord, was perched over a diagram he'd scribbled with "yes" and "no."

Considering Claire was perhaps the greatest witch alive, at least at the moment, she knew perilously little about her own culture.[2] Henry had become something of a consultant to her—and now that she'd kicked off Ozarik's pre-Assumption world tour, she needed him more than ever.

Henry, of course, knew none of this. He simply strolled into his living room hunting for his shoes, and stopped short.

"Oh!" A surprised smile overtook his lips. "Claire Bishop. To what do I owe the pleasure?"

She wrinkled her nose. "You know perfectly well why I'm here, Henry."

"I know Jenifer was immensely pleased our wedding had a celebrity appearance. Perhaps she finally sent you a dinner invite? She's been threatening one for days." Amusement played on his lips, and he plucked one sneaker from behind the couch.

Claire arched one perfectly manicured eyebrow. "What happened to your shoes?"

"Three words. Zero gravity room." Henry began hunting for the second one.

"That was days ago."

Henry smirked. "We had fun in the meantime."

Claire wrinkled her nose and rolled her eyes simultaneously. "Disgusting. Where is Jenifer, anyway?"

---

1. Henry's pendulum had nothing to do with the invisible pendulum that swung between Claire and Ozarik, and was used for making decisions like "should he give Jenifer flowers?" and "should he get a mullet?" One answer was yes, the other a resounding no.

2. To be fair, witch "culture" was an ever-growing, ever-changing thing. With so many influences around the world, and so many different abilities from witch to witch, everyone had a different definition of it. Henry delighted in consuming them all.

He shrugged. "Normal people work, Claire. She's at the office, elbow-deep in tax law." Now he dropped to the ground, peering under the coffee table. "Between her and me, I'm obviously the adventurous one."

Considering how he and Jenifer met—him bumping into her at jury duty, then realizing they had a common friend in one of Jenifer's sisters—, his statement wasn't as true as he probably hoped. Claire rolled her eyes and meandered to the bookshelf.

He had a few spell books on various witchy topics—tarot, reading tea leaves, banking—but most of these were fiction. She chose a romance novel, noted the cover of a man with washboard abs wearing only a pointy black hat, and cast Henry a sly glance.

"Jenifer's?"

"Don't be absurd. That's mine," Henry replied unapologetically. Claire snorted, but he'd already moved on: "The market's open in Henderson. You coming?" He fished out his other shoe, laced them up, then tugged a set of keys from his pocket.

"Why not?" Claire replied, keeping her tone casual. It was a feat, considering her thoughts were anything but. Every nerve was screaming to get back to Ozarik, even as her mind reverberated with the ramifications of what she'd done.

She'd only impersonated Ozarik one other time—when she'd fought the wildfire to save Henry's aunt's home—and it resulted in their break-up. Who knew what today's actions might prompt?

But even though she *should* be poofing back to Javarini, she just... couldn't. Not yet.

So, she followed Henry outside and piled in his tiny car. They drove for a few minutes before Henry remarked, "I saw the newsfeed. Ozarik's first public appearance since Reiki's death."

Claire didn't stiffen, didn't flinch, didn't give any indication of what she'd done. She just shrugged. "Mhmm. He did well."

Henry cast her a quick glance.

Claire frowned, daring him to protest.

Unluckily for her, accepting Claire Bishop's dares was a favored pastime. Henry returned his eyes to the road. "I was surprised at his composure, considering that horrible announcement earlier. But in Kyoto, he really seemed to understand what the world's witches need to hear." A weighted pause. "It was uncanny, how different the two speeches were. The second seemed... almost theatrical."

"Are you enjoying this?"

Henry smirked. "Maybe a little."

Claire rubbed her forehead, staring out the window as he slowed for a stop light. Off the Strip, Vegas lost its luster, dissolving into dull concrete and asphalt. The suburbs were slightly nicer, golf communities wedged between dusty neighborhoods, but it still wasn't anywhere as scenic as Javarini—or even Spokane.

And yet, sitting here with Henry, Claire was more comfortable than at any home she'd known.

"Oz isn't handling it well," she finally admitted. "And I'm losing patience for it."

"You've helped a lot already, Claire. Considering how Reiki banned you from participating in that lifestyle, I'm surprised you're putting your life on hold."

Claire frowned. "I'm not putting my life on hold. I'm just... taking a vacation."

"Most vacations aren't three weeks." When Claire arched an eyebrow at him, Henry shrugged. "Come on. You're the biggest act on the Strip. Everyone noticed when the shows were canceled."

Claire subtly hoped no one put two-and-two together: how her show was canceled after Reiki died, and was scheduled to resume right after the Assumation Ceremony, when Ozarik fully claimed the title of Zaro.

Of course, by Las Vegas's standards, she wasn't a witch—so most visitors simply wrote this off as an uncanny coincidence.

"I can't just leave him, Henry," she said, quietly.

Henry merged into another lane. "I know. He's lucky to have you."

She shifted, suddenly uncomfortable. "Well, he doesn't *have* me. Not—not anymore."

"Have you as a friend, Claire." Henry paused. "You've been alone for most of your life, and that's hard. Ozarik is your one constant. But—" he trailed off, mustered his courage, and added, "but that doesn't mean you owe him more than what you're willing to give. You're still allowed to walk away. It doesn't make you a bad person."

Claire felt like a bad person just thinking about it.

"If I walk away, he's going to run the world into the ground."

"You have that little faith in him?"

Claire was beginning to regret visiting Henry. "No. He's been training for this. I guess I'm just surprised at how reluctant he is to take control of his life."

Henry pulled into a strip mall's parking lot, killing the engine with a twist of the key. "Sometimes, we forego what's important for what's easy."

"You sound like a fortune cookie."

"I get that a lot." He slid from the car, leading the way to a cavernous building adorned with a hand-painted sign that proudly boasted: *Witches' Market – Today Only*. People were streaming through the double doors dressed in all manner of odd outfits.

Her eyes trailed the banner. "I thought this place was open every Friday?"

Henry looked at her like she'd just declared the Queen of England was attending Thunder from Down Under. "Ah, you must be thinking of the Farmer's Market. The *Witches' Market* is only open on the third Friday of every month, provided it's also a full moon."

"Amazing they stay in business," Claire said drily.

"Amazing... or magic?" Henry winked, holding open one of the double doors.

A woman in a sleek black dress and an ornate, lace-adorned hat huffed at them as she muscled through at the same time. With a nasty glare, she adjusted the plastic crow glued to the brim and strolled into the market.

"Ah, the official dress of our people," Claire said.

Henry rolled his eyes. "*That* woman was human. You can tell by her sloppy spell work."

Claire hadn't realized she'd applied a spell, but another quick glance revealed what he meant. The woman had obviously applied a spell to smooth her makeup, but the magic sat heavy on her skin, refusing to absorb like it would for a witch. The result probably looked good to humans, but her makeup was clown-like to magical folk.

"Ah. I thought she just had terrible taste," Claire remarked.

"Well, you can tell that by the crow."

They set out, weaving through displays that were less like a market and more like a trade show. Rather than stands with different wares, there were stages with various witches on display. This one could illuminate every light bulb without external power—and at her feet were dozens of pre-illuminated bulbs for sale. That one was a crocodile tamer who was serenading his ward while eager children watched and waited for disaster. Clusters of people held their e-readers together, trading spells through the Windle app.

"Why are we here?" Claire finally asked.

Henry gestured to a woman arranging glass test tubes in a tiny box. "Midge, the salt collector. They say a sprinkle of her Arabic blend can convince an army to lay down their weapons."

"And you need that... why?"

He ignored Claire. "She's also a fortune teller, so watch yourself. Midge!" With a cheerful grin, he strolled up to the woman.

Midge crossed her arms over her massive chest, looking wholly unimpressed. "Henry Ballard. Should have known you'd be back. I told you, kid. You got a keeper—I ain't givin' you pink salt."

"Love salt," Henry stage-whispered to Claire. "Of course not, Midge. I married her, actually. You were right to let affection play its course."

Midge squinted at him. "And now you want to persuade her parents to like you. They already think you're bewitching young Jenifer. Didn't you learn your lesson?"

Claire snorted.

The woman glanced at her, as if noticing for the first time. Seconds ticked by as Midge simply stared. Then one thick eyebrow rose. "Oh, you're someone special."

After years in Las Vegas, Claire was used to living in the golden glow of fame. She momentarily forgot that she looked nothing like the Magnificent Claire Bishop, who was several inches shorter and brunette, and waved an unassuming hand. "Anyone can do my tricks. It's mirrors and light, that's all."

But the witch laughed loudly. Midge had met a lot of Vegas folks, and a performer pretending they weren't conceited was nothing new. Of course, they didn't usually have the power or connections to justify their arrogance—this one clearly did. "I ain't talkin' about your show. I'm talkin' about the note in your pocket. You got friends in high places."

Claire blinked, taken aback. In the chaos of Kyoto's address, she'd completely forgotten about Reiki's hidden scroll.

Midge waved a hand. "I see your apprehension. Don't open it here, but know—its contents are genuine, as are the emotions behind them." With a wink, she reached into the box and tossed Henry a vial of white salt.

One thing to know about Midge was that her witchy ability was actually recognizing what was unique about a person. Contrary to popular belief, it was *not* spelling magical salts. After all, perfectly-seasoned food could persuade a lover or kill an enemy just as easily.

Henry fumbled for his wallet, his words hopeful. "The Arabic blend?"

Midge laughed robustly. "No, boy! Givin' you that would be like givin' *her* praise." She gestured pointedly at Claire. "It'd go to her head. Fill her soul with lies."

"Hey," Claire said.

Midge rolled her eyes. "It's for your wife. She's gonna need the vitamins. A little on her eggs every morning, you hear? They ain't for you!"

Henry wilted, fishing an inordinate amount of money from his wallet. Midge collected it with a broad smile, then told Claire, "Fortune tellin's free. Specially for a friend of the Zaro."

Claire managed to wait until they were back inside his little green sedan before she plucked the scroll from her pocket. Her finger ran over the miniature dragon carving as Henry tucked the salt into his cup holder.

"What's it say?" he asked, absently.

She unfurled the note, her blood running cold at the gorgeous lettering. Reiki's handwriting.

Claire read it twice, three times, then carefully and quietly rolled it back into a tight scroll.

Henry quirked his head. "Was it good news, at least?"

"It's just a set of coordinates."

This was mostly true.

Claire huffed, shoving the scroll back into her pocket. "If she thinks I'm gallivanting across the world on some scavenger hunt, she's dead *and* wrong.[3] I have to get back to Javarini." Then, as an afterthought, "Tell Jenifer I said hi."

"She'll say hi back," Henry replied, but Claire had already poofed out of existence. Coughing, he rolled down a window.

---

3. Considering this was exactly what Claire had instructed several witches to do—this was a very ironic statement.

Chapter Eighteen

14 Years and 118 Days before Death Stopped

"Sapphires are heat con—" Kyle Flanderson hiccupped, cleared his throat, and tried again. "Heat conducers. D'you know what that means?"

Across the sticky and pockmarked folding table, five-year-old Claire blinked slowly, then shook her head. Her eyelids were drooping, her cheek pressed against one little fist. Maxwell was already asleep, but Claire wasn't allowed that yet.

Kyle rapped the table. "Focus, baby." Except, after an evening of cheap beer, it came out more like, *focush*. He fumbled for his drink, but his uncoordinated reach meant his fingers smacked the can to the floor instead. Claire jerked ramrod straight as the sound echoed through the house.

Kyle cursed under his breath—not at Claire, *never* at Claire—as he comprehended at the mess. Then his eyes snapped back to his daughter.

She swallowed under his piercing stare.

"Baby, be a dear?" he drawled, gesturing at the floor.

"Daddy, I can't." The magic came and went, much like the ebb and flow of the tide. Sometimes she had so much she could trick the postman into leaving packages at their door, or physically change the face of the cards Daddy slapped on the table. But it was unpredictable, because sometimes she couldn't even keep herself warm at night.

Today, the pendulum had swung in the other direction, landing squarely in Slovakia. So while Kyle's beer inched across the floor like a plague, filling the subtle indents of linoleum squares that hadn't been replaced since the '70's, Claire simply watched.

Kyle's face reddened.

"Clean it up, Claire."

She hunched her shoulders, clamping her mouth shut. Her blue eyes dropped to the pictures on the table before them, magazine cut-outs of various gemstones. They were pretty. She especially liked the sparkly white ones.

Meanwhile, Kyle was attempting his anger management techniques. After all, the house didn't like it when he yelled, so he'd been forced to adopt subtler methods of control as Claire grew.

The one method he had yet to perfect, regrettably, was listening.

"Claire, honeybee. Don't you want to save Daddy some time? A good girl would clean this up. You're a good girl, aren't you?"

His words still slurred, and his bloodshot eyes seemed to pin her to the table.

Claire wanted to be a good girl. She kept trying, hoping that one day, she'd do enough magic to make Daddy happy. So despite the empty well, she reached towards her heart again, exhaustion creeping into her fingers as she tried to coax some magic back to her side of the world.

It was 5am in Slovakia, and Ozarik was, ah, how to phrase it? *Otherwise occupied.* Their not-inconsiderable magic was clamped tightly in his grasp, forming a sloppy barrier as flames licked under his bedroom door. Ozarik coughed, a harsh, rattling sound, and fought past tears that *weren't* the result of the thick smoke.

Back in Spokane, Claire slumped to the table, swallowing a yawn. "There's no—no magic. Can I g'to bed, Daddy?"

"No, you can't," Kyle snarled. A shock of pain lanced through him, one he was intimately familiar with now that Noelle was gone. Been a few months since it had happened, but then again, it had been a few months since he drank this heavily. Fury twisted like a dark, angry poison, but he forced a smile to his face. "You can't, baby, because in one week, you'll be walking into that jewelry store, and I need to know you *understand what to do*."

Claire squirmed, fighting sudden, frustrated tears. "I know." When his intense stare didn't lessen, she fumbled for more. "I—I take the rocks." Now she pulled one of the magazine cutouts towards her, a bright red stone she'd already forgotten the name of. It was pretty too, but not as nice as the white ones.

"And how are you going to take the rocks if you can't use magic reliably?" he snapped, much more to himself than her. Another flinch of pain, and he drew a shaking breath, forcing his voice back to sickly-sweet territory. "Baby. You want Daddy to be happy, don't you? So show me. Show me how you'll get the, uh, rocks."

Now, he gestured at a glass box near his left arm—and at the single, actual rock inside it. He'd heard somewhere that kids were tactile learners, so this *should* be simple enough for her.[1] "Figure it out, Claire. Use your godda—" a pause, a correction, "ah, your precious magic."

Hot tears sprung to Claire's eyes. "No. I don't wanna. I wanna go to bed."

"Daddy? Aren't you done yet?" another tiny voice asked, and Kyle spun to see Maxwell standing in the doorway. The boy rubbed his eyes, clutched a ratty blanket a little closer to himself.

It was, unfortunately, the wrong move for Max. Because while Kyle worked to restrain himself around Claire, Reiki had neglected to provide any such protections for the human child in the house.

Kyle shoved to his feet. "*Enough!*"

At the kitchen table, Claire stiffened, eyes widening in desperation. Maxwell froze at the doorway, his shoulders beginning to shake.

---

1. If Kyle Flanderson had ever truly paid attention to his daughter, he'd have realized that—even at five years old—she understood far more than he ever did.

Kyle had followed through on his promise to Claire's mother: he'd found one way to control their daughter. Max's bruises may had faded, but they both knew what happened when Kyle snapped that word.

"Did you find some magic, baby girl?" Kyle's voice was soft as he approached Maxwell, who's eyes were darting between Claire and the safety of his bedroom. "Better show—"

The doorbell rang.

If the timing of this event seemed suspicious, it was important to note that not everything in the world was the result of magic. Sometimes, a series of very normal events took a very normal[2] amount of time, and culminated in a moment just like this.

Tonight, for example, was the pinnacle of five years of work on behalf of Spokane's Child Protective Services. Years of documenting Maxwell Flanderson, of performing sudden and invasive home visits, of forcing Kyle to maintain a certain standard of cleanliness and care for his children, all in one particular caseworker's hope that his "caring father" façade would slip.

Granted, this moment only culminated because Zaro Reiki filed a magical tip to CPS, that fateful day she met baby Claire. But that's a fact easily ignored.

On this night, it didn't matter what ruse Kyle Flanderson acted out—because Mary Alvarez rang the doorbell with a trump card. She'd spent so much time imagining this moment that when Kyle wrenched open the door, her voice didn't tremble at all.

In fact, her tone might have been a little bit smug.

"Kyle Flanderson, we're here to collect your son, Maxwell."

But a proud moment for Mary meant a world-shattering night for Max.

Claire had slipped off the kitchen chair when Kyle stomped to the front door, and now she pressed against Max's side, examining the people on their porch with curiosity.

---

2. Unreasonable, but regrettably normal.

Meanwhile, dread slipped up Max's spine. His trembling hand snaked into Claire's.

At the door, Kyle examined Mary and the two police officers flanking her and came to an immediate decision. A perplexed and moderately concerned smile flitted across his lips, and his drunken slur vanished under years of perfected grifting.

"I'm sorry... you want to take my son?"

Of all the CPS caseworkers, *Mary* was the bane of his existence. Mostly because, unlike the rest of them, she refused let this go—and she didn't buy his bullshit.

Mary made a show of sniffing the air. "Enjoying a late-night drink, Mr. Flanderson?" While the officers narrowed their eyes, she peered past Kyle, noting the two children. A kind smile crossed her lips, and she muscled Kyle aside to approach them.

Claire stepped behind her brother, who puffed up his chest at this new threat.

But Mary just knelt to their level, her voice gentle. "Maxwell, we found your grandparents. They're at the police station right now, ready to take you back to Scottsdale, Arizona. Do you know where Arizona is?"

Claire glanced at him sharply, finally realizing what was happening.

"Yeah," Max said, slowly. "I found it on a map." His hand tightened around Claire's.

Mary watched the interaction, then shifted her attentive gaze to Claire. "It's okay, sweetie. They're Max's grandparents, but they want to meet you too."

And that was the moment it clicked for Kyle. His concerned façade faltered, vanishing under a note of true panic. They couldn't take *Claire*. Not his daughter, his precious Future-Zaro. All that time, all that energy he'd invested? All the *magic* he would soon possess? His vision edged in red, and he squared his shoulders. "Now hang on a second—"

"Stay there, sir," one of the officers commanded, physically blocking his path.

Kyle pinched his lips together, fear cutting straight through the alcohol. "You can't just waltz in here and take my children. Look at them! They're

131

cared for, fed, clothed. Mary, we've done this over and over—you have *nothing*."

"Actually, now that I've tracked down your old in-laws, I have more than enough. They found your wife's last will and testament." Mary pushed to her feet. "She wanted Maxwell with her parents."

Last will and testament. Fancy words for an eight-year-old, but neither of Kyle's children were slow.

Max's eyes widened in horror.

His mother's death was completely new information, and something he probably shouldn't have discovered in this particular moment. But regrettably, Mary assumed he knew, and Kyle was too distracted to think about his son's emotional state, so this monumental discovery passed without a thought.

"Regardless of her will, I have custodial rights," Kyle snapped.

If this sounded impressively legal for Kyle Flanderson, it's worth noting that aspects of the law—especially when it came to parental rights—were something Kyle researched extensively. He didn't particularly care about Maxwell as his child or heir. Instead, his love was closer to that of a farmer and his stock: appealing only until the creature's purpose was served.

After all, if Maxwell was taken away, Kyle wouldn't be allowed to leave Claire unsupervised. His little girl wouldn't be properly... incentivized... to do magic on command.

And that simply didn't work with his lifestyle.

Mary, of course, didn't care about any of that. She met Kyle's furious gaze past wire-rimmed glasses. "Custodial rights only apply when it's in the child's best interest... and unfortunately for you, we have a documented history of neglect. Meanwhile, there's a very excited set of grandparents who've been decorating his Arizona bedroom for weeks. One guess who the judge will side with." Mary's smile was gone, her expression purely derisive now—although her tone remained soft for the children's sake. "You've lost, Mr. Flanderson."

For a long moment, Kyle looked between Mary and the officers. In his inebriated state, it was hard to remember why throwing a punch would be a bad idea. He fought for the last thing he had.

"Fine. But you're *not* taking Claire."

Mary hated his conviction, but his words wedged her into a tough spot. Because while they could remove Claire from this house tonight, *her* biological mother had vanished, and there was less legal standing unless Max's grandparents applied for guardianship. They'd expressed interest, but it was a lengthy process.

And yet, she'd be damned if she left either of these children in Kyle's care tonight. So she smoothed her expression and said, "You won't be able to stop us."

Kyle's face twisted for a brief moment, and then he knelt, holding open his arms. The police tensed, but he just crooned, "Claire. Claire, baby, come over here. You don't really want to leave me, do you? This is your home."

Claire winced, looking to Max for her cues. Her step-brother wrapped his arm around her shoulders and squeezed, but his brown eyes were centered on Mary. "We'll both go to Arizona?"

The woman hesitated.

Kyle pounced on the weakness. "No, of course not. Only Maxwell is allowed to go to Scottsdale, isn't that right? Claire's a witch. She's not even under your jurisdiction. So, Claire, would you rather go with this lady and be trapped at the police precinct... or stay here with Daddy?"

"I wanna stay with Max," Claire whispered.

"She can't come?" Maxwell stared into Mary's very soul, eyes watering.

The caseworker smiled, aiming to make this less traumatic for everyone. "Tonight, she can come with us, Max. Eventually we'll get her to Arizona. But for now, she might have to stay—"

"See, Max?" Kyle hissed. "Don't you believe her. What did I say about bureaucracy?"

Maxwell still didn't understand what bureaucracy was, but he knew it meant *bad*. He began to shake, fat tears streaming down his cheeks. "I don't want to go. I can't leave Claire. I won't go." When Mary looked like she might object, Max turned desperately to his little sister. "Claire. *Claire*! Make me a witch so I have to stay too."

Claire stared at him in shock, her own fear compounding into something uncontrollable. "I don't—"

"Max, that isn't going to change—" Mary tried to say.

But he wasn't listening. "You can do it, can't you?" Max bent to Claire's level, holding her gaze desperately. "*Please.*"

His heartbroken plea snapped something inside the five-year-old's heart. She'd never wanted anything more, and that desire spread through every vein in her body. A power, some witchy power for Maxwell. If she managed it, he wouldn't have to leave. She scrambled for her heartbeat, grabbed the depleted magic with more desperation than she had for anything in her life.

Across the sea, Ozarik had found his parents, huddled in their blazing home. They were screaming, their skin burning, bubbling in the heat. He desperately tried to wrap his magic in a protective bubble around them—

—and Claire yanked it away, shoving it with little decorum into her brother.

Maxwell gasped, collapsing to his knees. His olive skin went pale, his eyes rolled back into his skull, and he seemed to *glow.* Mary lunged for the boy, but he regained his senses just as fast.

A beat of silence.

Then Max blinked, dazed, and stammered, "D-Did it work?"

Claire scrubbed at her chest, which had begun to ache with such a force of magic. "He's a witch. You can—you can't take him!"

But only the Zaro had the power to bestow magic onto humans, and they used it so sparingly that the ability had been lost to general knowledge.[3] So while Kyle stared in wonderment at his daughter, feeling the electricity of magic in the air, Mary Alvarez—human—took it as a sign that Maxwell had low blood sugar, or was entering shock at this encounter.

---

3. After all, imagine the panic if humans everywhere realized that anyone could become a witch at the distant whim of an all-powerful empress. The world would be chaos.

Things like this scarred children; there was a procedure to retrieving a child from their home, and *this wasn't it.*

Once again, she blamed Kyle Flanderson for ruining everything.

"It's okay, Max. We're going. We'll get you a cookie and some juice and figure out Claire's situation at the precinct." Mary took Max's hand, carefully leading him away.

But the second she started towards the door, he began to scream. "You can't! No! Claire!" Mary desperately tried to regain his attention, but Maxwell had become utterly hysterical.

And Claire Flanderson, five years old, decided something truly horrifying.

If giving Max magical powers hadn't helped—the next best thing was to make him *forget.*

After all, she'd done it before. Mommy had forgotten all about them. And Daddy wasn't dangerous to Claire specifically; the house ensured that any pain he caused her, he felt too. At that young age, Claire didn't think about verbal abuse, about manipulation. All she knew was that sometimes, Daddy hit Maxwell because of her, and now that wouldn't happen anymore.

But she didn't want her brother to be sad about leaving, either.

So even though Mary stopped short, gestured desperately for one of the police officers to scoop Claire up, the cop hadn't taken three steps in her direction before another wave of magic pulsed through the house.

A far more devastating wave.

Instantly, every memory of Claire faded from the minds of the two police officers, from Mary Alvarez... and from Maxwell Flanderson. With one shove of magic, Claire wiped their thoughts of anything pertaining to the little blonde girl in the living room.

She almost forced it onto her father, too—but he still had that vicious look on his face and she *knew* what happened when she used her magic on him. His guttural, "*Enough,*" could stop her cold, kill her magic on the spot or activate it in a breath, and her young heart didn't dare test it.

For a long moment after the wave dispersed, there was silence.

Then, Kyle Flanderson watched in shock as Mary's grip tightened around the hand of the suddenly-docile boy. Her eyes glazed over Claire's head as she said, distantly, "Thank you for your cooperation, Mr. Flanderson."

Without another word, she strolled from the house, taking Maxwell with her.

The officers scanned the living room one final time, but Claire might as well have been a ghost to them. They filed onto the porch, through the front yard, into their squad cars. Silence filled the house while father and daughter listened for slamming car doors, engines revving, tires on gravel.

Then they were gone.

Kyle turned an incredulous gaze on Claire.

She scrubbed tearstained cheeks and refused to look at him.

Satisfaction bubbled in his chest. "Well, I think that was an excellent demonstration of magic. How about some ice cream, baby?"

Chapter Nineteen

13 Days before Death Stopped

F ive days after the Kyoto Consulate Reconciliation, the Future-Zaro prepared to board a plane to Rome to meet the pope.

Historically, the pope and the Zaro were on good terms. The Zaro had significantly more power in a magical sense, but one billion people worshipped the pope, while only about 630 million witches existed. And considering the ongoing historical debate of whether "witch" was a religion or a race, many witches were also practicing Catholics.

Naturally, the two leaders attempted to be amicable.

At least, they would be, if Ozarik actually deigned to visit.

Instead, right before they left for the Vatican, Clementine intercepted both Ozarik and Claire. They stopped short fifteen feet from the airstrip, and the aciradaan bowed, her voice stiff with barely-contained hatred.

"Apologies, Future-Zaro Ozarik, but the Vatican staff were specific. Only your chosen aciras are allowed to join you in this diplomatic mission."

"Claire is my oldest friend," Ozarik said, and Claire heard his hint of desperation. Her chest tightened; they'd spent the last four days preparing for this. He kept insisting he was ready, but now his protests had her doubting. "Surely—"

Claire cut him off. "Oz. It's fine. I'll just wait for you here."

His face paled, and his eyes darted from the aciras to Claire. After a moment's silence, where she thought he'd shove his fears down and smile like he was meant to, Ozarik instead ventured, "Claire, can I speak with you? Privately?"

"I'm not sure it's necessary." Now Claire was the one speaking through gritted teeth.

"Oh, it is." Ozarik grabbed her arm and towed her back into the castle.

Clementine pressed her lips together, exchanging a dark glance with Bao while Jorge tugged their bags up the awaiting jet's staircase. But it wasn't the aciras' place to question the Zaro, so they busied themselves with their tasks until he returned.

Inside the castle, the heavy wooden door slammed shut. Alone, Ozarik spun away from Claire, tilting his head towards the painted ceiling of the castle's foyer. It denoted a rather epic scene of a leviathan at sea, facing a Zaro of old. No one knew if it was myth or history.

"See, the thing is—" Ozarik began.

"You're still procrastinating?" Claire interrupted, deadpan.

"Possibly." He drew a breath. "I'm researching the—ah, the Assumation Ceremony. We're only a couple weeks away, but I think there's a chance we can permanently divvy our magic if—if we prepare properly."

He was lying. His eye twitched like it did when she tried to teach him poker. Claire crossed her arms.

"Oz."

"It's true. Reiki found a book on the subject. She was researching it too, but—but she didn't get to finish."

A book.

Claire knew exactly what book he was referencing. Did the ancient journal have a spell to separate magic like theirs? She thought it was something... darker. Something dangerous.

But she hadn't seen all its contents. No one had. That was why a certain hunt was ongoing at that very moment, scouring the internet for clues of the journal's whereabouts.

If the spell was to separate the persistent push-pull of their magic... if Ozarik could take most of it, leave Claire with just enough to make a living... well. Obligation to the Zaro and Javarini would be a thing of the past. She could be Ozarik's friend from afar, making her name as a stage magician without any of the world-altering footnotes.

Claire wanted that to be true.

But she also knew Ozarik too well. He was fumbling with his words, lying about his actions. Hiding behind the death of Reiki because he thought Claire wouldn't pry.

Irritation prickled her skin.

Ozarik noticed her aura souring. His voice turned soft, pleading. "Just a few more days. A little bit of time is all I need." And the unspoken words were there: this was an excuse, and he acknowledged it. But it didn't change the fact that he wasn't *ready* to meet the pope, to stand in as the Zaro and rub elbows with the most powerful people in the world.

The contents of the journal wouldn't change that.

Claire sighed. "You really don't want to do this?"

What she meant was, *you really would rather be hunting for a spellbook than out there, experiencing your destiny?*

Ozarik hesitated.

Anything that happened after that moment was inevitable, in Claire's mind.

With a long-suffering sigh, she waved a hand and the illusion was once again in place, shielding Claire Bishop from the prying eyes of the world, replaced with a perfect veneer of Ozarik. He could see the magic shimmering around her, but to everyone else, the Future-Zaro looked as predictable as ever.

"Thank you," he whispered.

She rolled her eyes—his eyes—and boarded the plane with no one the wiser.

It was immensely uncomfortable. Claire had only flown on a plane twice and cared for it even less the second time, so when they arrived in Rome to a sleek town car parked at the airport, she stumbled towards it gratefully.

Planes. What a useless concept for someone who could teleport—and teleport others, if they were prepared for the gut-churning consequences.[1]

But Reiki had never approved of fabulous displays of magic, and thus, traveled by plane almost exclusively. She used to claim it was to discuss current affairs with her aciras, undisturbed as they traveled from location to location. She claimed it was down-time, akin to meditation.

Nothing about this felt meditative.

"Are you feeling all right, Future-Zaro Ozarik?" Jorge asked.

In that moment, she hated him, and she hated Ozarik, and she hated all this pomp and circumstance. When she snapped, "Just fine," loathing filled her soul at the deep timber of her voice under this illusion.

She'd agreed to this, but a couple of miserable hours on a plane soured her charity. Why wasn't Ozarik here right now? Why was this *her* job?

They rode to the Vatican in near-silence, interrupted only by Clementine discussing the daily schedule. Apparently, the pope was a busy man. *Apparently*, he'd reworked his entire day to accommodate them after hearing the news of Reiki. A meeting at one to discuss world politics. Pre-dinner appetizers and a summary of Reiki's accomplishments at three. A public appearance at four, followed by dinner itself: a seven-course meal featuring the finest cuisine Rome had to offer.

Claire liked Rome, and she could appreciate the ancient architecture of the Vatican. She was looking forward to the food, once she could get her hands on some grape soda.

The rest of it... ehh. The older she got, the less she liked wining and dining. As a young act on the Strip, she'd had to make nice with the big players, play into the expected naivety—but now that *she* was top dog, she ignored all the social markers. Reiki had spent her life trading favors,

---

1. She was convinced grape soda would work just as well on common folk, witch or not. Henry, who didn't like grape soda one bit, had spent their spontaneous afternoon in Hawaii absolutely miserable and would debate that until he died.

negotiating peace over dinner tables and in board rooms. It was a lot of pretenses Claire didn't care for.

But the thing was, she was *good* at it. As the nausea faded, she replaced it with a dazzling smile and humble attitude. By the time they stepped into the pope's chambers, her illusion was perfectly in place.

"Your Holiness," Claire-as-Ozarik said, dipping into a formal bow. "It is my deepest and most sincere pleasure to meet you, despite the dark circumstances."

"My dearest Zaro," Pope Augustine pushed from his chair to meet her. An older man with a kind smile, it was no surprise why he was adored by billions. His easygoing attitude and forgiving nature made even Claire relax.

"I am so sorry to hear about Reiki." He waved her aciras and his own aides from the room. Clementine alone hesitated, but when every other aide filed out, she had no choice but to follow. Claire didn't miss how the woman frowned, like she knew Ozarik's appearance was merely an illusion.

There was no way she *could*, but it made Claire's skin prickle regardless.

The door closed gently behind Clementine. Finally alone, the pope motioned for Claire to sit. His old eyes seemed to peer into her soul. "How are you handling it? I know she was like a mother to you."

"She was. It—it's been hard." Claire, who was closer to Christianity than the witches' revered Universe, felt like there was a special place in Hell for lying to this man. But he was watching her earnestly, so she forced herself to continue, scrambling to mourn a woman she'd sworn to hate. "A lot of people are emptier now. I don't think any of us truly appreciated her presence until it vanished."

Pope Augustine's gaze softened. "I didn't ask about the rest of the world. I asked about you."

"Me?" Instantly, Claire was yanked back to the Bellagio's burning stage, to the horrifying moment when Reiki's death echoed through the universe. Had this holy man felt it too? The fracturing of souls, the screaming of hearts?

Reliving that moment, Claire's façade faltered. "When—when I heard the news, it was like the world rained fire." The words ghosted from her lips, surprising even her. "It's been weeks, and it still feels like it's raining. Like everything ignited and no one noticed, and I'm the only one who can put out the flames."

"It is a heavy responsibility, leading a nation." Pope Augustine took her hand. "But a heavier burden is keeping your grief bottled inside."

Claire laughed, choking on the sound. "I—I'm not grieving."

He gently touched her cheek, then pulled back to show the moisture on his single, crooked finger.

Claire stared at it, confusion and sadness compounding in her soul. She felt where he'd touched her, just to verify. Maybe something had broken in her mind, because in five sentences, this man had somehow managed to shatter walls she'd erected years ago.

It took a moment to recenter the illusion, now.

"Ah. I'm so sorry. T-this wasn't the point of today."

"To the contrary, this is *exactly* the point of today." Pope Augustine smiled, clasping his gnarled hands in his lap. "My advisors want me to discuss world politics, but that removes the humanity that is so necessary in our line of work. May I tell you a secret, Ozarik?"

Claire nodded.

The old man's eyes glistened. "Reiki was one of my dearest friends too. So, when it feels like the world is raining fire, please remember: you are not alone."

The two of them spent the afternoon chatting about Reiki, exchanging stories. For a rare moment, Claire placed herself in Ozarik's shoes, imagined what it was like to be raised by such an extraordinary woman. When the pope shared stories about why he admired her, Claire admired her too.

It didn't erase how Claire had been treated, but... it was a fitting tribute.

She ruminated all the way back to her suite, buried deep in the guest quarters of the Vatican, and stopped short on seeing Aciradaan Clementine perched beside her door. The woman swept into a practiced bow, more for appearances than anything. Claire nodded back, like she'd seen Ozarik do a thousand times.

Of course, the day's events had worn Claire raw, and her earlier unease manifested as a slightly cutting, "What do you need, Clementine?"

The woman's green eyes were almost unnerving, and her hand settled on the Chinese dao ever-present at her hip. "You seem... anxious. I wanted to check on you."

Claire saw right through that remark. The pope was partially right about Reiki mothering Ozarik, but he didn't realize that the aciradaan had an even bigger hand in Oz's life. Clementine took her unofficial "maternal figure" status seriously—which meant that Claire had always been the Other Girl. The threat.

Claire wasn't amused by it.

"Everything is fine," she replied tightly.

Clementine pushed away from the door, shoulders back. "I see." They were almost the same height, although with Claire's illusion in place, she would appear a few inches taller. The dao's black-hole magic seemed to pulse as the two women stared each other down.

And then... Clementine crumbled.

"I thought maybe—I mean, I know what h-happened... it wasn't your fault, Ozarik," Clementine said brokenly, and Claire nearly recoiled to see actual tears in the woman's eyes. "Reiki—oh, *Universe*, Reiki. I can't believe we're here right now, without her. I shouldn't have left that room. I should have been there."

Claire, who knew no details about Reiki's final moments and was starting to feel very awkward about it, forced her face into a semblance of sympathy. But anything she said here might disrupt their ruse, so she diverted.

"She always appreciated you, Clementine."

It felt hollow. Reiki had been perfectly friendly towards Clementine—but even as a teenager, Claire knew Clementine's feelings swayed into much deeper territory. She and Ozarik used to giggle about it in the secrecy of his bedroom, gossiping about the popes late into the night.

It didn't seem so funny now, watching Clementine's shoulders tremble with grief.

"I know. I know she did. She meant the world to me, Ozarik." Clementine pressed her palms into her eyes, hunching into herself.

It pulled at Claire's soul, reviving an empathy she'd thought was long gone.

It wasn't her place to comfort Clementine—she wasn't Ozarik, and she wasn't the Zaro, not really. But Claire couldn't ignore a witch in need. Her magic slipped into the aciradaan's soul, wrapping around her body like a warm hug. *It'll be okay*, the motion assured. It was powerful healing magic, a spell she wasn't even sure Ozarik knew about, but it made Clementine sob in earnest.

"Reiki—" the aciradaan whispered, hugging her arms over her chest as the spell soothed her grief, lessened the ache in her chest. "I haven't felt this kind of magic since... well. It's been years." Now she turned watery eyes to Claire. "T-Thank you. If you ever need to talk, to mourn... please know—"

"I'm not alone," Claire murmured.

It seemed to be a theme around Reiki's legacy.

Clementine nodded, bid her a fast goodbye, and vanished down the hallway before Claire could follow. She stared after the woman for a long moment, ruminating, before stepping into the privacy of her lavish suite. Once the curtains were drawn and the door was locked, Claire let the illusion fade, tugging something out of her pocket.

An intricate scroll with a dragon carved into one side, a moon in the other. She unfurled it, reading it for the second time.

The inky swirl of Reiki's perfect handwriting made her pause. At the witches' market, the woman's message had seemed contrite, mocking. Now, they assumed a different inflection—one that almost let Claire believe Reiki really meant those two little words.

I'm sorry.

"All right, Reiki," Claire said, turning her attention to the coordinates. "What do you want me to see?"

Chapter Twenty

2 Years and 204 Days before Death Stopped

Seventeen-year-old Claire consulted the apartment building's letter, then scanned the doors until she landed on a second-floor unit. It should have been obvious—its door was wide open, and pop music drifted into the common space. People were laughing and chatting and a handwritten sign above the door said, "Witches and other folk welcome!"

Claire snorted, then climbed the stairs. The typical Las Vegas heat was nonexistent today, which was a shame. One hundred fifteen degree temperatures[1] would have provided an easy excuse for why sweat dripped down the back of her neck.

Claire projected easy confidence most of the time, but today her chest tightened in fear. Stages and crowds, she could handle. All eyes on her? Just another Tuesday evening.

But a housewarming party? Henry knew a lot of people, had that easygoing air that everyone could befriend, but this was... intimate... by Claire's standards. And Claire didn't *do* intimate.

Still, he invited her, and she'd never refuse an invitation from Henry Ballard.

---

1. Which was 46.1 degrees Celsius, for everyone else.

She had barely raised her hand to knock on the doorframe when an older guy barreled past her. His shoulder slammed into hers, sending her careening over the threshold and into the living room. The guy skidded to a halt, a six-pack in his hands, and yelped, "Ah, sorry! Didn't see you!"

Claire caught her balance with the grace of a dancer, twisting to quirk an eyebrow at the guy. "You didn't *see* me?"

She spoke it with the exasperation of someone used to being seen.

Before he could reply, Henry called, "Well, it's better than you hovering there like a vampire waiting for permission."

Now Claire gasped in fake indignation, even as the guy with the beer roared in laughter. He tossed one to Henry, one to Claire, and dropped the rest on the coffee table, where they were snatched up by the other people in attendance. Three guys, two girls, plus Henry and Claire. One of them, interestingly enough, was actually a human. Claire wouldn't know it yet, but this was one of Jenifer Shield's siblings—and in half a year, the introduction would be made, and their resulting love would be one of ages.

For now, of course, Henry was quite content to entertain his friends, rather than a girlfriend. The beer *hissed*, and he raised the open can to cheers Claire. "Can't believe you made it. Figured you'd be busy with... ah, work." He quirked a grin.

Claire grinned back, already glad she came. She wasn't wearing The Magnificent Claire Bishop's brunette façade, and rarely did in Henry's presence, but he was the only resident of Las Vegas privy to the difference.

She opened her own can of beer, but he plucked it from her hands before she could take a swing. "Ah, ah. No underage drinking in my new apartment."

His guests burst into laughter, cajoling him to make an exception, but Claire simply waved at the fridge. "Lucky you, I prefer grape soda anyway."

"I don't have—"

She opened the fridge to reveal it absolutely *packed* with grape soda, to the point of sheer absurdity. Henry's shock, which almost instantly shifted to utter amusement, was priceless. Claire winked at him as she tugged out a bottle and popped the cap.

The night wore on, and it didn't take Claire long to learn that the guy who'd run into her was the infamous Milo, Henry's best friend. She met Alisha and Noah and Valentin and finally, Isabelle Shields, who was a waitress at one of the casinos Henry worked at. They welcomed her with drunken happiness, broke out a witchy card game about crafting new spells on the fly, and in the ensuing creative chaos, Claire found herself forgetting—just for a moment—the reality of her life, her magic, her choices.

Of course, it lasted exactly as long as it took Reiki to make a goddamn announcement into the brains of every witch in the world. Reiki didn't make announcements often, and when she did, she tried to keep them local—straight into the minds of the witches she needed to address.

Claire knew it was coming when her magic ebbed into Ozarik, like pulling a suction cup off your arm. She braced, and a second later, the witches present were wincing as Reiki intoned: *"To the witches of Los Angeles—violence is not the answer. Please calm your anger. I will personally get to the bottom of this."*

"Los Angeles?" Milo said as the Zaro's voice faded. He always thought it was unnerving to hear Reiki speaking to them through that map—like a god slapping someone upside the head. "She missed the mark a bit, didn't she? Geographically speaking."

"She probably just didn't want to miss any residents," Alisha replied.

"What happened in LA?"

"Homicide, I think? Some human murdered a witch. A white, Beverly Hills housewife human, so of course it's prompting a bigger discussion."

They chattered on about the Zaro and the murder in LA, but it was noise to Claire. She pushed to her feet, trembling, her drink forgotten. Because it *was* strange that Reiki cast such a wide net for that announcement.

Either she *meant* to encompass Claire—unlikely, since Reiki always knew where to find her, and Claire had nothing to do with the uproar in Los Angeles—or it was a genuine mistake to include Nevada in that announcement. And if it was the latter... it meant Zaro Reiki was starting to slip.

"Turn on the news, Henry," Valentin called.

Claire mumbled about needing something from her car—which was a lie, since she hadn't driven a car in her life and didn't intend to. Still, she slipped out while they argued, stumbling down the exterior staircase onto a carefully manicured common space.

She sunk into the grimy picnic bench at the center of it, drawing careful breaths. She prodded Ozarik's magic, but he sent a hasty reply: *busy now. Chat later.*

Of course he was busy, if there were riots in LA.

It left Claire feeling lonely, excluded.

"Claire. You okay?" Henry's footsteps stopped behind her, and Claire didn't twist around to see him. She should have known he'd follow, because of *course* he did—Henry Ballard was nothing if not reliable, nothing if not attentive to emotion.

"I'm fine," Claire said stonily.

Henry stepped around her, leaning against the table's edge. It was coated in some blue rubber-like material, more durable in the desert heat, and one hand absently ran over the holes on the tabletop. "Are you concerned about the murder? Or is it something more?"

Anyone else, and Claire would fake a smile, breezily cover up her emotions. But her fingers trembled with the loss of magic—with the fact that Ozarik had *stolen* her magic tonight—and she couldn't get that bugging thought from her brain. So, she sighed with the weight of the world and replied, "It's weird that Reiki made an announcement we could hear, too."

Henry frowned, tilting his head. "It is strange. But maybe that's how the magic works—" he cut himself off as she shook her head, turning his gaze to the metal ramada shading them. "Right. That's not how it works."

Henry Ballard didn't *quite* know everything about Claire, but he knew that she had the magic of a Zaro, that she was dating Future-Zaro Ozarik, and that she'd lived on Javarini before coming to Nevada. When Claire told him how magic worked, he believed her, no questions asked.

Claire pinched her brow. "If she meant to do it, fine. But if she didn't, it means... she's losing control."

"Scary thought."

"Not *dangerous* control. Just—losing her magic. It's seeping into Ozarik already."

"And into you."

Claire pressed her lips together, watching him carefully.

But Henry wasn't one to pry. He simply said, "So there will be an Assumption Ceremony sooner than later, is what I'm hearing?"

"It's possible."

"Are—will you both partake in that?"

Claire chuckled humorlessly. "It's not my future."

He pushed away from the table, taking a seat across from her instead. Whenever he stared at her like this, Claire was almost entirely certain he knew more than he let on. Hope flickered in her chest, but she kept quiet, waiting for him to piece things together.

Always waiting.

After a long moment, he said, "Do you *want* it to be your future?"

"I used to. Now I don't."

"Are you sure?"

No. "Ozarik will be a great Zaro. I just thought we had more time." More time for whimsical dates and deep conversations. More time of them being equals, even though they *hadn't* been equals for a while. More time of Claire swimming in magic that really shouldn't belong to her—not once Ozarik Assumed the title of Zaro.

With the announcement finished, her magic slipped back—not all of it, but enough to stop her hands from shaking. She drew a breath and smiled slightly. "Well. A problem for another day." She moved to stand.

"Claire," Henry said.

She paused.

"Not every problem vanishes with time."

Claire Bishop shook her head, and her voice was laced with exhaustion. "This one will."

And with that, she strolled back upstairs, her mask firmly back in place. Henry heaved a sigh of his own and followed. After all, there wasn't much else to do.

Chapter Twenty-One

12 Days before Death Stopped

Despite common understanding, all the magic in the world wouldn't give Claire an innate ability to find a location from coordinates on a scroll. She'd tried exactly once, when she was eleven and decided to study engineering as a last-ditch effort to be anything *but* the "Future-Zaro." Her father reluctantly promised her a set of expensive textbooks from the local community college... on the stipulation that she teleport into a bank in Seattle and secure the deed to a plot of supposedly very rich land.

Claire had splashed into the Sound in the dead of night instead, and wasn't eager to repeat the experience.

Instead, she poofed from the Vatican to Henry's place, utterly interrupting Jenifer's first attempt at breakfast in bed. It was probably a blessing for Henry—his new wife's pancakes were more like charred discs, and the orange juice was store-bought and maybe expired.

Jenifer nearly dropped the platter when Claire magically appeared in their bedroom. Although to her credit, she handled it better than 95% of humans would.

"Oh! Ah, w-welcome. Didn't expect you here." Jenifer couldn't decide what to call Claire: were they on a first-name basis, or would Ms. Bishop be more appropriate? Possibly "nearly-Zaro Claire"... or was that rude? The possibilities swirled as Jenifer's polite smile shifted into awkward panic, as

150

she clutched the breakfast platter tight enough to show the whites of her knuckles.

Claire, meanwhile, couldn't care less. Her desire for formality had vanished the day Reiki kicked her off Javarini.

"That bacon smells salty." Claire shot Henry a wry glance as she wrenched open his dresser drawer, rifling through his socks.

"Claire." Henry pulled his blanket up to his chest, although his tone was amicable and pleasant. "Remember when we talked about boundaries? It's Saturday morning. Who knows what we could have been doing."

Claire, who didn't like to think about sex on a *good* day, much less one possibly soon-to-be wrought with emotional trauma incurred by a dead woman's final message, wrinkled her nose.

Jenifer flushed deep red, averting her gaze as she crossed the room, nearly slamming the tray onto Henry's lap. She shot him a look that very clearly said, *stop embarrassing me*—one that Henry took as, *you're so cute in the morning*. He smiled wide while she spluttered, "He's exaggerating. We wouldn't—"

"I'm only here for a moment." Claire finally fished out Henry's GPS tracker. She'd gifted it to him two years ago, enhanced to magically and automatically record all rare stones he found in the Las Vegas desert. She flashed the oval device at him, then waved at Jenifer. "Enjoy your breakfast. Jen, that salt wa

s for you, not him. Maybe try some steak tonight."

Then she vanished again, leaving a whiff of purple smoke that had both human and witch coughing.

"S-Should we expect that a lot?" Jenifer Shields-Ballard asked, secretly pleased that not *only* were she and Claire on a first-name basis, they'd apparently graduated to nicknames at some undisclosed moment.

Henry shrugged, sawing into his burnt pancake. "With her? Impossible to know."

Meanwhile, deep in the forests of Mount Fuji, Claire entered the coordinates into the digital screen and checked the direction on the little map. This all seemed very intensive for Reiki—although arguably, Claire didn't know much about the woman before she hit her sixties.

In reality, Reiki had been an avid hiker in her youth, and possessed a particular reverence for the Japanese wilderness specifically. Although a Zaro's hiking reality was much, much different than that of a normal person, witch or otherwise. Branches tugged themselves out of her path, leaves parted like heavy drapes, and even the insects didn't dare enter a Zaro's aura or risk being crisped alive.

Yes, Reiki had rather loved the wilderness.

Claire, possessing only half her magic, was having exactly half the good time. She landed near the coordinates, not exactly on them, which was a mistake on her end. But her stomach churned unpleasantly and there was a disturbing lack of grape soda way out here, so Claire drew a frustrated breath and continued on foot, batting at branches and leaves that extended only as much weary effort to move aside as a performer waiting for an ovation that would never come.

Evening in the Vatican and early morning in Las Vegas meant that Mount Fuji was bathed in the late-night moon's glow—and it was cold as *balls* here. Even a bubble of magic didn't warm her soul, and Claire grumbled at Reiki's memory as she followed the GPS up the mountain's treacherous ledge.

"This had better be worth it," she said in multiple instances.

No one answered, obviously.

Two hours later, the sun peeked over the horizon and bathed the dense forest in golden light—one that would have most people in awe of the magnificence present in the Japanese wilderness. And yet, most people didn't awake to a luxury high-rise condo in Mandalay Bay, so Claire Bishop merely rolled her eyes and mumbled to the sun, "Finally. So glad you deigned to get up."

Thirty minutes after that, Claire found what *had* to be the destination; after all, the ancient temple was exactly Reiki's style. It was framed in stone lanterns that must have once been bold and angular, but now... weren't. A single, splintering torii gate loomed over an uneven, moss-covered platform. The temple was open to the elements, but despite the luscious vines creeping around the exterior, the platform itself was completely bare.

And no wonder. Magic—Reiki's magic and something even more ancient—rippled through the space. This wasn't a random destination.

It was a shrine to the Zaros of Japanese history.

Claire swallowed, feeling distinctly out of place. She was an imposter to the Zaro lifestyle on the best of days, but here...? This was a space for Zaros who'd changed the world. Even if she'd been born in Japan, Claire Bishop wouldn't have belonged.

"Okay." The word was lost in the sudden silence of the forest. It felt like everything nearby was holding its breath—the leaves stopped rustling, the creatures paused, and even the stone itself swelled in anticipation. Claire mustered her courage and carefully climbed the short staircase to the platform.

She reached the top.

One second passed.

Two.

Five.

Thirty-seven.

It was pretty anti-climactic.

"Very funny," Claire muttered, already calling her magic to poof back to the Vatican for a hot shower and sleep. But the second that spell became a concrete thought, her magic infiltrated the space—and a golden shape took form.

It solidified into glimmering light and stars... and then something truly human. Someone that looks exactly like Reiki.

Claire froze. Shit. This wasn't the plan. Reiki was *dead*; Claire had expected to find some token of her life here, something trite and probably unsatisfying. Not a magical hologram of her actual nemesis. Not a *conversation*.

Claire was not prepared to have a heart-to-heart with Reiki.

But the Zaro wasn't looking at her. The woman knelt, running her hands along the stone platform. Her voice sounded distant, like audio from an old recording. "It was inevitable you would sit in that chair. And I know your curiosity; of course, you followed the coordinates."

Claire stiffened.

Reiki blinked eyes made of light, finally looking towards the entrance of the shrine—towards Claire. She wasn't looking *at* her, but it was close enough.

"Even Ozarik hasn't been here." A note of regret filtered into Reiki's voice, and she pushed to her feet. "I should have brought him. This place was created millennia ago to honor the first Zaro that hailed from the islands. Since then, we've used it as a speaking place, a point of remembrance." Now Reiki trailed off, gazing skyward. "I wonder if Arjun had something similar in India. I imagine there are shrines like this across the world."

Claire stepped forward, warily. It was almost like Reiki was back again, alive and well, which filled her with all kinds of emotions. The last time she'd seen the woman was that night in Javarini, during their final argument.

Years hadn't seemed to dull the anger, at least on Claire's end. It had been the lowest point of her life, and worse, Reiki—so known for compassion and understanding—had demonstrated absolutely none.

Which was why her next words kept Claire from repeating the past, from storming out of Reiki's life—death—without a word.

"I'm so sorry, Claire."

The girl inhaled sharply. She must have been imagining it—*must* have—but with those words, she swore she could feel Reiki's true regret. It settled over her like a second skin, making her almost sympathetic.

Almost.

Reiki closed her eyes, then glanced again at the torii gate, where she clearly expected Claire would be standing. "The world viewed me favorably, which was a great honor. The Zaro is meant to be benevolent, but—a reputation can be tainted. Especially by the actions of someone beset with emotion."

Ozarik.

Cold sweat prickled Claire's neck.

"You've noticed it too," Reiki murmured. "You must have seen it, Claire. I always thought *you* were his problem. You were the reason he could never focus, the reason he lost sight of our life's work."

This was a familiar phrase, something that made Claire's hackles rise again. She crossed her arms, but Reiki continued uninterrupted.

"It was never you."

"No shit," Claire snapped, but even her ire was hollow.

After all, it took immense willpower and confidence to overcome the dark phrases of life—especially when they came from people of power. People who were supposed to show someone love and affection, and instead offered accusation.

Claire's heart had hardened well before this moment.

And yet, Reiki's pained gaze took a chisel to the stone.

"Ozarik resonated with our goals, but... he loves deeply. And I was unable to distance myself from his potential, unable to see the desperation growing in his heart." Reiki was wearing another traditional kimono, perfectly pressed despite the hike she'd probably taken to reach this place. Her hair was pinned in its usual bun, and her eyes glistened with sparkling tears. "I fear Ozarik might do something terrible, Claire. And if you're hearing this, it means I won't be present to stop him."

Claire set her jaw, thinking about a certain book.

But admitting that to Reiki felt like a betrayal to the one person she loved most. Instead, Claire took the offensive. "How is this my problem? You made it abundantly clear that I will never be the Zaro. I'm too selfish. Too materialistic. Too vain." She spit the words at the dead woman's feet, and fury curled in her chest.

This was a waste of time.

But in an eerie change, Reiki looked directly at her now. "I can feel your future anger. It reverberates through time and space." Now she drew a shaking breath. "I should have paid more attention when you were growing up. You wanted an explanation the night I exiled you, and ever since I've wracked my brain for an excuse."

At this point, Claire wasn't even sure what the woman could say to make things better.

Still, the child inside wanted to hear her try.

"Only a fool makes excuses." Reiki paced across the temple platform. "Here is the truth. I didn't believe your father's empty promises, but I believed in my own magic. I believed the spell I placed on that house would protect you. During my subsequent visits, his little performances told me everything. You weren't okay."

Claire was torn between defending her childhood, claiming everything was fine, and snarling, *Obviously.*

"By that point, however, my popes knew Ozarik would be Zaro. The *world* knew. And by introducing you as his equal, I feared the chaos that would follow."

"It might not have been chaos," Claire muttered stubbornly. It was an empty statement. Her childhood couldn't be changed, and wasting anger on "what ifs" only made her tired.

Reiki paused in her walk, facing the vast wilderness. Her sparkling visage faded as beams of early morning sunlight speckled through the trees. "I should have removed you from that house, but I was afraid. I didn't think you could live in my castle, under the noses of my popes, without someone realizing your magical potential. And when you showed the signs of abuse—arrogance to cover your fear, aloofness to protect your heart—it was easy to pretend that was your true personality."

It wasn't enough.

It was too late.

Claire stepped into Reiki's line of sight, for all that it mattered. "So, what I'm hearing is that you fucked up." Her voice pierced through the magic of the shrine, and Reiki's light faltered. "Surprise, surprise."

How *dare* she?

Claire took two steps towards the staircase, towards freedom, before Reiki appeared in front of her. "Wait—"

Claire growled, lashing out with her own magic. A *boom* echoed through the forest, a physical push of wind and magic. It absorbed into the temple, and the stone lanterns began to glow. Reiki's golden image vanished, leaving Claire alone, panting with exertion.

The sounds of the forest resumed. Claire's breathing quieted.

But Reiki wasn't going to back down so easily. Her magic slid back into the space like water sliding downhill, filling every crevice in the stone, every drop of Claire's blood. Claire struggled to contain it as it shoved against her soul.

For someone so mild, Reiki always had been too damn insistent.

Sweat trailed down Claire's face, and in a fit of frustration, she shouted: "I don't *care* what your reasons were! I didn't need your help. I grew up just fine on my own." She almost started listing off her accomplishments, but that felt like pandering.

Even her excuses sounded like that.

The magic shoved harder, for Reiki had never been able to be contained. Claire dropped to her knees, sweat pouring down her face. "Maybe I am vain. Materialistic. Greedy. It's what you expected, after all. Why try to be anything *better*?" She snarled the word, slammed her fist against the ground to punctuate.

The temple rippled with the force of it, stones shifting under her knees. Reiki's magic went silent.

Claire gasped, hunching lower. Her hair fell from its ponytail, sticking to her cheeks and temples. "I don't need your approval, or your advice, or your apologies. I don't need anything from you, Reiki. You hear me? *Nothing*."

Unconsciously, her magic barriers faded just enough that Reiki's could again occupy the sacred space. Except this time, warmth surrounded Claire, a magical hug sent through time and space. It wrapped around her soul, but it wasn't a force from within, begging for release.

It was like a knitted blanket and hot cocoa on a cold winter day.

"I'm so sorry, dear," Reiki whispered from all around her. The physical visage was still gone, but her words settled over Claire. The old Zaro's tears were evident in her tone. "I'm so, so sorry. Failing to help you was my biggest mistake, my only regret in life. Ozarik was never meant to be the Zaro, but I never gave you the chance... and now it's too late."

Claire's heart hurt. How would her life be different if Reiki had visited her house first, back when they were babies? How would their lives be different if she'd seen Claire first?

Reiki sounded quiet and sad. "You are the next Zaro, Claire. And I'm so sorry I didn't see it earlier."

Claire's breath hitched.

How long she'd waited to hear that.

Reiki's presence began to fade, her words drifting through into the morning light. "My time is over. I can sense it within the magic—dusk has descended into night. If I survive tomorrow's encounter, I will destroy this message and tell you myself. If not," a pause, a deep breath, "I can only hope *you* understand your own potential... for it's the one thing I never could."

And she vanished.

Trembling, Claire pushed to her feet, drawing her magic back into herself. Reiki's presence had dissipated into the constant, ancient magic of this shrine. The world was still and silent in her wake.

The old Zaro was gone forever.

Suddenly, desperately, Claire Bishop needed to know *why*.

Chapter Twenty-Two

3 Years and 324 Days before Death Stopped

In Henry Ballard's expert opinion, witchy casinos were best. Usually, they existed on the second floor[1] of certain shops—herbology, fortune telling, and the occasional accounting office—and the entry requirement was as simple as "be a witch." If this seemed discriminatory, it's important to remember that these casinos only existed because humans were a paranoid species.

After all, it was nearly impossible to tell if someone's magical ability happened to be winning card games.

Because of that, these specialty casinos were mostly a free-for-all. Instead of normal gambling games like poker and blackjack, they offered odd games that centered more around luck, intelligence, and a person's ability to pay attention... or lose attention. Henry's favorite was split between "Find the Cat"—where a witch was locked in a cluttered room while viewers bet on how fast they'd accomplish the name—and "the Fool's Pluck"—wherein a witch drew cards from a modified Tarot deck under the judgmental eyes of a raven, which had a tendency to attack if the victim—er, player—found a certain, unknown card.

---

1. After all, Las Vegas sat on very hard bedrock, so literal "underground" casinos were simply too expensive.

While inside these casinos, Henry operated under two parameters. First, he lied about his own ability of finding pretty stones, because history showed him—unkindly—that this magical skill was literally unheard of... and in a city of debt and addiction, it would gain favors with all the wrong people.

Second, Henry Ballard never drew attention to himself. Attention in Las Vegas could go from admiring to dangerous in a matter of seconds, and Henry rather liked preserving his health and wealth, thank you very much.

Which was why, when a blonde girl with sharp blue eyes emerged from the Cat Room in seven seconds, possessing both a standoffish tabby and a devious smirk, Henry strategically about-faced and sat at the salamander dueling table instead. He watched the amphibians circle each other in their small enclosure, mouths open, and slapped a stack of bills at the table. "Bets on blue."

The croupier was too busy staring, slack-jawed, at the blonde girl to accept his money.

The blue salamander—which wasn't actually blue, but had a tiny blue ribbon tied to its tail—lunged, taking the red creature by the back.

Henry tapped the table to get his attention. "Blue?"

The witch glanced back at him, huffed, and took the money. The match played out, and two minutes and thirty-three seconds later, Henry found himself out a stack of bills.

"Such is life." Henry shrugged good-naturedly, even as a raucous cheer arose from the table where the blonde girl had sat next.

The girl was trouble, and Henry found himself watching her. Not because of her outstanding ability to best every game, but rather because the more games she bested, the more *eyes* landed on her. And their hosts started muttering, and then grumbling, and soon she was fielding dark glares from every employee in the casino.

Including a couple of their bouncers.

Henry recognized them immediately, a nasty pair. Janice's magical ability was to always possess the sharpest knife. Marcus's ability had to do with knitting—he was notoriously close-lipped about it—but he valued his job more than anything.

And normally Henry wouldn't care, but this girl, the one flashing an obviously magical ability to *win every game* like it was a billboard in the desert, couldn't be more than sixteen years old.

Her age hardly mattered in this casino (recall the only entry requirement of "be a witch"). After all, the games made so little sense that no human regulator cared enough to intervene for underage "gambling," even though very real money was exchanging hands. In fact, Henry himself was only nineteen.

But at least he wasn't stupid about it.

When Janice and Marcus ominously flanked the girl, towering over her shoulders while she glanced up at them and smirked, Henry, against his better judgment, withdrew from his game. When they "escorted"—read: muscled—her down the stairs, through the quaint shop of flowers and house plants, and into the side alley, Henry, against his better judgment, followed.

And when Marcus shoved her against the rough brick wall and Janice pressed a too-sharp knife against the girl's throat, Henry, against his better judgment, intervened.

"Hey now," he said, forcing an amicable tone as he strolled towards them. "Janice. She's a little young for that, don't you think?"

"She's old enough to gamble, she's old enough to win... she's old enough to face consequences," Janice snarled.

The girl swallowed, and a thin drop of blood slipped down her neck. But despite the obviously perilous position she was in, her expression befuddled him. She almost looked... bored.

Unease prickled Henry's chest, but it was too late now. He was involved. He'd broken his second parameter, and now all eyes were on him. "Look, have you considered the fact that maybe, just maybe, she's *that good*?"

"Being 'good' doesn't matter in Vegas," Marcus said. He narrowed his eyes. "And we've lost a lot of money because of her."

"She's not claiming that money." Henry paused just inches from them. Janice still hadn't removed the knife, which made his gut tighten with fear. "Obviously, she's just messing with you."

"Henry. Leave before we're threatening *you* again too."

In fact, the reason Henry created Parameter Two at all was because of Janice and Marcus. He liked to think they were friends now, water under the bridge, but... it was possible that wasn't as true as he hoped.

The girl cleared her throat. "Ah, that's a misconception."

"That they'll threaten me too?" Henry quirked his head.

"That I'm not claiming the money. I won it, so I'm taking it. Also, you two don't scare me. This whole act is a bit amusing, to be honest." Now she smiled at them, a brilliant expression that almost made Henry believe she had this under control.

Except, oh yeah, she had a *knife to her throat*.

"Amusing?" Janice growled, and gently scraped the blade's edge against the girl's neck, pulling the small cut upwards. More blood beaded around the mark, sliding down, staining the girl's white button-down shirt.

Well, that was quite enough.

"Janice, stop!" Henry grabbed her arm, trying to yank her back, and in that breath two things happened.

First, Janice spun the knife on him instead, blade aimed to do far more damage than a simple scratch—and then, both Janice and Marcus disappeared in a puff of purple smoke. A strong, fruity scent filled the air as the girl shrugged off the brick wall. Her blue eyes seemed to glow for a second, but it might have been his imagination.

There was a strong chance this was *all* his imagination, because—because—

"You teleported them."

"Just a bit. Not far." The girl smiled at him, but it seemed vaguely malicious now. He stepped back, although she didn't seem to be directing the sentiment at him specifically. "That's right. You figured it out, didn't you?"

"Only the Zaro can teleport," he said.

The girl, who we know to be Claire Bishop, flipped her hair. "And Reiki said I couldn't keep a low profile." She laughed, a harsh, guttural sound brimming with anger, and looked at the sky. "Ugh, Ozarik is going to kill me. Fine. *Fine.*" A snap of her fingers, a glare at the sky. "Those two will never recognize me again. My secret identity is intact. And before you say anything, no, it's not mind manipulation—it's an illusion. Are you happy, you stupid Zaro?"

Henry was beginning to think he shouldn't be here. He cleared his throat and edged away. What he said was, "I'm glad you're all right," but what he thought was, *is she crazy... or am I?*

Desperate to let that mystery remain as such, Henry about-faced, calling over his shoulder, "Maybe don't collect your earnings at this particular casino. Those two will be back, and they're a lot less forgiving the second time around."

"Hang on," the girl said, and Henry stopped before he knew why. She strolled up to him, casual as if they were going out for ice cream. "That was pretty ballsy of you."

"Ballsy, or ball-ard?" Henry made the joke without thinking. It didn't even make sense—his surname was pronounced like the word "ballerina," and he got a lot of shit for it growing up. Although now that he thought about it, pronouncing it the other way probably wouldn't have helped in high school either.

The girl didn't laugh. She just stared at him, intensely enough that he cleared his throat and tugged his collar.

"Ah, sorry. Bad joke. My last name is Ballard, so—never mind. Anyway, flaunting magic like that in a city like this isn't a good idea. Just a tip."

But the girl's eyes had widened, and now *she* looked unnerved. She took a visible step backwards, like he was an angry ghost and she could ward him off with distance.

"Are you okay?"

"Ballard. H-Has your last name always been Ballard? He said your name is Henry."

"Well, Henry's my middle name." He tucked his hands in his pockets and rocked back on his heels.

"Your middle name." The girl scrubbed her face, and Henry realized her hands were shaking now. Blood stained the collar of her shirt, making her crisp appearance look like a Halloween costume. Probably an adrenaline crash. He distantly wondered if he should call someone—an adult with medical experience.

The girl continued: "I didn't expect to see you in Las Vegas."

Considering they'd never met before, Henry didn't expect to see her anywhere. He cleared his throat. "I moved here about a year ago."

"From Scottsdale."

He stiffened. First the gambling wins, then the teleportation spell, now mind reading? This was... unnatural.

Except for a Zaro.

With a nervous laugh, he shifted away from her. "Ah, yes."

"Henry." She rolled his name over her tongue. Then, she reached for him—seemed to realize it—and hugged her arms around her chest instead. It was such a subtle motion he should have missed it, but he didn't, and somehow that made it even more awkward. At some point, the blood had vanished from her shirt, the skin of her neck smooth as silk.

Like it never happened.

Henry backed up a few steps. "Look, you seem clever. If you need cash that badly, I bet you can figure something out. Something that doesn't involve robbing the local witches."

Claire squinted. "Is it robbing if they're a casino?"

"Well, the money has to come from somewitch."

She sighed, massaging her forehead. "Fine. I'll think of something else."

Something else. Alarm bells went off, and Henry frowned at her. "Do you live here?" She didn't seem neglected, underfed, or homeless—but he wasn't sure what adult would let their teenage daughter trump an entire casino on a Wednesday afternoon.

"Apparently," she replied, and that was the end of that discussion.

He cleared his throat. "Okay. Just... whatever you choose, maybe don't go flashing that magic around."

"But that's half the fun." Then she seemed to realize what he meant, the dismissal, and cleared her throat. "Never mind. You have places to be, I'm sure. You just... remind me of someone."

Henry relaxed. That, at least, made sense.

She held his gaze, then added, "I'm Claire."

The name filled the alley with a heavy weight. It was one of those rare moments most people found only once or twice in their entire lifetime, a moment where there was a right response... and a very, very wrong one. And Henry's reaction might change both of their lives.

Unfortunately for Henry Ballard, previously Maxwell Henry Flanderson, every memory relating to this moment had been carefully erased by Claire Bishop herself. Although he wanted to pass her test, he had no exposure to the material.

As a result, he offered a friendly smile and a firm handshake and a few empty words.

"Nice to meet you, Claire. Stay safe, okay?"

She forced a smile. "Right. You too."

They parted.

For Henry, it was a mildly intriguing, albeit odd night. Possibly more exciting than his best record of "Find the Cat."[2] Definitely better than dueling salamanders.

For Claire, the world shattered, and no one else noticed.

---

2. One minute, seventeen seconds. A new casino record, at the time.

Chapter Twenty-Three

Roughly 14 Years and 118 Days before Death Stopped

In the end, Zuzana Krajovičová's downfall was her own vanity.

She was a woman of pride. From the street, her home appeared pristine, with perfectly manicured rosebushes, expertly stamped concrete, and a freshly painted picket fence. She drove the most desirable car[1], maintained relationships with every socialite outside of Bratislava, and although her early-twenties career as a model was finished when she had Ozarik, Zuzana could still dominate conversation with regales of her worldwide travels.

But nothing, *nothing*, propelled her into the highest echelons of social standing faster than birthing the next Zaro.

In her immediate family, only Zuzana's great-uncle was a witch, and he'd accidentally driven off a cliff when she was young. Her parents used it as a tale of caution: don't associate with witches. They spent their days

---

1. A BMW 8 series coupe in the head-turning brokatrot metallic—highly ineffective for family life, and yet the most-whispered-about vehicle on her block.

worrying about whether thyme could be mixed with cat hair, and then they drove off cliffs.

But what her parents failed to mention was just how witches flocked around their ruler. When word spread that Reiki, *the* Zaro Reiki, had made a house call to Zuzana's cottage, witches from all over Europe were scrambling to glimpse their home.

It didn't take long for word to get out, even amongst the humans: Ozarik Krajovič was the Future-Zaro.

(Well, it took longer than Zuzana would have liked, but a few tasteful mentions to the right people finally gave the rumor legs.)

Zuzana used to think her previous life was grand, but it was nothing compared to this fame. It outgrew Europe—soon, people from all over the *world* were visiting Poprad, hoping to glimpse her child. They cornered her at the outdoor market and the flower-lined parks, eager to know... well, everything. Each of Ozarik's giggles had the crowds swooning, and every cry elicited empathetic concern.

Zuzana stole their devotion with pleasure, playing the perfect role of doting mother to her precious, precious boy.[2]

At dinner one night, her husband, Marek, grumbled over their meatloaf: "Another gift for Ozarik today."

"Petunias?" Zuzana asked. She'd put out the word that petunias would look just lovely in Ozzy's bedroom.

"Some toy from America."

"Well. We hardly need more of those." Zuzana waved a hand. "I'll have Jana take it to the children's hospital tomorrow. They do so love our donations." She took a delicate bite of her food, casting a glance at their two-year-old, perched in his high chair. "Eat your carrots, honey."

Ozarik's lower lip protruded, and he shoved the plate off the table instead.

---

2. Years later, Reiki would count her blessings that Ozarik hadn't been born two decades later. She could only imagine what Zuzana Krajovičová might have done with a Future-Zaro on social media.

It clattered to the floor, making Zuzana yelp.

Marek grunted, unmoving in his own seat. "Kid's gonna get a big head from all this. Unimaginable power, my ass. Whatever happened to a good, honest living?" He cast his son a derisive glance.

Zuzana scooped up the plastic plate, then retrieved a broom and dustpan. A cheery smile flitted across her face at the mention of "unimaginable power."

"Luckily, *one* of us still has that."

Marek wrongly assumed she meant *his* honest living, since he was still trundling through his day job as a banker, and grunted affirmation. He didn't realize that, to Zuzana, fostering their family's reputation was the most important job in the world.

She swept the uneaten pieces of carrot into the pan and disposed of it, continuing, "Ozzy will find his way."

"Sure. With that woman, on *Javatinia*," Marek muttered, aggressively stabbing his food.

The words settled over the house like a heavy blanket, because that was the razor's edge of this arrangement. Zuzana was able to raise her son, display him for the world—but there was a time limit. Everyone, adoring witches and humans alike, expected Ozarik to join Zaro Reiki on a foreign island at some indeterminate time.

Every one of Ozarik's birthdays seemed like another log on the fire. Eventually, her flame would burn out, and she'd be left trying to stoke the smoldering ashes.

"Well." Zuzana set a clean plate of carrots in front of Ozarik, kissed his chubby cheeks, and settled back into her chair. "We'll just have to see how that pans out, won't we?"

Zuzana's and Marek's final night on earth occurred the exact way Zuzana would have hoped: at a lavish party.

It was technically the Prime Minister of Slovakia's niece's *daughter's* birthday party, but considering the man's autocratic hold within the state, many viewed it as an opportunity to schmooze all the right people for all the right favors—which meant it was the place to be that fine summer afternoon. The Prime Minister's niece resided on a historic street of Košice, in a two-story home with a parlor decorated specifically for these kinds of soirees. Three waiters in tuxes flitted from guest to guest, offering the finest in cheeses from Switzerland and chocolates from Belgium.

All heads turned when Zuzana, Marek, and Ozarik arrived.

"Welcome," their hostess exclaimed.

Zuzana surveyed the room with a practiced eye and quickly discerned that *they* were the most famous guests in attendance. Instantly, she realized the whispers of this party had been greatly exaggerated. She'd hoped to rub elbows with the Prime Minister's wife, at the very least—but alas, she'd have to settle for the other guests rubbing elbows with *her*.

How very droll.

"Oh, it's our pleasure," Zuzana replied with a gracious smile. Marek muttered agreement, somewhat annoyed that he was missing a day's work for this, and strolled off to find the other men.

Ozarik, now five years old and eager for experiences outside Zuzana's reign, bounced on his heels. "Mother? May I go play?"

A few women nearby tittered at how *polite* the Future-Zaro was. What a beacon of light he'd be for the world, and how warmly that light would shine on the Slovak Republic. Zuzana basked in the praise, then pressed a pointed kiss on her son's forehead.

"Of course, sweetheart. Remember to be courteous and kind to our hosts."

"I will, mother," Ozarik replied, and trailed another child into the garden.

Zuzana counted the seconds of peace before the other parents swarmed her. She recognized a couple: there was the president's best friend's wife, Monika, who'd once invited Ozarik to a diplomat's dinner party, standing beside Katarína, wife of the owner of the fourth-richest clothing company in Slovakia. Her eyes glossed over the rest, tagging them with their points of influence: here, a middle-eastern oilman's wife, there, the girlfriend of a famous actor.

And yet, all of them merely *orbited* their points of power.

Zuzana, meanwhile, might as well have been the Virgin Mary.

"He's such a little gentleman," Monika said, handing Zuzana a crystal glass of champagne. She took a delicate sip of her own. "He'll be a charmer. He certainly has your good looks."

Zuzana flipped glossy hair over her shoulder, offering a humble wave. "Well, I can't take all the credit. Marek certainly gave Ozzy a few features." His nose, for one. Zuzana had always prayed Ozarik wouldn't get Marek's nose, but it would seem God couldn't gift her with *everything*.

Katarína plucked a chocolate-covered strawberry from a passing silver tray, pinching it between manicured fingers. "My neighbor is a witch. She told me Ozarik isn't long for Poprad. Is that true?" A hand to her forehead, a devastated swoon. "I would never let some foreign woman steal my little girl."

Zuzana pressed her lips together, forcing a tight smile.

"It's a point of pride, actually," she lied. "Ozarik will be representing our family all over the world. That kind of recognition can't be bought." Another subtle jab that even though these women had money, they'd never have what *Zuzana* had.

Of course, the other women weren't impressed by it. Monika's sister was a witch, and she'd heard *all* about the Zaro before this party began. As a personal friend of their hostess and godmother to the birthday girl, she also didn't appreciate Zuzana waltzing into their group and pretending she was better, somehow.

They all knew Ozarik would be famous and important, but Zuzana Krajovičová?

She was merely orbiting power.

"I heard it's highly unusual that a Zaro stays with his birth family this long," Monika said.

It was unusual. Reiki had been collected by her mentor at the young age of three... but her power had begun to manifest by that time. Ozarik and

Claire's perpetual transfer of magic meant neither currently had enough to cause any real harm.

Meanwhile, Reiki was a bit preoccupied researching the history of their power, scouring for a solution about why *two* Future-Zaros had been born instead of one. She wouldn't find any explanations, and her time spent buried in history books and ancient witchy journals was coming to a close.

But at the lavish party in Košice, Zuzana had no idea what her short future held. She simply flashed a suspicious smile. "You're correct; it's unprecedented. In fact, that's what makes Ozzy so unique. The Zaro herself told me that late-blooming witches gain substantially more power than their younger counterparts."

Reiki *had* told her something of the like, but only to pacify her vanity. A Zaro's power was something like sand on the beach, with a limited number of granules shifting between the tides of lucky participants. Ozarik could only possess whatever magic Claire wasn't using, and only after it seeped from Reiki over the years.

Monika hummed, sipping her champagne again.

Katarína chewed her strawberry, swallowing thoughtfully. "Isn't it true that a Zaro doesn't retain ties to their family of origin?" She framed it like a question, although—and she'd never admit it to *this* crowd—as the only witch in the room, Katarína knew that was true.

"Oh!" Monika was delighted. "Then once his powers develop, he'll shed the Krajovič name?" A pause. "However will he represent you?"

"Everyone knows he's my son," Zuzana replied curtly.

"Will they?" The words were innocent.

Katarína waved a hand. "Now, now. Birthing a Zaro is a high honor within witch culture." She added just the right amount of derision to hide amongst this particular popaloo of humans. "After all, Zaro Reiki's family has... ah..." she paused, tilting her head. "Well, we haven't seen much of them. But I suppose that's what you can expect from the Japanese."

Ozarik jogged back inside, his olive cheeks reddened with playful exertion. He waved at the ladies standing around Zuzana and tugged on her sleeve. "Mother, I'm thirsty."

"Of course, my little king." Zuzana flashed the other women a smug smile, then fetched him a glass. He drank deeply, handed the cup back, but before he could run off again, she pushed him into the center of the room. "Ozzy has perfected certain displays of magic. Even though his power isn't immense yet, he's still able to perform..." she glanced around the room, then chuckled, "parlor tricks."

After all, what was a better reminder of a Zaro's power than physical acts of magic? In the minds of most humans, Zaros were known for moving mountains, quelling storms, teleporting around. Big, physical displays with big, physical ramifications.

It was often why they were underestimated.

Only Katarína was appropriately concerned. She took an imperceptible step backwards, feigning indifference as Zuzana urged a five-year-old into magic far beyond his comprehension.

"Oh, I don't think that's necessary, Zuzana."

"Nonsense. Ozzy, will you do magic for your mother? Perhaps the fire magic?" Zuzana smiled broadly, telling the mothers: "He lights my candles all the time."

And Ozarik, ever the obedient child, nodded.

His magic failed to ignite, because Ozarik was young and it was rare a child could perform under such pressure. Zuzana collected her son and fled the party to the polite smiles and secret chortles of the attendees.

This failure would light a fire, so to speak, later that night. Faced with his mother's humiliation, Ozarik vowed to do better—and in the privacy of his own bedroom, deep within their house in Poprad, Ozarik played with sparks well into the morning.

And as the sun rose, Ozarik's world burned.

Zaro Reiki stared in disbelief at the charred remains of the Krajovič's pretty house in Poprad, a sick feeling of regret clutching her chest. At her left stood Jana, kneeling beside Ozarik's trembling form. The local witch whispered soothing words to the child, smoothing his ash-covered hair as he squinted against tears and the morning sun. On Reiki's right, Aciradaan Clementine made a note on a white pad of paper, then glanced over her shoulder at the approaching sound of sirens.

"The humans will be here soon, Reiki. We should probably leave."

"I'm so sorry, Zaro," Jana whispered, deathly quiet. Even she knew what a disaster Zuzana's party had been—gossip of Ozarik's failed magic spread far and wide. She should have known he'd try again. "It's my fault. You asked me to watch over him, and I—I wasn't paying attention."

Reiki inhaled slowly. "No." Both witches fell silent as their ruler spoke. "No, this is my fault. He had so little magic, I never thought—but it's irrelevant now. His parents are dead, and his training will begin."

The broken carcass of the home seemed to loom before them. The white paint around the door had blistered and faded as the wood frame splintered. The pretty rose bushes were charred and wilted. Only the grassy meadow beyond the cottage remained untouched.

At Reiki's abrasive words, Ozarik began to cry again in earnest. "I started the fire. It was me. Mother—" he squirmed from Jana's grasp, sprinting for the home.

As if he'd find his parents alive and well inside its broken walls.

Reiki intercepted him swiftly, radiating so much power that he stopped short, eyes widening. At his fear, her gaze softened. For a moment, she just stared down at him, at this little boy who'd lost *everything*. It was one thing to tell his parents, mature adults, that he'd disconnect from his country and his family.

It was another problem entirely to explain that to a five-year-old.

Reiki drew a breath, knelt beside Ozarik, and said, "Your parents are gone, young one. They've become one with the Universe, but they'll be watching over you always. For now, you're going to live with me, and we're going to make sure this never happens again. All right?"

He stared at her, dark eyes dazed and confused. As the words sank in one-by-one, his heart thumped harder and his anger grew. "No! They're not gone."

Jana covered her mouth with one hand, and Clementine lowered her eyes.

Reiki smoothed a wrinkle from his charred shirt. "They are, my child. I'm sorry."

"Bring them back!" Ozarik slammed a little fist into Reiki's arm. "You're a witch. Mother said so! Bring them *back*."

His anger would be a problem. Reiki had little experience with children, but she made a silent note of this tantrum: meditation would certainly be a focus of their training schedule. Her calm tone never wavered. "We do not meddle with those forces, Ozarik. What's done is done. The only thing we can do now is look to the future."

That meant little to a child, and Ozarik's devastated wails echoed off the stone walls of every house on this street.

The magic Reiki placed on their neighbors, keeping them placidly rooted in their homes instead of investigating this curiosity, began to fade as the sirens grew louder. She pushed to her feet and shook hands with Jana.

"I appreciate your service to our Future-Zaro. You are hereby relinquished from any responsibility."

Jana nodded silently.

Reiki felt her dissatisfaction, the fear that she'd failed somehow. Here was a woman who hadn't moved from this country lane in Poprad for five years, a woman who operated on the peripherals of fame out of unrelenting duty to her people and her ruler.

A simple thank you wasn't enough, although Jana would never ask for more.

In silent response, Reiki reached out to the woman's family—a husband and two young children—and bestowed them the greatest gift of all: long, healthy lives. She squeezed Jana's hand and added, "Thank you. You did an excellent job."

Jana, oblivious to the Zaro's gift, tried to take the words at face value. It was hard, considering they were standing near the previously-burning remains of her charge's house.

"Ah, Kio?" Clementine said, glancing over her shoulder as a fire truck careened around the corner. "Unless you want to explain this in more detail, it's time we leave."

She was right. An explanation would take more time than necessary, and unless the firemen were witches too, it was unlikely they'd understand Reiki's claim over the child. That would be a legal debate for her popes, not something to be conducted here.

The Zaro took Ozarik's hand. Her words were strong, almost optimistic. "All right, Future-Zaro Ozarik. Let us begin the next phase of your journey."

And with a puff of purple smoke, the three of them vanished.

After one last, forlorn glance at the burnt house, Jana trudged home.

Chapter Twenty-Four

3 Years and 291 Days before Death Stopped

Before Claire was the star act at the Strip, the darling of the Paris Las Vegas, she performed on a decaying stage in the backstreets of Nevada. This was impressive to Mr. Hiddles, her manager, who had truly believed Carson City was the greatest either of them would get—but Claire Bishop had a way of making magic.[1]

The first day she strolled into his office (although "office" might be a bit grand for the tiny cubby at the back of his husband's art studio), Mr. Hiddles nearly spilled his coffee. She walked like a star, carried herself with the confidence of someone twice her age—which was simply too young, too young to be represented, where were her *parents*—but even he saw the bags under her eyes.

"Ah, I think you're in the wrong place—"

"Evan Hiddles, right? Of Hiddles and Horses Talent Agency?"

"T-That's right," he said, his ears tingling at the mention of his business name. Once again, he cursed that ridiculously expensive bottle of merlot they'd devoured the night he filed for the LLC.

---

1. This was a pun Mr. Hiddles would often cite. Claire would always laugh good-naturedly. The Universe Itself would chuckle too at just how right Mr. Hiddles was.

Her ice-blue eyes scanned the studio, where several of his husband's equine paintings were on display. A slight smile quirked her lips. "Yes, this will do nicely. I'm Claire, and I humbly request representation."

"I don't—ah, you're a bit young—?"

"I'm old enough," she replied. Contrary to popular belief, there was no magic attached to this statement. Claire was simply that charismatic, *that* confident, that Mr. Hiddles took the words at face value.

From that moment on, Claire was eighteen—maybe even older—in his mind. And once they saw what she could do, no one bothered to question it.

Mr. Hiddles nodded emphatically. "Ah, of course. Erm, representation for what, exactly?"

Claire plucked out a deck of cards, and his heart sunk.

Magic. Of course, it was magic.

She fanned them in his direction. The second he reached for one, she snapped the deck closed and laughed. "I'm joking. Card tricks are so very bland. Mr. Hiddles, have you ever seen the Milky Way?"

It was, after all, one of her favorites.

He shook his head, and she gestured at the window. Under her command, the sunlight hastened to hide itself, offering a private glimpse of the silvery, star-speckled streak just for them. This, to be clear, *was* actual magic.

With Claire, it was sometimes hard to tell.

Mr. Hiddles yelped, nearly spilling his coffee a second time. He hastened to set down the cup, pushing out of his desk chair and rubbing his suddenly-sweaty palms on his jeans. It was *2:00 PM*. The sky had been clear and deep blue. Just to be sure, he checked the clock. Peeked at the forecast on his phone.

Claire snapped her fingers, and the glimpse disappeared.

"A magic show like nothing Vegas has ever seen, Mr. Hiddles," she said.

He blinked hard, rubbing his eyes, squinting at the bright glass. Then he looked at her, back outside, back to her. His desperate voice went small, almost scared. "A-Are you a witch? Is that your power? Illusions over the mind?"

Am I going crazy? was what he really wanted to ask.

Claire stiffened. To Mr. Hiddles, she looked offended, but in reality, she was disturbed at how fast her magic was seen as mind-manipulating. After all, Claire didn't *do* that kind of magic. None of them did.

Silently, she altered her plans for the new show, removing half the tricks for being too extravagant. Give the public what they want, plus a few delightful surprises. Not *stars*. Not yet, anyway.

Maybe she *would* do a card trick or two.

"No, sir," she lied through her teeth, flashing a dazzling smile—the look of someone who'd been dealt a shitty hand and was forced to make it into a winning pile. "I'm not a witch. I've just always wanted to perform on the Strip."

"The Strip?" He fumbled with his tie, tightening it as a nervous tic. "Ah, I don't *really* work in that field. H-Have you thought about Laughlin? They have very nice shows—"

Claire put a hand on his arm, stopping his movements. She looked deep into his eyes and replied, kindly, "With all due respect, sir, I'm not Laughlin material."

And she wasn't.

So, he pulled strings. Found her that theater, booked a month of shows, and promised to make it worth the owner's while. And when the owner asked her name for the brochures, Claire stopped short.

"Um..."

"The Magnificent Claire?" Mr. Hiddles suggested. He'd heard stage names like that before.

"It's too common. Give me a last name and we can make it work," the owner replied.

Claire went silent. Then, slowly, a smirk tugged her lips. Her thought process was: *The Zaro is kind of like the pope, right?*

But what she said was: "I guess that would make me a Bishop."

The men, who weren't privy to that line of thinking and wouldn't have understood it if they were, nodded along.

The Magnificent Claire Bishop performed in a very impressive manner on that very unimpressive stage for exactly thirty-six days. It took thirty of them to be noticed by a certain, vivacious celebrity, and another six for a flabbergasted Mr. Hiddles to declare a winner of the sudden, cutthroat casino bidding war.

The Paris Las Vegas, spearheaded by the feared Ms. Finch, walked away with the prize of the decade. To celebrate, the casino threw a gala.

Claire Bishop, previously Claire the Orphan, and before that, Claire Flanderson, accepted the gold-inlay invitation with a cool smile, closed the door to her crappy motel room, and shoved a thought into Ozarik's head from thousands of miles away.

Within seconds, he poofed into the room, as promised. His tone was slightly panicked. "Claire? Is everything okay?"

He looked disheveled, clearly in the middle of something important. She quirked an eyebrow, and he smoothed his embroidered jacket, a simpler version of Reiki's preferred kimonos. "Ah, civil unrest in the Amazon. A witch set fire to—well, it doesn't matter. What's wrong?"

Guilt pricked Claire's chest. But something more, too, something nastier. *Jealousy*. She smashed it down, deep down, covered the hole with forced reminders of what she had now. *She* was the most desired show on the Strip—or would be soon. *She* had just succeeded in earning an advance that would have made her father's head spin. And what's more, she had done it all on her own.

The Magnificent Claire Bishop was her stage name, and it was a title no one could take away.

"Claire?" Ozarik asked, stepping closer. His hand brushed against hers, a gentle movement as familiar as breathing at this point.

"Do you want to be my date?" Claire blurted.

Ozarik squinted at her. "A date? You hate romance."

"I don't *hate* romance. I just... don't have much use for it." Claire shifted, feeling awkward now. "I'm going to be performing on the Strip. Paris Las Vegas won the auction, and they're throwing a party."

"Auction?" Ozarik's eyebrows pinched together for a brief flash. Claire almost missed it, and it made her stomach twist even more. He ran his fingers along the embroidery at the base of his black jacket and frowned. Opened his mouth.

Claire braced herself.

He sighed, closed it again. "I'm sure you know what you're doing."

I'm sure you know how desperately we need you to hide your magic—how the world could be thrown into chaos if you don't, was left unsaid.

Still, Claire's mind drawled: *We all know who really wants my magic hid. Hint: it isn't me... and it isn't you.*

She didn't voice that either.

"I'm happy to be your date," he replied, and his eyes sparkled now. "I'll always be here for you, Claire. You know that. Even when you're forcing romance."

"I don't force anything with you." Claire pulled him into a hug, and his strong embrace calmed her thumping heart.

The night came, and Claire dressed to the nines. First, she needed an apartment worthy of the Strip's best act. Her father had excelled in faking it, hoping to make it one day. Claire, meanwhile, had no intention of faking anything. She'd have the grandest condo in Nevada, the best outfit for a debut performer, a confident smile, and a true friend on her arm.

Ozarik quirked an eyebrow when he poofed into her new home, soon enough after she purchased it that Mandalay Bay's walls were still locked in their post-renovation haze. Ozarik tilted his head. "I didn't know this casino had condos."

"I don't think it does." Claire smirked deviously.

His eyes settled on her hair, which now had a rich chocolate hue. Claire fidgeted under his gaze, but a warm smile broke out. "It's a nice color on you. I still prefer the blonde, but this is a great stage appearance."

She'd changed—ever so slightly, she'd changed. The Magnificent Claire Bishop's eyes were closer together, still ice blue, but framed by bangs, a square jaw, rosy cheeks. It was enough of an illusion that if anyone pulled tapes of Claire the Orphan, standing beside the benevolent Zaro

Reiki and their beloved witchy prince, Ozarik, no one would recognize the similarities.[2]

Now he glanced at her outfit. His cheeks darkened at the flashy red dress, one that hugged every curve. "That seems a bit much, though." The words were squeaked, and he seemed seconds from averting his gaze.

Claire rolled her eyes. "It's a *Las Vegas* stage, Oz. I'm giving the people what they want."

"Claire Bishop, magician?"

"Well, it certainly isn't Claire Bishop, Zaro," she replied, somewhat bitterly.

He didn't have anything to say to that, so off to the gala they went.

The party was as lavish as one would expect from a major hotel-casino in Nevada. They'd cleared out an entire wing for the event, invited only the best celebrities and stars, and plastered promotional banners over every square inch of overhead space. Claire and Ozarik arrived in a limousine, were escorted down a red carpet into the VIP section, and handed one thousand dollars in specialty chips, which had the logo for her upcoming show already etched onto them.

"Only the best for you, Ms. Bishop," Ms. Finch trilled. Claire could read her thoughts—not literally, as that would be a horrible intrusion—but rather through the too-wide smile on her lips and how it wrinkled her nose *just a bit* when she gestured them inside.

She didn't like Claire.

Which was fine. Claire didn't like her either.

Ozarik was holding the thin black box of golden chips like it contained a poison meant to kill an entire population. He forced a painful smile when Ms. Finch's eyes landed on him. "Ah, thank you. I don't need—"

"Then I'll help myself." Claire plucked the box out of his hands, much to his exasperation. But Claire grinned at him, and he found himself grinning

---

2. Mr. Hiddles recognized it, but she'd changed so soon after signing with him that he'd convinced himself, over years, that first meeting had been a trick of the light.

back, and Ms. Finch glanced between them with another barely-evident look of disgust.

"And whom do we have the pleasure of hosting tonight?" Ms. Finch asked, because it seemed like the thing to do. Keep the performers happy, and she kept the customers happy—and spending money.

Ozarik had slipped into an illusion himself. His hair was nearly orange now, his jaw wider, his nose a little crooked. Claire wasn't a fan of gingers, but when Ozarik smiled dazzlingly at Ms. Finch, her heart flipped just a bit.

"Ah, I'm Claire's friend."

"Boyfriend," Claire interjected, hooking her arm through his.

He glanced at her, sharply, eyes widening. One of their infamous telepathic conversations occurred in that moment, which might have actually formed mental words, or could have just happened between slight twitches of their lips and eyebrows.

Boyfriend? He said, wryly.

Claire squeezed his arm. *You're my best friend. My other half. The only family I have now. Up to you.*

Ozarik didn't hesitate. He turned back to Ms. Finch and laughed good-naturedly. "Secret's out, I guess. Nice to meet you."

"A pleasure," Ms. Finch drawled, inwardly rolling her eyes at this young, *so-in-love* couple. She gestured broadly to the bustling room. "Enjoy your evening, you two."

It was one of those nights where Claire remembered only flashes the next day, and not because they'd been drinking. For one brief, pristine evening, one fabulous party, Claire earned a glimpse into the life her father had always imagined—one she'd never truly expected to achieve. All that glittered was, in fact, gold, and Claire walked away with a bag of metallic chips, sunset memories, and the molten knowledge that Ozarik was hers, *all hers*.

Nothing and no one could intervene.

The Magnificent Claire Bishop's life in Las Vegas had officially begun.

Chapter Twenty-Five

12 Days before Death Stopped

Instead of returning to Rome from Japan, Claire tracked Ozarik to his castle in the Tatras mountains of Slovakia—and arrived there in a poof of huckleberry smoke and a churning stomach. Her eyes cast over the impending structure, its huge stone walls reflecting the bright moonlight in an almost eerie fashion. Although Zaros—or those lucky enough to possess their magic—didn't fear much, a shiver crept up Claire's spine.

She'd never liked this place, and now, in the echoes of Reiki's postmortem confession, it seemed even more ominous. She couldn't know it at the time, but the chill surrounding the castle was an echo inside itself—a hint of the future reverberating two weeks earlier—a whisper through time to prepare herself.

Claire had never been very in-tune with these whispers. Instead, she shoved open the wooden door with a flick of magic, muttering, "And Oz thinks *I'm* flamboyant."

The unnamed castle, which had never really liked Claire, shifted in vexation, its stones groaning in the mild wind. After all, Claire wasn't *its* Zaro. Claire didn't understand. The old structure took a perverse pleasure in how Claire tensed, glancing over her shoulder like a ghost were on her heels.

Of course, to Claire, there *was* a ghost on her heels.

She snatched a grape soda from the beverage cooler by the door, a courteous afterthought when Ozarik, then thirteen, first revealed his "secret retreat" and noticed her blanching from the teleportation spell, which they'd only just perfected over long distances. He kept it stocked, always hoping she'd come by for another visit.

Exhaustion hung under her burning eyes, but Claire blinked heavily and took a deep swig of the soda to force herself awake. Tediously, muscles aching from her surprise hike, she climbed the heavy wooden staircase to the second floor. "Ozarik! Oz, we need to talk."

Silence answered, which only made her more irate. There was no mistaking his magic.

He was here.

She slammed open the door to his bedroom, but found it empty. Her jaw set, and she cast a glance over the banister towards the massive library—arguably his favorite space on earth. But there wasn't any sign of light down there. The silvery shadows of not-yet-morning stretched through the arching stained glass windows, reaching like fingers along the scuffed floor.

Claire rooted herself to this spot and snapped, "*Ozarik.*" Her word took the candor of magic, slamming through the vicinity with the force of a gleeful great-aunt kissing their now-adult niece on Christmas.

A second passed, and a door further down the hall wrenched open.

It was Claire's bedroom, back when she and Ozarik dared to spend a night away from Javarini, back when having a secret hideout was considered exciting and dangerous. It hadn't been used in years, but Ozarik had clearly chosen to sleep there.

Claire couldn't decide how she felt about that.

He stepped into the hallway, scrubbing his face. "Claire? Aren't you supposed to be at the Vatican?"

"What's wrong with *your* bedroom?" She quirked an eyebrow.

His cheeks colored, and he lied: "Ah, bedbugs."

"Hmm."

Silence, while Claire recalled Reiki's ominous message—"*he loves deeply. Beset with emotion,*"—and Ozarik tried to put distance between his chosen sleeping quarters and her derision. He strode past her, stepping down the stairs until she had no choice but to follow, if just to keep the conversation going.

"You found the soda, I see," he remarked, stepping into his study. A wave of his hand illuminated lightbulbs dangling from the ceiling with twine and absolutely nothing electrical. "Did something happen with the pope?"

Maybe on another night, Claire would have the patience for this pretense. Tonight, she did not. Her fingers dented the can of soda, and her eyes flashed.

"How did Reiki die?"

Ozarik froze.

One might remember his overstep in Kyoto—the moment he forced Claire's curiosity from her mind. Fiddling with a person's thoughts was a grave offense, something Reiki refused to utilize on the grounds of its ethically dubious nature. Claire, meanwhile, had used that ability twice. First, the moment she'd compelled her mother to walk out of their house and their lives. And second, with Maxwell, on the night he was taken away.

Ozarik, the beloved prince of the world's witches, had never needed to try it. Not until he had something to hide.

What's more, when Ozarik had perched on the tatami mats in Kyoto's unofficial embassy, staring at the furious crowds outside and recalling Claire's blank, placid expression after his magic took hold, he'd sworn he would never try it again.

That vow would last for precisely sixty-seven more seconds.

"She was killed." Ozarik paused between two heavy wooden chairs, the kinds with the absurdly tall backs meant for royalty in the Middle Ages. He leaned over the long table, which was spread with yellowing pages of parchment and glowing e-readers alike. His voice was thick with misery and grief. "It w-was an accident."

That was true... in the same way that choosing to bungee jump tied to a spool of thread would be an accident.

Unfortunately for Ozarik, Claire was raised on long cons and poker games. His left eyebrow twitched, his lip downturned for just a second, and it was enough to know that, for the second time tonight, he was lying.

Her words were curt, unforgiving. "That's not good enough; I want specifics. Who killed her? Where did it happen? You *must* have been there."

"I wasn't," he tried hastily.

Desperately.

Claire wasn't a fan of this new, dishonest friend. She narrowed her eyes. "Oz. Enough."

"Isn't the pope expecting you?"

"*Ozarik.*"

All of this boiled to a culmination of panic in Ozarik's very soul. Magic pierced the air around him, a dark aura of fear. He slammed his hands on the tabletop, sending a pot of ink spilling onto a bright red tablet. Its dimly lit screen soured with heavy black stains.

"*Don't* speak to me like I'm a child, Claire. Did you ever think that maybe I don't want to tell you? Maybe it's none of your business."

"That," Claire said, calmly, irately, "is not your decision to make."

Which left Ozarik no choice. Claire's eyes were gleaming—the same gleam when she said, "I won't return to Javarini," or "I *will* be the best show in Vegas." It was determination, tried and true, and it became the *thump* of a trunk's heavy lid, locking the vestiges of his happiness in a dark, devastating prison.

If she pressed here, it would break him.

Out of anger, fear, desperation, Ozarik abandoned his earlier vow. His words were careful now, measured, drenched in the most powerful magic known to mankind.

"You will forget this, Claire. *Forever.*"

Two things happened in rapid succession.

First, the magic slammed into Claire's mind, a shark smelling blood, intent on devouring her intentions whole and leaving nothing but pleasant thoughts in its wake.

And a breath later, that same magic exploded outward in a blast powerful enough to send ancient, leatherbound tomes flying off the floor-to-ceiling shelves, powerful enough to crack the stained-glass windows, powerful enough to knock the Future-Zaro off his feet. He slammed into that heavy chair, and both him and it went crashing to the floor.

When the burst of light faded, Claire was left standing over Ozarik. He'd never seen anything so beautiful—or so terrifying. Her blue eyes shone in the dim light, her hair whipping in a golden halo around her head, but it was her *magic* that made him freeze.

Magic so powerful that it could devour him, just as he'd tried with her. Magic that, if directed appropriately, could wipe his very mind from this planet.

Except where his spell failed, he knew with confidence that hers... wouldn't.

For a long moment, neither of them spoke.

Then, the magic ebbed. It drained from her, slowly, meticulously, slipping through the castle's parquet floor, into the sturdy mountain that protected this sanctuary, then into the earth far, far beneath.

"You will *never* attack me like that again." Each of her words echoed not with magic, but with promise.

Ozarik had nothing left to say.

Claire offered a hand, which he took. His fingers were trembling. She ignored it, feeling particularly uncharitable at the moment. Instead, she held his gaze and ordered, "Tell me the truth about Reiki, Oz. It's time."

He hung his head, shame filling every crevice of his soul. "It... it was my fault. *My* suggestion. I thought you'd be excited. I thought it'd fix things. But—" a hollow laugh. "I was blind. I didn't understand what he was like. What you went through."

Claire stiffened. All this time, and she'd never considered that Reiki's death might directly relate to *her*.

"What did you do?"

"I found him," Ozarik said, eyes brimming with tears. "I tracked down your father. And I arranged a meeting."

And suddenly, Claire knew exactly what happened.

Chapter Twenty-Six

3 Years and 320 Days before Death Stopped

The most vulnerable day of Claire's life didn't happen during an altercation with her father, or that final fight with Reiki. No, despite everything, her breaking point wasn't nearly as loud. It happened the same way the wind shifts before a thunderstorm, just a vague scent of petrichor before the gales began.

The scent of petrichor in this metaphor occurred seven days after she left Javarini, and four days after she met Maxwell Flanderson—now Henry Ballard—in that witchy casino.

In front of the Bellagio's fountains, a teenage boy hugged his sister.

Claire saw, and tears welled in her eyes. To us, this might seem like an obvious connection, but someone like Claire was not in-tune with her emotions. She'd spent a lifetime stuffing her anguish deep, deep down, assuming a confident façade until that façade was all she could be.

Claire Bishop didn't cry.

And she certainly never broke.

The tears on her cheeks caused a responding surge of spite, her go-to emotion when threatened with loneliness. She scrubbed her eyes with the sleeve of her low-cut shirt[1], spinning away from the family.

"What kind of parents bring their kids to Las Vegas?" Claire snapped to no one in particular.

The crowds swarming around her didn't answer. She had enjoyed the sheer volume of people after three years on Javarini, a remote island populated by maybe a hundred witches at any given point. The bustle of the Strip was everything she imagined: boisterous, adventurous, exciting. She loved that everyone emerged when the sun began to set, loved that the party didn't start until past Reiki's bedtime.

But now, her chest clenched in dark hatred, and she suddenly felt like she couldn't breathe. Her blue eyes kept cutting to the siblings, watching the sister shove her brother away, watching the parents laughing at their antics. The mother brandished tickets to one of the shows and the four of them headed for the Bellagio.

It wasn't fair.

Claire glared after them, her magic electrifying the air around her. It caused a bubble of unease, and people began avoiding her. She began to tremble, clenching her fists tighter.

The family slowed to a stop.

No one else seemed to notice, but the family's auras shifted from excitement and joy to something darker—fear. They couldn't *move*. For no discernable reason, they'd simply been frozen solid, paralyzed in a sea of drunken fools.

The father was a witch, and his magic pushed against Claire's. But his power was training fantastic dogs, which essentially meant that "pushing" was less of a shove, more of a poke.

Petrichor.

---

1. Which had once been a very modest article on Javarini, but sympathized with Claire's plight and shifted for her sake.

Claire found herself striding forward, her mind a buzzing, trembling mess. Tears streaked down her cheeks, and she stopped right in front of the family, stared right into the daughter's eyes. They were about the same age of sixteen. The girl was wearing a backpack with flair on the strap: a pride pin, a roaring lion and letters that said LHS, and an open book with a swirly bookmark.

She was normal.

And that made Claire hurt even more.

"Why do *you* get this?" Claire whispered to her frozen face. The girl's eyes twitched imperceptibly, until magic firmed even that movement. Claire, meanwhile, didn't even notice, too blinded to care. "What the hell did you do to deserve a family vacation? Or a brother who knows your *goddamn name?*"

Normally, this sort of thing would draw attention—but nothing about this situation was normal. Claire's magic settled over the crowds like a fog, blinding them to what was happening several feet away. It was a surge Reiki would absolutely feel, but in that moment, Claire didn't *care.*

She didn't care about anything.

She just wanted someone to hurt the way she was hurting.

"You know what I'll be doing tonight?" The girl, of course, couldn't answer, so Claire did for her: "I'll poof across town, to an abandoned motel on the north side. I'll sit on a bed usually reserved for people high out of their mind. I'll stare at those moldy walls and know there's nowhere b-better for me." Her voice had risen in pitch, cracked a bit at the end.

The daughter stared back, tears beginning to pool in her eyes too.

For a moment, Claire could almost imagine she was sharing sympathy. But it fell as flat as every other hope Claire had. She scoffed, turning away from the family, although her magic held them tight. For a long moment, she stared hollowly at the gleaming golden doors of the Bellagio, listening to the persistent cacophony of bells and shouts just past the doors.

"It's not fair," she said.

Then, when no one replied, she screamed, "*It's not fair!*"

The scent of huckleberry filled the air, and Claire was *certain* it was Reiki appearing to rain hell on her and her terrible decisions. And in that split second, Claire decided she *was not having it*. She flinched, spinning, her magic swelling in a violent wave to attack Reiki—only to meet Ozarik's gaze. He swiftly countered the push, sucking her magic into his own for a mere second before easing it back to her like a gentle caress.

Seconds ticked by. Tears dampened her face. His gaze was raw.

Then, without a word, he pulled her into a tight hug.

Claire choked on a sob, falling against him.

Ozarik clutched her, stroking her hair with one hand while his magic swiftly undid the spell over the family, distracted their minds so the experience would feel less like a memory, more like a dream. The fog shifted over the two of them, hiding them from view, and Ozarik watched over Claire's shoulder as the parents paused, shook their heads, and once again began leading their kids towards the Bellagio.

The daughter alone paused at the doors, brows knitted as she scanned the crowds.

But Claire Bishop was forgotten by the time the curtain rose for their show.

"Come on, Claire," Ozarik whispered.

The winds died down as he took her hand and led her down the street. To be honest, Ozarik wasn't even sure where he was going, had spent so little time in Las Vegas that he couldn't find it on a map when Claire mentioned it last year, but he knew Claire needed comfort—and what better comfort than food?

He paused at a 50's themed diner just off the Strip, letting the protective magic around them vanish as they stepped inside. Few people were here so early in the evening, but the waitress waved them to a booth, and Ozarik slid in, letting Claire choose where she wanted to sit.

The fury had faded, morphing into absolute, abject misery—and crippling embarrassment. Claire scrubbed her face again, glanced at the floor. "Y-You didn't have to come." She hated how her voice tripped.

"You were hurting, Claire. I'd never ignore that." Ozarik tilted his head. "We don't have to eat here, if you don't want to."

She was still standing at the table, her body shaking with leftover emotion.

"It's fine," Claire mumbled, and slid into his side of the booth, shoulder to shoulder with him. Just like she'd done hundreds of times on Javarini.

Ozarik pressed his shoulder against hers, then casually pushed a menu in front of her. He smelled like sea salt and linen, a scent that reassured Claire just via proximity. She wondered if he'd use their magic to ease her emotions, calm her down. They'd done it a few times for each other during high-stakes situations: worldly negotiations and the like.

But Claire had to work through *this* without magic, and they both knew it.

After a long moment of scanning the menu, where Ozarik remarked on their late-night breakfast food and Claire quietly composed herself, the subject was broached. Claire hung her head. "I didn't mean to freeze them."

"I know." Ozarik smiled slightly. "I sent them on their way. It's okay."

He had deep bags under his eyes—it was early morning in Javarini, she knew. Her magic must have woken him up. She couldn't even muster the energy to feel guilty about that. All that remained was shame... and a deep, agonizing loneliness.

Claire thought again to Henry Ballard, recalled his easygoing smile, how he'd leapt in to protect her, which was so very reminiscent. They'd laughed, he'd joked. She'd revealed her magic, watched his face for any sign of recognition.

But even at five years old, Claire Bishop had been incredibly adept—and when she made someone forget, it was permanent.

Deep sorrow settled into her bones, and only now, perched in this booth beside Ozarik, did Claire realize she was mourning her brother all over again. She traced the dessert portion of the menu, blinking back fresh tears.

The waitress, who'd been strolling over to take their orders, subtly decided now wasn't the time.

Ozarik carefully placed his hand over hers. "Want to talk about it?"

He'd lost people, so he would understand. His parents were a consistent, devastating memory for Ozarik.

But memories rarely showed the whole picture, and in that moment Reiki's final accusation—the one that truly convinced Claire she couldn't stay on Javarini, with or without Reiki's permission—slammed back into focus. She hunched over the table, shaking again. "I keep messing up. I thought being on Javarini would *fix* things. But it didn't. It just made me worse."

Worse because she'd gotten to meet Ozarik, her supposed nemesis, her competitor for the coveted position of Zaro.

Worse because he was everything she'd hoped he might be, everything she was too afraid to voice to her father when they plotted her infiltration.

Worse because now, even Ozarik had been ripped from her life... just like Maxwell.

Ozarik didn't know any of that, so earnest optimism filled his voice: "Are you kidding? Having you on Javarini after so many years of feeling your magic—it was like a dream. Claire, I bet if we ask Reiki, she'd let you—"

"No." Claire pulled her hand away, averting her gaze. Then, softer, "I can't go back there, Oz. Javarini was never the place for me."

Ozarik inhaled slowly, softly. "Okay. I understand." He didn't, actually, because both Reiki and Claire were notoriously tight-lipped about that argument. But at this point in time, Ozarik prided himself on being a calm, understanding individual.

That would *not* be the case in 3 years and 320 days.

For now, though, he simply let Claire be. Silence filled the air for a moment, where the waitress stopped by and took their orders. Eggs for Ozarik, a milkshake for Claire. Once she was gone, Ozarik dared to say, "It seems like you're lonely."

Claire's defenses had been slowly rebuilding themselves over the last hour, and now she scoffed. "I'm fine. Everything is fine."

Her words hitched.

Ozarik turned back to the table, fishing a quarter out of his pocket. It was actually a Japanese 100 yen, but when he pressed it into the table's karaoke machine, the machine decided not to squabble over apples and oranges. Its screen illuminated, offering a choice of music.

"What do you think?"

For a 50s diner, they had a very wide selection. Claire numbly reached over Ozarik to press the button for an Aly & AJ song, her cheeks coloring when it filtered over the loudspeakers. Ozarik grinned, and she stared him down. "It's a good choice."

"I agree," he answered easily.

More silence.

"I'll be here for you, no matter what." Ozarik drummed his fingers in time with the beat. "Distance doesn't mean much for us, you know."

"Reiki said I can't come visit you," Claire said sullenly.

He shrugged. "Luckily, that's not a two-way street."

Happiness flared in her chest, bright and dangerous, and Claire was too miserable to quell the hope. She glanced at him with guarded desperation. "Promise?"

Ozarik held her gaze, and their magic seemed to tremble with the weight of his words. It wasn't a spell, but it felt just as binding. "Claire, as long as you need me, I'll be here. Okay? You're not alone."

Quietly, tentatively, Claire reached out to intertwine their fingers. "Okay."

Chapter Twenty-Seven

9 Years and 12 Days before Death Stopped

Claire Flanderson met the Zaro when she was ten years old.

Obviously, the Zaro met *Claire* when she was days old, but much like an elephant remembers, baby Claire forgot. Therefore, we'll operate on the idea that in Claire's reality, her first true meeting with Zaro Reiki occurred a decade into her life.

This wasn't to say Reiki hadn't stopped by their home in Spokane many other times. She had, and each time she tweaked her spell to accommodate the child within. After all, that "never leave her alone" order wasn't practical long-term, especially for a growing girl with a temper and demands for privacy.

For extra protection, Reiki asked the witch down the street—a kindly old woman with very few hobbies—to keep an eye on Claire, much like she'd asked of Jana when Ozarik was young. Margaret, the old woman, had reported multiple times that everything was fine and Claire was aging beautifully, and Reiki took those statements at face value—which was grimly amusing, as Margaret was both scatterbrained and suffering from early stage dementia.

From the outside, Kyle kept his nose clean and never attempted anything that would get him in the papers or flag the Zaro's attention. His heists occurred far from the prying awareness of his now-magical house, and were only barely enough to keep their family afloat.

As a result, Claire spent her childhood as the source of their financial woes.

They could afford an instrument at school... if Claire would *actually* perform street magic, instead of just flicking cards with sloppy gestures.

They could have three meals a day... if Claire would *actually* persuade the grocery store clerk that they'd already paid.

They could move somewhere bigger, with better opportunities... if Claire could *actually* figure out how to teleport. That boy Ozarik had perfected it already, if the media outlets were to be believed.[1]

For those reasons, Claire blamed Zaro Reiki for a lot, long before she ever grasped the gravity of what the woman had done (or, in Claire's unique case, *didn't* do). So when she felt the Zaro's immensely heavy magic drape over Coeur d'Alene, Idaho, just a hop, skip, and jump from their house in Spokane, Claire towed her father to the car.

"'M not takin' you to the library again," he grumbled, reaching for one last swig of his cheap, flat beer. "You got books. Read 'em a second time."

Claire glared in the way only a young girl could. "*Dad*, this is important."

He scowled at her, drawled: "Really."

"Really."

And the heft of her reply, the odd gravity of her eyes, made him pluck his car keys off the counter.

---

1. They were. Claire could feel her magic shifting like paint on a canvas whenever Ozarik attempted bigger and bigger spells. Sometimes, she'd trace them to him, probe for details on the spell or the caster. Once, she managed to get a flash of his face, almost like she'd placed herself at his feet and their souls connected for a single, solid moment. He'd smiled, expression a bit confused but mostly intrigued, and her heart soared. She'd never managed that again.

Zaro Reiki had overtaken the Well-Read Otter, a quaint local bookstore Claire had the pleasure of visiting on her seventh birthday, when she learned to persuade card faces to shift before Kyle's eyes and he rewarded her with three books and a scoop of mint ice cream. Now, it looked entirely different, walled off by police barricades with a curious crowd peering through the decaled glass doors. The interior was dark, the bookshelves towering like statues as a shadowed figure stepped between them.

Kyle was intrigued, wondering if his daughter had finally started planning her own heists, right up until a bystander whispered, *"—the Zaro in there."* At that, he went rigid, his grip tightening on Claire's shoulder. For the most part, he'd outgrown petty violence, but there were still moments where he slipped.

She winced, pulling out of his painful hold. "We have to get in there."

"No way," Kyle hissed, grabbing her arm instead.

"Dad," she said, desperately.

"Enough."

Claire stiffened, went still.

He towed her from the crowd, around the side of the building and into an alley that faced the parking lot. His gaunt face was fierce. "Look. That '*Zaro*' has done nothing but ignore you. We're not givin' her the time of day." He spat on the ground, glared at the bookstore's brick structure, and stomped back to his truck.

For the first time in her life, Claire didn't follow, despite the feeling of intense unease at disobeying her father.

But curiosity burned—at the Zaro's insanely strong magic, at their unrecognized connection, and at the thought that maybe, just maybe, this was all a big misunderstanding.

Maybe Claire would have a chance to realize her destiny, a chance to get out of Spokane, if the Zaro just got to know her better.

Plus, she bet *Zaro Reiki* would never grab her like that.

In a swift moment of bravery, Claire slid towards the innocuous metal door braced in the brick wall. She'd learned to tease locks open when she was six years old, and now she played this one's pins with the encouraging, magical tone of a trainer coaxing a puppy to dinner. A little exasperated at her effort,[2] the lock *clicked* open, and Claire was inside the bookstore before her father realized she'd left.

Kyle should have been proud.

He wasn't.

A sick feeling spread through the pit of her stomach, but she locked the door behind her—magically, because her father could *pick* locks in seconds—and plowed forward. Too late to regret now.

She'd entered a tiny storeroom far from the windows and the lights and the crowds. Cheap metal shelving lined the walls, covered in books of every genre. Claire paused for only a second, eyeing a particular novel with a unicorn on the cover. Her eyes darted upwards to look for cameras, and upon seeing none, she shoved it into her backpack.

Something to occupy her the next time her father was passed out... if he wasn't too furious at her after this.

Swift as a fish swimming downstream, Claire slipped out of the storeroom, using her magic to pad her footsteps as she stepped down a hallway with two empty bathrooms. She turned the corner into the bookstore proper—and came face to face with a ghost.

Literally.

Claire screamed, her backpack slipping from her fingers.

The ghost vanished in a puff of golden sparkles, but the chatter outside the bookstore grew in urgency. Sharp flashlights shone through the glass, police looking for the disturbance. Claire instinctively ducked away from them, shaking hard.

And then a hand clamped down on her shoulder.

Her father. Claire braced herself for a painful squeeze, maybe a vicious tweak of her ear or a cuff on the head. She'd disobeyed, and while she wasn't *afraid* of him—*she wasn't*, and she'd chant every night that he tucked her into bed with that possessive smile—Claire had decided long ago to treat her father with a dose of healthy caution.

---

2. She could have just asked.

But then a woman's voice filled the space. "Claire. What are you doing here?"

The Zaro.

Reiki.

Claire took this trip to see her, had even tried praying to the witchy Universe for no interruptions during a meeting like this. But now that the woman, the queen, the *goddess*, was standing beside her, all Claire could manage was shocked silence.

"Never mind," Reiki said, lifting her hand off Claire's shoulder. She gently pushed the girl back towards the hallway. "You shouldn't be here. Go home, child."

"You know my name."

That wasn't what Claire meant to say.

Reiki paused, glancing at her. "I know everything about you." (This was a lie, one Reiki told herself until the day she died.) "And because of that, I know that this bookstore, especially at this moment, is no place for your magic."

And sure enough, an eerie wail began echoing through the bookshelves. The ghost. Claire had convinced herself she'd imagined it, but now she yelped, almost hiding behind the Zaro.

Except her father *hated* Zaro Reiki, and had spent years telling Claire all of the woman's shortcomings. So Claire instead forced herself to stand strong: an independent, immovable wall. If she trembled a bit, neither commented on it.

Reiki turned towards the ceiling, a deep frown crevassing her old face, before a blinding police light flashed over her eyes. She turned away, blinking hard, then muttered, "By the Universe, I told them not to help." And with a swift spell, a wall of inky blackness spread over the front windows.

The entire bookstore went dark.

Fear crept up Claire's spine, causing her to go absolutely rigid. She almost wished her father *had* followed her inside—but the lock had only opened with her magic, and wouldn't entertain her father's attempt at forced entry. For now, she was alone.

In total blackness.

With the world's most powerful witch.

And a ghost.

Suddenly, the unicorn adventure novel Claire stuffed in her backpack seemed trite in comparison. At the vague reminder, Claire bent to retrieve her dropped backpack, clutching it to her chest with the desperation of someone holding a life raft in an ocean.

And then Reiki snapped her fingers, and warm light illuminated the space. The spell was so advanced that Claire couldn't even tell where the light was coming from—she expected a floating ball, or maybe flames in the woman's hand, but instead she was merely facing the opposite of darkness.

It hurt Claire's eyes, and she scrubbed them with a palm.

"Now we have a little privacy, at least," Reiki said. "Claire, sweetie, don't cry."

The very idea offended Claire to her core. "I'm *not* crying. And I'm not scared."

"You shouldn't be," the Zaro said in a soothing tone—and then the light she'd established flickered. A flash of surprise crossed her features, and the two witches barely had time to exchange a glance before the ghost slammed into existence right between them.

Claire yelped, skittering backwards until her back pressed against a bookshelf. Hard shelves dug into her spine as the golden ghost took a human's form, as the wailing increased in volume and tempo until she had to cover her ears, as the Zaro raised her open palms towards the figure in a display that surely was meant to accomplish something.

It didn't, which was the opposite of comforting to Claire.

"Your magic," Zaro Reiki shouted over the wailing, which had become more of a scream now. "You have to shield your magic, Claire. Imagine a wall of ice protecting you, containing your aura. Tell your magic to stay within it."

This was advanced, even for Ozarik—so Reiki was flat-out shocked when Claire closed her eyes... and did it.

Within a breath, the scream petered into words: "AAAAHHHHHHHHhhhhhhhiiiiiiIIII can't believe it isn't out yet. I've waited twelve years. *Twelve.* And K. Almond couldn't seem to figure out an ending for these characters. It's like she didn't even *read* my fanfiction. Well. If I die before it comes out, I swear I am going to haunt her bookstore—"

Reiki waved a hand, and in a burst of sparkles, the golden form vanished. Ringing silence stood in its wake.

"Well. That's new." Reiki hummed.

"What *was* that?"

The Zaro clapped her hands together, massaging the air. Which looked... very odd, to Claire. Except now that the girl was concentrating, it was easy to feel the magic she was diffusing, like easing a tangle out of hair. Claire could almost see the strands of magic beginning to smooth around them again—she hadn't even realized it had been matted before now.

"An echo," Reiki replied.

"Oh. Okay." Claire's voice dripped sarcasm.

The Zaro glanced at her, lips downturned in disapproval at her tone. "The world does not owe you explanations, young one."

Claire bristled. "I know that."

Of course, Claire was one of the brightest students in her class, when she could be bothered to sit down and focus on a problem. Now, just to spite Reiki, Claire turned that dedication to this conundrum. She noted the magic flowing between Reiki's fingers, noted how it wrapped around the bookstore and beyond, recalled the ghost's words and the short explanation of an "echo."

"That witch died—and her magic took physical form here on her final wish. Right?"

Zaro Reiki stopped short, then swiveled to face her fully. For a long, long moment, wherein Reiki grew more perplexed and Claire basked in arrogance, neither spoke. Finally, Reiki said, slowly, "That's right. Although it's doubtful that was her final wish. More likely, it was a powerful emotion she experienced very close to death. Something she recited with passion in the moments or days leading up to it, something that imprinted in her soul. Echoes like this are found all over the world, and if they aren't dealt with, they become... problematic."

An actual explanation. Claire didn't know what to feel more smug about—the fact that she'd guessed correctly, or the fact that she'd manipulated clarification out of a woman who'd *just* told her she wasn't owed any.

Reiki tilted her head, and now Claire felt the woman prodding her own magic, poking holes in the ice-bubble she'd just managed to form.

"That was an impeccable shield," Reiki mused. "Your magic was bleeding into this place, heightening that echo's imprint. And you merely… boxed it up." A pause. "I would recommend you practice keeping that spell in place. Your magic will become dangerous if Ozarik doesn't succeed in siphoning it away as you both age."

She said it casually, oh so casually, but to Claire it was like she'd backed into a sarcophagus of spikes, and Reiki was poised overhead ready to slam down the lid. Her entire body ran cold, then hot with rage.

Claire knew of Ozarik. *Everyone* knew of Ozarik at this point—he was the prince of witches, the Future-Zaro, always smiling at Reiki's side during public appearances. Even at their age, he was allowed small displays of magic, things like gathering storm clouds for crops or calming a rampaging animal.

Claire could do those things too. She just didn't have a camera capturing it—and she was somewhat bitter about that fact. After all, if Reiki had chosen *her* as the Future-Zaro, her father wouldn't constantly complain that they were dead-ass broke.

She was starting to see why her father disliked this woman.

"Ozarik can't have my magic. It's mine."

The Zaro arched one perfect eyebrow. "An unfortunate error in the cosmic scheme." Reiki meant this to be comforting, but she might as well have slapped Claire in the face. Oblivious to that fact, she continued: "My hope is that Ozarik will eventually manage to pull your magic into his soul, and you will be able to live a long, healthy, human life."

"And he'll be the Zaro," Claire said, coldly.

Reiki frowned. "My dear, you want this title for the wrong reasons."

"Then show me the right reasons!" On a whim, thinking briefly of her fuming father waiting outside, Claire tried something desperate. "Take me with you. You—you can teach me like you're teaching Ozarik. I promise I can learn."

For a long moment, the Zaro merely stared down at her. In Claire's mind, she was considering the request, giving it due diligence; in the absence of an outright refusal, hope blossomed. In Reiki's mind, however, she was standing petrified in fear, imagining all the terrible things that would happen, all the immensely difficult conversations she'd have to conduct, if she allowed this girl to set foot on Javarini.

Her words were meant to be tactful. "Your place is here, Claire. If you truly want to be considered a Future-Zaro, you must learn how to be selfless."

Denial. Claire's hope squashed flat, like a new butterfly having its wings crushed by a careless child. In its place, anger surged, so hot and intense it made her shield spell flicker out of existence. Her magic filled the room like boiling water.

"I am selfless." Claire clenched her fists.

Reiki was unconcerned. She tamped the magic down, then waved a hand, lifting the dark veil over the front windows. Instantly, the police lights and curious crowd chatter resumed, even as Reiki turned on the bookstore's lights with a snap of her fingers. They were near the back of the store, hidden by bookshelves, but the front doors opened at the cue, and a woman's voice called, "Zaro Reiki? Have you expelled the echo?"

"Yes, Clementine," Reiki called. Her expression firmed, and she said to Claire: "Child, if you were truly selfless—you wouldn't have a stolen book in your backpack, nor ulterior motives for tracking me down."

Claire stiffened.

Seen.

Reiki offered a kind smile, wholly unaware of how much it made Claire hate her. "Benevolence is a difficult attitude—one with which people far older than you struggle. Remember that you are not your family, and it is never too late to become someone people will admire."

Claire watched, numbly, as Zaro Reiki strolled towards the front of the Well-Read Otter, out the double doors, into the adoring crowd.

Quietly, she slid the unicorn book out of her backpack and set it on a nearby shelf.

Then the girl padded outside to her furious, awaiting father.

Chapter Twenty-Eight

9 Days before Death Stopped

Back in the present, Ozarik's devastated confession rang through Claire's mind hours after their discussion ended. It left her with a glaring question: how to proceed from here.

Claire thought about confronting her father. He was trapped in a prison northwest of Oklahoma City—now that she was paying attention, she knew it, could feel his puny magic pulsing across the globe.[1] It'd be easy, "visiting" him. Teleport in, possibly on the opposite side of those bars to remind him that he was incarcerated, and she absolutely wasn't.

After all, Kyle Flanderson belonged in a cell. Claire didn't care that Reiki had to die to put him there.[2]

But when Claire thought about poofing to America, actually confronting the demons of her past, a cold sweat pricked the back of her neck and her heart began to pound. She wouldn't admit it to anyone, not

---

1. There once was a time when Claire would never let herself forget where Kyle Flanderson physically was, and why she cared. That time had faded proportionally with her success on the Strip, and she wasn't pleased it had roared back to life.

2. This was a lie.

even under the persuasion of magic, but—Claire Bishop was afraid of her father. She couldn't face him.

Not yet, anyway.

Maybe never.

And so, after Ozarik's confession, after her quiet, "oh," in the face of his miserable expression, after the world shifted and realigned and Claire was forced to accept that her father wasn't just a monster, but also a murderer—after all that, Claire simply returned to the Vatican. Caught a few hours of restless sleep. Then spent two more days smiling and waving alongside the pope to adoring crowds who thought she was Ozarik.

After all, there wasn't much else to do.

At the end of it all, the pope took her hands and offered his knowing smile. "Thank you for visiting, Future-Zaro. You will do incredible things, just like our dear Reiki."

Claire smiled, trying to ignore the very real pain in her chest. Then she boarded another horrid plane with the popes and pretended to sleep through the jarring bumps of turbulence.

Ozarik hadn't returned to Javarini; his magic was absent when she staggered off the airplane. Instead, it pulsed from his castle in Slovakia, thousands of miles away. A dark part of Claire was relieved. After all these years, she honestly wasn't sure what else to say to him.

Her next step was to hide "Ozarik" in his study and take a few hours to herself. The whirlwind of the last few days was plenty, thank you, and Claire was dying for a hot bath and a good book. But as she paced across the tarmac, Clementine swiftly intercepted. Her dark eyes were narrowed, piercing.

"I haven't received reports on Claire Bishop's whereabouts. I'm concerned she's meddling somewhere on the island."

Claire had actually forgotten that her alter-ego was supposedly killing time on Javarini. Nauseated from the airplane and thoroughly done wearing Ozarik's body, Claire voice was sharper than normal. "Go find her, then."

Clementine stiffened, but gradually nodded. "Yes, Future-Zaro Ozarik. Of course."

Now, we could follow Claire as she slipped into Ozarik's rooms and shed his façade, as she strolled to her own, drew a bath, and sunk into the waters with a raunchy romance novel, but frankly, it wouldn't be very interesting.

After all, Claire had convinced herself that she didn't care about Reiki's death, and was studiously ignoring signs to the contrary.

Clementine, however, was not. As Claire-as-Ozarik strolled towards the first castle's massive doors, Clementine accepted her new role as Claire Bishop's keeper and began her hunt.

Jorge happened to be alongside her at that moment, gathering bags off the plane. Clementine caught his eye. "I want a log of everywhere Bishop went this weekend. Tell Otso and Säde to pull security footage. Down to the minute, understand?"

He nodded, even though he secretly thought Clementine's obsession with this random ex-orphan girl was... a little absurd, to be honest. Jorge had been looking forward to a calm evening playing poker, and Claire used to be his best opponent. Frankly, he'd been hoping to steal her for a game at some point.

Clementine didn't know that, and had already flagged down Bao. "Search the second castle for her. I'll canvass the first castle and grounds."

"Straight to the second castle?" Bao whined, his eyes cutting to the massive structure. He swore he could hear the meowing from here. "She told me she's allergic to cats."

"That was a lie, just like everything else out of her mouth."

Bao hung his head and trudged off.

Clementine briskly entered the first castle, sweeping through the rooms with an almost militaristic efficiency. Thirty years on this island meant there was nowhere for Claire to hide.[3] She'd fallen into such determined movement that it was almost a disappointment to hear Claire drawing a bath in her old room.

---

3. Of course, Claire had a way of opening doors that didn't exist for anyone else. Thus, if Claire were truly hiding, Clementine would never, ever find her.

Clementine checked the time, made a silent note of the girl's location for her report, and left the wing. The next hour was filled with housekeeping duties—checking with the popes responsible for cleaning while they'd been gone, any maintenance items she'd ordered repaired, and finally, a visit to the mailroom.

The current attendant, Francesca, was a middle-aged woman who baked excellent cookies and loved a shot of whiskey in the evenings. She was also one of the longest-standing popes, besides Clementine herself. She straightened when Clementine entered the room, one step short of a salute.

"Aciradaan Clementine. A pleasure."

"What do you have for us, Francesca? Anything of note?" Clementine's words were standard, but her eyes traced the room, looking for a specific stack of letters. It was a losing task: the room was absolute chaos. Long tables were blanketed in letters of all kinds. A few junior popes sliced the letters open, reading them briefly before folding them back up and filing them either into a pile, or one of the massive trash cans.

Sometimes a Zaro insisted on reading and responding to fan mail themselves. Reiki had rarely been one of those Zaros, and if Clementine had her way, Ozarik wouldn't be either. There were more valuable uses of his precious time.

Francesca offered a knowing look. "Gifts to Future-Zaro Ozarik were sent to his rooms. Requests for the Zaro's intervention were left on your desk this morning. Fan mail has been discarded." A pause, a soft sigh. "We're getting so many letters mourning her, Clementine."

Clementine's shoulders slumped, like a balloon losing air. Against her better judgment, against her absolute will, she began to tremble. "Of—Of course we are. She was... outstanding. The best Zaro in centuries, maybe millennia."

Her words were rich with love, thick with loss.

Francesca crossed the space, wrapped Clementine in a hug. "She was," the woman agreed, pulling back once Clementine seemed more stable. "Would you like me to send the condolence letters to your room? It might help to... well, to know you're not alone."

"None of them knew her like I did," Clementine murmured, wiping her eyes with a rough palm.

None of them cared like I did.

Francesca didn't argue. She simply said, "The gravestone arrived while you were gone."

It was a dagger to the heart.

"I see," Clementine whispered. "Thank you."

Francesca patted her hand and bowed her head, and no one protested when Clementine swept out of the mail room, her duties as the aciradaan forgotten in her haste. She strode with purpose across the carefully paved paths that sliced the jungle landscape, climbing to the western shore.

To the clearing, marked with a towering arch rimmed with flowers.

To the cemetery of Zaros, with gravesites arranged in order from the first Zaro to the most recent, markers ranging from careful stacks of rocks to elaborate mausoleums, each depending on the culture and choice of the Zaro buried beneath. Some were buried with familiars—Zaro Victoria was near the front of the line, and her headstone had a tiny cross beside it for a dog named Grimoire. Their lives were an enigma, but Clementine could guess some details.

Beyond, the ocean glimmered in the early afternoon sun, casting orange light over the luscious grass landscape. There was a lovely vantage point to watch the sunset on the nearby mountain, a short hike from here. Clementine's eyes landed on the cliff's face, on the outcropping above it, tears stinging as she remembered Reiki patting the spot beside her, pouring a cup of tea for her aciradaan.

"*Long way to go for tea,*" Clementine had gasped, winded from the climb.

Reiki merely smiled. "*If we do not pay respect to the dead, who will?*" Clementine had realized that the Zaro wasn't watching the sunset, but rather, the cemetery far below them.

Now, Clementine entered the solemn space, approaching the most recent gravesite. Her breath vanished as the stone column's lettering caught her eye. Like most of their tombs, the inscription was simple: merely her name, her country of origin, and the dates she lived. Zaros were humble even in death.

Grief overwhelmed Clementine. It was as raw as a physical wound, slicing through her heart, shredding any pretenses, once again reducing her to little more than heaving sobs. Clementine sank to her knees in front of Reiki's grave, and revealed to the cemetery what could never have been revealed to the world.

Aciradaan Clementine's heart shattered, just like it had the instant that bullet pierced Reiki's chest, sent the Zaro slamming to that cheaply carpeted floor. She'd heard the shot from the motel's empty hallway, where Reiki had asked her to stand watch. When Clementine burst into the room, it was already too late. Kyle Flanderson was incapacitated, trapped by Ozarik's magic, and Reiki died before she could say goodbye.

Clementine's agony mirrored Reiki's blood, gushing from her body despite all attempts to stem the flow.

Back then, Ozarik had poofed halfway across the world, riddled with grief himself. Clementine alone was left to pick up the pieces—left to guide the police to Kyle Flanderson's incapacitated form, left to watch as they loaded him into a police vehicle, left to sob as they carried Reiki's body into a hearse. She ensured Kyle was trapped in a cell without bail. She ensured Reiki's corpse would be cremated, her ashes returned for a burial so private, it was merely her, Ozarik, and Javarini's popes in attendance.

Clementine coordinated all of that... alone.

It was something she'd feared on the dark nights, listening to Reiki sleeping in the adjoining bedroom. Everyone knew the Zaro lived a dangerous lifestyle. Clementine specifically knew exactly how dangerous, had made a point to examine each and every unnatural Zaro death.

By the Universe, there were *so many* of them.

"It's always a possibility," Reiki had said with a serene smile. *"But that is simply the will of the Universe, Clementine. We cannot fight it."*

Now Clementine wailed, gripping the obelisk gravestone, her fingers curling against its sharp edges as she rocked back and forth. Reiki's ashes were buried beneath this monument: a woman of peace and salvation reduced to a simple mound of dirt and stone.

Reiki, her light, her love, her other half, fallen prey to one man's avarice.

Clementine's eyes traced the letters. She knew Japanese, of course, was as fluent in Kanji as a woman from the English countryside could be. She always thought Reiki's written name looked beautiful.

Reiki always looked beautiful.

"R-Remember the night in Oslo?" She surprised herself with the words.

And yet, the mere mention of Oslo brought memories with it: Clementine's first year as an pope, perched across the table from a woman not much older than she. Reiki had seemed larger than life, barely in her mid-twenties, a bit defiant in her youth. It had faded with time, matured into something stalwart and calm, but Clementine still remembered her devious smirk as the waitress strolled up and made a snide remark in Norwegian.

"You never told me what she said." Clementine told the grave, choking on a laugh. "B-But I fathomed a guess." After all, homosexuality had recently been decriminalized... and they were two women having an intimate dinner. Nevermind that Zaros didn't form attachments: their personal love was directed at every witch in the world.

But that was easy to forget when Reiki trailed her fingers over Clementine's palm and spoke in flawless Norwegian, challenging the waitress to say more.

"She was so angry. I'm sure she spit in my soup," Clementine murmured now, lost in the past. "I never told you, but I could feel your hand in mine for days."

Silence was her answer. A gentle breeze blew off the ocean, tinged with sea salt, and Clementine could almost imagine it was Reiki carding her hair. She leaned against the gravestone, shoulders trembling. "I miss you so much. Ozarik does too. I was—well, I was worried he wouldn't be able to take control. But you should have seen him in Rome. By the Universe, you'd have been so proud. *I* was so proud." A pause, like she was gathering her courage. "We raised a good one, Kio."

If Zuzana Krajovičová had been alive to hear that sentence, she would have bristled in contempt. If Zaro Reiki had been alive to hear it, she'd have patted Clementine's shoulder and said gently, *"He was never ours to raise."*

But neither of those women heard Clementine's statement, and thus, the aciradaan continued believing that she'd been instrumental in shaping Ozarik as he was today.

This was a shame, because, as the afternoon wore on and Clementine spoke to the grave as if Reiki were still alive, her erroneous motherly instincts cemented. She recalled how he used to call her "Teenie" as a child, how his youthful behaviors morphed into a calm, collected young man. She recalled every moment he looked to her for guidance, and believed she was essential to his growth.

She hadn't been able to protect Reiki, and now Ozarik was all she had left.

He was going through a rough patch, but she'd seen him step up: in Kyoto, in Rome. He would be a wonderful Zaro.

And Clementine would make damned certain no one—especially a certain young woman—got in his way.

Chapter Twenty-Nine

7 Years and 43 Days before Death Stopped

There was a dark secret in the Flanderson residence—one buried deeper than Claire sharing a Zaro's magic, deeper than a spelled house that (poorly) countered abuse, deeper than a con artist pretending to be an upstanding citizen.

The secret was that, as Claire aged, Kyle Flanderson saw himself losing control.

After all, a Zaro's magic was limitless—once Claire reached her full potential, she could teleport to the other side of the globe and he'd never have a *chance* of finding her. Controlling her when she was young had been easy, but slowly, she was showing signs of rebellion. Slowly, her hatred was festering, and he couldn't patch the wound.

His nightmare was realized one afternoon when Claire, then twelve years old, stayed late at school... despite his plans to drive to Boise for a counterfeit job. He waited outside the brick building in his rickety truck as preteens streamed around him, laughing and joking. A half hour later, he continued to wait, staring hard at the double doors, even though they stayed firmly shut.

Claire was disobeying him, and she didn't even have the guts to do it to his face.

In reality, none of that was true: Claire was getting extra help on her math homework. But Kyle Flanderson hadn't been in school in decades, and certainly never stayed late for tutoring, so he didn't understand this.

When she finally emerged, it was too late to make his appointment. Claire took one look at his stormy expression and swallowed her apologies. They drove in tense silence until her father pulled off the freeway. Claire tensed, holding her breath as he parked in an empty lot near the river.

The silence felt like he'd driven *into* the river, like dark, cold, suffocating water was gushing into the cab. Claire's heart pounded. She couldn't breathe.

One desperate attempt to pacify him.

"Dad, I'm—"

Kyle smacked the back of her head, taking sick satisfaction in how her skull jerked forward. (As stated earlier, he'd *mostly* outgrown violence—but he could still utilize it when they weren't inside his house.) "I told you we had a job. When I give you an order, you listen, you hear me? You don't dick around in some fuckin' school."

Tears sprang to Claire's eyes, but she stared dispassionately ahead. The only sign that she'd heard was how her fingers crept to the spot he'd hit, massaging it gently.

He clenched his fists around the steering wheel. "Answer me, Claire."

"Okay," she replied after a long beat.

Too long.

A test.

"'Okay,' *what*."

He counted seconds.

She swallowed, blue eyes finally darting to his white knuckles. But although he thought he'd seen fear, felt relief that she was obeying as always—Claire's tone was now mildly sarcastic.

"Okay. I won't learn anything after hours at school. Sorry for assuming that was fine."

Kyle Flanderson had a trigger, and it revolved around *respect*. And when Claire disrespected him, well. Not much could interrupt him after that.

He lunged—fist clenched, cursing that goddamn spell on his house that he couldn't handle private matters in true privacy—but suddenly, his entire body froze. It was like he'd been pinned by the cops, or shoved in a block of ice.

Or bound in magic.

In the passenger seat, Claire trembled. Her face drained of color, and she pressed flush against the opposite door. As far from him as possible.

Through the magic, his eyes blazed. He had to admire her, truthfully. Claire was becoming a master at using her magic, which was exactly what he'd been pushing her to learn.

The issue was when she used magic *against him*.

After a long second, Claire flicked a finger—this was a flawless spell, one he'd definitely remember for later, and the control she had, fucking fantastic—and his mouth relaxed, just enough for him to speak.

Kyle broke out his trump card. In a guttural tone, one he'd been using strategically since she was old enough to understand words, old enough to be scared by a sharp noise, Kyle snarled, "*Enough.*"

And as always, Claire stiffened—and her magic vanished in an instant.

For a long moment, there was silence as Kyle twitched his muscles, checked his reflexes, and recentered his attention on his daughter. Claire, meanwhile, hadn't budged from her spot against the window. Her fingers rested on the door's handle, but she didn't open it.

Good girl.

"You will *never* use that against me again," Kyle said, and his calm tone was only the result of a decade of practice reigning his instincts. "Do you understand me?"

Claire nodded, slowly.

"Apologize."

"I'm—I'm sorry."

Fearful, more than truly apologetic. But Kyle could work with that.

He smiled, warmly, pointedly. "That, honeybee, is a very useful spell. You did good work. Maybe we can salvage the day after all."

Claire settled uneasily back into the passenger seat, and Kyle began to whistle as he eased the truck back onto the road. But although he'd dismissed his anger and moved on, irritation still sat heavy in his stomach. An asset out of his control was no asset at all.

In Claire's defense, she thought it would work. It seemed so blindingly simple to her, even at twelve years old. Her father even told her to do it: "If the music's too loud for you, honeybee," he shouted over the din, even as Claire—going on 52 hours without sleep—sobbed heavy tears, "just teleport away. Nice and quiet in the woods."

"What if I just freeze you again?" she'd screamed, barely noticing how she slurred her words. Exhaustion was making her magic jittery, shifting the normal, soothing waves into something shaky and impulsive. It vibrated around her, amping her anxiety to eleven even as the pounding bass against her bedroom wall threatened to shatter her completely.

Her father's expression went dark and dangerous in the span of a second. His tone went low, guttural, as he snapped, *"Enough."*

As always, the word seemed to cut through her soul. She stiffened, suddenly wide awake as adrenaline slammed into her already chaotic system. The result was a heavy shudder, one that made Kyle smirk slightly, gone before she could really register it.

He smiled sweetly, even as his stupid music shook the walls of their house. "Ozarik has been teleporting for years now. Do it right, Claire. Show me you're the better witch." He slammed her bedroom door shut.

And so, Claire yanked magic so hard from Ozarik that he felt it half a world away, wrenching upright in bed, drenched in cold sweat. Claire felt his probing concern through time and space, but her only concern was escape.

Now.

She'd practiced in the same room before, and had basically boiled the spell down to her magic parting the space between souls, offering a single thread to her destination of choice. All she had to do was follow that thread through a location that *didn't exist*, and she could teleport.

This was a somewhat simplified explanation—the reality was that the nowhere space between souls was *filled with souls*, which was kind of like following a temperamental cat through a sewer dripping with acid—but Reiki hadn't bothered to explain these functions to Claire like she had to Ozarik. As a result, Claire's rudimentary attempt at this spell, fueled by desperation and hysteria, had her stomping souls like a rumbling bear stomped dandelions.

What that meant was that a large population of the western United States awoke with very bad hangovers. Humans blamed the witches. Witches blamed the moon.

Claire, meanwhile, slammed into existence in blessed silence—and that was where it went downhill. Because for once, her life wasn't carefully guarded. Her whereabouts weren't controlled by her father's oppressive words. His truck wasn't following her down the street.

She landed in the next neighborhood over, silenced their German shepherd with a scowl, and realized three things: first, she'd done it. She'd teleported.

Second, her stomach *really* didn't feel good.

Third, her father couldn't possibly know where she was.

And right then, Claire, twelve years old, immensely sleep deprived, insanely nauseated, and resoundingly vindictive, realized she could run. And without a second to question if she *should*, she'd already yanked open the space between souls again and stepped inside.

She crashed to the ground in a thick forest this time, gasping for breath as sweat poured down her face. After a long moment, staring at the glimmering Milky Way, basking in the absolute, blessed sound of nature's silence, Claire laughed. And then she flipped off the direction she thought was Spokane, for good measure.[1]

After all that, she slept—long enough that night turned into day, and almost turned into night once again. When she awoke, Claire expected

---

1. It was actually the direction of Bend, Oregon, and the town was flummoxed at what it had done to deserve a Future-Zaro's wrath.

regret, but all that filled her soul was crippling relief and an odd burst of happiness. With a swing in her step and magic flooding her aura, Claire Flanderson set off through the wilderness.

And two blissful days later, her freedom came crashing to a halt.

It started when she broached a cliff, grinning down the valley at a small town far below—definitely not Spokane, but certainly a town with things to eat that weren't berries[2] —and her pocket started to burn.

It was somewhat alarming.

Claire yelped, reaching into her jacket for the red-hot object. Instead of a lighter or something that made *sense*, she tugged out three slim leaves, which glowed orange as they fell from her hand, burning to ash before they hit the ground.

A sense of foreboding prickled along her spine.

But the leaves were gone and there was nothing else to do, so she stumbled down the mountain and into the town. Turned out, she'd landed in McCall, Idaho, which was honestly very pretty, with a glacier lake that rivaled Coeur d'Alene and a small-town feel Claire could tolerate for a few days. Better than sleeping in another tree, anyway.

She snuck into the local motel, coaxed its paper-thin walls into revealing which room was vacant, and set up shop. A few minor thefts later, and she had food, television access, and all the solitude she could want.

Claire propped up her feet and fell asleep on the springy, stained mattress.

And when someone pounded on her door four hours later, Claire blearily opened it without thinking, because never in her wildest dreams would Kyle Flanderson be standing on the other side.

---

2. Twice, Claire had accidentally picked poisonous berries, but her magic swiftly and automatically stepped in to revive the age-old Zaro protection of neutralizing bad food. Lucky for her, this spell had been encoded into a Zaro's existence in the Middle Ages, back when Europeans favored alcohol in pewter cups and blamed the resulting coma on a vindictive Universe.

But he was.

And all he had to do was say, sharply, "*Enough*," and Claire was rooted to the flattened carpet, even though her magic, her desperate mind, begged her to teleport one more time. Instead, she simply watched as her father stepped into the room like he owned it.

Like the last few days hadn't even happened.

Kyle whistled. "You learn fast, honeybee. I'm impressed. Missed you lately, though. House is awful quiet without ya."

"H-How did you find me?"

"Met a witch travelin' through Spokane. Had a special ability to spell objects, use 'em to track people. More reliable than GPS, she said." He smirked, gesturing at her pocket. "Worked like a charm. But magic always does."

At the word, another burning scent filled the air, and Claire flinched, snatching a fourth leaf out of her shoe before it burned her heel. It, too, vanished in a puff of smoke.

Claire never had a chance.

The realization was devastating, slipping through her veins like a snake's poison. In that moment, she thought of Maxwell, of his glazed, compliant expression as he stepped after that woman from CPS. Not for the first time, she wished she could have gone too.

She wished for a lot of things, truth be told.

Claire set her jaw, quelled her trembling. "I'm not—going back." Despite her best efforts, she still stumbled over the words.

Kyle glanced at her, offered a smile that was somehow almost worse than a physical hit. "Oh, never. Course not. You're striking out alone, learnin' to live your own way. I respect it." It didn't sound like that was true. "Thing is, though, magic like yours is dangerous unsupervised."

"I can handle it."

"Maybe. Or maybe not. I can stop it with a word... or you could take your chances alone and wind up setting a town on fire."

Claire stiffened, offended. "I'm not going to hurt anyone." A pause, a defiant lift of her chin. "And you can't stop me from teleporting away again. How many leaves did you get, anyway?"

For a brief moment, fury flashed in Kyle's eyes. But instead of shouting, or raising a fist, or doing any number of things Claire expected, he simply fished out a short stack of Polaroids. The top one denoted a skinny kid with dark hair reading by a brick school.

At first, Claire squinted at it in bemusement. Then, slowly, it clicked into place.

Dread slipped through her entire body.

No.

Kyle tilted his head. "Found your brother. Looks like he's doing well. Last name is Ballard, now. Straight A student, but a bit socially distant. I have a friend in Arizona who's keepin' an eye on him."

He flicked her the Polaroids, and she desperately flipped through them. Here, Maxwell lounging on a bench at school, surrounded by laughing teenagers. There, him marching with the band on a football field—he played clarinet now, apparently. He volunteered at the public library, sorting books with a satisfied smile. He played tabletop RPGs at the local gaming store. And the final one, the most unnerving, was a photograph of him perched on a bed, books strewn around him, deep in thought.

That one was taken through an open window at his new house.

Fury surged in Claire's chest, warming her entire body. Her magic crackled. "Leave him alone. You don't *touch* him."

"Well, I wouldn't waste my time. But my friend—he can be violent sometimes."

Claire's breath caught. If she were an adult, she might have called his bluff. If she could teleport further than one state, she'd find Maxwell and warn him. If she thought the cops would do anything at all, she'd make the call.

But she wasn't older, she couldn't teleport, and police had failed her time and time again. She gripped the Polaroids like a lifeline, staring hard at her older brother. No fear in his eyes anymore. No bruises covering his body. In every photo, a common theme: he looked *happy*.

She would never, *ever*, risk Maxwell's happiness.

Kyle stepped into her space, looming. "I'm sure you'll be a good girl and do as you're told, now that we understand each other. Is that something you can do, honeybee?" He affectionately tousled her hair, smirking when she tugged away.

Claire felt icy now. Her magic stilled the air around them.

But really, the decision was easy.

"Okay." The word was mumbled, and Claire lowered her gaze so she didn't have to look at the photos anymore. She didn't hand them back, though. "I'll go back. I'll be good."

"You always are," Kyle crooned, and gently, ever so gently, led her out of the room. But although she stiffly climbed into his passenger seat, numbly watched as the town of McCall faded into their rearview mirror, a decision was made.

If she couldn't leave without permission, Claire would concoct a plan to leave with her father's blessing. Her eyes drifted to the newspaper at the floor of the truck, one that magically rearranged into a headline she needed to see: *ZARO TO VISIT NEW YORK CITY FOR ONE WEEK.*

Ah, yes. The Zaro's visit.

Claire smiled, cold and precise, and everything slid into place.

Chapter Thirty

4 Years and 16 Days before Death Stopped

"Claire, don't sit in that," Reiki said absently.

Claire, who'd been migrating ever-so-subtly towards the ornate wooden chair in the corner of Reiki's Kyoto office, cleared her throat and spun away. In the doorway, Ozarik chuckled, offering her an exasperated smile. She winked at him.

"Worth a shot," she mouthed.

He shrugged, stepping closer to Reiki's desk. The Zaro was buried in paperwork, and Clementine was perched behind her, pinning an ornate flower kanzashi in her hair. Down the hall, four of her popes were prepping the front room for a traditional Japanese tea. Anticipation ignited the air as everyone prepared for the Emperor's arrival.

"Kio, you'll need to change soon," Clementine murmured.

"I know, my dear." Reiki offered her a smile, then glanced at the two of them. "Ozarik, have you reviewed these proposals? His Majesty will have questions, and it will reflect well if you're able to answer them."

"Yes, Zaro. I've read them twice," Ozarik said, pulling his shoulders back.

Claire tried to straighten too, lifting her chin. "Well, I read them three times."

She meant it as a joke, but also... wasn't joking. They were proposing a new law that identified witches as dual citizens within the country of Japan, which would offer magical folk legal protections in the event their abilities got them into trouble. Reiki had made incredible progress over the decades with this, and this moment was the culmination of her trials.

Claire was thrilled to be in the room during these negotiations, and had consumed the paperwork with a voracity she hadn't shown in years.

Now, she stiffened under Clementine's irritated glare, under Ozarik's shifting magic, twisting in hue from an earnest yellow into slightly blue-tinged sadness. Something was wrong, and Claire had overstepped somehow.

Again.

"I—It was a joke." She forced a smile.

"I know, Claire." Zaro Reiki sighed, pushing to her feet. She walked around the desk and said, "Ozarik, Clementine, will you leave us for a moment?"

Ozarik's fingers brushed Claire's, a brief moment of comfort before he obeyed Reiki's request. Clementine closed the door behind them, offering one final scowl at Claire. The resulting silence had Claire dancing from foot to foot.

"What's wrong?"

The Zaro leaned against her desk, although she kept her posture open and apologetic. "We received a message from His Majesty this morning. He's requested that only the Zaro, Future-Zaro, and aciradaan be present for the tea ceremony. Even my aciras will be vacating the building while we speak with him."

Claire went stiff. She and her father had a deal—and the deal only worked if Claire was making progress towards becoming the true Zaro. Cold fear slipped down her spine, and she laughed slightly. "Well, good thing I'm a Future-Zaro too."

Reiki didn't respond. Her expression was as calm as stagnant water.

On the heels of fear came irritation. Claire scowled. "So you didn't tell him the truth. Why would you? The whole world is still oblivious to who I am... and that's never going to change, is it?"

"Child, you've taken part of many things since coming to Javarini. But this negotiation will be a huge positive step for our peoples' rights."

"And it will be Ozarik's and my job to ensure what happens today actually takes effect over the next decade. We should both be present for this!"

Reiki pinched her brow. "*Ozarik* needs to be present for this, yes. You will have your chance—"

"Will I?"

Silence.

Claire scoffed, spinning on her toes. "Whatever. I get it." Tears pricked her eyes as she slammed the door open, stomped past Clementine and Ozarik. Her mood had Clementine pressing a hand to the sword ever-present at her hip, as if Claire would turn around and attack the Zaro at any moment, but the girl didn't even break stride. She simply stormed out of the embassy and into the street.

In her mind, she was already constructing a fabricated lie for her next letter to Kyle Flanderson. She *hated* lying to him, though—not because she respected him, but because of the repercussions if he found out. Her hands trembled at the thought.

"Claire!" Ozarik called, running after her.

She wiped her eyes with a sleeve, spinning on him. "Forget it, Oz. You can't help."

You won't help, is what she wanted to say.

Ozarik reached for her, then seemed to think better of it. He'd obviously been eavesdropping through the door, because he pleaded, "I didn't know. I swear."

"It's okay," Claire clenched her fists, drew a deep, tense breath. "It's not your fault. And I know it isn't Reiki's either." This was untrue, but Claire was *trying* to see the best in people, to have faith in their leader. "It's just frustrating. I—I'm starting to think she's never going to tell the world about me. Oz, what if it's easier for her to keep quiet forever?"

"It will never be forever," Ozarik swore, vehemently. He took her hands, squeezing them tight. "Once we're the Zaros, all this will change. I promise."

Claire smiled tightly. "I would love to believe that. Go on. You've got worlds to change." She tugged her hands from him, gestured back at the embassy.

He hesitated, but returned inside.

Claire briefly considered eavesdropping from a cat café down the street, but ultimately decided she couldn't bear it. She ducked into an empty alley, then poofed herself into her favorite Japanese destination—the small mountain town of Hakone.

The air was chilly here, and she tugged her jacket's collar higher around her neck. She considered visiting one of their onsen, but without realizing it, her feet took her to Lake Ashi's edge instead. Mount Fuji was invisible today, hidden beneath a low-hanging layer of clouds. Across the water, a torii gate stood proudly—the Hakone Shrine was nestled in the forest behind it, but Claire didn't feel like being surrounded by people right now.

Instead, she dropped to the concrete steps, heaving a sigh.

Loneliness ached in her soul, and she tried to tamp it down before it affected her magic. So focused on that, she wasn't paying attention, and utterly missed the old man who hobbled up to her.

His clothes were far too thin for this weather, his gnarled hands tucked in the folds of a ratty scarf. Despite his persistent shivering, he eased down beside her, then said in accented English, "American?" and gestured at her blonde hair.

Claire shrugged and replied in magically flawless Japanese: "Some days."

A smile split his face, and he laughed. It was a hoarse sound, riddled with sickness, but he didn't seem bothered by that fact. "It's very beautiful. How are you liking Hakone?"

It was an innocent question, but something gravitas shifted.

He was a witch, possessing the ability to sculpt the perfect bonsai, to coax the most intricate shapes from any seed. It was a beautiful power, and in that moment, his magic nudged hers, reassuring the Future-Zaro—and through her, the Universe at large—that it had been an ability well-used and loved.

But she'd been able to sense abilities for years. No, what overwhelmed Claire was the *vision* that accompanied it. How, in a flash, she saw the greenhouse he'd established decades earlier, saw the joy in his customers' eyes as he presented them with treasured gifts, the calm in his demeanor as he coaxed the bark to darken, the leaves to brighten, the roots to dig into their small pots.

And she saw the day his son banished him from the family business, sentenced him to a lackluster retirement in a cramped apartment far from everything he loved.

All of this information flooded Claire, nearly drowning her senses. She'd felt emotions of witches in the past, but this—this was something new. Reiki's magic had been waning as the months and years slipped past, and now, suddenly, Claire understood why she traveled the world, how the Zaro remained so empathetic to humans and witches alike.

She *saw* them.

If their magic didn't spill secrets, their souls did.

Maybe the man realized it, because his bare-toothed smile widened. "You are also a witch. Aren't you?"

Claire shifted to face him fully, one hand reaching out to encompass his forearm. "Yes. Your magical ability... It's something rare."

The man turned incandescent now. "I know. I am blessed."

"You don't need your greenhouse or your son's permission to follow your passion," Claire said, suddenly, vehemently.

The man's eyes widened, and he shifted uncomfortably, bowing his head. "I am afraid that is no longer true." Now he held up his hands. "My fingers ache. My bones are old. A new generation is assuming the world, and I have no place in it anymore."

Claire took his hands in hers, running her fingers over his paper-thin skin. Like a woman possessed, she sunk into a trance, feeling the spaces where his magic had thinned, where sickness overtook him. She slipped her own magic into those gaps, revitalizing his body, soothing his pain, strengthening his muscles. It wouldn't prolong his life, but it would ensure he was comfortable right until the end.

"That should help," she said, softly.

He clenched his hands in wonder, and fat tears welled in his eyes. "You—you are the next, aren't you? The child to replace the revered Zaro Reiki?"

Shit. Claire's heartbeat slammed in her chest. "N-No. No. This is my magical ability—"

"I will not tell." His dark eyes held her gaze. "Your secret. It's safe here."

With nothing else to say, she muttered, "Ah. Thank you."

He bowed at her then, deeply, his forehead nearly touching the concrete step. The wind cut over the lake, sending him into another round of shivers, but he didn't even seem to notice. "You are a blessing upon the world. And you *also* deserve to follow your passion."

Hundreds of miles away, Ozarik tugged on their connection: the meeting with the Emperor was winding down, and she was free to return. Claire suddenly didn't regret missing the tea ceremony—suddenly, she was inordinately grateful the Universe or God or whoever moved her here, to this step, by this lake, to meet this man.

"I don't even know what my passion is." Claire forced a laugh.

"It will show itself when the time is right. Magic always does." The man climbed to his feet, moving far more fluidly than he had before. It sent a shower of pride through Claire's soul. She'd helped. She'd *helped* a witch in need.

It felt good.

Fantastic, really.

And in her soul, a flicker of passion ignited.

Chapter Thirty-One

7 Years and 22 Days before Death Stopped

C laire Flanderson was clever. She took pride in creating solutions out of problems, in identifying and conquering the path less traveled. She offered charming smiles and effortless poise and watched as people bent over backwards to accommodate her. But those people didn't realize that, beneath her popularity, spite smoldered.

It began the day she ran to the small Idaho town of McCall, and was smacked in the face with her father's blackmail—and it burned in her gut every year moving forward. After all, determination could only get someone so far.

Spite, however, could conquer the world.

Kyle Flanderson and his quietly scheming daughter returned to their house in Spokane, and in Kyle's mind, her rebellious phase had come to a close. But Kyle also wasn't stupid, so he left hints around the house. Photos of Maxwell Flanderson in Arizona, a longstanding history of pictures that began the day Maxwell moved in with his grandparents. Kyle had less-than-savory connections just about everywhere, and he'd suspected, in the weeks after CPS collected his son, that he might need a new method of keeping Claire in line.

It paid off, in his mind. From the moment he showed his trump card, secretly smirked as Claire's expression shifted from furious to submissive, he'd won. The new photos were simply a means of retaining that victory:

an image of Maxwell celebrating a birthday at a pizza place haphazardly left by the fridge here; a school essay his friend had secured via dumpster diving discarded on the coffee table there.

They all disappeared, which told Kyle Flanderson that his method was working.

Everything would be fine.

In her bedroom, Claire Flanderson hunched over the images, spread across her floor like a conspiracy board, and spite curdled in her belly. She traced Maxwell's face in one particularly close-up photo, simultaneously disgusted and devastated. Then she set her jaw and launched her own method of warfare: tactical manipulation.

Her magic wove seamlessly through the house. The TV channel would shift to a news station when her father wasn't paying attention, and the broadcast was always focused on New York City's preparations for the Zaro's arrival. Articles in the newspaper he pretended to read surfaced—about how the marching band from some Seattle high school had been chosen to perform in the witchy parade, and how honored the northwest was to be represented.

And then there were the conversations.

At first, she merely planted the seed. One rare, sunny day a week after she'd returned to Spokane in her father's truck, she commented, "Ozarik is learning how to quell tsunamis."

Her father stiffened. "So?"

"It's just an impressive display of magic. That's all." Claire went back to eating the stale mac and cheese he'd "cooked" for her a week ago.

Kyle Flanderson, meanwhile, gripped his beer bottle a little tighter. "That ain't an impressive display. You can do that too. We'll go to the river—you already know how to divert it."

The day she'd diverted the river, her magic fled to Ozarik for an entire week. It was too much, too soon, and she'd been left with a magical hangover that garnered absolutely no sympathy from her father. He'd been too busy cackling in glee that a police officer's house had been flooded, and made the news.

"A tsunami is a lot bigger than a river," Claire mumbled, doubtfully.

"Fine then. I'll drive ya to the coast and you can try there." It sounded vaguely like a threat.

Claire stabbed her food, silent for a moment. "Maybe." Then she said, feigning bitterness, "I just wish Reiki would teach me too. I'm better than Ozarik. I bet I'd have a chance at being the Zaro if she compared us side by side."

Kyle frowned, but she'd already swallowed the last of her meal and was carrying the bowl to the sink.

From there, she didn't mention it again, but a gentle suggestion pitched the topic into the minds of carefully-selected bystanders.

The woman shopping for cantaloupe at the store made an off-handed comment to her friend: "Did you hear the Zaro is going to be in New York in two weeks? My cousin is going to see her."

The mechanic at the shop her father took his truck to: "Wish I was like Zaro Reiki, eh? Snap my fingers and the engine'd be fixed. Wonder how long it'll take that boy Ozarik to figure it out."

The kids swarming the school as her father dropped her off: "It'd be so cool to have magic like Ozarik! He's going to be the best Zaro ever."

Claire didn't have to wait long. Eight days before Reiki and Ozarik were slated to arrive in New York City, her father slammed open her bedroom door. The house grumbled at the brazen display, but ultimately allowed Kyle to stalk up to her desk, where she was dutifully hunched over her homework.

"You're goin' to New York," he snapped.

Claire's expression was a carefully manicured mix of surprise and confusion. "Huh?"

"Don't talk back. You're goin' to New York City, and you're gonna show that no-good Zaro who the real talent is. You hear me?"

"I don't—but I can't teleport to New York," Claire said, channeling all the panic a normal preteen would feel if they were being kicked out of their home. It was a very convincing display.

It was also the exact wrong[1] thing to say, because Ozarik was the same age, and he'd been able to teleport across countries for a year now. Kyle had been pleased at Claire teleporting across the state—but that was a week ago, back before everyone in town started singing Ozarik's praise.

Now, he slammed his fist on her desk. "You'll *figure it out*. Understand me?"

The house pulsed with warning magic, and he withdrew his hand, taking a step back before it smacked him with a wave of pain.

"And what do I do once I'm there?" Claire snapped back, emboldened by his retreat. "I tried walking up to stupid Reiki in that bookstore, and she told me off. She doesn't *like* me, Dad. She's not going to help."

She waited, praying to God or the Universe or whoever that he'd puzzle through it.

And her prayers were answered.

Kind of.

"We'll blow somethin' up."

Claire paled, and that wasn't acting. "W-What?"

"Oh, sure. Magic outta control, future Zaro on the loose. That's the kinda thing that'll get Reiki's attention. She won't have a choice but to cart you back to Javarini for proper trainin'." Now Kyle grinned, wondering why he hadn't thought of this before. His little girl would become the Zaro, as promised, and he'd be out of babysitting duty—fucking finally.

Never once did Kyle worry about how he'd get Claire under control once she was out of his house. After all, he knew exactly where Maxwell lived.

Claire, meanwhile, was trying to quell her panic. "I'm not causing an explosion." She wasn't even sure how to do that, unless she was coaxing a propane tank to utterly reject its safety protocols. It sounded dangerous. It sounded *stupid*.

"I'll do it, then say it was magic."

---

1. Or right.

"Can't Reiki feel my magic?" Claire wasn't sure if that was how it worked, but based on how she could feel Reiki's and Ozarik's magic, she suspected so.

Kyle scowled. "Then *you'll* do an equally large display of somethin' at the same time. It'll be easy. Pack a bag, honeybee."

He swept from the room without a word, leaving Claire's heart thudding in her chest.

It turned out her magical display wasn't hard to fake.

This was because Kyle's explosion was out of control, and Claire *knew* it. The moment her father chucked the modified Molotov cocktail into the store's window, she felt the explosion pulse, a magical warning to *clear the vicinity because this will be bad.*

It was late at night, on a dark street in downtown Spokane, but there was a homeless couple around the corner and a retail worker closing the shop next door. Forgetting her planned magical display of clearing the storm clouds overhead, Claire pivoted. She positively *yanked* the magic from Ozarik in the milliseconds before it blew and threw protective bubbles around all three of the innocent bystanders.

The force of the blast threw her and her father into the street, and Claire smacked her head on the concrete. Stars burst in her eyes, blinding her for a second, and then a fierce wave of heat washed over them. Claire's bubbles screamed in protest, but she strengthened them, holding tight on the shielding magic even as her own consciousness faded.

The homeless couple pounded the pavement, fleeing the scene. The retail worker found a broken window and crawled through it, somehow miraculously unharmed. In the distance, sirens wailed.

Kyle grabbed Claire's arm and hauled her upright. "There. You tell Reiki you caused this. Tell her it was magic."

She could already feel the tizzy of wonder from the three people she'd saved, and had no doubt they'd be citing a miracle soon. And if they didn't, Ozarik surely noticed her yanking the magic. By saving those people, she'd aided her father's idiotic plan. Claire blinked hard to recenter her vision, swaying in her father's grasp.

"Claire! Listen to me." He shook her roughly.

The back of her head felt tacky with blood. She touched it gently, rubbed the crimson smear between her fingers. For a moment, just one, she imagined what it'd be like to have a parent who would kiss it, make it better.

Maxwell would have helped.

That reignited the spite in her belly, reminding her *why* she'd put this idea in Kyle's head at all. Three weeks ago, he'd blackmailed her into returning home. Now he was nearly shoving her out the door.

It worked.

The flames billowed behind them, eagerly engulfing the buildings on either side too. Claire tried to reach out, coax them into submission, but they flared out of reach with a taunting, "*Nya nya nya nya nyaaaa.*"

Flames. The most stubborn of all elemental magic.

She *really* needed a teacher.

"I hear you," she said faintly, planting her feet so she wouldn't topple over. "Get to New York. Find Reiki. I understand."

"If you deviate, I'll find you. But *not* before I find Maxwell," he whispered, towing her into an alley as firefighters careened onto the scene. He grabbed her shoulders, tilted her chin to meet his gaze. "One week to get to New York, Claire. It won't take you longer than that."

The bus tickets he'd bought her burned in her pocket. She nodded silently, flames reflecting in her eyes.

"And Claire."

His low tone made her entire body tense.

"If you can't beat Ozarik—kill him."

Claire physically recoiled. "I'm not going to kill anyone."

Her father's face went hard, and he grabbed her chin so roughly he was almost strangling her throat. She choked for breath, eyes widening, but her magic was depleted after saving those people, and she couldn't do anything but claw at his hands.

He didn't relinquish his grasp. "Allow me to be clear. You have *one* shot to keep your brother alive. Don't make me regret it."

And he shoved her towards the bus station. By the time she'd regained her balance, he was gone. With fear curdling in her gut, she hiked the backpack over her shoulder, tugged her hood over her bloody hair, and staggered to New York.

Chapter Thirty-Two

9 Days before Death Stopped

After visiting the pope, Claire Bishop relaxed in the first castle on Javarini while Clementine visited Reiki's gravesite. Claire knew little of Clementine's grief, and cared even less, which was why she was wrapped in a bathrobe reading a book when Ozarik poofed into her bedroom with an excited grin.

"You're *killing* it, Claire," he said, eyes alight in a way she hadn't seen in months. He noticed her in a fluffy robe and his cheeks colored. "Ah, sorry." And he turned around.

Claire magicked into some real clothes, glaring at his back. He was acting like his confession about her father—her *murdering* father—hadn't happened. Like he thought they were fine now that the secrets had been revealed.

Before she could address it, Ozarik saw she was finished changing and launched into his original topic. "Look at this. Look at these articles. Every witch in the world was watching your interactions with the pope, and the responses are excellent!"

He tried to shove a tablet into her hands. She tossed it onto her bland bedding instead, strode past him to the open window.

"Bully for you."

Ozarik paused. "You're still angry."

Claire stopped bothering to hide her anger years ago. Now, she crossed her arms, set her jaw. "Of course, I'm angry."

"About your father?" Ozarik's expression crumbled. "Claire, I'm s-so sorry about that. By the Universe, if I'd *known*—"

This was an ironic statement; by all intents and purposes, Ozarik *did* know. But in the same way that a river doesn't respond to a rock disrupting its waters, Ozarik progressed on his chosen path as if nothing had been disturbed. As if Reiki hadn't echoed warnings to avoid Kyle Flanderson. As if Claire hadn't written the man out of her life *for a reason*.

And despite this rather solid argument, Claire stiffly brushed off his comment for one of her own.

"Not about that. I'm angry that you keep lying."

"I'm not—"

"Oz."

He went silent.

Claire turned from the window, staring at him again. Her eyes were cold. "The world expects *you* as their new Zaro. Witches all over the world relying on you to bolster hope. It doesn't matter that I impressed them at the Vatican. It was an illusion—and these aren't people visiting my show in Vegas, hoping to be fooled. You seem to forget that."

"Nothing is more important to me than doing right by the world's witches," Ozarik insisted.

"Really? Because when they need you most, you're spending an awful lot of time 'researching.' You're not actually planning to split our magic—stop lying to me."

Now he stiffened, caught. "There was a time, once, when you'd be furious about the idea of me permanently stealing your magic."

"That was before you started hiding *behind* it." The words cut through the air, but she didn't take them back. Instead, she shook her head. "It's impossible, isn't it? If Reiki could have permanently fractured our connection, she'd have done it already."

The fact that Ozarik didn't have an answer for it told Claire enough.

"That wasn't what occupied your time lately anyway. You're hunting for Zaro Victoria's old journal, aren't you?"

Now Ozarik stiffened. "What do you know about that?"

Claire rolled her eyes. "Enough."

They stared at each other, neither willing to divulge what they'd discovered about the journal... and the spell inside it. Determination overrode fear in Claire's chest—more than ever, she needed to mobilize the world's witches and *find* the fucking thing.

More than ever, she needed to keep it out of Ozarik's hands.

Ozarik clearly didn't want her dwelling on it, because he waved it away. "The journal isn't important. And it doesn't *matter* that the Vatican was an illusion. You proved a point: we can rule with two Zaros."

Claire hadn't heard that sentence in a while.

But now Ozarik scooped up the tablet on her bed, brandished an article from Dubai. The words translated before her eyes, an optimistic headline reading: FUTURE-ZARO TAKES PLACE AMONG WORLD LEADERS.

Her expression didn't change, but Ozarik laughed, gleeful again. Heavy bags sat under his eyes, an obvious sign he hadn't been sleeping. "Claire, don't you get it? *Reiki was wrong.* With the proper application of magic, we can keep this charade going for decades. Our entire lifetimes! Standing side by side, just like we always dreamed."

Claire felt her insides curling like the charred ends of burning paper. Her room was oppressively hot; Javarini had the benefits of a temperate climate coupled with never-ending ocean breezes that bordered on chilly—but despite her open window, the room felt like she'd stoked a fireplace to full blaze.

Because they *had* dreamed that, right here, huddled under a protective bubble to keep Reiki from eavesdropping. How maybe they could tag-team their rule, shifting magic between them depending on the crisis they were facing. Two Zaros. Double the global coverage.

But only if they both showed up.

Her voice was icy. "You think it's my dream to live as *you* all my life? To hide under an illusion every time the public eye turns my way?"

Ozarik frowned slightly. "That's how you handle your stage persona in Vegas. I just thought—"

"I gave up wanting to be Zaro," Claire said. "Remember? The night Reiki banished me, that dream died. I'm only here for you, Ozarik. I wanted to help, but you don't seem to care."

"You are helping me." Ozarik strode across the room, pulling her into a firm, almost desperate hug. When she stiffened in his grasp, he released her, looking more hurt than if she'd slapped him.

A mere breath apart, they held each other's gaze.

"You're helping," he repeated, softer now.

Claire stepped backwards. "I don't think that's true." Reiki's apology, her ghostly urging to claim the title of Zaro, flickered in the back of Claire's mind. It was serendipitous how there'd be one last act of defiance, one last order from the dead Zaro that Claire could resoundingly ignore.

After all, she didn't want this title anymore.

This life was never for her.

She tugged back her shoulders, held her head high, and made a decision. Not Reiki's, not Ozarik's. Her own.

"I'm going back home."

"You are home," Ozarik said automatically. Too late, he shook his head, pinched the bridge of his nose. "Sorry. I just meant—you always have a home on Javarini. Please, Claire. The Assumation Ceremony is nearly here. Please stay until then."

But she was done being his crutch. She shook her head, then pulled *him* into a hug. Unlike her response, Ozarik melted against her, fitting like puzzle pieces. Their bodies remembered seeking this kind of comfort in times of stress. His scent—today, it was sandalwood and a hint of musty books—made her wish, briefly, that things were different.

That they weren't all-powerful witches.

That they'd just met in Times Square at thirteen years old, and the rest was history.

But life wasn't like that. She pulled back, offered a slight smile, and said, "You're going to be great, Oz. Get to it."

And before he could argue, she poofed to the other side of the world.

Chapter Thirty-Three

6 Years and 122 Days before Death Stopped

Before Claire learned to *feel* a witch's ability, before she understood the Zaro's true purpose in the world, before Reiki stomped on her firelight of passion and exiled her from Javarini—Claire was an absolute monster of a teenager.

At thirteen years old, nearly seven months after arriving on Javarini as an "orphan" plucked from the cruel streets of New York City by the benevolent Zaro Reiki, she'd simultaneously coated Clementine in Jell-O and milked her last ounce of sympathy. Ozarik followed on her heels as they tore through the castle hallways, his chest swelling at Claire's bright amusement.

"I can't believe we did that!" As always, he was torn between absolute horror and infectious enthusiasm at Claire's daily antics. After a childhood of people telling him to watch his magic, his magic could be dangerous, always maintain control—well, Claire went against all of that. She was like no one he'd ever met.

And her callous displays of magic terrified him—left him late at night with nightmares of his parent's charred corpses, of the acrid stench of burning flesh. He'd wake up screaming, Claire would poof into his bedroom, and they'd huddle beneath the covers whispering about anything and everything until Ozarik's shuddering stopped.

In all honesty, his reaction was *why* Claire kept pushing the boundaries of their magic and what it "should" be used for. A Zaro's power was nearly limitless, but only if the Zaro wasn't perpetually afraid of his gift.

Ozarik may have no trouble performing under Reiki's careful gaze, but big displays outside the Zaro's scope caused him to break out in a cold sweat.

So, Claire started small, with harmless pranks around the castle.

And considering she'd never been afforded this kind of freedom without dangerous repercussions... the pranks evolved.

Today was the final straw. Clementine's screams of fury bounced off the stone hallways, and Claire giggled, yanking Ozarik into one of the music rooms. They slammed the door shut, chests heaving as they pressed against the heavy wood.

"Think we lost her?"

Ozarik buried his head in his hands. "I think I'm going to be grounded."

Barely a breath passed before the room filled with the strong scent of huckleberry, and Reiki appeared from a plume of purple smoke. "That is accurate." She crossed her arms over her chest, looking down her nose at them.

No, not *them*.

Claire.

Of course, although her accusing gaze was obvious, Reiki's eyes cut to Ozarik when she started to speak: "I worry, children, that you are losing sight of what your purpose on this island is."

"We—"

She held up a hand, cutting Ozarik off.

"This is not magic camp, or some whimsical retreat." Her eyes pierced into Ozarik, addressing him alone now. "*You* are supposed to be a beacon of light and hope. You represent the dreams of every witch alive."

Claire subtly tried to step closer, place herself in Reiki's view, even as her father's warnings echoed in her ears. *Beat Ozarik—or kill him.* She wouldn't do the latter; that, she knew from the moment her father vanished down that alley in Spokane.

Claire was a lot of things, but "murderer" wasn't one of them.

She'd been able to stall her father for months with written promises of grandiose magic displays in the privacy of Javarini's forests, with media photos of her standing in the Zaro's peripheral, of false assurances that she was getting equal treatment as Ozarik.

By his letters, he was satisfied. After all, Kyle Flanderson had always been known to play the long game. And yet, his letters held an unspoken threat—and Maxwell was the one in the crosshairs.

Now, Reiki had noticed her, even though it was with mild distaste. This conversation felt like a victory, however small.

"Claire. Ozarik. Your magic will be used for many things. Dumping flavored gelatin over my aciradaan is *not* one of them." Somehow, she got through that with a straight face. Claire wasn't sure if that was magic, or if Reiki actually did lack any sense of humor.

Probably both.

"It was my idea," Claire said, puffing her chest.

Notice me.

"Claire, my dear, it's always your idea." And yet, Reiki's eyes slid again to Ozarik. "I expect better of you, however."

Oz hunched into himself.

Panic flared in Claire's chest. This was the closest they'd gotten to a real conversation about the future, and she was barely being included. "Wait. Why don't you expect better of *me*? I'm half Zaro too."

Reiki shook her head, disappointment evident in her deep-set frown. "I expect you both to conduct yourself in a mature manner while on our sacred island and abroad. But the fact remains that Ozarik is a clear representation of the future, and this is not the kind of activity that inspires collaboration with world leaders."

Past the thick wooden door, footsteps pounded down the hall. Clementine's stiff voice shouted, "Ozarik. *Claire*! You aren't being sneaky!"

All three Zaros went silent until the aciradaan stepped past. This time, Claire couldn't even enjoy it. She glared.

She wasn't expecting Reiki to whisper, softly: "Do you truly believe this is the best use of your time, Claire?"

The genuine curiosity in the question caught her off-guard. "Um, n-no? I mean. I guess I'm just... bored."

"Bored."

"Well, yeah," Claire snapped, emboldened. "I've been here for seven months, and you still won't include me in your magic lessons. I can *do* what he's doing. It just seems like you don't believe in me."

Beside her, Ozarik shifted awkwardly. He knew all of this—they'd spent months whispering about it. But he wasn't willing to stand up to Reiki. Claire, however, had no such reservations.

Reiki frowned. "I believe you can perform magic. What I worry about is your self-control."

Ouch. Claire flinched, her fingers unconsciously coming up to the slight scar on the back of her skull, leftover from slamming her head into pavement during the Spokane explosion.

Kyle's plan worked, but Reiki had *not* been happy about that.

To this day, Claire didn't know how much of their plan the Zaro had pieced together. It was like playing chess with a grand master, but half the pieces were invisible to Claire. She moved across the board cautiously, bracing for a checkmate.

"I can learn. I *want* to learn. That's why I found you in New York in the first place—I need help." Claire shoved all the desperation, all the determination she could into that sentence. "*Please*. Teach me what I need to know."

Keep my brother safe a little longer.

Long seconds ticked past. Reiki pursed her lips.

Ozarik piped in. "Claire would do really well in our classes, Reiki. We've been practicing in my room. She's a quick study."

"In your room." Now the Zaro massaged her eyes. "Late at night, I presume. That is inappropriate, children. There is a curfew for a reason."

Claire felt her chance slipping away. She grabbed it again. "If you're teaching me, I won't need to sneak into Ozarik's room. I'll stop. I promise."

"Leveraging me with the promise of honoring the rules is a fool's errand. You will follow my curfew, or you will leave Javarini."

Claire stiffened. "Okay," she said, too quickly.

242

"Reiki," Ozarik pleaded. "She just wants to learn. You never turn away from a witch in need, right? Claire is just as deserving of your time."

That seemed to make her pause. Claire held her breath as the Zaro considered.

"Hmm. I suppose… it would be beneficial. Something to give your magic structure, at the very least." Reiki narrowed her eyes. "All you've wanted from the day I brought you to Javarini is consideration for the Zaro's title. Am I correct in assuming that is still your goal?"

Ozarik glanced at her curiously, but determination had overridden her features. In her chest, spite coiled tightly.

"Yes."

Reiki nodded once, even though her insides had tightened at the confirmation. At what Claire's ambition represented. Still, under the gazes of both her protégés, she did the proper thing.

"Then you begin with us Monday morning. But allow me to make myself crystal clear here: your mischief will cease immediately. My aciras will not be terrorized in their home. My aciradaan will not be made a fool. It's a poor reflection of your true spirit, Claire."

The girl nodded, a little too vehemently. "Done. No more pranks."

Ozarik gaped. "Just like that? I've been asking you to stop for months!"

"Well, you aren't teaching me magic."

"Yes I am!"

Reiki held up a hand, and their bickering stopped abruptly. "I believe you will do great things, Claire. But from this moment on, your future is solely in your own grasp. Show me you emulate what a Zaro is meant to be, and you'll have everything you desire."

She left the alternative unsaid: *fail my expectations, and what you desire will be placed on a pedestal, far out of your reach.*

Claire, for better or worse, remained oblivious to this unspoken caveat, for in that moment she was too dazzled by the grandeur of this possible future. A world where her father held no control over her, where Kyle couldn't reach her brother because her magic was so strong, nothing could hurt Maxwell. A future where Claire was free, truly free, to pursue whatever she liked, simply because no adult had a hold over her.

"Thank you," she gasped, grinning wide. Then she spun past Ozarik to yank the door open.

"Where are you going?" Reiki tilted her head.

Claire's reply was immediate: "Clementine is owed an apology. And someone has to disassemble the backup we set in her bedroom. See you Monday!"

And she was gone, a flash of blonde hair sprinting down the hallway.

Ozarik ran after her, as always.

Reiki watched them go, massaged her temples, and murmured, "Universe help me."

Chapter Thirty-Four

23 Hours before Death Stopped

The Magnificent Claire Bishop's ice blue eyes swept across the audience, a cool smile tilting her features as she strode to center stage. Her dress was sparkling gold tonight, hugging every curve and plunging at her neckline. Black feather accents spread from her shoulder, tickling her left ear in their extravagance. A top hat crowned the luscious brunette hair that cascaded down her back.

From the audience's perspective, crammed into the Paris Las Vegas's theater like plastic cups in a cross-country flight's trash can, Claire was every bit the performer.

From our perspective, this was every bit an act.

Claire put a hand on her hip, smirking at the drunken audience. "Well. This must be a theater filled with adoring fans, because I've been told my grand reopening sold out in twelve minutes." A quirked eyebrow, a dry laugh. "So, you're the rabid ones, huh."

Raucous laughter, enhanced generously by the free liquor pouring from the Paris Las Vegas's bars for this exclusive event, swelled to the ceiling. The entire place felt alive, vibrant with the anticipation of hundreds of fans.

It was a feeling that *used* to sweep Claire off her feet. Alcohol had nothing on the intoxication of hundreds of eyes, hundreds of cameras, poised to film her incredible feats. It didn't feel like that now, and so she waited for it, like an astronomer waiting for a meteor shower. She was confident she'd get that rush.

But tonight, her chest was hollow, her heart beating simply because it was the thing to do. That metaphorical astronomer had messed up the dates, and the happiness of a passion manifested faded into the darkest corners of the theater. Tonight, as Claire smiled at the audience—for the first time in her performing life, fear choked her.

Because Ozarik was focused on a goal, but it wasn't completing the Assumation Ceremony. He had no interest in being the next Zaro.

Not alone.

This was a fact to Claire, although witches around the world would gasp at the heresy. It was his desperate stare the day she left, the stunning silence that followed, ten whole days where Future-Zaro Ozarik vanished off the face of the planet. It was the way he'd stolen the journal, without a word or a care, as if she wouldn't notice.

It was the simple fact that he wasn't here tonight, cheering her on.

Ms. Finch was thrilled at Claire's return, sweeping Mr. Hiddles into planning "*The* Event" of the Strip to celebrate. New costume to accommodate a repertoire of never-before-seen tricks, tricks Claire had developed as an afterthought five days ago. Pyrotechnics, lasers, holograms; her show had moved so far past mirrors and light. None of it was fooling her, not even the hope that withered and died as she examined the audience.

Ozarik was suffering, and halfway around the globe, it left a throbbing wound in the fabric of the Universe.

The show must go on.

How did no one notice? Claire thought desperately.

In the audience, front row center, Jenifer Shields-Ballard gasped in delight as The Magnificent Claire Bishop produced a comically large magic wand from... somewhere within her top hat. Henry's best man, Milo—who had spent the last month living his own life, a life that had nothing to do with this story until this moment, thank you very much—cackled at the witty remark Claire made about "being a true magician" now that she had a wand.

Yet perched between them, *Henry* noticed. He saw her hesitation, watched Claire's eyes flicker to the black and white rod, watched her lips curl in agitation—and then it was gone, replaced with her trademark dazzling smile. Henry's brow knitted together, his finger tapping a curious rhythm on his leg.

On stage, Claire scoffed at the wand, perfectly rehearsed, and drawled, "Okay, this is a joke. Unless you actually want me to saw someone in half?" A pause, a devious smirk. "Kidding. I don't think my manager could handle the stress."

Behind the lavish curtains, Mr. Hiddles began to sweat.

With a pointed flick, Claire tossed the wand into the crowd—but before it hit anyone, it exploded into a pair of white doves. They soared high above Claire, finding refuge in the rafters.[1] The audience cheered, and Claire's smile spread a little wider.

Her tone was vibrant, yet her eyes were blank. "*That* impresses you? Okay, great. This will be easy."

More laughter.

Henry wasn't sure she was joking.

Claire went through the motions of her show, moving from trick to trick while the tension soared. Would she drown? Would she fall? Would she burn? The audience pressed to the front of their seats, breathless for the answer.

And as always, Claire Bishop obliged.

Right until, forty-seven minutes into the show, Claire's eyes fell onto a certain woman in the audience.

To be clear, this woman was no one special. Her name was Alex Amphiana. She lived in Nashville, worked at a bank, and was here for her friend's second bachelorette party. Alex's face was flushed with excitement, waiting to see the final trick of the night—a trick that took inspiration from

---

1. And there they would stay until an acrophobic stagehand managed to secure them two days later.

the falling meteor shower *disaster* of a show the night Reiki died, a trick that was *supposed* to sweep the theater in ice-blue flames.

But that woman changed the entire script, simply because Alex's features were eerily similar to Reiki's.

The odd thing was that to anyone but Claire, this statement would be laughably false. While Alex had Japanese roots, they were generations removed. She carried none of Reiki's grace, none of her quiet poise, her generous smile.

But on stage, Claire's face paled, her speech stumbled. She tucked the lighter into her pocket and stared straight at this woman, feeling Reiki's soul piercing her heart.

You are the next Zaro, Claire.

"It's time to switch gears," Claire said without thinking, tearing her eyes from Alex. The theater was silent, waiting. She basked in their stares as that familiar sense of rebellion sparked in her soul.

"Uh oh," Henry muttered.

"Uh oh?" Jenifer asked.

Claire's smile had become a little more mischievous, a little more real. "We would be remiss to host a magic show without paying homage to the late, great Zaro Reiki."

"Oh no," Henry muttered.

"I think she's doing fantastic," Milo said obliviously.

Claire ignored the stagehands waiting for her to ignite the first flame, ignored Mr. Hiddles waving to get her back on track, ignored Ms. Finch's narrowed eyes from her position in one of the boxes high, high above the hoi polloi.

But the Magnificent Claire Bishop had deviated now, and Universe-bless the poor soul tasked with getting her back on track.

"The Zaro is known for many things, and I'm certain Ozarik will make a mark for himself. But one thing that always perplexed me was Reiki's aversion to teleportation. That seems like the best spell, doesn't it? A free, immediate pass to anywhere in the world."

A ripple of appreciation spread through the crowd as witches and humans alike agreed that it did indeed seem like the best spell.

"Reiki preferred to fly. On an *airplane*." Claire shuddered. "Can't imagine why. If I could teleport, I'd do it all the time."

And with a puff of huckleberry smoke, Claire appeared suddenly on the opposite side of the stage.

Henry swallowed a groan as Jenifer's jaw dropped. Milo leaned closer and said, "Oh. She's—not supposed to do that, is she?"

"What was your first clue?" Henry scrubbed his face, glancing desperately around the theater.

But of course, the audience had exploded into exuberant applause.

On stage, Claire's expression darkened like the sun during an eclipse. "Of course. It's all just a trick, isn't it? A puff of colored smoke, trap doors, and I can make it happen, huh? Pretend I'm a Zaro, right here on stage."

The audience held their breaths, waiting to see her expand the trick.

Claire didn't disappoint. Henry groaned as she strode forward, spreading her arms.

"And if I poof to the back of the theater—"

Another cloud of smoke, and she called from beside an emergency exit: "—how do you explain that?"

Perplexed silence. For a moment, one might expect the witches in this audience to *get* it, to truly comprehend what was happening. Maybe be a little suspicion, mild alarm. But to those witches, there was only one Zaro now—and it was Ozarik.

Meanwhile, humans have always been oblivious.

Explosive cheers erupted, because this particular audience, drunk on liquor and life, literally couldn't care less about the *how*. They'd arrived to be amazed, and Claire had just performed a trick mimicking the most powerful person on Earth. In their minds, this night was absolutely worth the expensive ticket.

As they craned in their seats to see her better, Claire's smile dropped. Her microphone scrambled to cover her whisper, to amplify it into the corners of the huge theater, suddenly and vividly yanked back from its extended vacation as Claire's magic—once pulsing and impending and huge—sucked back into her soul and anchored there.

All that remained was the Magnificent Claire Bishop... a magician who could almost pretend to be human.

"It's impossible to explain," she said quietly, and the auditorium hushed to hear her. Claire strolled back towards the stage, and to the three people in the front row who knew her—to the brother who used to know her better than anyone else—Claire's shoulders were slumped in defeat. "I suppose that's why the Zaro commands attention. She's impossible."

It was unclear if Claire was speaking of Reiki.

The magic show ended shortly after, with people murmuring about how *real* her teleportation trick had been, how even Future-Zaro Ozarik surely would have been impressed, how they couldn't wait to visit Las Vegas again, sit in her auditorium again, and really look at how she'd done it.

They would never guess.

Numb, Claire attended the afterparty, a bougie soiree brimming with the biggest names in Nevada—and several big names from Kansas, oddly enough. She shook hands and smiled when spoken to and spent the rest of her evening at the blackjack table, inexplicably losing every hand.

Henry found her there, peering over her shoulder as she somehow, impossibly, lost a set of 2s to the dealer's perfect twenty-one. The table murmured that it wasn't her night, but Henry swore he saw her cards flicker back to their original state of true blackjack before resigning themselves to the unglamorous life of the lower numbers.

Well, Henry saw them flicker. The rest was supposition.

He put a hand on her shoulder, offering a firm, comforting squeeze. "Great show, Claire. You, ah, really wowed them with that last trick."

Their gazes locked.

He had their father's eyes.

Claire heaved a sigh and pushed away from the table, plucking the single chip she had left off the velvet. Like her first party, this was inlaid with gold, a special souvenir to remind her that this time, Ozarik wasn't here.

He'd missed most of her performances... but none that mattered. Not until tonight.

"Where's Jenifer?" Claire asked.

"Ah, somehow beating Milo at slots. She claims it's all statistics." Henry offered a kind smile, draping his arm over her shoulders. "Let's get some air, huh?"

Claire offered a deadened smile. "Sure." She raised her voice. "Pay close attention, folks. Time for an encore." And before he could protest, with the eyes of hundreds of partygoers locked onto them, she poofed herself and Henry onto the roof.

He coughed, waving away the huckleberry smoke as Claire smoothed her dress. The final day in September should have been a chilly evening, but the desert wasn't known for its cool temperatures. The scent of dust lingered, and the vibrant shouts of the Strip seemed distant, muted. Below, it was bright and loud and vivacious. Here, it was shadows and darkness—and a passing glimpse of glamour.

"Just going all-out, aren't you?"

Claire cast him a wry glance, but he didn't miss the darkness in her eyes. She leaned against the concrete barrier of the Paris Las Vegas's rooftop, peering over the edge. Henry's palms were sweating, but Claire looked as relaxed as if she were in a hammock in the woods.

"Ozarik isn't going to do it."

"Do what? The Assumation Ceremony?" Henry frowned. He'd suspected as much, but hadn't wanted to pry for details. And as a newlywed, he'd been preoccupied whenever Claire wasn't physically popping into his life. "I thought he was ready. He seemed ready."

The look she gave him now could burn an ocean.

He cleared his throat. "It was you, wasn't it?"

She shrugged, seeming a thousand years old and somehow so, so young.

Long beats passed. Claire watched the partying far below them and sighed. "I think I've been pretending this entire time. Trying to create a life grand enough to replace the one I wasn't allowed to have."

"Did—did you always know Ozarik would be Zaro?"

This was a new topic, one Claire tended to avoid. Whenever he'd tried to bring it up at first, she used to smile and divert attention—just like she did on stage. Eventually, Henry accepted he was meddling with gods and stopped asking.

251

And now, she stared at the stars far above while a cool breeze tousled her fake brunette hair. "Ozarik was lucky. Reiki visited his house first, announced him first, and then it was too late." She chuckled. "Ironic that I'd settle for this city when my luck was so bad, isn't it? I'm surprised Vegas didn't chew me up and spit me out."

"You'd succeed anywhere, Claire. Luck has nothing to do with it."

"I couldn't succeed on Javarini."

"Yet."

Tears pricked her eyes, and she turned away from him, staring down at the Strip now. Stretch limos every few cars, crowds of people with oversized drinks ogling at fountains, horns and sirens and flashing neon. "I can't take his destiny away, Henry."

Henry tilted his head. "Did Ozarik ever say he wanted it? Or was he just unlucky enough to be forced into the role?"

Claire went silent, foreboding slipping through her veins. "That's not it. He wants it. He just doesn't want it alone."

"So... try together, maybe?"

Claire scrubbed her face, smearing the tears away. "I think I would have enjoyed that once. But now, Oz thinks I'm someone else. He expects me to *be* someone else. I'll never be able to live up to his fantasy, even if we forced the world to accept both of us." She paused, deathly quiet. "I don't know what to do."

Henry was struck with the sudden, devastating realization that *this*? Worldly power and all the magic in the Universe? The lingering question of who would rule an entire subsect of people?

This was a lot to put on a nineteen-year-old.

Which meant that in Claire's moment of need, it wasn't Ozarik who stepped in to comfort her. It was Henry Ballard, the boy who'd rescued her from thugs in an alley when she was new to town, the boy who'd protected her from their father and her own magic, right up until she removed the ability to remember that was his job.

He pulled her into a hug, resting his chin on her head, and said, "I wish you'd never sent me away from Spokane, Claire."

She stiffened, jerking backwards. Her eyes were wide, her heart stuttering.

"W-What?"

Because Henry wasn't supposed to remember. *Maxwell* didn't have a sister, as far as anyone was concerned.

It didn't change the expression he wore now, one of cautious, protective optimism. One she'd seen over and over as they aged—right until the moment she removed him from her life. Her breath caught as she realized she hadn't misheard him.

Henry smiled. "The memories came back slowly. It started... well, I think it happened when Reiki died." He laughed now, self-deprecating. "For most of my life, something always felt *off*. I didn't know it was you until we met at the casino. My magic told me to stay close... that you'd need me. Now I remember why."

Claire's face had reddened, and she fumbled for words. "B-But I erased it. I erased everything."

"Please don't take this the wrong way, but I think you have a better command over your magic now than you did at five years old."

More tears spilled from her eyes, slipping down her cheeks. "I never meant to remind you. You had a good life in Arizona."

"I had a great life in Arizona. I just wish you'd been there too." Henry opened his arms, offering another embrace, and this time Claire didn't resist. This time, she sunk into his arms.

She didn't realize she was shaking until he tightened his grasp.

"The world would be lucky to have you as a Zaro, Claire. But even if you decide to be selfish, you always have a place in Las Vegas. You always have a family here."

Claire clenched her eyes shut, fighting the dread that crept through her veins. But that night, perched on a rooftop beneath a blanket of stars, she clutched her brother and felt a little less alone.

Chapter Thirty-Five

85 Days before Death Stopped

B efore he attacked the world, Ozarik descended into chaos.

Like most tragic cases, this was a slow occurrence. After all, a gradual decline caused more damage than one loud, personality-altering moment. Ozarik experienced both, but if the moment Reiki was shot became the nail in Death's coffin, he built the casket over the months preceding it.

This descent began, specifically, on the day he and Claire severed their years-old relationship. After she casually ended him, Claire returned to her Las Vegas stage and her adoring crowds, and Ozarik returned to a cold, empty castle on a warm, empty island in a vast, empty ocean. And he ruminated.[1]

He was perched on the edge of his bed, staring wistfully at a photo of teenage Claire and himself exploring a small cave further up Javarini's mountain, when it clicked into place. For Ozarik, this was a revelation, akin to Newton's laws of motion or Einstein's theory of special relativity. And considering only *one* of those men were a witch, possessing the ability

---

1. In case it wasn't apparent, for someone like Ozarik, rumination is never wise.

to perfectly chill a beverage at any time, this was remarkably pathetic for someone with a Zaro's power.

Nevertheless, the revelation persisted:

Claire never spoke of her family, but her father was still alive.

Reiki spoke of Claire's family often, but Reiki didn't respect Claire's father.

Clearly, Claire's father was the key to their faltering relationship.

This made perfect sense to Ozarik. After all, he spent a decade convinced that the simplest reason *he* was collected for Zaro training, rather than Claire, was that his parents had died[2] ... and hers didn't. Obviously, if Ozarik's parents were had survived, Reiki would have trained them together, far earlier than the day she'd accepted Claire in New York City.

If this seemed like flawed logic, it's important to remember that Ozarik worshipped Reiki, and never truly entertained the idea that she would play favorites. This was an easy thing to believe, as Reiki's favorite.

So, as Ozarik stared at Claire's young face, smeared in dirt from their adventures in the golden years, he decided that Claire's father was the lynchpin to all of this. Claire must love her father dearly, but her budding magic forced her from home. Reiki expressed obvious dislike for Claire's father—which put Claire in a difficult position. That rift ultimately drove them apart.

None of this was true, but careening into madness often occurred within the crumbling foundation of erroneous beliefs.

Ozarik hatched a plan.

It began simply, with sneaky questions to Clementine and internet searches at Spokane's local library. Claire's birth records were discovered, her mother MIA, but a single address was listed. Granted, the old house was a mess now, left to rot in the elements after its family abandoned it. Ozarik stood in the overgrown yard, squinting at the askew front door, and squished down his uneasiness.

---

2. "Been killed" was more appropriate, but we won't quibble semantics.

Claire never mentioned she was abused. This must have happened *after* her father moved.

Did she even know where her father had left? Heartache—projected memories of his own family—renewed his determination. Ozarik would reunite them. He would present Claire's father to Reiki, and together, they would invite Claire to visit.

One big, happy family.

One day, he was seated at the long wooden table in Javarini's grand dining hall, articles spread around him. They were from local papers across the western United States, stories of petty theft, larceny, break-ins. Ozarik set his jaw, tapping his pencil against the table in a rhythmic fashion.

Reiki had the unfortunate end result of strolling into the room at this exact moment. She paused, noting the articles, and wrongly assumed Ozarik was researching the history of civil unrest in the Republic of Rwanda.

He looked up—saw her gaze—and pounced.

"Is Claire's father a criminal?"

Reiki stiffened at the ambush. She scanned the papers again, saw the headlines for what they were, and mentally planned a response. After all, only someone highly irresponsible and selfish would leave a child such as Claire alone with a known criminal. But in her defense, Kyle Flanderson had mostly kept his nose clean while Claire lived with him. After all, his top priority had been keeping Claire with him. Cared, fed... controlled.

She knew this. Deep in her soul, after almost 19 years of ignoring that fact, Reiki knew this was true. And yet, knowing and facing the fact that she'd been so, so wrong were two very different things.

Ozarik's respect was one thing she couldn't afford to lose.

So, she nodded curtly. "Regretfully, he tends to err on the side of easy, rather than right."

Ozarik set his jaw, sifting through the papers. "They think he stabbed a woman in Seattle. He paid bail before the trial and vanished."

"That's almost certainly exaggerated," Reiki said sharply. "People who choose physical violence have a history of it, and Kyle Flanderson opted for a quieter path." Universe forbid someone—*Ozarik*—thought she'd left Claire with a physical abuser. Her magic ensured that was never the case.

Ozarik visibly relaxed. "Of course. Yes, that makes sense. There's always another side to someone's story. No one wakes up and chooses crime like this, not unless they were prompted." But his eyes dropped again to the newspapers, a visible trail of Kyle's poor decisions. "I wonder what happened in his past to lead him here..."

"I fear Kyle Flanderson is a person never satisfied with the blessings life has given him." Reiki's tone was slightly bitter, but mostly sad.

"I'm sure he's not that bad." Ozarik tilted his head, watching his mentor carefully. "I bet Claire would love to reconnect with him. I bet you'd be surprised at the goodness in his soul, if you just gave him a chance to prove—"

"*Enough.*" Reiki said, and the irony of using this statement in this manner would go unnoticed.

It worked exactly as Kyle Flanderson's command did, silencing Ozarik immediately.

Reiki's gaze had turned sharp, impending, backed by the waning power of a once-mighty Zaro. In truth, she was disturbed that he continually affixed on Claire, even years after the young girl had moved on. In truth, moments like these made her question... everything.

She continued, fighting the dread sitting hot in her chest: "Claire demanded her privacy when she left our island. She's had every opportunity to reconnect with her father, and to my knowledge, she has not."

Ozarik frowned. "Maybe she doesn't know where he is. Or—or she's afraid too much time has passed."

Reiki pinched the bridge of her nose. "Ozarik, I will not speak of this further. I'm sorry that Claire hurt you, and I know you miss her dearly, but prying into her family history is not the way to repair that relationship."

That made him flinch. His face reddened in humiliation, and he gathered up the newspapers. But his eyes flashed briefly as he met her gaze. "You could be right, Reiki. But it's disappointing to hear you aren't willing to give one of our witches the benefit of the doubt."

Reiki watched him storm out of the room, her mouth set in a grim line.

Fifty-eight days later, he snapped at her outside a Canadian hospital, abandoned his Future-Zaro duties to arrange a meeting with a criminal, and Reiki no longer had the luxury of lying to herself.

Unfortunately, Ozarik retained that luxury until the very day death stopped.

Chapter Thirty-Six

3 Years and 327 Days before Death Stopped

Reiki stared at the newspaper article, trembling—in what? Anger? Fear? She paused for a moment to puzzle through the emotion, before settling on *betrayal*. The headline seared her eyes. It was a small local newspaper in Colombia, the audience barely noteworthy, and would almost certainly be written off as lies or conspiracy.

And yet, the fact that an article had been written at all set betrayal so deep in her veins that Reiki felt fire coursing into each appendage. Her magic tingled in the air, electrifying everything.

A soft knock at the door.

Reiki drew a calming breath, then another. This required action, and she needed to be of sound mind before handling it. When her voice was steady, her heartbeat even, she called, "Come in, dear."

Clementine stepped inside. The aciradaan's smile was soft, knowing. Her fingers rested on the Chinese dao at her hip. "Are you alright?"

"I believe that is my line."

"I—it's probably crazy, but I swore I felt your magic pulse. I thought you were upset."

Reiki regarded her carefully, weighing her response. After all, Clementine was especially fine-tuned in sensing emotion. That was her magical ability.

Unfortunately, "sensing emotion" didn't extend to revealing lies, something Reiki knew all too well.

The Zaro was no longer in a position to reveal Claire Flanderson's magic. Reiki's ruse had progressed years past the point when explaining her conundrum would have been reasonable, and now she had no choice but to power through.

So, even though Clementine—her oldest, dearest friend—was staring at her with questioning eyes, Reiki simply... lied. She showed her the paper's headline, which had rearranged itself moments ago. "I was merely concerned with the drought in Bogotá. I'm unsure Ozarik's recent visit was sufficient."

"Of course. I'll add it to our list," Clementine replied, barely glancing at the new headline. She made a notation in her notebook. "Anything else?"

"Is Claire in her room?"

"Well, it's past curfew, so she'd better be. But that's *never enough* with that girl, so I have Bao monitoring the corridor. He hasn't reported a disturbance."

Reiki inhaled, held the breath, and exhaled slowly. "All right. I need a moment alone with her, if you please. Mark that area off-limits until I'm finished."

Clementine frowned, but made another notation. "Yes, of course."

"Thank you, my dear."

"It's my pleasure." A weighted pause, a slight shift. "If you need anything, Kio... anything at all, please don't hesitate to find me."

Kio. Clementine's affectionate nickname. Reiki's heart warmed at it, and not for the first time, she truly regretted their positions in life. But the Zaro was never meant to form attachment, and so Reiki merely smiled and left Clementine alone.

Claire was indeed in her bedroom, which surprised Reiki. Despite her promises years ago, the girl had a bad habit of poofing into Ozarik's room late in the evening.[1]

(In truth, the only reason Claire disobeyed was because those were the nights Ozarik had nightmares. Now, they simply poofed to the other side of the island to talk, a spell simple enough to hide from Reiki's dulling perceptions.)

When Claire opened the door, Reiki drew a breath—bracing herself—and tried to ignore the sinking feeling in her stomach.

On the other side of the doorframe, Claire did the same.

This was because they could sense the magical ramifications of this conversation rippling through time. Tonight, everything would change. There was only one direction this conversation would go, and the result would haunt Reiki for the rest of her days.

"You don't usually visit this late." Claire forced a casual tone. She wanted to feel comfortable around Reiki, but the pinched lines of the woman's brow, the slight downturn of her lips, implied it wasn't merely a check-up.

Reiki crossed her arms, the newspaper hidden from view. "May I come in?"

"I mean, it's your castle."

Sarcasm. Reiki pressed her lips more tightly together to keep from retorting that it wasn't, not really, it belonged to all Zaros across time and space and therefore was as much Claire's as Reiki's, but that defense only mattered if Reiki believed it.

She didn't.

She stepped past Claire, into the cluttered space. The girl had blatantly ignored their rulings of minimalism, and her bedroom was nothing less than a distraction. She had huge posters of American bands hanging

---

1. The wards Reiki had established to enforce curfew were working perfectly. Granted, they functioned by sucking Claire's magic away, but Reiki had learned early and often that if the punishment wasn't strong enough to make Claire think twice... she wouldn't.

on the walls; books on gambling, card games, long cons—no doubt the influence of her father—stacked in the corners; a thick, luxurious blanket that appeared to be crafted of merino wool; and—

Well, at least the widescreen TV was gone. For now, anyway.

Claire squinted at her, but reluctantly dropped into her desk chair, folding her arms over the back of it. "To what do I owe the pleasure?"

Reiki almost thought about pushing this off. Having another lecture tomorrow with Claire *and* Ozarik about the responsibility of the Zaro, smiling distantly as Ozarik vehemently agreed and Claire nodded along. The girl would already be daydreaming.

No. Enough was enough.

Reiki dropped the newspaper onto Claire's desk. The headline was still rearranged, asserting the drought in Bogotá. Claire's brow pinched in confusion. She prodded the newspaper with her own magic, which was way too much pressure. The headline choked, reverting back almost immediately:

AMERICAN GIRL CLAIMS TO BE SECOND ZARO

"So, this is what you were doing in Colombia?" Reiki asked evenly.

Maintain calm.

Claire's cheeks colored. "I was helping Ozarik."

"Ozarik is a competent young witch. He needs your *magic*, not your help. That is the only reason I sent you along—and if I'd known you would sneak off for an interview, I would have personally escorted you home."

Claire hunched into herself, but anger once again sparked in her chest. "He has his own magic."

"It's stronger when he's retrieving yours."

Retrieving. Not borrowing.

Claire frowned. "Maybe that's because we can do more together than we can alone."

Reiki pinched her nose. "Claire, with that mindset, you are going to cause a worldwide revolt."

"Catastrophizing, much?"

"You think I'm outdated, but history educates anyone patient enough to learn. The masses panic when things change too abruptly, and wars have sparked over less." Reiki shook her head. "You made a promise to me all those years ago. Don't you remember? You swore to keep your magic ability secret."

"Why the hell should I keep that promise?" Claire averted her eyes, picking at a thread on her sleeve, and added, quieter: "You've ignored yours."

Reiki, the beloved Zaro, a beacon of hope and light, valued her integrity over all else. She bristled against Claire's words. "I have given you a safe home, good company, and an education second to none. You have traveled to nearly every country in the world by now. What promise haven't I fulfilled?"

"You promised to give me a fair chance at being the next Zaro." Claire's words were bolder now, challenging. "And we both know that was a lie."

The words sat between them, and finally, Claire met Reiki's gaze. Her ice-blue eyes were suddenly as crushing as the deepest ocean depth, as hot as the surface of the sun.

Reiki, for once, didn't have a response.

The girl pushed to her feet. "Someone saw me saving Ozarik from that rockslide. She confronted me. I could either rewrite her memories... or tell the truth. And you always said we don't manipulate minds." The words hung in the air, and Claire's expression darkened. "It's not like they believed me anyway."

Even still, it was intriguing enough to make the front page.

"You have as much a chance as Ozarik to be Zaro. You merely have to prove your worth."

Even to Reiki, the words sounded strangled. Forced.

Claire snorted. "Ah, great. So you're lying to yourself, too."

Reiki was losing control of this conversation—something that was happening more and more frequently when Claire was involved. The Zaro wished she'd worn an outfit more impending than her evening robes.

"Claire, I am not the one stifling your abilities. I have taught you alongside Ozarik. You are the one making the decision to collect extraneous things—" Reiki gestured around the disorderly bedroom, "—and use your Universe-given magic for... well, side-show tricks."

Now the Zaro tugged at the tangled spellwork against the far wall. It vanished instantly, revealing a widescreen TV Reiki had removed from Claire's room no less than seventeen times this month.

Claire huffed. "These things don't change who I can become."

"These *things* are distractions. And they prove your commitment only to your own immediate pleasure." There. This was safe, familiar territory. For a dark, desolate moment, Reiki thanked the Universe for giving Claire such selfishness. It made Reiki's decision that much easier.

After all, Claire was proving her right every single day.

Claire clenched her fists on her lap. "I'm not a bad person just because I like owning a TV."

"No. But it shows me you don't have the self-discipline of a Zaro."

"I could be a great Zaro if you'd give me a chance," Claire snapped, shoving to her feet.

And in that moment, Reiki's final thread of patience snapped too. She'd kept this secret for so many years. She had been generous and given this girl chances, *so* many chances, and tonight proved that every single one was hurled back in her face.

Soon Claire would understand that her lies never fooled anyone.

Reiki stepped forward, dark eyes blazing. "Let's stop pretending for a moment. There's a reason you're here on the island, isn't there?" When Claire stiffened, Reiki knew she'd been right all along. "You have an ulterior motive to supersede Ozarik... by any means possible."

Their chess game was over, and the grand master had won.

"Do you think I am truly that oblivious?" Reiki said, dangerously quiet. "That I wouldn't discern Kyle Flanderson's true reason for sending you to New York City all those years ago?"

"I ran away."

The Zaro narrowed her eyes at the juvenile challenge. "The odds of you finding your way to New York exactly when Ozarik and I arrived were slim... unless you already knew we were coming."

"I knew, but there wasn't some hidden purpose for finding you. I needed a teacher, and I didn't know where else to go." Now Claire's expression had twisted into something ugly, something dark.

Dishonesty all around.

"My first mistake was failing to remove you from that home, I'll admit. However, it's becoming apparent that my second was believing you had nowhere else to go." Reiki folded her arms. "Clementine researched your family, and your half-brother was relocated to Arizona. If you truly were a runaway, why not find him?"

Reiki didn't hear what Claire thought: *Because I couldn't have protected him back then.*

What the girl said was, "Don't mention my brother. Don't you *dare* bring him up."

In reality, this conversation terrified her—but not in the same way it did before. Three years ago, when Claire begged Reiki to teach her, she was doing it to continue the ruse and keep Maxwell safe. Now, it was apparent her father was content to wait as long as she needed to secure the Zaro's title, time that had only allowed her magical comprehension to improve.

She couldn't have protected Maxwell back then, but now...

Now, Claire could do just about anything.

It didn't mean she wanted to be forced into that position, though.

"Your father's letters have always been delivered directly to you, not our mail room. Why is that? What did the contents say?" Reiki asked.

Claire pressed her lips into a firm line. "And here I figured I'd be allowed to have some privacy."

"That depends on why you'd need it. Kyle Flanderson is not one to *give up*, and he has always been convinced you are his final meal ticket." Reiki folded her arms. "Now, I want to hear the truth. If I don't award you the title, what does your father want you to do to Ozarik?"

Murder him.

Claire's expression said it all. Reiki fought the chill that slid down her spine, fought to keep her tone coldly dispassionate. "I suspected as much."

"I'd never hurt Oz," Claire snarled, hating the woman with every fiber of her being. "I love him more than anything. You know that! You *have* to know that."

Reiki stood impassively still, her expression infuriatingly blank. "I know your father's greed. I finally understand how you were raised. None of that is your fault. But even years removed from that influence, it is evident, based on displays like this—" a brief gesture at the newspaper headline, "—that you will never be happy with second place."

Claire knew, in that moment, that everything was about to change. And yet, she couldn't stop herself from continuing the argument, walking straight down the path Reiki set for her—right to her inevitable destruction.

"And why *should* I be happy with it?"

Reiki tensed at her tone, at the way she shouted. "Claire. Enough."

It was the exact wrong word to use. Flashes of Kyle Flanderson throwing that word in her face, using it to control her until it physically couldn't anymore, made Claire snap.

"Fuck you, Reiki. I'm as powerful as Ozarik. I talk with our witches while you tout Ozarik to kings and emperors. You just don't want to see that I'd be an *amazing* Zaro, because that means you've been wrong this whole time!"

As she spoke, Claire's magic sliced through the air again, lashing at Reiki. Framed posters flung off the walls, crashing into the bed. Gambling manuals and fake casino chips flew around the room. The TV hid itself under her invisibility spell again, just in case.

And Reiki stood in the center of it, the eye of the storm, wholly unperturbed.

It was infuriating. The woman had *never* cared.

So, Claire flung more magic at Reiki, violent waves that bounced off her shields. "Admit I'm right. Admit you messed up. Go on. Admit that the only reason Ozarik is your favorite is because you *saw him first.*"

Reiki waved a hand, and all the magic sucked out of the room. Claire felt some of it siphon back into Ozarik, sleeping two floors up, oblivious to all of this. The rest, magic that rightfully belonged to Claire, was held in an iron fist by the Zaro herself.

She loomed over Claire, dark eyes blazing. "You act like the world owes you a favor. You were already given the greatest gift in the Universe, and you squander it on tantrums. Your motivations for coming to Javarini are irrelevant now. I've seen enough."

"Seen enough of what? The truth? Your own failings?" Claire's words were vitriolic.

Reiki's own fury tipped into a boil. "I never dreamed you would be able to steal his magic—and yet, on the night his parents burned, that's exactly what happened. I had *planned* to collect you both for training, but when you made Ozarik an orphan, everything changed."

Reiki might as well have sucker-punched her.

"W-What? I—I didn't kill—"

"The magic swinging between you both is a dangerous thing, Claire. If you think it isn't, you haven't been paying attention." Reiki narrowed her eyes. "People have already died as a result of your power, and that is the world's fate if you are announced as a candidate for the Zaro's title."

Claire's world was shattering around her. She gripped her arms, backing away from the Zaro. "I never meant to kill anyone." Her father's words came back to her: *if you can't beat Ozarik, kill him.*

All this time, she thought she'd *avoided* being a murderer.

She was wrong.

The night she'd wiped Maxwell's memory and saved him from her father slammed into Claire with little courtesy. Never once in the years after did she think of Ozarik, of how he so *clearly* hadn't wanted to relinquish his magic that night. She hadn't given him a choice. She was stronger, more powerful, and she'd yanked his magic away in the moment he needed it most.

His parents had died.

She'd killed them.

All those nights he gasped awake to nightmares of his parents' charred flesh and dying screams, Claire was responsible. She suddenly and violently felt sick.

"The title will go to Ozarik, and you will have to make your peace with that."

A roaring sound in her ears drowned out Reiki's statement, and for a moment, Claire actually thought she might faint. She gripped the desk chair, shaking like a leaf, almost too distraught to respond. All she managed to whisper was, "D-Does Ozarik—"

"Ozarik doesn't know, and never will." Reiki finally seemed to realize Claire's state, and sympathy overrode her features. "You were young, Claire. It was a mistake. But you have to understand how *dangerous* mistakes can be with your magic."

"I—" Claire sunk into her chair, her stomach churning worse than if she'd poofed around the world. Her voice was barely whispered: "I understand."

Reiki sighed in relief. "Good."

"I can't stay here, Reiki."

Now the Zaro raised an eyebrow. "Excuse me?"

But the look Claire gave her, so raw and desperate, pinned her in place. "*Please.* Send me somewhere. Anywhere. I'll start a new life. I'll keep quiet about my magic. But Reiki, I can't *face* him every day and act like nothing's wrong. I can't—I—" Fat tears slipped down Claire's cheeks. If Ozarik found out, he'd never love her like now. He'd look at her with vindication, with anger, and then he'd leave.

Everyone she loved left, for one reason or another. This time, and this time alone, Claire could leave first.

"Please. Help me."

This response, this moment, almost flipped Reiki's opinion. She hadn't expected Claire to break so spectacularly, hadn't expected this raw, desperate emotion. She reluctantly allowed Claire to reclaim her magic, loosened her hold so it eked back to its rightful place. "My dear, no one is asking you to leave."

"*I* am. You were right. You're right about everything. I c-can't be Zaro. Ozarik can have it."

Reiki's mind whirled. The answer to her prayers, presented so neatly. And because Reiki was a kind and benevolent witch, but still somehow entirely human... she took it. "All right. But Claire, if you leave—you won't be allowed back."

A new chapter, for all of them.

Claire nodded. "Okay. T-Tell him you thought it was best. *We* thought it was best. I'm sure he'll find me soon, but... if you talk to him first..."

"I will."

It was because of how *easily* Reiki accepted this excuse that Claire would stew in fury about this fight later. The reality was that Claire should never have known about Ozarik's parents, or taken responsibility for a moment of reckless magic when she was a child. Reiki *should* have protected them both from this truth, rather than wielding it like a weapon.

Instead, she carved the life she wanted for Ozarik... and left Claire a bleeding shell.

This moment would be analyzed over and over in the coming days, weeks, months, until Claire settled on hatred, until she loathed the Zaro and everything Reiki stood for.

But Claire would never tell Ozarik the truth.

Claire would never drag him down in the same way.

So, when Claire packed a bag and teleported across the world, Reiki didn't interrupt. When Ozarik awoke for breakfast the next morning and realized she was gone, then furiously poofed to her new location in Las Vegas, Nevada, he would return empty-handed. When Reiki expanded her magic-sucking wards from Ozarik's bedroom to the entire island, she told herself it was for the best.

And life went on.

Chapter Thirty-Seven

The Day Death Stopped

The day death stopped dawned warm and sunny, as one might expect.

A brisk ocean breeze ruffled the meticulous outfits of the world leaders in attendance. Many of them clutched hats to their head or tightened scarves around their hair as they strolled down the ornate breezeway to the seaside dais, where Clementine and her fellow aciras were putting the final touches on the Assumation Ceremony's traditional décor.

Exactly nine cats—the best trained of the entire second castle—were perched in a semi-circle around the marble platform, which itself was overgrown with thick vines. An upbeat pop song by a well-known Australian witch played over cleverly-hidden loudspeakers. Meanwhile, a spot of light danced across the dais as one of the aciras fiddled with the sacred mirror anchored to the neighboring cliffside. When the time was right, that acira would be in charge of shining a Universe-beholden light on Ozarik, upon which Clementine would utter the formal words and place an ancient stone pendant around his neck.

Ozarik's neck, to be clear—not the acira in charge of the mirror.

It was very pomp and circumstance, and Claire was already annoyed. Her eyes swept across the rows of chairs carefully set up before the dais. It looked like a wedding ceremony, although this was significantly less fun than Henry's. She vehemently wished for Milo's absurdly large margarita, and bitterly took a swig of her grape soda as she wove through the crowds.

Of course, she hadn't made it four steps before Acira Bao intercepted her.

"Ah. Long time, no see," Claire said casually.

"You're not supposed to be here."

She glanced over his shoulder to see Clementine setting an ancient tome on the pedestal, glaring at Claire all the while. Claire waggled a few fingers in response, which only seemed to make the aciradaan angrier. She set a threatening hand on the Chinese dao at her hip, and turned red when Claire winked.

It was deeply satisfying.

"I think you'll find I'm exactly where I'm supposed to be." Claire offered a dazzling smile. "Or didn't Ozarik tell you? I'm the entertainment for tonight's party. The Magnificent Claire Bishop. You know, the most popular act in Las Vegas?"

Bao was from Vietnam, truly hated Acira Jorge's propensity to gamble, and loathed the fact that America had an entire *city* dedicated to it. He scoffed, crossing broad arms over his chest. "Zaro Ozarik is preparing for the ceremony in solitude. He didn't mention you."

"Already calling him 'Zaro,' huh?"

Bao's cheeks tinged red. "He will be soon enough." The words held a threat.

"That's a bit hostile."

"You're not welcome here. Aciradaan Clementine made it very clear—"

"Look, find Ozarik and *ask* him, if you're in such a tizzy." Her words were flippant, irate... right up until Bao's earlier statement sunk in. Claire's fingers clenched around the soda can, denting the soft aluminum. "Wait. Ozarik is in solitude?"

"He's preparing—"

"Has anyone actually *seen* him?"

Bao opened his mouth to protest.

And Claire had all the answer she needed. Her exasperation skyrocketed, and she spun away from Bao without another word, stomping back towards the island's airstrip. Bao watched her go, right until the hot sun made her shimmer and vanish on the horizon. He turned away just as a puff of huckleberry smoke wisped into the air, smugly satisfied at his enforcing duties.

Meanwhile, Claire poofed into Reiki's old study, the one place Ozarik would have paid his respects before Assuming the dead Zaro's title. And sure enough, the Zaro's traditional robes, deep blue stitched in gold so ancient it seemed to gleam with memories, were hanging beside the window.

But the room was empty.

Claire approached the robes. Far below, the procession was getting seated. aciras flitted between the bodyguards and dignitaries, offering water, wine, and coffee. Several more checked invitations before welcoming people down the paved path to the dais. A few lucky newscasters were setting up expensive cameras and performing sound checks for the broadcast.

The ceremony was about to begin.

Exasperation bubbled into actual irritation, and Claire snatched the robes off the hanger. "Ozarik, I swear, I'm going to—" But a paper fluttering to the floor cut her off. She knelt to retrieve it, recognizing Ozarik's scrawl immediately.

Back tonight. Stand in for me?

Claire stared at the note, meant only for her, as her heart thudding in her chest. The room seemed to spin, white noise roaring in her ears, drowning her in responsibility. She knew it. She fucking *knew* it. But a deep, hopeful part of her had wanted to believe she was wrong—right until he proved her very, very right.

Ozarik never planned to be present for this ceremony.

He just *expected* her to show up instead.

Expected her to fill in.

Expected to arrive whenever was convenient and pretend he'd been present all along.

Not only was it a massive jab to Reiki, a Zaro who honored tradition, it was an actual slap in the face to Claire herself. His theft of Zaro Victoria's journal, the thing she'd been hunting for all month, was concerning—but she expected it would come to a head *after* the ceremony. He didn't have time to play with dangerous spells, not while the world waited for him to receive a crown.

Apparently, whatever was written in the final pages of that leatherbound book was more important than the *most important day of his life.*

Anger crawled along her skin, seeping into her veins, hardening her heart. Ice washed over her. Cold disconnect. For a moment, she considered magicking literally anywhere else, avoiding this ceremony, letting the consequences of his actions bite Ozarik in the ass.

But it wasn't just Ozarik who'd suffer from that. The witches of the world were only protected under a Zaro's power. History showed that if Ozarik was absent, *they* would suffer, not him.

So, seething in anger, she slipped on the robes. Magicked into Ozarik's visage. Covering for him... one last time.

She made her way into the belly of the castle, met the aciras faithfully waiting in the lobby to escort her to the dais. One of the aciras bowed low and murmured, "Zaro Ozarik," and another wiped tears from his eyes, and it became dangerously apparent that Ozarik wasn't just missing the culmination of his life's work: he was actively failing every witch in the world.

She was going to *kill him* when this was over.

The acira watching the crowds outside, watching for Clementine's signal, finally gestured her forward. And without much else to do, Claire followed the procession down the path.

Between the chairs, under the eyes of all the world's leaders.

Onto the dais, where Clementine bowed so deeply she nearly folded in half.

Claire turned towards the crowd, sweat trickling down her neck, sick to her stomach. The absolute *audacity* Ozarik had, to pull a stunt like this. Claire knew how to perform—but she also knew when the performance should stop.

They were well past that point now.

Clementine gave her the warmest smile she'd ever seen, a smile meant for her pride and joy, for the prince of witches, not for the scrawny orphan girl Reiki scooped off the streets of New York City at thirteen years old.

"Are you ready to begin?"

Claire wasn't a perfect person, and spite made her feign confusion. As Ozarik, she asked in a deep, falsely confused voice, "Where's Claire?"

The aciradaan blinked, eyes flicking to the observing crowd. "She never showed, Future-Zaro Ozarik. Shall we?"

She never showed.

Such a seamless lie.

With those three words, Claire's heart ignited, beating with new fervor. A smile—a real one—split her face, and she started to laugh. The sound pealed through the open air, resonating off the cliff face until the crowd shifted uncomfortably. Her eyes sought the pope's, sitting in the front row, and she grinned at him.

He looked thoroughly perplexed, the poor man.

She couldn't blame him. She was perplexed too. Part of her couldn't believe what she was doing—but the rest had never felt more certain of anything in her life.

"Oh, I'm ready."

Clementine, eager to get back on track, opened the massive tome in her hands.

Claire cleared her throat. "No. Not yet. What I meant was, I'm ready to stop living a lie. I'm ready to take what's rightfully mine—what's *always* been mine." She snapped a finger, and the illusion vanished away.

What was left was Claire Bishop, adorning the Zaro's sacred robes.

Her robes.

It felt *damn* good.

Clementine gasped, falling backwards. She nearly tripped, but recovered at the last second, face white as a ghost. "H-How dare you—"

"How dare I Assume the title of Zaro when I hold half the power? Ah, yes. How arrogant of me. Then again, I've always been a bit audacious." A feral smirk, a light in her eyes that hadn't existed in weeks. She reveled in their shock, their confusion.

If only Ozarik were here to see it—but if he was, none of this would be happening at all.

She finally stepped into her destiny.

Claire swept her arms out like she was performing on a stage: "I am Claire Bishop, magician on the Las Vegas Strip, ex-Javarini resident, and commander of half the Zaro's magic. Ozarik, my other half, apparently had something more important to do. So, with Reiki's encouragement and blessing, I will be Assuming the position of Zaro myself."

Clementine's cheeks flushed. "Reiki's *blessing*? You—You're a fraud! Where is Ozarik? What did you do with him?"

"All I've done this month is encourage him to take responsibility," Claire snapped, rounding on her. "But he's been gone for a while, hasn't he? Actually, let me guess. You haven't seen him in... eleven days." When Clementine flinched, Claire smirked. "Ozarik has made it clear: he doesn't want the position. Luckily for him, I have equal ownership to it. And lucky for you all, I'm willing to step up."

Clementine dropped the tome. It landed with a heavy *thud*, a puff of dust settling between them. "She's attempting to overthrow Zaro Ozarik!" Clementine drew her sword in a rather threatening manner.[1]

A few of the aciras surged forward in time with Clementine, but Claire muttered, "For God's sake," and swept a hand, manipulating the air into fine mist. It settled over the dais, blinding them. As they stumbled, Claire flicked her fingers in their directions, and the wind effortlessly shoved them back into the grass.

As the mist cleared, a few bodyguards in the crowd reached for their weapons, but no one was brave enough—or stupid enough—to shoot someone claiming to be the next leader of the world's witches.

"My business is all about the suspension of belief, but this is a bit ridiculous," Claire replied, her voice amplifying to impossible levels. Even Clementine, pushed back several feet, was stunned into silence. Claire held

---

1. Although, admittedly, it was hard to draw a sword in an unthreatening manner.

her arms wide. "Lucky for you, I'm all about showmanship. So, let's see what the Zaro could really do, huh?"

With an upwards motion, Claire pulled the remaining mist into the sky. It bubbled into dark clouds, blotting out the sun. She tugged at the magic a bit, and fat drops of rain transformed into a shower of flower petals, which swirled in a lazy breeze around her. The ground rumbled, and far away, a tsunami rose from the ocean. It crested over the dais, but what crashed to the ground was a literal rainbow. When everything calmed, Claire posed as if expecting applause.

Instead, she got silence.

Well, she couldn't win them all.

Claire chuckled at the crowds, then faced Clementine. "I have the same magic that Ozarik does. Why do you think Reiki brought me here all those years ago?"

"She kicked you off the island," Clementine snarled. "She told me it was a mistake."

"Funny. She told *me* her entire response to my life was a mistake."

Clementine shuddered. The dao's tip angled towards Claire, its black-hole magic pulsing the air. "*Sacrilege*! You attend this ceremony, detain Ozarik, and pull a few fancy illusions to make us think you're his equal? Where is he? Is he safe?"

"He's probably buried nose-deep in a leatherbound journal that could end the world. But I'll address that soon." Claire's patience was waning. "What more do you need to see, *aciradaan*? Do you want me to teleport you to Slovakia myself?"

Clementine shook with anger, a woman pushed to the brink. "No. I want you *gone*."

And then, faster than Claire could react, Clementine surged forward—

—and pierced the ancient dao into the Zaro's chest.

Chapter Thirty-Eight

The Day Death Stopped

The day death stopped was cloudy and rainy in Slovakia. This was a subtle ploy from the Universe to propel Ozarik into activity, to shove him away from his dreary mountain study and into the bright, social sunshine of Javarini—where Clementine and the aciras were setting up the island for his Assumation Ceremony.

He ignored it.

Truth be told, he'd ignored many things in the past week and a half.

Claire's parting words ran through his mind: *You're going to be great, Oz. Get to it.*

"Not without you," he muttered for the seventeenth time, flipping through the pages of a certain journal. The power to stop death was, in theory, simple—it was a persuasion of souls, commanding them to remain anchored to their bodies. But human souls weren't chipmunk souls, and *human* souls thrived on questioning, arguing, and disobeying. And that made this very simple theory immensely complicated in practice.

He'd been wrong about Kyle Flanderson. The man was an asshole, a black mark on the bright note of Claire's existence, and Ozarik could acknowledge it. What he couldn't acknowledge was that Reiki—*Reiki*—died by his command.

He couldn't acknowledge that, in his desperation to hold onto Claire Bishop, to keep her in his life forever, he'd made a choice: Reiki, or Claire.

The Zaro, or his life partner.

Responsibility, or love.

The responsibility was soured for him, and even as his magic pulsed with warning—*the Assumation Ceremony nears, you are encouraged to Javarini, please return to your home and claim your title*—Ozarik felt sick whenever he considered the Assumation Ceremony. Being swathed in formal blue robes, robes Reiki had worn decades ago. Standing beside Clementine, who'd always looked at him so proudly, and knowing that she'd lost the most important person in her life because of *his* mistake.

And then there was Claire.

Reiki wanted to sweep her under the rug, keep her hidden from the world's eyes. Ozarik absolutely refused that life for her. Claire thrived in the spotlight, and once he became Zaro, no one would exist to dispute that.

He would present her to the world.

And she would be at risk.

Every Universe-damned day, Claire would be at risk—because every day, people like Kyle Flanderson prowled on the peripherals of her life. Ozarik had ensured the man was trapped by magic, apprehended by authorities, no bail, no freedom. Kyle Flanderson awaited a trial where the world would declare him guilty, and he would suffer for his crimes.

But there were others. How long after Ozarik's announcement would Claire come under fire? Governments, leaders, witches... everyone would want answers. Some would be angry. Ozarik was no longer naïve enough to think they would quietly stand by as Claire joined him on the throne.

He massaged a centuries-old spell into being. One final spell to tether one single, stubborn soul to her body. Claire's soul would argue, and thus, his spellwork had to be foolproof. He stared feverishly at his pendulum, scribbling into a notebook with his left hand as the golden weight swung from a simple chain pinched between his right finger and thumb.

(To be clear, this was a physical pendulum. While it wasn't Ozarik's preferred form of dowsing[1], it *was* effective in linking his demands to the inner magic below his Slovakian castle. This simple pendulum should not be confused with the metaphysical one perpetually swinging between Claire and Ozarik.)

He'd nearly perfected it. Just a few simple parameters remained to be attached, guidelines that would bind Claire's soul to this world forever.

And if they bound Claire's soul to *him* forever, well. He wouldn't complain.

He shoved a map underneath the pendulum and said, "Show me the terminology I need to lock her down."

But now, for the first time ever, his pendulum stilled.

This was because, across the world, Claire had just discovered Ozarik was resoundingly *not* on Javarini.

Her magic pulsed furiously, and it spread like a wildfire over Europe. He winced, sweat beading on his neck. "In a minute, Claire. You'll thank me for this later." He gently swung the pendulum again. "Where can I find the exact phrase?"

Despite his fingers motioning the pendulum, its golden weight stayed perfectly anchored to the center of the map—which, of course, happened to be over Javarini. A pointed statement. Claire's magic washed over him again, poking him, needling him. Unlike his magic, which offered gentle encouragement, hers was akin to a knife in the chest.

Get your ass over here, it said irately.

He snarled, frustration boiling over in waves, and threw the pendulum to the floor. It skittered across the stone, sliding under one of his many bookshelves. Ozarik shoved to his feet, desperation and anxiety compounding in his soul.

"Leave me *alone*, Claire. I'm working," he snapped at the walls.

---

1. As a Zaro, Ozarik's favorite form of dowsing was to merely reach into the magic of the Universe and demand answers—most of which were provided hastily.

While their magic could communicate and she most certainly felt his dismissive irritation, his verbal cues were purposefully left unheard—because Universe forbid Claire actually *respond*. Instead, they made Ozarik into a raving lunatic, buried in dangerous research within a crumbling castle somewhere deep in the woods.

Moments passed, long breaths where Ozarik paced his study, slammed to his knees by the bookshelf, and fumbled for the golden pendulum. He needed those and he wasn't willing to wait for it. The spell was almost complete.

In Javarini, Claire resolutely donned the robes and joined the aciras.

In Slovakia, Ozarik sat at his table again, pouring magic into the pendulum.

In Javarini, Claire stook on the dais and announced herself to the world.

In Slovakia, the gold fractured, then melted over Ozarik's precious map.

In Javarini, Clementine plunged the magical dao into Claire's chest.

In Slovakia, the world shattered.

It happened violently, a snapping akin to breaking a bone, or crashing your car into oncoming traffic. One moment, things seemed to be fine. And the next breath, everything magical was bleeding and moaning and explosions of light and color flashed in a devastating display and souls across the world screamed as a Zaro was killed.

Except the magic didn't transfer from Claire to a newborn baby somewhere else. This was because, unlike past Zaros, *two* existed—and the sacred Chinese dao merely shoved her magic into Ozarik.

It drowned him in a shock of cold water.

His immediate thought was: *No. Not her too.*

One couldn't be sure what he was expecting when he vanished on the day of the Assumation Ceremony.

Nevertheless, he grabbed the leatherbound journal inscribed with *ZV*, abandoned the melted pendulum, and poofed in a blind panic to Claire's location: the dais on Javarini's grassy beach.

The spell wasn't complete. The parameters weren't set.

None of it mattered when he saw the dais covered in Claire's slippery crimson blood.

Chapter Thirty-Nine

The Day Death Stopped

Clementine withdrew the sword from Claire's chest, finding little resistance of skin against the sharp blade. The *schwick* sound seemed to echo across the suddenly-silent beach.

Claire dropped to her knees and wheezed two words:

"You *bitch*."

Above her, brandishing the bloodstained sword meant for this exact scenario, Aciradaan Clementine was red-faced with fury.

Her rage had nothing on Ozarik's.

Time seemed to *freeze*. Actually, "seemed to" was a bit of an understatement. It literally slowed, suddenly terrified to keep marching forward at a steady pace, terrified of disobeying a person wrought with grief and anger so deep he could destroy countries, burn worlds. So, when a pulse of the most powerful, dangerous magic in the world spread across the grass, stopping the wind, blinding the sun, time simply bowed its head in submission.

Everything washed in greyscale as Ozarik sprinted to Claire's side, catching her seconds before she crashed to the reddened stone.

"Claire. *Claire*!!"

In a perfect world, the dao would suck the magic from the current Zaro and deposit it into that Zaro's replacement—but this was far from a perfect world. Because in this world, Ozarik *was* Claire's replacement. The pendulum swung, and he effortlessly shoved it back towards her.

She hissed, seizing for a breath that didn't come, but the magic did form a sort of patch over the wound in her chest.

It wasn't a healing spell, but it was good enough for now. After all, *now*, there were more pressing concerns. Ozarik spun, his ferocious glare pinning Clementine to the spot.

"*You.*"

A dark, all-encompassing fear washed over her. It stabbed her spine, holding her upright, as frozen as the time around them. She wanted to step back, to scream, to run, but the dao remained pointed at Claire's body, trembling violently in a suddenly immovable grasp.

Ozarik's eyes dropped to the sword, and it began to burn. The stamped metal turned white-hot, ripping a scream from Clementine's throat—but everything moved too slowly, and painful blisters blotted her palm before she was physically able to drop the weapon. The dao, too magical to be destroyed, clattered to the ground, stained with shiny crimson.

"You *stabbed* her." Ozarik was wholly unconcerned with the intense burns searing Clementine's hand. Wholly unconcerned with how terrified she looked, eyes wide like a deer in the highway seconds before impact. His fingers tightened around Claire, who's own ice-blue eyes were slipping shut, even as she attempted to manipulate the magic around them.

The world wouldn't know it, but she was casting that spell she'd discovered at Lake Ashi, in Hakone—the spell to calm Ozarik, soothe the anger in his soul... and barring that, to contain his suddenly malicious magic.

Unfortunately for the bystanders, it didn't work. He hadn't returned enough magic for her to do much more than survive.

Clementine stammered, "I—I was protecting you—"

Although time had slowed, his magic had not. In a violent, extraordinarily fast act, the island *splintered*, gaping chasms gorging a perfect circle around the dais. The visiting dignitaries all screamed, scrambling over themselves to flee the Zaro's wrath, no matter how futile the effort.

After all, mortals could never outrun a god.

Claire, nearing her final thought, barely resisted rolling her eyes. *Christ, Oz,* she tried to say, but in that moment his magical patch fractured. Blood burned her esophagus, painted her organs, spilled from her heart, and Claire could do nothing but fight for every single gasp.

Meanwhile, time had managed to bolster its courage, walking now instead of crawling.

Ozarik didn't notice any of that. For all the instances he'd replayed Reiki's death, imagined his intervention, now rage overwrote logic. Claire lay unobserved.

"*Protecting* me?" Fire roared from the depths of the splintered earth, burning Clementine's hair, drowning the dais with threats. "I am not a child, and you are not my parent. Don't you dare pretend you know what's best for us."

This statement hurt Clementine more than the burns. She crashed to her knees in the pool of blood, covering her head from the onslaught of nature. "I'm sorry! She cast an illusion spell, and tried to—"

"I told her to do that, Clementine! She's done *everything* for me, and look—" Ozarik choked on the words, his fingers bruising Claire's shoulders now. Noting almost too late that her skin was ashen grey, her eyelids barely open. Panic surged, his magic flaring as he hunched over her, fumbling for the journal. His words were a guttural scream. "Look at what you've done!"

Above them, thunder exploded. The grassy area behind the dais was empty now, and even the light seemed to shatter. The sky vanished under a sea of black grief. When Ozarik met the woman's terrified gaze, Clementine knew without a doubt she would be killed.

"She's—she's not the Zaro," the aciradaan tried to say, feebly.

Because if Claire *was* the Zaro, that would mean... Reiki lied.

Clementine's very soul fractured at the thought.

Ozarik didn't care. "She's more a Zaro than I'll ever be. And if you can't see that, you have *no purpose here.*" With a seething smack of wind, he sent Clementine hurling into the fire-smoked chasm. She screamed, grabbing the jagged edge just in time. Her skin bubbled from the heat, and she quickly lost control of her limbs.

Only a clap of magic saved her life.

Claire's magic.

It ballooned around Clementine, one last, desperate breath of hope, shoving her into the hot grass on the opposite side of the chasm. The ex-aciradaan writhed in agony, her mind slipping into chaos, but she was alive.

Claire, fading fast, took mild comfort in that, because Ozarik did love the woman... even if he didn't remember right now. On the dais, shaking with effort, ice-cold from blood loss, Claire's hand dropped back to her side.

And she died.

It came as a sigh, rather than a storm—nothing like Reiki's, where her magic flooded the Universe and informed every witch of her death. No, Claire Bishop died softly, her magic simply returning to Ozarik, the pendulum shifting back into the ornate set of scales it was always meant to be.

And that was resoundingly *not okay* for Ozarik. His agonizing scream filled the air, somehow more painful a sound than a thousand avalanches. But this time, he didn't simply watch in horror.

No, this time, he slammed open the journal and located the spell that both caused and completed all of this, words Zaro Victoria had tried to hide over a century ago for the good of the Universe.

"You don't get to die, Claire."

And he recited the spell.

Once he uttered the final verse, everything fell silent. Not mute, but true, aching silence, as if the world had stopped to ponder its decisions and found them severely lacking. And then a shockwave of magic slammed into Claire's soul, binding her to her corpse in the most agonizing way impossible.

Clementine's agony had nothing on Claire's, but it was silenced by the absolute lack of breath in her body. Her back arched out of Ozarik's hold, her skin glowed white, her eyes opened black and soulless before the alien orbs rolled into her skull, replaced finally with her typical blue irises.

She shuddered violently as her heart moaned in despair, but reluctantly began to beat again.

Her lungs constricted, then yanked themselves apart, forcing a gasping breath.

Her throat convulsed, shoving blood out of her mouth in a waterfall.

Ozarik leaned over her, anxiously.

Stay in your body, his spell ordered. *There's nowhere else to go.*

Claire's soul called bullshit, personally, but coming back from the brink of death had a way of disorienting even the most articulate mind. She blinked slowly, painfully, and Ozarik laughed like a child hugging his first teddy bear.

"You're okay. You're okay!" His voice was bright.

"Oz—" she coughed, words wet with blood. "You *moron*."

And that's when their magic pulsed again, spreading over Javarini and the oceans and the continents and the planet, splintering every single soul who dared to die at the same time as Claire Bishop. It pierced all 86 of them in turn, dozens of wounds, immeasurable pain, spiking in every direction and utterly overwhelming Ozarik's tenuous hold on the spell's parameters.

While drafting the spell, he didn't care that restrictions were done carefully. He just cared that it worked.

Like most things, haste came back to bite him in the ass.

"Oh no," Ozarik whispered.

"W-What did you *do*?" Claire wheezed, pushing out of his grasp.

He leapt up, reaching out with invisible fingers to prod the threads of the spell, feel how far they vibrated around Earth. "Nothing. It wasn't supposed to—"

Another pulse, another fresh wave of souls trapped in their bodies.

"I didn't—"

"*Fuck*, Ozarik," Claire snarled, wiping her mouth as she shoved to her feet. She suddenly didn't have the luxury of writhing in pain.

"It's fine. I'll figure it out." And Ozarik yanked most of her magic away, poofing to his beloved, mortified castle in the Tatras mountains, journal in hand.

Claire remained, swaying dangerously on the dais, one hand over the oozing wound in her chest. The Zaro robes were stained in blood, and the world swam. She flicked a finger and slowly coaxed the circle of flames down into the earth, begged the island to knit itself back together. It grumbled, annoyed at the dramatics, but rearranged itself under her will.

Her magic stores were now dangerously low, and another pulse had her crashing to her knees. It took precious minutes, but Claire managed to stagger to Clementine's blistering body. The older woman was sobbing, hunched into herself. Claire eased the feeble remnants of her magic over the aciradaan's skin to soothe her burns.

"Are you okay?"

"H-How could she lie to me?" Clementine shivered, eyes glazed with pain.

Claire, in that moment, felt very, very tired. "I think... we've all made mistakes."

Over the hill, towards the castle, Aciras Bao and Jorge were running towards them. Claire left her protective magic in place to keep Clementine from going into shock, and then stepped back a respectable amount. The dao had been forgotten on the dais, but she had no intention of getting stabbed again, or shot, or whatever they cared to try.

"I'll find Oz," she said, feigning more confidence than she felt. "We'll stop this."

Clementine clenched her eyes shut.

With nothing left here, Claire summoned her quickly-dwindling magic to poof to the other side of the world. But instead of appearing at the Slovakian castle, she opened her eyes to... Henry's apartment.

Without really understanding how she got here, or why, Claire stumbled to the entry. Rapped twice on the door. And when Henry wrenched it open and gasped, "*Claire?*" she couldn't stop herself from collapsing against him.

His arms were around her immediately, towing her inside, and despite everything, she felt safer than she had all day.

Jenifer yelped as she saw Claire's state. "What happened?" The human began tossing pillows off the couch, mumbling in a panic, "Oh my god. Oh *my god*."

"Yeah, I don't think he can hear you," Claire muttered, gripping Henry's arm as he eased her onto the cushions.

Her brother knelt beside her, eyes wide, his normally cool temperament fracturing under fear. "Are you okay? Do you need a hospital? Jenifer, call 911!"

"Don't bother. This isn't our most pressing concern."

"The *blood* isn't—"

With a wave, Claire switched their television from the previously live, chaotic footage of the Assumation Ceremony, landing on a local news station instead. It had been eleven minutes since death stopped, and witches everywhere could feel the pulsing magic of Ozarik's spell. Even the humans were catching on, reports flooding social media about "near-death" experiences.

Or rather, "not-death" experiences.

The reporters were baffled, sifting through reports as footage of car wrecks and burned buildings and hospitals cycled through, everyone drowning in carnage and chaos. Jenifer covered her mouth, and Henry stilled.

Beside him, Claire narrowed her eyes. "He didn't just bring *me* back. He brought everyone back." Another pulse, and she cringed at the power it drew from her. Sweat beaded across her brow as she grasped the couch's armrest with bloodied fingers. "It's still happening. Fuck. *Fuck*. I need a phone."

"What? How will that help?"

"Well, I have to distract him *somehow*." Claire clenched her eyes shut as a wave of pain washed over her. Henry handed her his cell, worry pinching his face as she dialed a number that didn't exist.

"It's okay." She offered him a bright—perfectly fake—smile. "I'll fix this."

He didn't return it. "Don't tell me that."

"Would you rather I sit back and let death stop?"

Henry's voice was uncharacteristically hard as he waved a hand at the TV. "I don't give a shit about this, Claire. I care that you're safe. Promise me you'll *stay safe*."

Tears sprang to Claire's eyes, and she tore her gaze from his. Her brother, her guardian, her moral compass. But today, in this moment, he couldn't help her. She had more important things to do, things he couldn't fathom yet.

"I'm sorry, Henry," she whispered.

And she pressed the phone to her ear.

Chapter Forty

The Day Death Stopped

A nd so, we arrive at the moment of truth, the moment used to lure you into this ageless story of heartbreak, love, and agony. For after this moment, the world was never the same, and we can finally understand why.

Ozarik went to his castle in Slovakia, realized the extent of his spell—and decided he simply didn't care.

Claire poofed to his side, as always. She yanked her magic back, restarting the gentle swing of their pendulum. Tried to reason with him, and failed miserably. The two of them faced each other, their magic pulsing around the world as readily as it swelled from each of their souls, preparing for battle.

They were both brutally aware of it.

"I guess it's my job to make you," Claire said. "You shouldn't have brought me back, Oz. You shouldn't have done any of this."

"Please, Claire. I've never been more certain in my life, and you'll see it too... with time. A world without death is the new standard. The spell is already stabilizing."

Beside him, the old journal glowed with power, and Claire thought briefly about lighting it on fire. But of course, it did nothing wrong, except to have the misfortune of existing as written proof of one Zaro's grief.

Ozarik had been studious, a perfect apprentice—any spell he articulated couldn't be so easily undone.

He was right about it stabilizing. Their pulsing magic had slowed the moment Claire poofed into the castle. Her wound stopped bleeding, although it remained a gaping, grotesque hole under her bloodied robes. The construct of death was relenting under Ozarik's powerful corruption, slowly and surely deciding now might be a great time to take a well-deserved vacation... or rather, retirement.

Don't you dare, Claire snapped at it.

It shrugged, lazily bowing to the spell's whim.

Ozarik smiled, feeling it settle. "There we go. If stopping death were so unnatural, wouldn't this be harder?"

"It will be once I'm through with you." And with time running out, Claire did exactly what her father always wanted—and attacked her other half.

Ozarik didn't see her coming. Or rather, he was expecting a slower response, considering she'd been stabbed twenty-three minutes ago. But Claire had spent years on stage, performing physically demanding feats of illusion, and her magic spread through her arms and legs like an elixir.

She was suddenly unstoppable, and her fist cracked into Ozarik's jaw.

His head snapped back, and he crashed into a row of bookshelves. They started to tip, but he threw a shield around himself—one Claire unstitched strand by strand before he could blink. She let gravity take control: the heavy tomes slammed into him, burying him under a bookshelf of painful knowledge.

The pendulum swayed closer to her, and she grabbed the power in her mind's eye, storing it away. But Ozarik was stirring, and she couldn't give him the chance to regain command. She ripped her hands outwards, and the earth undid itself below her feet. The castle moaned as its foundation crumbled, as Ozarik plummeted into a dungeon that didn't exist before.

He didn't land; instead, he poofed behind her. Unlike Claire, he pulled his punches, wrapping his arms around her body to pin her in place.

But his magic spread into her like a disease, greedy and desperate, and everywhere it touched pain ignited. Claire swallowed a scream, which caused him to loosen his physical hold, but his magic continued leeching hers, unrelenting. Sucking her dry.

Claire elbowed him in the stomach, slammed her foot into his shin, and spun from his grasp. As her wound throbbed, as sweat poured down her brow, she attacked him in a different way.

"Reiki would be *ashamed* of what you've become."

"If I'd become this sooner, she'd still be alive," he snapped, hunching over his waist, grimacing at the force of her blow. "Reiki was always afraid to disrupt the status quo. She never pushed our magic as far as we have. She never wanted us to be together."

Claire put some distance between them. "I don't want us together like *this*."

"The details don't matter. It's done, and now nothing can stop us from following our destiny." His feverish eyes shone bright, desperate.

"Restart death. Then, *maybe* you can talk to me about 'destiny.'"

The spell pulsed again, and when his magic was momentarily weakened, his tendrils briefly lifting their parasitic hold, Claire erected a barrier so powerful it sent a gust of wind through the collapsing castle. Her magic locked into place, inaccessible to him. But it was temporary at best; her body was failing, which meant she needed to be clever, not strong.

Around them, heavy stone bricks fractured and fell, their crashes booming through the forest. Claire dodged one, thinking fast as Ozarik advanced on her. His magic pawed at the barrier, desperate for more power, even as the spell to stop death trembled with the loss.

"You're unraveling it," he cried, and made his decision. He'd been trying not to hurt her, but the point of no return had arrived: there would only be one winner here.

Ozarik lashed out instead, fingers clenching painfully around her arm. With a vicious yank, he threw her to the ground. A jagged rock bruised her back, and she swallowed a yelp. For a brief flicker, Ozarik seemed to come back to himself, but then his spell tightened the noose around his neck and his expression twisted into determination.

"*Enough*, Claire! Let me save you."

The word held no power anymore. Claire rolled out of his way, forcing herself to her feet. "I don't n-need saving."

He lunged at her again, and for the first time, fear chilled her skin. Her best friend was gone. Ozarik was no more—all that remained was a young man blinded by his vision of a better world. One day soon, the loss would reverberate so potently that mountains would crumble beneath her grief, but today, there was no time for that.

Claire suddenly knew what she'd have to do.

Two spells. One, Claire had been using like a second breath from the moment she met Reiki in that bookstore in Coeur d'Alene. The second, she hadn't used since she was five.

It was such a simple solution, but it ripped Claire's soul in two.

Ozarik had spent a maniacal month lying to her, pretending like he was hunting for a spell to separate their magic, even as she suspected more. Reiki had been convinced *one* of them would become more proficient in magic, and the separation would happen naturally as they aged. By the time the old Zaro realized her error, it was too late.

Claire knew the truth, and she would fix it all.

His magic slammed against her barrier, but it didn't splinter. Her power was locked away, and she set her sights on the push-pull ever perpetuating between them.

Before he could move back, she surged forward, grabbing his arms and holding him in place. At the same time, the earth leapt upwards to engulf him, pinning his body in a cage of rock. Only his head was visible now, and he snarled, frothing like a rabid animal, spewing anger with every word.

It was background noise, nothing more.

Claire's voice was quiet as she gave him one final chance.

"Ozarik, please. If you really do love me, you'll stop this."

"All I've ever *done* is love you," he hissed, and cracks spiderwebbed along the stone that held him in place.

Claire sighed, clenching her eyes shut for a bare second. Solidifying her resolve. Then she stepped forward, gently pressing her forehead to his.

He stilled against her touch.

And in that moment of surprise, Claire viciously wrenched his magic away. She left nothing behind, not even a glimmer for him to rely on, and slammed her impenetrable barrier back in place. In the same way she gave Henry a magical ability—she stripped Ozarik of his.

The pendulum's chain snapped, and the golden weight vanished into the cosmos of the Universe.

Claire Bishop had become the Zaro—permanently.

It was both the simplest thing she'd ever done, and the most devastating choice of her life.

Ozarik, utterly devoid of magic, gasped at the sudden emptiness. He wrenched his head as his massive, death-stopping spell dismantled around him, eyes widening as Claire sent new instructions into the world: *Follow your spirits home.*

"No," he screamed.

But the not-dead souls obeyed her command, sobbing gratefully as they soared upwards, as their corpses dropped, as balance returned. Meanwhile, Claire glanced at Zaro Victoria's battered journal, offering a bare apology before it burst into flames. Breath by breath, each book in Ozarik's crumbling castle followed suit, until flames raged around them and a dark silence took hold.

Her own wound throbbed suddenly, vividly, but she'd never before held the full power of a Zaro at her fingertips, and it was immense. She brushed her thumb across the wound, and it hastily stitched itself shut. Her organs cleaned themselves, her lungs stopped aching, and Claire had never felt so alive.

Ozarik trembled before her, tears springing to his eyes. "*Claire,*" he whispered, and the word held the agony of a thousand lives.

She let the earth around him sink back into the ground, and he staggered, dropped to his knees. She physically *felt* his ache—but this time, she didn't attempt to intervene. Her comfort spell was buried deep beneath the agony of what they'd both done, and for once, Claire needed them both to acknowledge this pain.

Instead, she sunk to the ground beside him, intertwining her hand in his.

"I'm sorry," she said, quietly.

He didn't respond, but sobs wracked his entire body. She wasn't sure how long they sat like that, him curled against her chest, his magic pressing against her impenetrable walls, never to return. Her own magic wrapped around it, slowly twisted it from Ozarik's optimistic yellow hue to hers, a brilliant gold.

Soon, the magic would forget it ever belonged to him.

Claire waited for Ozarik to speak, rubbing his back while her heart lay in pieces around them. When he finally shifted, his tone was low, surprisingly accepting. "I'm not... getting it back."

"No," she whispered. "I can't risk it."

His eyes had returned to their typical green color, and his skin had lost its feverish tint. He looked perfectly and utterly normal. And sad. So, so sad. "Then what do we do now?"

She closed her eyes, burying her nose into his shoulder. "I don't know, Oz."

More silence.

Neither of them wanted to admit the reality of their lives now. Left alone, Claire never would. If he asked, she'd probably instate him as her aciradaan, give him that stupid sword, let him monitor her choices and live his life in peace on her island. She'd consult him with worldly problems and let him research to his heart's content and they'd be together, just like he wanted.

But he never wanted it like this. And Claire Bishop knew firsthand that living on the peripherals of a world where you desperately yearned to belong... well.

That didn't work for long.

Ozarik reached the same conclusion. His voice trembled. "Then I'll decide. You have to let me go."

"You can go anywhere. Wherever you want."

"No, Claire." He pulled away from her, traced her cheek. Their hearts broke in tandem—the final moment where they'd ever synchronize. "You have to *let me go*. I can't live as the Almost-Zaro." His sad smile was weighted with the loss of their bond. "I'm not as strong as you. I'll break.

And if that's the case—" his voice fractured, "—I'd rather live whole, in your memories."

Claire suddenly realized what he was asking. Her voice got sharp, her magic pulsed. "I'm not going to kill you. And you aren't allowed to kill yourself." The words became a spell, but she hesitated before setting it on his shoulders. "Y-You don't want that, right?"

"I don't know what I want anymore," he said.

She'd hoped for a better solution, but neither of them could take back their actions. His words revealed the truth: they would never be together again. They couldn't. The Universe was in peril when they were linked.

Claire, as the witch who'd severed that link, had to finish the job. "I—I can persuade your memories. Convince you it never happened."

Convince you that we were never two halves of the same whole.

Ozarik hesitated, but they both knew there wasn't another choice. This heartache would twist him to do something dangerous later, whether Claire and their magic was present for it or not. It took a long moment of silence, but then he cupped her face, pressed a kiss to her forehead.

"I love you, Claire. That will never change."

Claire held his gaze, breathless, devastated, because it absolutely would.

"Give me a good life, okay?" Ozarik tried to laugh, but it became a shuddering sob.

"The best life." Claire hugged him. "Like you gave me that day in New York."

He gripped her like a lifeline, eyes tracing her face like he couldn't get enough of her, even as his castle, his soul, burned around them. Claire memorized his face, his personality right now, because she alone would bear the responsibility of recalling who Ozarik the Almost-Zaro had been.

And then her magic slipped into his mind, winding through his synapses, rewriting old memories, paving the path for new ones, slowly convincing him that he'd never been a Zaro at all. There was no resistance. He willingly accepted her magic, even as it erased everything he was.

And only once he looked placidly at her, a blank slate awaiting instruction, did she send that same persuasion outward, into the minds of every witch and human on the planet.

Ozarik never existed, she said, feeling sick inside. *I am your Zaro.*

It wasn't a voiced command, nothing so explicit that it would require the ancient map they'd used before visiting Kyoto all those weeks ago. This order was utterly intangible, utterly encompassing, and every nameless soul blinked, shrugged, and replied: *okay, then.*

The *named* souls would be harder to convince, but Claire would cross that bridge when she came to it. For now, the world at large accepted her as Zaro, and Ozarik... well. Ozarik would never remember what they were.

Claire untangled herself from her partner, her best friend, her lifeline, and helped him stand.

He dusted off his arms, blinking in confusion. His eyebrow arched at the decaying, smoldering castle around them. "This, ah... this is something." Forest-green eyes settled on her, on the blood of her robes, the bags under her eyes, and he surged forward, mildly alarmed. "Are you okay?"

"I'm fine," she lied.

He heard the subtext of her tone, and tilted his head. "Do we know each other?"

She smiled, a perfect, stage-worthy smile, even as her eyes burned with tears.

"We actually haven't met. I am Zaro Claire."

Chapter Forty-One

7 Years and 1 Day before Death Stopped

An eternity ago, Claire shoved past an absolute wall of humans, fighting to reach the front of the massive crowd packing Times Square to glimpse the Zaro and her entourage. She elbowed more than a few stomachs, gasped hasty apologies, and used their surprise to claw further forward.

She had one shot at this. One brief moment to ensure Reiki *saw* her, ensure guilt truly took hold, ensure she was brought to that stupid island just like her father wanted. He'd be watching—he had eyes across the country. Someone would tell him if she failed.

And she couldn't poof to Arizona fast enough to save Maxwell then.

Luckily, the last week had been hell, so she wouldn't have to try very hard to convince the Zaro she needed help. Her clothes were ripped, grimy with stains she'd collected even before days traveling on a public bus. Her hair felt greasy and sticky, even in the hasty bun she'd used to get it off her neck. Her skin was grainy, salty with sweat and fear. It took four days and seven busses to reach New York City, and she'd spent the last three sleeping in an alley with only her magic keeping her warm.

She didn't dare use her magic to manipulate a place to stay, not when she desperately needed Zaro Reiki to feel sorry for her.

When she finally reached the front of the crowd, Claire was confident in her ability to get noticed. What she wasn't confident about was the wild card: Ozarik. Her other half, her competition. He had to know what she was trying to do.

All it would take was a word from him, and Reiki would turn away. Claire *knew* it.

But their magic pulsed as she watched the stage where the Zaro would make her appearance. Traffic had been diverted from here, and the televisions framing Times Square displayed the empty stage. Anticipation layered heavily in the air, with enough witches craning to get a peek that their magic swirled like an ocean around them.

It was nothing compared to Claire's magic as she stood so physically close to Ozarik. For the first time, they were in the same city, the same street, mere feet from each other. Their magic hugged like long-lost friends, and it filled her with a warmth she didn't want to believe.

After all, Ozarik was her enemy. Her father had made that quite clear.

Reiki appeared, her face serene and smiling as she waved at the crowd, and her aciradaan trailed behind her, hand on that magical Chinese dao, and finally Ozarik arrived, perched at Reiki's right hand, eyes wide as he glanced over the crowd.

And forest-green met ice-blue.

And the world *stopped*.[1]

A shiver rippled through them both, and Reiki followed his gaze, and Claire didn't miss the look of shock, of horror, as she recognized the dirty blonde girl nestled in the adoring crowds. Claire held her gaze, her own expression hard—*take a good look, Reiki. This is what you've done to me.*

But her anger softened as Reiki's eyes knitted together, as her magic settled over Claire's like a warm blanket. *I see you, child, and we'll talk soon*, it said. Claire rooted to the spot as Reiki addressed the crowds, as she introduced Ozarik, as she stepped back to allow him a brief display of magic.

---

1. Not literally, not this time. But it still felt quite immense to those involved.

He called storm clouds to the center of the city, an old classic for a Future-Zaro, but this time his magic intertwined with Claire's, and lightning flashed. Ozarik's eyes widened, but Reiki swiftly set in, establishing parameters around the spell so the crowd was none the wiser.

An impressive display. Claire couldn't help but think maybe the Future-Zaro should try magic shows, just for kicks.

After the clouds dissipated, as everyone cheered, Reiki whispered something to her aciradaan. Minutes later, two women clad in subtle gray uniforms approached Claire. Aciras. A thrill swept through the girl as she was led backstage, past a slew of police and staff, and into a private room within the building behind the stage.

She was given a glass of water, which she subtly changed to grape soda when no one was looking. Then she flopped into an armchair, feigning a confidence she didn't feel as the door opened and Reiki and Ozarik entered.

The aciradaan took position by the door outside, and closed it behind them. A magical, soundproof barrier erected itself, and Claire swallowed a laugh. Sure. Best not to let anyone know about her magic, huh? Not even the aciradaan.

Whatever.

Zaro Reiki looked exactly as Claire remembered, her makeup perfect, her hair pinned in a tight bun, her robes flawless. In contrast, Ozarik looked nothing like Claire imagined, mostly because he entered the room with a huge, friendly smile.

"You," he breathed, walking forward as if entranced. "You're the one. The girl who has my magic."

Claire stiffened, pushing out of the armchair. "It's my magic."

"Our magic," he corrected, grinning wider.

What an idiot.

But already, Claire's defenses were crumbling. She hadn't expected to *want* to like him. She was supposed to hate him. Maybe—maybe even kill him.

Well, forget that. What did her dad know anyway?

Reiki, meanwhile, was watching her carefully. "Child, did you come all the way from Spokane? Alone?" The last word held weight, a warning.

"I ran away." Claire lifted her chin in defiance. Her fingers curled around the cup of grape soda.

"So I see." Suspicion laced the Zaro's tone now. "What prompted that?"

"My dad's an asshole."

Reiki stiffened at the language, and Ozarik coughed a laugh.

The Zaro recovered first. "I heard there was an explosion in Spokane. The official story is a malfunctioning propane tank... but no one was hurt, even though at least one human should have been."

"Sounds magical," Claire muttered, offhandedly.

"It does, doesn't it?" Reiki narrowed her eyes. "Were you involved?"

Claire had spent the last seven days imagining this conversation. She'd meant to infuse her voice with fear, spin a story about how her magic had turned dangerous, how it scared her, how she had nowhere else to go and was afraid she'd hurt someone.

But that was a lie. Claire had control of her magic. She needed instruction, but she wasn't a danger to anyone. And what's worse, Reiki's tone clearly implied that she expected Claire to *be* that menace to society.

Irritation curled in Claire's soul, blackening like burnt paper.

"What if I was?"

Reiki frowned. "Was it intentional?"

"Everything's intentional," Claire snapped. "Like the fact that you knew about it, but didn't bother to check in on me. *Ever*. Like the fact that I was sleeping on the ground the last few days, and you still took your sweet time arriving in New York, even though you can teleport anywhere in the world with a snap of your fingers."

Ozarik's eyes widened. He probably never talked to Reiki like that.

Was that why he was her favorite?

Reiki inhaled through her nose. "I'm sorry, Claire."

She didn't *sound* sorry.

"So what? What are you going to do about it?" Claire took another swig of her grape soda, then tossed the cup in the trash. A few drops spilled, staining the carpet purple. She stepped over it, driving the stain into the thick fibers as she glared up at the Zaro. "I have the same magic as Ozarik. I'm dangerous. Unhinged, right? So now you have a choice to make. I'm not going away."

Silence.

Ozarik fidgeted, then cleared his throat. "Reiki. W-We can't leave her here. She doesn't have a home."

"She has a home," Reiki said, but she sounded contemplative now. Her eyes scoured Claire, and her magic prodded the cracks of Claire's façade.

Claire flinched away, and Reiki's brows knitted together.

"You saved them. Those humans."

Well, crap. Claire huffed, her bad-girl exterior fracturing. "No. I caused the explosion. You'd better reign me in before I hurt someone."

"Hmm." Reiki sighed, pinching her nose. "All right. You'll return to Javarini with us. I suppose it is about time. Ozarik, take Claire to the jet, please. We'll fly home today."

Ozarik was blindingly excited. His magic flared so brightly Claire needed to shield her eyes from looking at him. "Really? She's coming back with us? I thought she was supposed to be a secret."

"You are the Future-Zaro, Ozarik, but that doesn't mean Claire cannot learn with us. At least for now, her magic needs to be controlled."

Claire hated everything about this sentence, and almost snapped a vitriolic retort. But her father's warning kept her in line: get to Javarini, win over Reiki, claim the title. Or Maxwell would be in trouble. So, she swallowed her retort, forced a smile, and let Ozarik take her hand.

The fact that he could teleport them *both* several miles away showed how far ahead he was, magically speaking. Her stomach churned as he practically skipped to the awaiting jet, waving at the acira standing watch. The poor woman blinked in shock when he said, "This is Claire! She's coming to stay with us."

Claire waved halfheartedly, cut between crippling relief that her plan had *worked*, and the new weight of what her father would expect now. She'd bought Maxwell some time, but she had no idea how much.

Ozarik offered her a glass of water, chatted a mile a minute about their future together. "This is going to be fantastic. We'll get you a room in the castle—we live in a castle, it's really nice and big and has artifacts from just about everywhere in the world. And the island is so cool; you'll love exploring it. Plus, Reiki will be so excited to have another student—"

"I'm not her student," Claire said, sharply.

Ozarik frowned. "But you have my magic. Ah, *our* magic."

Claire sunk into one of the jet's plush leather seats, clenching her fists against her ripped jeans. "That doesn't mean she'll train me. You heard her. I'm not the next Zaro."

"You could be, though," he said, ever the optimist. "We can rule together. I bet Reiki is discussing how to make it happen with Clementine right now. We'll probably announce it to the world in a few weeks, and then you'll have a lot of great experience with—"

"Shut up!"

Ozarik clamped his lips together.

Claire's cheeks colored. "I don't want to be Zaro, okay? I just—I just wanted to get away from my dad."

For the first time in weeks, she doubted this was the right move after all.

Ozarik perched in the seat beside her. His magic meshed against hers, and it felt like a hug on every plane of existence. Claire relaxed unwillingly, swallowing past the lump in her throat as Ozarik tentatively squeezed her hand.

"I bet it was hard, leaving what you knew. I did that too, once. But you'll love it on Javarini." Ozarik smiled warmly, and Claire could see why the world fawned over him. He brightened people's moods just by existing. "And no matter what, we have each other. Okay?"

Claire stared at their intertwined hands, and a flicker of his optimism ignited in her soul.

Maybe things *would* be better, if she could be with Ozarik.

"Claire?"

"Yeah. We'll always have each other."

Epilogue

Three Months after Death Stopped

Zaro Claire stood in the foyer of her massive Mandalay Bay condo, surveying the gold-tinted windows and heavy furniture and granite counters with a hint of nostalgia and a healthy dose of sadness. The condo itself reverberated with it, aching at the thought of reverting back to normal guest suites, of hosting people who felt that they deserved grandeur simply for existing. The palm trees that framed her front door leaned towards her, as if their fronds might trap her there.

She brushed them aside, offering a rare, honest smile. "I'll miss you too. But this is the next step."

"I mean, I don't think anyone would complain if you decided to keep an office in the States," Henry said from the kitchen, hefting a box of crystal glasses onto the countertop. He wiped sweat from his brow, offered a sly glance. "On a side note, Jenifer has been hoping for crystal glasses."

"Take them." Claire rolled her eyes. "But don't lie about who really wants to be drinking in luxury."

Henry grinned sheepishly and handed the box to a burly mover loading up a dolly. "This goes to my place too." The mover snorted, but dutifully added it to the expansive pile. Meanwhile, Henry joined Claire in the foyer, stretching his arms above his head. "Just saying, Claire. Nevada is really going to miss you."

"I think Mr. Hiddles is happy for the early retirement."

"You know what I mean."

Claire smiled, sadly. "There's no time for it, Henry. Oz—Ozarik divided his attention, and it was disaster." Those who knew Ozarik personally—the aciras, the world leaders, Henry and Jenifer and Milo—hadn't fallen for her persuasion.[1] Luckily, they were also quite aware of how much devastation Ozarik had caused, and how Claire alone had fixed things, so very few were upset to see her taking control.

It still hurt, saying his name out loud.

"I need to be working at the Zaro's headquarters. Clementine is helping, but she can't do much if I'm not around."

"I still can't believe you're keeping her on," Henry muttered. He'd made his opinions on the newly reinstated Aciradaan Clementine *very* clear.

But Claire didn't hate the woman anymore. In fact, the more she learned about Clementine, the more understanding Claire held for a life lived in the shadow of someone great. Clementine had believed her love to be pure, believed Claire's love corrupt, and that alone was a vivid reminder of how disillusioned people could become.

Claire healed Clementine's burns, but she couldn't cure the woman's frayed mind. Only now, months later, had the aciradaan slowly begun reclaiming responsibilities—all under the approval of Zaro Claire.

Claire ignored Henry's comment. "The movers are almost done. Are you ready? We'll be late otherwise."

"I didn't think a Zaro *could* be late." As he took her arm, Henry called to the mover: "When you get to my house, please don't let my wife lift any boxes. She's pregnant."

"That *is* our job," the guy replied, almost sarcastic.

Claire poofed them out of the condo before Henry could retort.

---

1. To be fair, she hadn't tried very hard to persuade them all. She liked that some people remembered Ozarik—the old Ozarik—so she focused her attention on anyone likely to cause problems, and let the rest accept his new fate.

They landed in a prison near Oklahoma City, in a private room arranged for the Zaro's personal use. The two guards by the door jolted as Claire waved away huckleberry smoke, as Henry moaned and hunched over his stomach. She magicked him a grape soda, popping the can open with a flick of her finger.

"It helps," she said.

"Next time, I'm driving."

"Feel free. This will be my last time here." Claire took a deep swig of her own soda, then sat at the table, motioning to the guards. "Bring him in."

They nodded, and a few minutes later hauled Kyle Flanderson into the windowless room. Henry stiffened at Claire's back, but Claire herself remained relaxed, offering a cold smile as their father took a seat across from her. The guards handcuffed him to metal rings soldered to the tabletop—a useless gesture for an ex-criminal turned murderer. Kyle entertained it, though, offering a snide wave as the guards retreated to the wall.

"Actually, you can leave," Claire said.

They hesitated, but the senior guard was a witch and knew far better than to test this particular Zaro. He nodded, and they stepped from the room, but not before he said, "Call if he acts out."

"Oh, I'm sure that won't be necessary," Claire replied, and the door *thunked* closed.

Finally, they were alone.

"It's about time, Claire." Kyle's lips upturned as he rapped his fingers in a rhythm on the tabletop. His eyes skirted to Henry, still standing awkwardly, and the smirk became a feral grin. "Maxwell. You've grown."

"Fuck you," Henry said.

Claire leaned backwards, the picture of ease. "How's prison life treating you?"

"Cut the bullshit, honeybee. We both know you're not here for that."

"Oh? Then what am I here for?"

Kyle didn't notice her tone, or the way his son choked on a laugh, or how he had suddenly seemed the fool. This was because, throughout his life, Kyle Flanderson believed he was owed something, which was a blinding assumption on the best of people.

After all, Kyle grew up in a decent house that, in his mind, should have been a *great* one. His parents showed love and affection, but not *enough*. While his siblings—perfectly pleasant people who went on to live perfectly pleasant lives—worked hard for their accomplishments, Kyle felt he'd already earned life's praise. And the fact that no one gave him that praise...

It didn't sit well.

And thus, he took shortcuts.

When Claire said, "Oh? Then what am I here for?" Kyle Flanderson laughed outright and gestured at his cuffed wrists.

"You're finally gettin' me out." He spoke with the unerring confidence of someone conversing with an idiot when *they*, in fact, were the idiot. "About time, too. I've been here for months. Figured you'd be more grateful for what I did."

The absolute audacity of it wiped all the humor from the situation.

Claire straightened, leaning forward now. The room seemed to shift, tension rippling like heat waves in the desert.

"Grateful that you shot Reiki and paved the way to my success? Grateful that your actions sent Ozarik into a spiral? Grateful for that?"

Kyle wouldn't admit it, but her predatory expression had the hair on his neck rising. But this was his daughter, so he forced himself to maintain easy body language, forced his tone to remain smugly confident. "You know I ain't admitting to shit."

"Why would you care about incriminating yourself if you know I'm plucking you out of prison?" Claire took another swig of her soda. "Unless, of course, you suspect this is a ruse. That I'm trapping you into a confession."

Silence filled the room.

Kyle's eyes slid to the cameras trained on his position.

Claire leaned closer and whispered, "How much do you trust me, Dad?"

"*Enough*," Kyle snarled.

Henry put a hand on her shoulder, squeezing.

Under his encouragement, Claire pushed to her feet. Her magic swept over her father, settling into his very bones with a mere thought. He flinched as his luck vanished, as magic twisted his destiny until all that remained were the cold, hard consequences of his actions.

"You're going to waste away in this prison, in case that wasn't clear."

Claire crushed the empty soda can and tossed it on the table. It skid to a rest between his hands, still cuffed to the metal table. "Call it a protective spell—protecting the entire world from your influence." A pause, a tilt of her head. "Actually, let's make it official. From today forward, your words will fall on deaf ears. You will be given the barest necessities to survive and dwindling hope that you might escape your cell. And if you do get a taste of freedom, it will come with the knowledge that I'm always watching you."

This was eerily similar to the spell Reiki placed on Kyle and his family when she'd first visited that bungalow in Spokane. By some standards, it was oppressive, eliminating his ability to choose his own path.

Reiki hadn't cared.

Turned out, Claire didn't either.

The Zaro pressed a hand to the table, leaning until she was eye level with her father now. "If you manage to run, it will only be a matter of time before I kill you myself."

The curse slammed over him like coffin's lid, and fury ignited in his soul.

"You are *nothing* without me," Kyle hissed.

Lithely, without warning, Henry stepped around the table and slammed his fist into Kyle's cheek. His father's chair nearly tipped over from the force of it, and when Kyle snarled at him, Henry grabbed his orange prison shirt, hauling him into an awkward standing position.

"I'm starting to think that you're nothing without *her*," Henry said.

Kyle glared at his son, blood trickling from his split lip.

Claire rapped on the door, beckoning the two guards inside. They flanked Kyle, shoving him back in his chair before he could lunge at Henry.

"Truth hurts, doesn't it?" Henry offered a winning smile. "Thanks for all the life lessons."

Meanwhile, Claire told the guards, "You're going to want to watch the recording of this. His confession is shocking."

The cameras, which recorded no such thing, hastily rewrote the video to the Zaro's whim. After all, everyone knew Kyle Flanderson killed Zaro Reiki—and now there was irrefutable, albeit magical, proof.

"That's a damn lie. Claire, *enough. ENOUGH!*"

"Come on, Dad." Claire looped her arm through Henry's again. "I've never been enough for you." And without another word, they poofed away, leaving Kyle Flanderson at the mercy of the American justice system.

Back in Las Vegas, Henry hesitated at his apartment's open front door. Inside, the movers had arrived and were unloading the many boxes he'd claimed of Claire's things. Jenifer wove between them, saying, "Ugh, why did Henry take this? Here, let me help—"

Henry winced. "I'd better go explain myself. But Claire? You were right. That was... well, pretty cathartic."

"Thanks for coming with me." Claire rubbed her arms. For all her earlier bluster, her heart still twisted at her father's commands. "It helped. Knowing he couldn't threaten you anymore."

"I doubt he ever had the reach we thought. But just in case he did... thanks for not testing it." Henry pulled his sister into a hug, and she squeezed him like a lifeline. "Don't be a stranger, okay? Jenifer wants to make a pot roast this Sunday. It should be a disaster. You're welcome to join us."

Claire laughed, brightly. "I have some wrongs to right in the world first. But if I'm free, I'll stop by."

Henry tilted his head. "Philanthropy is a good look on you, Zaro Claire."

Her cheeks colored.

Henry waved, strolling inside his apartment.

Claire poofed away—but she didn't land in Javarini. After all, there was one final puzzle piece to complete this picture, one final stop before she could begin this new chapter of her life. Knowing that, she arrived in the city of Bratislava, appearing between two limestone buildings about four stories tall. The alley was thin, barely wide enough for her shoulders, but she didn't stay put for long. Instead, she followed the yearning in her soul until she found a tiny bookshop perched beneath modest apartments.

Shelves crammed with old books stood proudly beneath dim lighting. A pair of velvet armchairs were placed below the window, and a long desk with an old cash register lined one wall. A gold-painted sign written in a Slovak rearranged itself under Claire's eye, boasting something along the lines of *Books Old and New*.

And behind the counter was Ozarik.

Claire drew a deep breath, striding across the street. His magic pulsed along her soul, but more out of curiosity than an urge to reunite with its original person. After all, it was a Zaro's magic—and Claire was the Zaro.

A tiny bell rang as she stepped into the shop, slipping into the façade of a short brunette with a wide jaw and small nose. Just some anonymous woman, browsing the wares. Ozarik looked up from the cash register and smiled, as warm and bright as he had that day in New York City.

"Welcome," he said. "Let me know if you need anything."

"Of course." Claire stepped between the shelves, running her fingers along the books. She'd spared no expense in magicking this place for Oz, adding details that bolstered his fake memories. Initials scratched into the wood of one bookshelf, belonging to his "parents." Books from around the world, hand-collected by a great-aunt that never existed. A cat canvassed the store, a volunteer from Javarini's second castle, the creature's magic pulsing quietly as it protected Ozarik from afar.

Claire used to have allergies, but now, she scratched the feline's chin. "I like your cat."

And she did.

Ozarik's voice settled over the store. "Yeah, she just kind of... wandered in here one day. Can't really blame her. I'd want to live in a bookstore, too." Amusement filled his tone. She wasn't supposed to know it, but his apartment was upstairs.

Claire picked a book off a shelf, and for a moment, she thought it was a certain leatherbound journal. But of course, that wasn't true—where Zaro Victoria had been too nostalgic to manage, Claire had no such reservations. She'd burned the journal, its separated pages, and the death-stopping spell inside.

Now, she turned the leatherbound book over in her hands, her heart calming. It was just an old spellbook. Claire's dark brown eyes traced the gold lettering, and she tucked it under her arm, strolling to the counter. "I'll take this one."

"Huh. Didn't think I had any books for witches here." He chuckled. "You hear about the new Zaro? People say she's wonderful."

"I haven't seen much of her." But the compliment falling from his lips made her cheeks warm. She almost expected him to flash her a private, knowing look, to take her hand and pull her close and tell her everything would be okay.

But none of that happened. He just accepted her cash, offered change, and scribbled a handwritten receipt. When she risked a glance at it, all he'd written was the book title and cost. Nothing else.

She'd done her part perfectly—and the Ozarik she knew was gone.

Her heart broke as she offered a stage-worthy smile. "Thanks for everything. I appreciate it."

I miss you.

The cat leapt onto his counter, and he pet between its ears. "Come back anytime."

Claire wouldn't be back. She didn't trust herself not to reverse everything, to recall memories she'd buried, to convince his magic to go home. Instead, the Zaro nodded pleasantly, tucked the book under her arm, and left.

After all, the show must go on.

The End

The #WitchyHunt Journal Pages

In September 2023, Claire Bishop joined TikTok to beg for help finding a certain spellbook—one we later learned contained the spell to stop death. Participants banded together to puzzle through the location of Zaro Victoria's spellbook, a relic from the 1800s. In the end... they lost the spellbook to Ozarik anyway.

These are the journal entries they uncovered along the hunt, a snapshot into the life of an old Zaro.

———ele———

18 Nov 1814

Jane got me a puppy.

I should have known. Despite decades of friendship, Jane thinks I'm "lonely." She is concerned that I never married—never mind that she herself is a widow. She "has a son," as she is so apt to remind me.

She forgets that a Zaro needs no partner. My magic is my heart, and the world's witches, my soul.

With that and Jane, I have everything I need.

And yet, I am penning this, staring at this puppy. His ears are too floppy for a proper terrier's, and he keeps attempting to chew my armoire.

How much would Jane loathe me if I slid his bow back on, set him back inside that basket, and left him on her stoop?

Hmm. It's likely not worth her ire.

20 Nov 1814

The puppy's name is Grimoire.

2 Dec 1814

Jane's son is following in her footsteps. "London's Great Oddities & Inventions," he calls it. I call it a shed, not a business. Despite my recalcitration, he wants to journey to America. I tried to assure him America is nothing of note. They cannot decide on a culture of their own, much less any sort of political state.

He insists.

Worse, Jane is encouraging it. I fear she isn't considering life without him. While I transport around the world on business, she will be left alone in that gloomy home.

I worry.

Perhaps I can relocate her to Javarini...

313

11 Jan 1815

Grimoire can teleport with me. A human takes considerably more effort, but he simply fits in my tote and the Universe includes him—an extension of my magic. I am beginning to suspect he's become a true familiar, which will greatly insult the cats of Javarini.

Jane is jealous—of Grimoire's ability to see the world, or his proximity to me, I could not say.

6 April 1815

Something is very wrong.

The magic of the Earth itself screams to me, like boiling water spilling between the edges of a pot and its lid.

A volcano.

An eruption.

Ash is falling in East Java, and I fear I will not be enough to stop it.

Ivan, my Aciradaan, is mobilizing the Aciras. Javarini will be barren while we race to stop a global catastrophe. I fear that my dear Grimoire is not suited for this work. Jane has reassured me she and her son will take excellent care of him.

Universe bless our path.

13 April 1815

My magic was not enough.

Another Zaro might have done better, but—

Well. Too late now. I am fatigued from the effort, depleted of magic, but I must persevere. If we do not cleanse the sky of ash, more will perish. The world will suffer. Ivan is injured, half my Aciras have perished, but we continue on.

I need to continue on. But I cannot help but wonder... What is the purpose of world-altering magic if I cannot *alter the world* with it?

There were so many dead. Could I have prevented that?

21 Aug 1815

Nothing is relaxing in my line of work, but... Grimoire and I are on a beach in Greece, angling toward something of the like. Jane is beside me in a hat so ridiculously large, I am convinced she is angling to be admired by the stars themselves.

They probably would. Her personality is very much like a sun.

She and her son have invented something new. They somehow compressed two telescopes into a much smaller handheld. They call them "ocular scopes." Considering their purpose is to enhance sight, I am concerned they haven't looked in a mirror yet.

She plans to gift me a pair.

For now, my dog and I shall sit on the beach, "relax," and intervene only when Jane uses these ocular monstrosities to stare somewhere she shouldn't.

Which, realistically, should not take long.

27 Nov 1815

A year has passed with my darling Grimoire, and I have belatedly realized that I missed his birthday.

Naturally, I summoned the Aciras to coordinate a Zaro-sanctioned worldwide celebration.

I am just now returning from the party. Grimoire shone like a star. He kissed children, pranced between buffet tables stealing food, and was adored for his mischievous soul. I am hearing similar reports from all over the world, according to Aciradaan Ivan.

It has been a rough year. The witches of the world didn't need much reason to celebrate.

Grimoire and I will return to Javarini tomorrow, but tonight, I am perched in my childhood home, Grimoire sleeping at my side, watching Jane attempt to translate *Pride & Prejudice* into French.

I am fairly certain someone has already translated that novel, but it is fun to watch her suffer.

26 Dec 1815

Jane has developed a cough. She assures me it is nothing, but my magic tells another story. It infests her blood and seeps through her lungs like ash in the sky.

And I know firsthand how ash can poison.

I do not want to worry her.

But something must be done.

30 Feb 1816

The witches of Egypt have proved an invaluable help.

Past Zaros have fabricated spells to counter disease. Zaro Teva spent decades working on the cure for malaria. Before that, the Black Death and others were magically addressed. Considering the malicious way diseases pivot, these spells take time, energy, and magical persuasion.

My dearest Jane doesn't have time for that.

And so, I turned to Egypt, where I'd heard rumors of a witch with the power to heal. In actuality, her power is maintaining a dust-free home, but she *is* immensely knowledgeable of local herbs.

The dryroot only grows in the deepest bed of the Nile. I have retrieved the finest supply for my spell.

In the meantime, Grimoire is keeping Jane company. Nothing lifts her spirits like a good game of fetch.

18 Mar 1816

The spell worked!

It is a small win, but I will happily bask in it. Jane is back in her shed—ah, apologies, "the establishment of London's Great Oddities & Inventions," tinkering with her son. Grimoire moves fluidly between our houses, as I am back to work.

The eruption has disrupted Earth's balance, and famine is imminent. Much to do.

4 Jan 1820

Universe bless, the time passes, doesn't it.

It doesn't help that I placed this journal in my study, only for an Acira to sweep through on a cleaning spree. Ivan assures me it will not happen again, but this journal found itself in Javarini's "unclaimed" pile for the better part of four years.

Perhaps a spell to locate lost items...

Regardless, a summary for my own aging mind:

Jane's son visited America, but believes a move will take longer to coordinate. Jane is now beginning to think this "might be a bad idea."

My protégé has been located: the son of a freed woman, a boy named William. The magic in our Future-Zaro is strong—and I can already feel my own magic siphoning into him. It is an odd sensation.

He will face a fight with the color of his skin, but a Zaro of his caliber might be just what America needs.

Ivan has retired, and a new Aciradaan has taken his place. Wiebke is young but determined, and I trust her to adhere to her duty. I do wish she'd stop pointing the sacred dao at me "for practice," but it is important that she feels capable of stopping me, if I were to go rogue.

That sounds like strenuous effort at my age, to be frank.

Meanwhile, Grimoire continues to be my constant companion.

18 Jan 1820

Today, Grimoire discovered he adores sticks. Considering Javarini hosts an impressive pine forest, I am frankly shocked it took him so long.

The cats of the second castle seem to be stalking him. I might have Wiebke address that.

... if she can.

19 July 1820

I am a fool.

I wrongly assumed that Jane was cured. I assumed that after 3 months of work, my spell would be perfect.

I assumed the disease wouldn't adapt.

And now Jane is—

Jane...

Universe bless, what can I do?

24 July 1820

A spell to cure needs time to be perfected. Perhaps a Future Zaro will accomplish it, but for my purposes, it will be too late.

I need more. All this magic has to be suitable for something.

Commanding the Universe's lifeblood *must* mean something.

Disease is complicated... but death is glaringly simple. One moment, they are present. The next, their soul drifts away. It is reabsorbed into the fabric of all things, and fades into something greater.

I am Zaro Victoria. My magic commands oceans, quells fires, persuades minds.

I am the closest thing to a deity on Earth itself.

And Jane *will not die.*

25 July 1820

2 dryroot, crushed into powder

   1 silver chalice of old

   ~~*7 sprigs of lavender, to calm the stench of death*~~

   No good—lavender calms the soul. Impossible to communicate with it

1 golden pendulum, blessed by a Zaro
1 map of residence in question
1 spoon of honey

Mix.
Leave in sun to dry.
Bake into cookies and feed to loved one

Result: Jane did not take this well.

7 Aug 1820

I have ripped out several pages of this journal and burned the spells inside. My initial attempt at stopping death was... lackluster. Future attempts were tested on mice instead of Jane, and all had the opposite intended effect.

I am beginning to wonder if this requires something less than physical.

I will expose myself to death on a global scale and explore the effects.

In the meantime, I have placed a spell on this journal. Certain pages—spelled pages—can only be viewed with the "ocular scopes" Jane gifted me all those years ago. She was right; their invention caught on, and it's a must-have for any discerning opera attendee in London. But only my set holds the key to these pages.

Her son has abandoned plans for America.

Times like this make me wish William was aging faster. Had he been born earlier, I could divert my attention to—

Well. It hardly matters now. William will become the next Zaro when I perish, and not a moment sooner.

Until then, this task falls on me.

17 Aug 1820

All my fervor, and Jane is gone.

What am I to do?

26 Nov 1820

I miss her smile. She used to snort when she laughed, and the men of London found it abhorrent, and I would call them fools, and we would giggle like schoolgirls.

Even when I left for training on Javarini, Zaro Teva would teleport her to visit me. He knew how important she was. How special.

She was my closest friend.

Now, for the first time, I feel alone.

4 Dec 1820

Grimoire helps.

8 Jan 1821

Her son has decided to stay in England, manage the house a bit longer. The Universe has placed a woman in his path, a witch who would make Jane proud. She is wary of me, I think, but I find myself fiercely protective of him.

I believe they will marry. It is a good match.

William's power is growing, and I must shift my focus to his training before a disaster strikes. More visits to America will be warranted until he is old enough to train at Javarini. The Aciras are very excited to meet him.

I wish Jane had the chance.

28 April 1821

I experienced a fever dream last night.

Jane was back on her deathbed, picking at the sheets and bemoaning the fact that she'd stained them with wine moments earlier. I was at her side, longing to take her hand—and fearing it at the same time.

Her eyes met mine. And in a rare, lucid moment, she tells me, "The soul doesn't leave. Not right away. Contain it, and you can save me."

But that wasn't how it went.

Her death.

The sheets, perhaps. She craved one last drink. But that—

I haven't explored my spell to stop death in months. Clearly, I need to revisit it.

4 Nov 1821

Jane might have been onto something.

19 Mar 1824

I continue to forget this journal's existence... except when the spell to stop death resurfaces.

The pain of Jane's death has quieted. Less of a volcano spewing ash that darkens all skies... more the quiet simmer of a pot cooling off. The ache is constant, and there is no peace in her death, but the world continues.

William is growing into the brightest boy I have had the pleasure of knowing. He keeps contact with his mother, which I would normally disapprove—except that I was allowed to keep contact with Jane, and I cannot... would not... deprive another of a consistent love.

The soul, meanwhile, is a tangible thing for a Zaro's magic. It requires thinking of a human body as a compilation of magic, upon which the soul is infused. During death, that soul separates from its physical form—which is a slower process.

Jane was right inside my dream.

It takes time.

23 Oct 1824

Jane's son had his firstborn. He still talks occasionally of America, but his family is content thus far. His inventing has slowed, but not ceased, and he continues to create... memorable... oddities.

The Earth spins.

I spin alongside it, hollow.

Jane's laughter made things so bright.

19 May 1826

My spell's instructions are complete... and I am unsure of how to proceed.

It will stop death. I've tested it on countless flora and fauna, and now am biding my time to see how it affects humans. Obviously, I will need a very specific circumstance to attempt it on a person.

I don't want a repeat of July 25th.

The spell is fine. Its implications are less so.

I spent so long attempting ~~fruitlessly~~ to stop death that I didn't pause to think if I *should*. This spell is as refined as I can make it, and still, it hits like a hammer to the skull. It does not discriminate. Any creature intending to be saved, *will* be saved.

But when I think of Jane in those final days... sometimes, death is the greater mercy.

21 May 1826

The spell to stop death is both complex, and frighteningly simple.

This can only be performed by a Zaro.

Our magic is different, and thus, this is far more than a physical spell. Ingredients and incantations ignore the facts: the soul, its connection to a body, and how magic intertwines them. It's the equivalent of playing with building blocks versus exploring a new dimension.

[Author Note: The spell has been removed from this record permanently, under Zaro Claire's orders.]

Using these channels, winding along that path, the magic will obey.

And you will become a god.

22 May 1826

Jane visited me again last night. Perhaps death isn't as final as it felt. She begged me to hide this book, begged me to reconsider its uses.

She told me, "No one should be a god."

I must wrestle with the implications of this. I will store this book for a time... and debate whether to destroy it.

14 Dec 1827

Grimoire had a fit.

He is thirteen—a good life for any dog. Universe bless, it feels like yesterday that Jane surprised me with this child of mine. That big red bow around his tiny neck, the basket padded with a hand-crocheted blanket. My armoire in England still has the bite marks on its leg.

He is my last personal connection to Jane. He is my best friend, my witch familiar. My mischievous little puppy fighting for space in a castle of cats.

I... am not entirely certain I can let him go.

27 Dec 1827

I did something terrible.

I am now convinced this book needs to be hidden. It is my one connection to Grimoire, to Jane, and I am not strong enough to destroy it. But William, or the Future Zaros after him—this will be their responsibility.

This spell is dangerous. It should never be used.

Grimoire passed, and I lunged for his soul—and it obeyed me. I spoke the incantation and set framework around his tiny body, and he survived.

And he was in agony.

His body did not stop dying. I did not *heal* him. I merely tethered his soul to torment.

I shattered the spell, and have not stopped crying in days. He licked my nose before he died properly, and I could not accurately convey my adoration for him—and my sincerest, excruciating regret for what I'd tried in my most vulnerable moment.

He did not understand.

I do.

15 June 1828

I have determined a path to hide this journal.

I have to rip out the early pages—memories of my greatest friends, and our lives together—and keep them close. I never thought myself sentimental, but... well. On my death, I will ensure the pages spelled and scattered, located only by those who need them most.

The physical journal, however, and the spell it houses...

It is the culmination of almost a decade of work. It is everything Jane died for. I simply cannot wipe it clean—even though that would be the wisest decision.

Instead, I will hand the journal to someone who understands its risk: Jane's own son.

He is planning to move to America in a few years, once his children are old enough. Good. The further from my legacy it is, the safer it will be.

And once William Assumes the role of Zaro, after my passing, he will track down Jane's son and his family in America.

He will destroy this spell.

I hope.

Until then, may the Universe itself pardon my atrocities.

Acknowledgements

Everyone helped with this book.

I'm not joking. I plotted it with sticky notes and a diagram with my best friend back in 2019, and spent 2 years over the pandemic writing it on and off. My friends read it chapter by chapter over years and offered feedback. My first agent edited it for a submission this book never got to see. Then my friends edited it again, and I poured over it, and sensitivity readers scanned its pages, and now it's here in your hands.

So, since this book is already weird enough, I'll make the acknowledgements equally weird.

THANK YOU.

To everyone who ever took the time to support me, to anyone who fell in love with Claire's story, to every soul who made this book great. Thank you, from the bottom of my heart.

Special shout-out to Chris, Andria, and the entire Constructed Adventures team for helping me plan the #witchyhunt scavenger hunt. Huge thanks to all the amazing participants who rallied in September to make this book launch so exciting. #witchyhunt was a blast!

About the Author

Rebecca Thorne is an author of all things fantasy, sci-fi, and romantic. She thrives on deadlines, averages 2,700 words a day, and tries to write at least 3 books a year. (She also might be a *little* hyper-focused ADHD.)

When she's not writing—or avoiding writing—Rebecca can be found traveling the country as a flight attendant, or doing her best impression of a granola-girl hermit with her two dogs.

Also By Rebecca Thorne

Cozy Fantasies

CAN'T SPELL TREASON WITHOUT TEA
A PIRATE'S LIFE FOR TEA

Science Fantasy

THIS GILDED ABYSS

Middle Grade Sci-Fi

THE SECRETS OF STAR WHALES